12 SHADES OF
SURRENDER

12 SHADES OF
SURRENDER

ANNE CALHOUN

ADELAIDE COLE

EMELIA ELMWOOD

MEGAN HART

LISA RENEE JONES

EDEN BRADLEY

ALISON TYLER

SASKIA WALKER

ALEGRA VERDE

PORTIA DA COSTA

ELISA ADAMS

TIFFANY REISZ

HARLEQUIN®

entertain, enrich, inspire™

ISBN-13: 978-0-7783-1494-3

12 SHADES OF SURRENDER
Copyright © 2012 by Harlequin MIRA

The publisher acknowledges the copyright holders of the individual works as follows:

UNDER HIS HAND
Copyright © 2011 by Anne Calhoun

A PARIS AFFAIR
Copyright © 2011 by Adelaide Cole

THE ENVELOPE INCIDENT
Copyright © 2009 by Emelia Elmwood

THE CHALLENGE
Copyright © 2010 by Megan Hart

TASTE OF PLEASURE
Copyright © 2011 by Lisa Renee Jones

NIGHT MOVES
Copyright © 2010 by Eden Bradley

CUFFING KATE
Copyright © 2012 by Alison Tyler

GOING DOWN
Copyright © 2012 by Saskia Walker

TAKING HER BOSS
Copyright © 2011 by Esperanza Cintrón

CHANCE OF A LIFETIME
Copyright © 2008 by Portia Da Costa

FOR YOUR PLEASURE
Copyright © 2010 by Elisa Adams

SEVEN DAY LOAN
Copyright © 2010 by Tiffany Reisz

Recycling programs for this product may not exist in your area.

For questions and comments about the quality of this book, please contact us at CustomerService@Harlequin.com.

www.Harlequin.com

Printed in U.S.A.

CONTENTS

UNDER HIS HAND
ANNE CALHOUN

CHAPTER ONE

Tess Weston soaked a facecloth with cold water, then bent forward, drew her hair over one shoulder and held the cloth to the nape of her neck. Rivulets trickled down her back, merging with the sweat seeping from her pores. Even with the windows open, and a fan oscillating as languidly as a spoon through soup, the temperature on the second floor of her house was hotter than the ambient air outside.

She swiped the now-tepid cloth down her throat and paused at her collarbone. The washcloth soaked the thin ribbed fabric over her breasts while she considered the sheer curtains hanging lank beside the open window. Such an unremarkable thing, an open window, a simple pleasure people generally took for granted. Drew Norwood, her navy SEAL boyfriend, had extensive experience managing risks of all shapes, sizes and situations. Given her borderline neighborhood, he'd weighed simple pleasures against physical safety and insisted on windows and doors locked tight at night. However, Drew had disappeared almost a month ago, as usual with no warning. Three times in the six months they'd been dating, he'd simply vanished into thin air, reappearing weeks later sunburned, thinner and exhausted.

The disappearing act didn't bother her. It came with dating
an active-duty SEAL, and she was used to people walking out
of her life. The reappearing, as abrupt and unannounced as
the disappearing, still set her back on her heels.

Not much else did, but a brutal heat wave, an AC unit that
had frankly become an ugly pile of scrap metal three days
earlier and no money for repairs left her with two choices:
sleep in a situation Drew adamantly opposed or melt into a
puddle in her bed. She preferred to dissolve into liquid bliss
when he was the one heating her up, and she flat-out didn't
have the money to fix the AC.

What Drew didn't know wouldn't hurt him.

She scrubbed at her breastbone as if she could wipe away
the disloyal thought, then draped the washcloth over the edge
of the sink. When she shut off the bathroom light and stepped
into the moonlight illuminating a path along the scratched
hardwood floor, a shadow disengaged itself from the dark
corner behind the bathroom door, clamped a hand around
her wrist and spun her face-first into the wall. The callused
palm clapped unceremoniously over her mouth muffled her
instinctive shriek. With her free hand braced at shoulder height,
and a strength born of sheer terror, she pushed back into an
iron-hard body. Her captor didn't move an inch. Instead, he
knocked her off balance by wedging one leg between hers
and with minimal effort forced her flat. He had superior size
and strength, the advantage of surprise, and she was trapped.

Eyes wide with panic, she twisted her head and peered over
the big hand engulfing the lower half of her face, but her vision
only confirmed the input from the quivering nerves in her
hypersensitive body. Heavy shoulders and a broad chest clad
in black pinned her torso, and a ridged abdomen trapped the
arm bent behind her back. Squirming futilely in an effort to
regain her balance only ground her bottom against his hips,

and her thin cotton bikini panties provided no protection from the insistent erection shoved firmly against her ass.

Knowing it was futile, she inhaled sharp and hard, drawing breath to scream. The air rushing through her nose carried with it the familiar scent of musky skin and the sharp odor of no-frills soap used at Coronado. In a millisecond she plunged from ice-cold fear to weak-kneed relief and sagged against the restraining body.

Drew. Back with no warning. In her bedroom, scaring her half to death.

But how?

She'd been working downstairs all night, the front and back doors secured with the handle lock and dead bolt. He had a key, but hadn't used it; the door would have caught on the chain. The downstairs windows were so warped that opening or closing one was a noisy process that took effort, even from Drew. But upstairs the windows were unlocked and slid, loose and flimsy, in their frames. Discarding the possibility he'd slithered under the front door, he must have clambered in through the damned open window in her bedroom.

"Tess, you are in so much trouble."

Silky menace simmered under the growled words as he shoved off his black stocking cap and tossed it behind him. His thick, sweat-dampened hair, bleached near-silver by hours in the sun and salt water, gleamed even in the midnight-blue of her bedroom. With a wickedly accurate sense of timing, he'd caught her at her most vulnerable, dressed for bed in one of his tank undershirts, and string bikini panties. Her feet were bare, her body crushed between his and the wall, and she stood no chance of breaking free from his tight grip.

"I can explain," she said, but his palm muffled her words.

"What?"

The barked question told her that having the living daylights scared out of her hadn't atoned for her sin. She tossed her head back, away from his hand, and he lifted his palm just enough to let sound escape. "I said I can explain!"

His hand mashed down over her mouth again. "I don't want an explanation," he growled. "I've been gone for twenty-six days. I want *you*. Now."

A bolt of hot lust shot through her when his gorgeous tenor drawl, laced with rough need and tightly controlled ire, tumbled into her ear. She jumped when he nipped the sensitive rim of her lobe, then slapped her other hand up against the wall. Docile, trembling, she stood still for him as he pushed her panties down her thighs, then went to work on the buttons of his cargo pants. Sensations zinged through her as his abraded knuckles brushed against the soft, rounded flesh of her bottom. He made room for himself between her legs, the width of his thighs urging her feet farther apart, her thin panties straining against the muscles quivering in her legs.

Disconcerting, palpable desire streamed along nerves lit up by the adrenaline rush from his unorthodox appearance. Need coiled tight and hot between her thighs. Without conscious thought she arched her back and tilted her hips toward him.

His low, dry chuckle didn't mask the sound of a condom wrapper tearing. After a pause he settled big hands on her hips and lifted her up and forward, to the very tips of her toes. Turning her face to the side to rest her hot cheek on the cracked plaster, she closed her eyes as fear, the unintentional aphrodisiac, heightened the sensations swamping her. His rough black BDU pants chafing her inner thighs. The soft brush of his cotton T-shirt against her shoulder blades and back. Sweat slicking the skin of her bottom and his lower abdomen where he leaned into her. Whirling, sharp sparks settling low in her belly, ready for him to strike the tinder and set her on fire.

"Miss me?"

Did doubt linger under his taunting question? It was so

hard to think with his hand pressed flat to her abdomen, his cock hot and hard against her bottom. Nuances aside, the answer flowed easily from her parted lips. "I always do," she whispered and felt his breath hitch in response.

The eight-inch difference in their heights didn't deter him. He simply bent his knees, wrapped one arm around her waist to hold her up on her toes and braced the other arm next to her face. His thick cock parted sensitive flesh only beginning to swell and dampen with arousal. He drove in, and she winced.

He went still. "You okay?" he asked, his voice roughened, strained.

No… Maybe… "I… Yes."

A soft, almost unwilling groan eased out of him, then he began to thrust, deep and hard. Experience had taught her that although the first time would be fast and furious, she could come from the intensity alone, riding the waves of Drew's weeks-long adrenaline rush. Sometimes they made it upstairs before he was buried deep inside her, but more often than not he had her up against the door or on her rickety kitchen table. Watching Drew drive into her body, then shudder in her arms, reduced her to *female* at its most primitive. Taken. Possessed. The spoils of battle, even. She would come under the sting of his teeth on her shoulder, the brutal grip of his hand on her hip.

Tonight was different. Tonight the remnants of shock entwined with lust in her veins, and she added *submissive* to the list of adjectives describing how she felt when he had her spread and penetrated within thirty seconds of walking in the door, or, as the case may be, climbing through the still-open window. The unorthodox position left her off balance, straining up on tiptoe with her forearms braced in front of her face, pushing back into each thrust to avoid smacking her forehead on the wall. Her helpless acceptance made him growl again, low and deep in his throat.

His strokes were relentless, almost punishing, as was his arm around her waist, clamped down on her slippery flesh. The fingers of his other hand gathered her loose, sweat-dampened waves of hair at her nape and turned her head to the side so he could look at her. Her eyelids fluttered, on their way to closing as desire surged with each slick stroke, but an unfamiliar tenseness flashed behind the familiar hot need in his blue eyes.

For a brief moment she surfaced from the whirlpool of erotic sensation, but he angled his hips forward, stroking over a spot inside her that sent hot, electric pulses zinging through her. She succumbed to the immediate. The ribbed undershirt chafed her nipples each time they brushed the wall, and pleasure swelled in her clit. She shivered and moaned over the sound of his abdomen slapping against her ass.

With an inadvertent tug that made her gasp, his damp hand stroked down through her hair and across her rib cage to cup the top of her sex. One fingertip circled her taut, slick nub. She threw her head back, straining into his unmovable body as he maintained his pace, fast and hard. Her orgasm slammed into her a split second before he ground his hips against her bare bottom and gave a stuttering groan. His cock swelled and pulsed inside her convulsing channel as he mouthed her jaw and neck through slow, jerky orgasmic strokes. Then he exhaled against her shoulder, letting his weight slump into her body.

As the waves subsided, she sagged in his grip, waiting for her jellylike muscles to firm up enough to hold her weight. When they did, she tossed a languid smile over her shoulder, her needy gasps turning soft with satisfaction. That was beyond the heat of a normal welcome-home fuck, well into incendiary, and surely sex that amazing negated the issue of the naughtily open windows.

He didn't smile back. A deep red flush stood high on

his cheekbones, visible even under his perpetual tan. Sweat trickled through the blond stubble on his jaw. "I missed you, too, Tess. Now you can explain about the windows."

Oh, shit.

He withdrew as he spoke. Given the hint of steel under his soft tone, she did *not* want to be naked for this conversation, so she pushed herself upright and yanked up her panties. The cotton resisted, clinging to her damp skin as she peered at his back, headed for the bathroom.

"Don't move." The words were tossed over his shoulder in a curt fashion that made her freeze.

Definitely a panties-up conversation.

When he came back into the bedroom, he stopped in the same strip of moonlight she'd occupied when he'd ambushed her. His short blond hair lay plastered forward, serious stubble shadowed his jaw, and the planes and curves of his face were expressionless in the pale swath of light as he considered her. She expected him to look at her body. Her tank—his tank, really—was soaked with water and sweat and therefore practically see-through, and her nipples pushed pertly against the material. Tiny white string-bikini panties cut high on her hip covered her trimmed curls, and her legs were bare all the way to her painted toenails. Under normal circumstances his gaze would be all over her, but instead he focused intently on her face.

She twisted her hair into a loose knot at her nape, crossed her arms and stared right back. His black cargo pants were up and buttoned, his T-shirt plastered to his muscled torso. Bizarrely, he was barefoot. It was on the tip of her tongue to ask him where his boots were, but she bit back the question as irrelevant, given the currents swirling in the hot night. His first hours back were always dark and intense—whether from long-suppressed need or a sheer human desire to reestablish a connection, she didn't know or care. Usually by this point they were sharing a shower, but his distant demeanor felt like a bucket of ice water poured over her head.

After a solemn, purposeful glance at the windows, he looked back at her, his blue eyes glinting in the darkness. "What am I going to do with you?"

Tess kept quiet. He'd told her what he'd do if she slept with the windows open, but if he didn't remember, she wasn't giving him any hints.

He approached her with measured strides, his eyes never leaving her face. His palms closed hot and firm around her wrists, turned her and lifted her hands back to the wall, just above shoulder height. With a gentle tap of his bare foot against her ankle, he urged her legs a little wider apart. Heat flamed in her cheeks as she bent forward, her ass tipped toward him. Having sex like this was one thing, but it was quite another to have a conversation with him at her back. This was a power play, a conscious and unsubtle one. Drew knew exactly what he did and, worse, how she'd respond.

"Didn't we just do this? And what the *hell* were you thinking to scare me like that?" she asked, nerves stiffening her spine, vertebra by vertebra.

He didn't answer, and if he wanted to avoid a fight about the windows, he'd gone about it the wrong way. She drew breath to lay into him, but when he shifted between her spread legs and laid his warm, damp chest along her spine, she softened back into the sensual aftermath. His movements calm and easy, he gathered her hair in one hand and sent it cascading in dark waves over her left shoulder.

"Your hair was pink when I left."

Okay, she could talk about her hair. "I felt like a change," she said, breathless and again off balance.

He braced his hands just outside of hers, bent his head and pressed a kiss into her right shoulder, making his torturously slow way to her neck before nudging her head to the side and kissing along the soft skin under her jaw. Each openmouthed kiss, the only point of contact between his body and hers, resonated in her hard nipples and, more potently, in her still-eager clit.

"How long do you think it took me to climb up onto the porch roof, open the window and get in here?"

Dammit. She wasn't going to be able to duck this or make it up to him the old-fashioned way. Worse for her, one hard, fast fuck hadn't been enough—not in her sultry, stifling bedroom, not after twenty-six days without him, not after the scare of her life—so distracting heat licked at her skin while she tried to estimate how long she'd been in the bathroom, brushing her teeth. Thirty seconds? The American Dental Association recommended brushing for two minutes, twice a day, but she never lasted that long. She gave up and split the difference. "A minute?"

He set his teeth against her slick shoulder before replying. "Ten seconds, Tess. Ten seconds to pull myself up onto the roof, walk across the peak, open the screen and climb in. It takes longer to describe it than to do it. You didn't even see me when you came into the bedroom."

"You were already in the room when I came up? I didn't hear anything," she said, peering over her shoulder.

He met her eyes without expression. "One, opening a screen doesn't make much noise. Any kid who's snuck out of a house could do it. Two, as loud as you were playing Nickelback, you wouldn't have heard an M16 firing. Not safe, Tess. Not safe at all."

Sheer embarrassment heated her cheeks and closed her eyes as she turned back to the wall. She'd had "Far Away" on repeat for over an hour, ostensibly for background noise as she sketched versions of an ornate spiral staircase destined for a downtown loft. The developer knew her earlier work and asked for designs; if she got the commission, she'd create twenty unique staircases and add to her growing reputation for custom work. The payment would buy a new HVAC system and put a little extra in the bank. But between Drew's prolonged absence and the vulnerability in the song, the pages were half sketches of intricate decorative work, half rough drawings of his face in ten different attitudes.

With a firm but gentle grip, he turned her head to the corner, still hung in dark shadows. "I watched you. You took off that sexy skirt I love and put on this undershirt," he said. Her belly jumped as he fingered the hem of the tight white tank he wore under his uniform. "Then you made the bed just so you could get in it, brushed your teeth and tried to cool off with that wet cloth. Water trickled down your neck and over your breasts, Tess."

He drew a deep breath, and she took the moment of respite from his hot, hard voice to try to slow her pounding heart. He'd been close, less than two feet from her. Watching her, getting hard for her. The images were flat-out carnal, but what if someone other than Drew had been hidden in the corner?

Despite the heat, goose bumps shimmered over her skin. "I see your point."

"Do you? Put yourself in my place and then tell me you see my point."

He was taut against her back, biceps bulging in the deceptively lean arms braced on either side of her face, and she tried to imagine the scene from his perspective. Driving up her street after a month away, exhausted, hungry for sex and food and comfort, in that order, eager to see her, but finding the windows open late at night when he'd specifically told her it was too dangerous. But what was his *place?*

He was her boyfriend, which could mean a great deal or not much at all. He took her out to eat. She packed picnic lunches for days at the beach. They went to street fairs and outdoor concerts and the movies. He slept at her house when he could. She kept him apprised of her ever-changing work schedule. They were exclusive and had been for six months, but when did exclusivity go from *I won't see anyone else* to *I accept your right to make demands of me?*

She went rigid at the thought of such dangerous intimacies. "Do you want to hear my side of the story?"

Smart, smart Drew knew all too well how to handle her. Only when he'd gently pulled her back against him and licked a delicate path along the rim of her ear, then down to her soft earlobe, did he whisper, "I'm listening."

"The air conditioner broke last week."

She owned her aging house, a tiny, slightly off-kilter two-story painted a fading, funky shade of lavender unremarkable for the eclectic neighborhood near her studio space in the warehouse district. *Eclectic* meant affordable prices for interesting-if-dilapidated architecture, and diverse, opinionated neighbors who were passionate about the neighborhood, its causes and people. It also meant she walked home from her studio past addicts, dealers and drunks, hookers and pimps, homeless families and groups of aimless young men. Break-ins were frequent. After one weekend with her, Drew was already on friendly terms with her neighbor, Mrs. Delgado, given his polite manners and Southern drawl. But with his well-honed sense for trouble, he'd recognized the neighborhood's good and bad elements and formed a decidedly negative opinion about her ancient air conditioner and the windows.

"I figured as much," he said, his voice dry.

"And you still scared the daylights out of me?"

He ignored her question, or at least she thought he did. "Why didn't you get it fixed?"

She threw a glare over her shoulder. "I need to pick up extra shifts at The Blue Dog to come up with the money."

"How much?"

"More than I have until I work the extra shifts."

"You said they were overstaffed and tips were down. How much, Tess?"

This relentless Drew was new to her, as if a stranger had come home in her boyfriend's body. "Six hundred dollars," she said, knowing he wouldn't like the answer.

His teeth ground, then he shifted his weight behind her. "I left money for you."

This was true. He'd tried to give her a thousand dollars in twenties and the names of two navy buddies she could call day or night, for any reason, when he was gone. She'd refused both. A short, tense "discussion" ensued, one she'd thought she'd won when he stuffed the neatly rolled money into the pocket of his cargo shorts. She'd turned her back on him for less than a minute to retrieve his wallet from her nightstand. On his way back to the base, he'd called to inform her that in the sixty seconds she'd left him alone in her kitchen, he'd put the cash in an empty Folgers Instant can at the back of her narrow pantry and the phone numbers in her cell phone. The next day he'd left on his most recent mission.

She had no intention of using the phone numbers, let alone the money.

"This is my life, Drew, not an emergency. I won't take your money. If I used it I'd need months to earn enough to pay you back, and besides…"

Her voice trailed off when his head dropped forward to rest on her shoulder.

"You don't have to pay me back."

"I do." This was important, although for reasons that grew hazier with each passing day.

There was a pause while his even breaths merged with the sweat trickling down her back. "Tess," he said, his voice totally without heat, "what do I have to do to earn your trust? Because I can't keep going like this."

The words, their empty tone, sent a shiver down her spine. She pulled her hands free of his and spun to face him. "You can trust someone and not take money from them, Drew!"

"You think I'm going to count up favors and make you work them off on your back?"

Her eyes widened at his crass question. "Of course not!"

He kept his arms on either side of her head while his blue eyes, somehow both sad and curious, searched hers. "Because it's not just the money. For all practical purposes, I live here, and yeah, I buy groceries or fix things around the house, but it's a dirt-in-the-eyes, bare-knuckles street fight to get you to take anything I offer. You work harder than just about anyone I know, but half the time I come over here and you've got four cans of corn in the cupboard and nothing in the fridge. Christ, you won't use six hundred dollars to be safe, not to mention comfortable. It's hot as hell in here!" He took a deep breath. "I know how you grew up, Tess. I respect your independence. I'm just trying to do the right thing here. If I can't, I can't stick around."

She'd dated her share of losers—artists, bartenders, even a couple of suits—and none of them, not a single one, looked in her cupboards, let alone gave a rat's ass about honor. Doing the right thing. But the problem wasn't that taking the money felt wrong. It was how right it felt, how easily she could add to his burden by letting him shoulder some of hers. Serving his country was the ultimate honor, but no one got rich doing it.

"You don't have all that much more money than I do," she protested, cravenly sidestepping the far more important issue he'd laid at her feet.

For a moment his normal laid-back sense of humor surfaced. "Damn, you're hard on a guy's ego," he said, but just as quickly the smile disappeared into the firm line of his full lips. He shrugged. "I have enough to fix the air conditioner. You don't.

I'd give it to you with no strings attached because I love you, but you won't take it."

Shock once again flooded her veins. He pushed away from the wall, and a fear more potent than the icy torrent that had immobilized her when he'd stalked out of the shadows settled in the pit of her stomach. "Drew, wait!" she said and grabbed his arm.

Her grip was strong from lifting kegs and welding heavy, awkward pieces of metal, but he stopped because he wanted to stop. He stopped because she asked.

"You love me?" God, could she sound any more doubtful? Prickly?

"Yeah, Tess. I love you." Soft, even words. She marveled at the strength it took to casually put himself in harm's way, both on duty and off. Right now the soft underbelly of his soul was totally exposed to her, easy to lay open with a few brittle, indifferent words. Until Drew, she'd defined strength by the thickness of walls she built around her heart, the barbed-wire fences draping her personality. Compared to his willingness to walk into physical and emotional danger, she was weak. A coward, even.

"You…" She stopped, slid her hand down to clasp his, thinking through how best to handle the hidden sharp edges of another person's feelings. "You've never said that before. Why say it now?"

After a moment, a very long moment, he returned her grip with a gentle squeeze. "I'm a play-the-odds kind of guy, Tess. Odds weren't good I'd hear the words back. Tonight I needed to say it. You don't have to love me back, not right now, but if you can't let me in even a little bit, I can't stay."

The words could have sounded like an ultimatum, an effort to control her through an all-or-nothing choice, but he sounded taut, tightly wound, pushed to the point of no return. She wondered where he'd been and what he'd seen or done that made him lay it all on the line. Not ready to walk away, but prepared to do so if she kept her defenses up.

Her choice. She swallowed against the ache in her throat, looked at their linked hands, then down farther to their feet, his braced wide, hers snugged together, the right foot curled over the left.

"I don't know how to do this," she said to the chipped, bright blue nail polish on her toes. Hard to admit, but true.

"You don't have to do anything, Tess. I just want to take care of you. Fix your air conditioner. Make sure you stay safe when I'm gone. It won't suck, I promise." He said the words with a crooked smile, tipping her chin up so she met his eyes as he spoke.

"Why?" It was unfathomable to her. In foster care from the time she was eleven, on her own from the day she turned eighteen and the state no longer provided money to cover her food or clothes, she'd long since accepted that if she wanted something—a house no one could make her leave, a degree in industrial art, a client base—she had to scrap for it by herself. "Nobody's wanted to take care of me my whole life. Why would you?"

"Because you're you."

Unable to help herself, she laughed, the sound mocking, derisive. "Yeah, right."

He shrugged, the pain back in his eyes. "This is where the trust part comes in. What's it going to be, Tess?"

Dammit, she'd rather handle rusty scrap metal without gloves than do this, but for the very first time in her life, someone wanted her company on a permanent basis, and not because the state paid for her upkeep. All he wanted her to do was put herself into his hands, into his care.

Terrifying.

Even more terrifying was the thought of holding back and losing him.

Tension thickened and heated the air around them. Little dots danced at the edges of her vision, and she realized she was holding her breath. After a shaky exhalation, she took a deep breath, and the scent of him—clean sweat and musk over the harsh tang of no-frills soap—swept through her nostrils, triggering the memory of his unique taste, the silky-smooth skin under his wrists, stretched over his hip bones, the underside of his cock. The tension in her muscles eased from her body again. She didn't know how to do this, but Drew had good hands and limitless patience. He'd catch her if she fell.

"Okay," she said, with a nod and a small, tremulous smile.

Fierce exultation gleamed in his eyes. He bent his head and brushed his lips over hers, a sultry kiss that started as the merest pressure, just the tantalizing possibility of something more. Then his tongue lazily traced her lower lip and she opened to him, her breath coming faster, mingling with his. She shifted restlessly as the promise in his mouth trickled down her jaw, hardened her nipples and settled between her thighs.

Then he pulled back. Tess waited a few racing heartbeats, then opened her eyes to find hot, possessive emotion surging in his. In his smooth, easy way, he slid his hand into the hair at the nape of her neck. "Okay, what?"

"Okay, I'll take the money to get the air conditioner fixed," she said.

He began a gentle massage, right at the spot where her neck met her skull, the spot where she held all her stress after hours bent over a sketchpad or a project. A thrill shot down her spine even as her shoulders slackened with pleasure.

"And?"

"Hmm?" That was all she could get out, given his magic touch on her nape.

Her eyes widened at his pointed glance over his shoulder to the open window. At the same time, his other hand slid down her arm to encircle her wrist, where he rubbed his thumb over the quickening thump of her pulse. She felt the throb of blood now leaping against his gentle, unyielding pressure. The dark, hot, implacable look in his eyes dropped her gaze to her wrist captured in the cuff of his fingers.

"I'm sorry I slept with the windows open." She was proud of her steady voice, even as her heart thudded hard against her breastbone and fresh sweat broke out under her arms and at the small of her back. *Please let him have forgotten, please, please let him have forgotten...*

"What did I say I'd do if I caught you doing exactly that?" He hadn't forgotten.

Suddenly his hands on her body felt less like sensual preparation and more like a devious softening up for an interrogation. She didn't need to look into his eyes to note the preternatural energy humming under his skin.

"Drew. No."

"What did I say, Tess? Do you remember the conversation?" The words were liquid, so soft, which was a little scary. Despite the drawl, the sense of humor and the unflinching Southern honor, Drew was anything but soft.

She stayed stubbornly silent through ten pounding heartbeats, twenty, because if she kept quiet, his promise didn't exist. Thirty more beats passed with her gaze focused resolutely on the place where her pulse pounded against the circle of his fingers. Finally, she surrendered.

"We'd been in bed all day and we'd soaked the sheets even though the AC was on. You said it was on its last legs. I said I didn't care because I'd just sleep with the windows open. I'd done it before, and I'd do it again." Unwilling to show fear, she dragged her gaze up to meet his. "And then you said...if I did...you'd spank me until I couldn't sit for a week."

With his back to the windows, stark shadows lay across the planes and angles of his face, concealing most of his expression. His eyes, however, were such a pale blue she could see emotion flickering through them, too fast for her to decipher. His bent head and wide shoulders offered her no protection from the moonlight, but she didn't look away as her heart hammered in her chest and her stomach alternated between circus flip-flops and plummeting to the bottom of her abdomen. And yet at the same time, her nipples swelled against the soft material of her tank top and a traitorous heat throbbed in her womb.

In a voice as thick and dark as the still air coalescing into moisture on her skin, he said, "Good thing you don't have a desk job."

Not funny.

She stepped back, twisting her head and arm to pull free, but came up short with her back to the wall. "Drew, you can't possibly mean it. It's…archaic! It's crazy!"

He moved closer, boxing her in. "I meant it, Tess. You knew I meant it when I said it."

Her jaw dropped. A minute ago he was a rational twenty-first-century male whose mother had earned her law degree studying nights and weekends, and whose sisters juggled work and kids. That man had disappeared, leaving behind a Drew she recognized only at some level so primitive she hadn't been aware it existed.

"You need this—"

She gasped, somewhere between astonished and outraged. "I do *not!*"

His gentle smile almost hid the intractable look in his eye. "Yes, you do, Tess."

CHAPTER TWO

For the third time in thirty minutes, shock ran, electric and searing, through her veins. Suddenly she was as motionless as he was, with no heartbeat, no breathing as she searched his eyes, pale blue and unreadable in the dim light. The hand that had rested lightly on her nape now cupped her cheek, while his thumb brushed her full lips. Then his roughened fingertips trailed along her neck, into the hollow where her collarbones met, then slid down her breastbone before detouring along the lower edge of her ribs and finally dropping to the swell of her hip. He wound his thumb in the string stretched taut there, pulled the thin strip away from her body and slid his fingers into the back of her panties to curve around her bottom.

"You're trembling."

"You're scaring me. Again." She might have sounded believable if her voice had quavered rather than snapped.

"I'm not scaring you. I'm making you mad," he said, calling her bluff without a hint of remorse. "You know nothing bad's gonna happen here. I, on the other hand, came up the street and saw the windows open and half the neighborhood's Latin Kings drinking and hanging around in Mrs. Delgado's driveway."

An impromptu party she hadn't heard over the music. She turned her head to the side, away from the look in his eyes. "I said I was sorry."

"Apology accepted, Tess, but you still get the spanking." His hand tightened on her hip, the pressure constant until she opened her eyes again. He looked back at her, his gaze part wry amusement, part serious intent. "Sometimes pain can feel really, really good."

A dozen smart-mouthed comebacks trembled on the tip of her tongue, but in the end the agitation roiling inside her kept her from voicing a single one. She shoved at his shoulder and ducked under his arm, hurrying down the stairs and across the peeling linoleum to the kitchen sink. She opened the faucet as far as it would go. Cold water streamed into the scratched aluminum bowl. She scooped handfuls of water to her mouth, then splashed her face.

He'd lost his mind. That was the only explanation. He was completely insane if he thought she'd let him spank her. Yes, she'd left the windows open, but that was no reason for him to make good on a lazy promise made at the tail end of four hours of sex. Truth be told, they were nowhere near vanilla in bed, but let a navy SEAL spank her, for God's sake? He was certifiable!

Except he sounded sane, assured and totally in control.

Expecting him hard on her heels, she shut off the water and turned, but the stairs were empty, the creaky floorboards above her silent. Would he forget about it? He looked haggard with exhaustion, dark smudges under his eyes visible even in the dim light of her room. Maybe if she gave him enough time he'd fall asleep and they could laugh this off in the morning. Or maybe he'd storm down the stairs, drag her to the sofa and blister her butt. Moments passed, then stretched into a minute without sound or movement.

Fine. He could sit up there until he roasted.

Her mind replayed his words...*put yourself in my place...not as badly as you scared me...half the neighborhood's Latin Kings drinking and hanging around in Mrs. Delgado's driveway...not as badly as you scared me...*

Well, that was an accomplishment to put on her résumé. She'd managed to scare a SEAL, an individual trained to handle any circumstance at any time with whatever meager tools and resources he had at hand. She'd scared him.

But she'd known when she wedged open the windows with a small shim that she wasn't just dealing with her poverty-line life. She was defying the only rule he'd felt strongly enough to voice. Despite his current incarnation as a dominant alpha male, Drew was laid-back, relaxed, beyond tolerant of her unusual hours, jobs, hair color and friends. Besides the windows, he simply let her be. Of course, a highly trained, professional special operative in the United States Navy should have more on his mind than fussing over her rainbow hair and shabby wardrobe.

Okay, she got it. This had to be about his job, which called for extended, unbroken focus, and if he was worried about her, he might falter at a very deadly task. Given the life-and-death scenarios he faced, the last thing she wanted to do was distract him. She'd let him down, wronged him by disobeying a very specific request. If he felt that strongly about this, then fine. He wouldn't hurt her. She knew that.

Best to get it over with.

She turned and climbed the stairs with far more reluctance than she'd shown on her way down. Drew sat on the bed in her room, his eyes closed, his back to the wall, one leg stretched out in front of him, the other pulled up. His arm rested on his bent knee, the hand dangling forward while the other hand lay on his thigh. A wide swath of moonlight illuminated his face and body, and she saw the tendons of his hands running under skin dusted with fine, white-blond hair. Three knuckles were bruised, nothing unusual.

His hands had fascinated her from their first meeting—on a brilliantly sunny, late-winter San Diego day after a storm, when the surf pounded the beach in waves the length and height of tractor-trailers and the sand was damp from rain. Drawn to the crash of the surf and the clouds scudding across the sky, she'd spent the entire day sculpting an enormous, whimsical castle complete with thick walls, a moat, drawbridges and turrets with gargoyles, perched atop a mound of sand carved into unassailable cliffs. Late in the afternoon, several surfers who'd survived despite their death wish stopped to examine her work.

Drew was one of them. A couple inches under six feet, he was so leanly muscled that in his unzipped wet suit she could see veins, tendons, ligaments running under his skin. It was his hands she'd watched, however, as he and his friends circled the castle, sizing up the fanciful structure before identifying weak points and strategizing an attack. Nicks, scabs and scars covered his long, tapering fingers and the backs of his hands, while his palms and fingertips bore calluses from physical use. His hands skimmed over the packed sand, almost but not quite touching the painstakingly molded shapes as he argued with a buddy about climbing techniques. Muscles roped around his wrists and forearms, and his biceps, triceps, deltoid, trapezius and abdominal muscles flexed and released under his skin.

Any San Diego—raised girl knew navy when she saw it. Marriage-minded girls could pick out officers blocks away. After three years of bartending near the base, Tess correctly guessed rank with nine out of ten guys and knew the SEALs from the wannabes. Drew was the real deal, and guys like him, with their pick of the beach bunnies, normally didn't give her the time of day. But he'd looked at her, then at the castle, then back at her again.

"You did this?"

She surveyed seven hours of work that would wash away with the next rain, and shrugged. "Yes."

"Nobody helped you?"

"No."

He took in her rolled-up jeans with the muddy knees, her bare, dirty feet with bright purple toenails matching the purple streaks in her blond-for-now hair, windblown from two braids, her shapeless hoodie sweater. His eyes showed a frank interest her petite, semi-Goth self rarely attracted.

"Impressive."

After a murmured conversation, he transferred his board to a buddy. She stood silently next to him and watched his friends load up their trucks and leave.

She smiled at him, ready to play the game that would put him in his place at arm's length. "How are you going to get back to the base?"

He squinted into the setting sun, then at the nearly empty parking lot, then finally at her. A quirky grin crossed his face. "I was hoping if I bought you dinner you'd give me a ride."

"I'd think about it, except I don't have a car."

This time she spoke without a hint of emotion, as if his unexpected invitation hadn't sent a secret thrill through her. In return she expected disbelief, irritation, even a bit of blame for being so pathetic as to ride the bus. Instead, he threw back his head and laughed at himself, at her, at life, it didn't matter, because she was done. With his self-deprecating sense of humor and deft, confident hands, he'd won this round.

While she stood beside him and tried not to gawk at his hands or the gorgeous, anatomy-textbook planes of his torso, he pulled a cell phone out of his backpack and sent a quick text message. Then he introduced himself, helped her rinse her tools and pack them in the canvas tote that held the trash from her picnic lunch. Almost right away a black truck and a red sports car pulled into the nearly empty parking lot. Silent and efficient, a bulky bald guy got out of the truck, tossed a set of keys to Drew and slid into the passenger seat of the *sports car. With a spray of gravel and mud, the red vehicle zoomed back onto the highway.*

He palmed the keys and looked at her. *"Mexican? Thai? Italian? Your choice."*

Game over.

"Well?"

The brusque question called her back from the windy day by the ocean to the stifling confines of her bedroom and the black-clad man waiting silently on her bed.

She spoke in an even, measured tone of voice intended to hide the exasperation simmering inside her. "I get it. You asked me not to do something. I did it, anyway. That was disrespectful. If we're going to be together, I can't be a burden while you're...working. In the future I'll do whatever it takes to stay as safe as possible. And if you need to...spank me...to work this out, I'm ready."

There. An admission of guilt plus the proper recognition for his demanding career. That ought to do it.

After another snort of disbelief, he opened his eyes and turned his head, fixing her with an uncompromising look. "You think I'm doing this for me? Wrong, Tess. Your apology was sincere. I trust you won't do this again. The spanking is for you."

Exasperation exploded into slit-eyed irritation. "I cannot believe you think I need—"

His lifted hand cut off her words, then he turned his wrist and beckoned her forward. "You said you were ready. Come here."

The temper that got her screamed at, or worse, in every foster home she'd lived in surged red-hot in her throat, but she drew breath, closed her eyes and let it out as she counted to ten. He had a point. She didn't *get* his point, but dominating or hurting her wasn't the issue. She knew that. "Fine, fine.

Let's just get this over with," she muttered under her breath as she stepped through the doorway and stalked toward the bed.

A hint of a smile danced around the corners of his mouth before the beckoning hand switched to the closed fist meaning *halt*. "Take off your top."

The heat in his eyes and his intractable tone flipped a switch in her brain. All the confused protests tumbling around in her rational mind sputtered in a crackle of static, then shut off, but her body reacted automatically. She tugged the wet, clinging fabric over her head and let the shirt drop to the floor as she bent forward.

While she'd intended nothing more than using her hair to hide the aroused flush flooding her cheekbones, a hitch in Drew's even breathing as he beckoned to her again told her he wasn't immune to her downcast eyes and nearly naked body. Her hair fell dark against the upper swells of her breasts, and her white panties stood out even against her pale skin. As politically incorrect as it was, she couldn't blame her thudding heart and watery knees on nerves alone. The stark reality was she was all but naked as she crawled up onto the bed to accept his punishment for her disobedience, and her female, animal body seemed to be operating on an entirely different frequency from her rational brain. Sheer erotic arousal pumped through her veins.

Drew lifted his hands out of the way so she could lie facedown across his lap in a strange, awkward and more than a little embarrassing alignment of their bodies.

"Move forward," he said, his voice soft yet firm.

In response to his command, she shimmied forward, centering her bottom directly over his thighs. His discarded black watchman's cap lay a few inches away. She gathered it to her and rested her face on her folded forearms as images of how this looked flashed against the movie screen of her mind.

Mostly naked, over his lap, her bottom perfectly situated for swats.

"Pull down your panties."

Red, telling heat bloomed in her cheeks at the thought of reaching back and baring her bottom for him. The pendulum of her emotions swung wildly between a rather disturbing excitement and sheer vexation. She clenched her teeth to bite back a furious response, then turned her face away from him and reached back to hook her thumbs in the elastic edge of the string-bikini briefs. With a little squirming and some help from him, she got her panties down, lifting just enough to let him tug the soaked panel from between her legs. She expected him to slide them down and off, but he left the white fabric at midthigh.

He stroked his palm over the curve of first one cheek, then the other, the touch soft, gentle, so seductive she let out her breath in a trembling rush and, with the exhalation, melted into his powerful thighs. A lush blend of arousal, embarrassment and nerves made her wiggle her hips in a figure eight on his lap. When she made contact with his erection, hard and ready against his fly, his hand tightened briefly on her ass.

"Let's try again. Why did you leave the windows open?"

Fuck counting to ten. For that matter, fuck *him!* Hot, aroused, sweating, confused and emotionally reeling, she sucked in air and pushed up onto her hands and knees. "Damn it, Drew!" she all but shouted as she turned to look at him. "You know why!"

The muscles in his arm flexed as the hand at the small of her back forced her flat, then *crack!* A resounding smack landed on the left side of her bottom. Tess jumped and yelped as fire spread from the point of impact.

"Wrong answer."

"Drew, you can't—"

Crack! She yelped again, a shock wave of pain blistering through her ass.

"Whatever you think I can't do, I can. The windows, Tess. Why?"

If he intended to keep this up until he got the answer he wanted, she could see the benefit of coming around to his point of view. The only problem was she didn't know what he wanted her to say, and she told him that.

Crack! "Think about it, Tess," he said, with a low, peremptory chuckle. "Take as long as you need."

He was *amused?* "You...you...*jerk!*"

The crack of flesh against flesh ricocheted around her bedroom. She jumped again, felt his hand spread in warning against her lower back and muffled her startled cry in her folded arms.

It *hurt.*

Another measured smack landed in the same place, flat on her bottom. Raw sensation expanded in pulsing waves as he moved to the other cheek and administered five smacks there. A hot ache swelled and spread, much as pleasure did during long, lazy afternoons in bed. He switched sides again, settling into a methodical pace, not so hard and rapid that she felt battered in either body or soul, yet not slow and light enough for her to surface from the pain of each smack's sharp impact.

He worked at his task while she twitched and wriggled with each stroke, gripping his cap and trying to choke back the gasps fluttering from her throat. The weight of his hand near her center of gravity anchored her, body and soul. The strength of his thighs under her stomach and legs, the solidity of his abdomen at her side all kept her focused on the painful, erotically charged, emotionally laden moment.

What the *hell* was this all about if it wasn't about her dogged independence and how that affected him? She wouldn't do it again. He trusted her to keep her word, and he was certainly keeping his. He'd said he would spank her, and here she was, naked and facedown on her quilt, while his relentless hand moved from cheek to cheek and he steadfastly ignored her stifled yelps, which threatened to become sobs as the stinging grew to burning. Despite the undeniably sexy undertone, she knew this wasn't his first choice of activities on his first night home. He could have ignored the windows, the broken air conditioner and her crushing financial strain in favor of simple sex, pizza delivery and sleep. He could have yelled at her and left. Worse, he could have just turned around in the street.

But here he was. Doing what he'd said he'd do.

He hadn't left when he found the evidence of her disobedience. He'd stayed, and as painful as it was, he'd kept his word. He'd stayed.

He would stay. No matter what she did.

The smacks continued inexorably, but realization broke through the burgeoning ache. Deep down, she'd doubted his commitment. She thought he would disappear for real, not because he was mobilized. He'd just leave one day and not come back. Like her father, and then her mother. If she goaded him into it, then she could control when it happened.

That's why she'd needed the spanking, both for her lack of trust and as physical proof that he would keep his word. She could trust him to give her what he said he would. What she needed.

"I get it," she gasped over the rhythmic slaps. "I get it! Drew, please!"

His hand came to rest again on her now stinging, heated bottom, leaving an expectant, vibrant silence. Slowly, carefully, she relaxed her taut, quivering muscles, subsiding into his lap, but while the muscle tension eased, liquid flame burned in her swollen, wet folds. He reached out and gathered her hair in his hand, sending it spilling over her shoulder. Surprised by the temperate touch, she turned her face and looked back at him.

"Why did you leave the windows open?" he asked gently. The truth hurt. It really, really did. More than her ass, in fact. "Because I wanted to see what you'd do if I did."

"Even though I told you what I'd do." He wasn't asking. He knew. He'd known before she even walked into her bedroom.

There was a time and place for obstinate defiance. This wasn't it. "Yes."

"And what did you learn, Tess?" His voice was so soft and open she could hardly believe it came from the same man who'd purposefully paddled her into next week.

"To trust you." She took a deep breath and let it rush out onto the thin quilt under her hot cheek. "I learned you always keep your word."

"Always." The single word hummed with the unshakable confidence of a United States Navy SEAL. "You tell me to go and I'm gone. But you can't make me abandon you because you act up." He caressed her stinging butt. "You can earn yourself another spanking, no problem. But I'm here for the duration."

She let out another shuddering sigh as his words sank deep into her psyche, absolution and commitment rushing in to replace fear and abandonment. But her body still had a pressing need for relief. Undulating on his lap generated a sharp, longing twinge when her pubic bone made contact with his hard thigh. She'd never felt this way before, never had urgent, immediate desire thumping under her skin while she lay limp and pliable against his hard body. Soft give and sharp need melting together, and oh, how she wanted him to assuage the ache between her thighs.

Possessive admiration softened the line of his jaw as Drew slowly scanned her from toes to calves to thighs, lingering at her ass before sliding his gaze up the length of her spine, to her brown hair draped around her sweaty shoulders, then to her face. She didn't turn away, but let the heat throbbing in her bottom reflect in her eyes as she lifted her butt against his hand.

Admiration gave way to molten lust. "You want me to finish this," he said, but he wasn't asking.

All she could do was nod.

He raised his hand and she closed her eyes again, but this time she lifted into the stroke that fell not on the marked, throbbing skin, but rather on the soft inner curve where her buttocks met her thighs. The blow, lighter than the others but carefully placed, sent a sharp shard of heat flashing into her pussy. Once again she jumped and gasped, but even to her own ears the gasp wasn't one of pain or shock but the sound she made when he flicked his tongue against her clit. Which was exactly how this felt, except from the inside out. It felt as if he'd struck sparks in her clit, and the tender flesh swelled in demand.

She peered over her shoulder again. His eyes locked with hers and he deliberately raised his hand, landing another smack in the same place, but on the opposite cheek. Sharp, swift pleasure speared through her. The slap was different, the landing spot different, the sensations different, the moan different. Deeper. Throatier. Could have been lust, could have been pain.

He paused. "Too much?"

Yes, but oh, so good. "Don't stop," she groaned, winding her fingers through the hair gathered at the nape of her neck before she buried her face in her arm again.

His cock pulsed hard against her hip bone before his hand fell. The pace was slower, giving the pleasure time to build through the fire that exploded with each crack of his hand against her bottom. She found herself rocking back into each stroke, waiting for each one to fall, focusing on the ache expanding in her throbbing clit. The soles of her feet burned, and her nipples rubbed against the worn cotton quilt as she gasped and writhed under each blow.

Finally, when the ache threatened to destroy her, when she teetered on the edge of all-consuming pleasure, a smack landed that detonated the burgeoning heat. Orgasm flashed bright inside her and rolled to the tips of her fingers and toes as she threw her head back and let out a soft, high-pitched moan.

When she could rouse herself, she felt his hands stroking her back, bottom and thighs. Little tingles chased through the steady pulsations in her ass. She let her arms fall beside her face, gathered her strength and pushed back. As she moved, he pulled her panties off, then put his hands under her elbows to help her upright, supporting her but letting her situate herself as she pleased.

What pleased her was to straddle his lap, *carefully* ease her bottom back against his thighs and look him right in the eye while she tucked her hair behind her ears, wiped at her own eyes with the heels of her hands, licked her swollen lips. He watched each movement, then cupped her cheek and brushed his thumb over her mouth. He threaded his hand through her hair and pulled her down for a hot, swift kiss, his tongue flickering over her lips until she softened against him.

His gaze searched hers; his fingers gently rubbed her scalp. She returned the look, hiding nothing, avoiding nothing. What he saw must have pleased him because his lips quirked into a grin.

"You okay?"

Good question. Her heart pounded, whether from the exertion in the hot, muggy, still air or from the pitch and heave of her emotions in the past hour, she couldn't say. The rough material of his damp BDUs chafed her tender skin. A new tenderness drifted inside her, unfamiliar yet not the slightest bit scary.

"My ass hurts," she said bluntly, "but yeah, I'm okay. Tomorrow I'll make an appointment to get the air conditioner fixed. And…um…thank you. For loaning me—"

"Giving me," he corrected.

"Giving me the money."

"My pleasure," he said, but the wicked gleam in his eye betrayed the formal tone and words.

She trailed her fingers across his beautiful cheekbones and lips, down over the glittering gold scruff on his chin to dab at the sweat pooling in the hollow of his throat, then down his abdomen to snag her fingers in his waistband and press her pussy against the hard ridge in his pants. His shirt was so sodden she could probably wring it out like a wet rag. The gleam in his eyes went from wicked to intent.

"You liked that," she said, but the accusation was a mild one. There was a thin line between play and punishment.

He wasn't a liar, so he just gave her a wink.

"How red is my ass?"

"A pretty rosy-pink," he said huskily, as he throbbed hard against her soft folds.

Interesting. "You going to spank me again?"

Heat flared in his eyes and he tightened his grip on her hips. "If you need it or if you ask me very, very nicely."

"That sounds promising," she started, as she leaned forward and set her hands on his ribs. The quick, indrawn breath he gave at the pressure of her hands on his chest made her stop, then sit back. He loosened his grasp, but his lips pulled tight over clenched teeth. A couple seconds later, his breath eased out and his jaw relaxed.

Oh, God, oh, God… "Drew?" she asked and began to tug his sweat-saturated T-shirt from his pants.

"Easy, Tess," he said, but his voice was resigned as he submitted to her efforts to undress him, sitting forward and lifting his arms over his head so she could pull his shirt off and toss it to the floor with a wet thud.

Once again, icy fear wicked through her veins. The left side of his torso was a mass of bruises, some faded to yellowish-green, others the fresh deep purple of recent blows. A gash too deep to be a scratch but not deep enough to need stitches bisected his torso from just under his right pectoral down to his left hip bone. Much deeper and he would have been gutted.

"Drew," she breathed, her fingers trailing over the abused skin. "What happened? Did somebody *hit* you?"

The words sounded astonishingly stupid as they left her mouth, but he just gave a little smile at the incredulous tone of her voice. "A little dustup. Ain't no big thing, baby," he said, mocking mortal danger in the Alabama drawl that lingered despite nine years in California.

Which meant he couldn't talk about it. He'd matter-of-factly explained that anything really serious would mean members of his team at her front door and an introductory meeting with his family next to a flag-draped casket.

"Are your ribs broken?"

"Not even cracked," he said.

She looked back at the vicious, spreading bruises and quirked an eyebrow at him, but let it slide. There was no point in pestering him for details he couldn't provide. If someone got close enough to do this kind of intimate damage, whatever he'd done hadn't been the usual clockwork "in and out without a shot fired" mission. With her hand at his nape, she kissed his forehead, then rested hers against his.

"I love you, Tess," he said, his voice husky. "It's good to be home."

He needed a shower, a meal, twelve hours of sleep and about half a tube of antibacterial ointment, but fussing and hand-wringing went over as well as sleeping with the windows open. She pushed her concern aside, sat up and affected a disbelieving pout. "Really? Because from my perspective, you being home means me scared witless and spanked. But I'm glad it was good for you."

One golden eyebrow quirked up at her sassing. "That wasn't good for you? Because it sounded damned good at the end there."

"Okay, it was pretty good," she said with a mock eye roll.

"Pretty good? I can do better," he promised, then those seductive, dangerous hands went to the fly of his cargo pants and began to slip buttons from holes to free his straining shaft. His knuckles brushed against her damp mound, coming closer with each undone button. He pushed himself off the bed with both hands, lifting his hips for Tess to tug the clinging, sweaty fabric down. The pants made a louder, squishier thud than his shirt had when she flung them heedlessly behind her. From her crouched position, she kissed her way up his long, leanly muscled legs. After a brief, assessing look at his cock, straining thick and dark red from the blond nest of curls, she ran her tongue up the underside, the taste and scent of sex and sweat a heady aphrodisiac.

She kissed each hip bone, then licked the ridges of muscle forming his abdomen. Each wicked bruise received a gentle touch of her lips, as did the edges of the slice through his skin. She poured words not yet spoken into the caress of her breath, the flutter of her tongue against his skin, the not-quite-gentle pressure of her teeth against each nipple in turn. His breathing had slowed and softened with her ministrations but stopped altogether at the sharp pressure before easing out in a guttural groan.

She peeked down to see his cock pulse away from his abdomen as a pearly bead formed at the tip. "Wow," she said as she straddled him again. "You did miss me."

"I always do," he said, cupping her ass to pull her snug against his erection.

She affected a wince as his big hands flexed against her tender bottom. "Think twice before you work over your favorite playground," she said, the admonishment negated by her breathy voice…and the explosive orgasm.

Laughter gleamed in his eyes as he obediently slid his hands up her rib cage to her breasts, teasing her nipples as he massaged the soft flesh. "I like to play here, too."

"Mmm…yes," she whispered as he pinched and rolled the tender buds. Electric sensation flashed from her nipples to her clit. She bent forward, this time resting her hands on his shoulders, grinding a little as she kissed him. His tongue flicked against her parted lips, and with a soft moan she opened to him. Heat flashed between them as she rubbed her tongue against his, letting out a little sob as he nipped at her lower lip, then slid one hand into her hair to hold her for his mouth.

"Drew, please," she moaned. "I want to come with you inside me."

God, did she want that. She didn't idealize a relationship with any active-duty naval officer, let alone a SEAL. *Relationship* meant deployments, mobilizations, missions. It meant unexplained absences and weeks of worry. It meant seeing bruises, scrapes and scars on his body, pain and blankness in his eyes. It meant nightmares.

But with Drew *relationship* meant a love as strong and fierce as the commitment he made to his country and his team. It meant a soft place to land. It meant living with a wild, focused intensity when he was home, starting here in their bed. For now, empty solo orgasms were a thing of the past. She wanted to drop into the abyss with him as deep in her body as he was in her heart.

He unfisted his hand from her hair and set it on her hip as she reached for the condoms in the nightstand, then scooted back a bit to tear one open. Their fingers tangled as they rolled it down his shaft, but after that it was all her. She braced one hand on his shoulder and used the other to pull his erection away from his ridged abdomen. His breathing harshened, quickened as he looked down and watched her center her wet, open body over his tip and slowly engulf him.

His eyelids dropped as she slid down. "Fuck, yeah," he growled as she began to move. His head fell back, coming to rest against the white plaster wall behind her bed. "Oh, fuck, Tess. So good."

The first fast, furious time had taken the edge off, but only the second session, with its prolonged, intimate connection, smoothed all the emotional edges roughened by his absence. She kept her tempo fluid and relentless, building the pleasure for him in thin, fine layers, much as she would use heat and compounds to add a patina to metalwork. His throat worked as his eyes slid shut and his lips parted, his breath easing out in one long, soft exhalation. She flicked her tongue against his lower lip as she tweaked his nipples, and he inhaled and arched, thudding into her with enough force to make her squeak.

"So how nicely do I have to ask to get another spanking?"

His head snapped forward at the question, a hot, tortured gleam in his eyes. "Very nicely," he said, low and rough.

She spread her legs and ground against him on the next downstroke, burying him to the hilt in her hot, wet passage. "I'm not asking now, you understand," she whispered. "Just getting an idea for next time. You want me on my knees when I ask?"

He fisted his hands in her loose, damp hair before his head dropped back against the wall again, exposing the pulse pounding in the base of his throat. His cock throbbed inside her. "Jesus, Tess."

"I'll take that as a yes," she said, then pressed her lips to his jaw. "Let's see…me on my knees…naked…my mouth wet from sucking your cock…would that be nice enough for you? I'd say please."

"Ask like that and I'll give you anything you want," he said as he shifted, surging forward and pulling her head back to suck not quite gently at the skin over her collarbone.

She rode his movements, arching into him, skin slick and slippery as she rubbed against his torso. Her orgasm swelled, gathering strength with each gliding, increasingly heated move. "You going to spank me for teasing you?"

That was the final straw. Strong and sure, he rolled her to her back, then pulled out, spreading her legs wide with his hard thighs and pressing her hands into the bed beside her head. "I'm going to fuck you for teasing me," he growled. "Eventually."

He braced himself above her, their only points of contact his hair-roughened thighs against her sore bottom, and his fingers, interlocked with hers. Hard kisses dropped onto her plump lips, stifling her fretful moans, as sweat dropped from his collarbone and temples. When she quieted, he held himself above her with taut control, surveying her wet, pert breasts. He bent his head and blew gently on one nipple, watched it tighten, then treated the other to the same torture.

"They're almost as pink as your ass," he said.

She shuddered at the image. When his teeth closed on an erect nipple, she let out a whimper, but the insistent pressure and his flickering licks against the trapped bud quickly made her moan. The rough stubble on his cheeks rasped against her soft skin as he worked, moving from one nipple to the other until both were raspberry-red.

"Perfect," he said, as she desperately yanked against his tight grip, trying to free their locked fingers.

He left her nipples throbbing in the heated night air and licked his way down her breastbone to her navel, moving their joined hands as he shifted between her legs. Their interlaced fingers ended up under her sore ass, and she trembled at the submissive sensuality of using her hands to lift her wet, aching pussy to his mouth. The breadth of his shoulders spread her legs wide for the lash of his tongue. He flicked, he licked, he nibbled, all in his own time, driving her up the ladder of desire until she arched and fell away into blackness.

The luscious, slick stroke of his cock into her satiated body brought her back into the moonlit room. Poised above her, sheer possessive agony etched into his face, he plunged into her, his elbow braced at her shoulder to keep her from sliding away on the sweat-dampened sheets, his hand gripping her bottom without mercy, his hips spreading her open to his pounding body. Mindful of his bruised ribs, she gripped the small of his back, then wrapped her heels around his calves and arched to meet him.

When her orgasm came, there was no falling this time, only annihilation. She exploded, sinking her teeth into his shoulder as she flew apart. With one last, tremendous thrust he buried himself to the hilt inside her. He shuddered, sweat dripping from his jaw to plunk on her collarbone, then he buried his head in the curve of her neck, his shoulders heaving. Long minutes passed while she simply stroked the damp skin of his back, breathing slowly to encourage the subtle loosening of his muscles, his heart rate returning to its normal slow thud against his breastbone.

Eventually he rolled off her and staggered into the bathroom, giving a muffled curse when he banged his shoulder on the door frame. She giggled and flopped onto her stomach. He came back and eased himself down next to her, on his back. His uninjured side was closest, so she cuddled into him and felt his arm come around her.

"Damn, Tess. You pack a powerhouse punch for a hundred pounds and change."

"It's not me. Those ribs are cracked and you probably haven't slept more than an hour a day for the last four weeks." She kissed him, soft and slow and sweet, then gave in to curiosity. "Where are your boots?"

"Locked in the trunk of my car with my duffel. I'll get 'em in a minute," he said. "You working tomorrow?"

"In my studio, but I switched shifts at The Blue Dog. The developer called while you were gone. He really liked the balcony I did for that house in Balboa Park. He wants to see staircase designs by Monday."

Drew lifted his head to look at her, a delighted grin splitting his face. "Tess, that's fantastic." His head dropped back and sweat trickled down his temple. "Fuck, it's hot in here. Let's grab a quick shower and go celebrate. Somewhere air-conditioned."

He slid his legs over the edge of the bed and sat up with a wince. Before he could get to his feet, she went to her knees, slipped her arms around his neck and whispered into his ear the words she'd doodled in swirling calligraphy with the sketches of staircases and his face. "I love you, too, Drew."

Despite injuries, exhaustion and exertion, he pulled her around him, into his lap. "Yeah?" he asked, his eyes searching hers.

She gave him a soft smile. "Yeah. Welcome home."

★ ★ ★ ★ ★

A PARIS AFFAIR

ADELAIDE COLE

THE STREETS OF PARIS

"Oh-laaa! Tu me fais chier quoi, Paris de merde! Ville des putain de lumières! Tu m'emmerdes!"

Valérie swore angrily as she tried to wipe the thick smear of soft, fetid dog shit off her shoes. "City of fucking Light! Go fuck yourself!" she muttered. The quaint Paris cobblestones, and in fact all the streets of Paris, were a landmine of dog turds. And they were a racing course of nasty little speeding four-cylinder cars, and of scooters driven by rude and careless teenagers.

She found the building. With Mathieu trailing, she entered the courtyard and tried to wipe her dirty shoe on a mat. She and her son made their way up the four flights to the medical specialist's office.

The receptionist looked at Valérie with undisguised boredom. "I'm sorry, *madame,* but there's nothing I can do for you. Your son requires *this* form—" she held one up in the same manner that a primary-school teacher would use with a pint-size pupil "—*before* he can have this appointment with the doctor."

"But I have the appointment *already.* This is *it.* It is *now,*"

Valérie said, pointing to her watch for effect. "How can some- one have given me an appointment that I'm not allowed to have? It makes no sense." Mathieu was whining at her side. He'd been complaining for most of their errands. *"Maman, juice!* Thirsty! Juice!" he repeated, tugging at her pant leg.

Valérie rummaged in her handbag and found a small bottle of water and handed it to him. He drank. The break in his whining felt like a release of some of the overwhelming, exhausting pressure in her head. Mathieu, her younger of two children, was almost five, and should have been speaking in complete sentences. But he wasn't, and when her veil of self- denial was finally lifted by the primary school's refusal to admit him because of language development issues, she'd unhappily begun to travel the routes of help for developmentally delayed children.

The receptionist sighed heavily. "The appointments are given six weeks ahead. *Madame, all* the families understand that they have those six weeks to have their *assessment* done before they are permitted their initial follow-up here. *Every- one* knows that before they arrive here. I'm terribly sorry you didn't understand that, *madame,* but it's commonly understood by all the doctor's patients."

Valérie had fought so many of these grinding, bureaucratic battles since they'd returned to Paris that she knew it was ut- terly pointless to continue any exchange with the receptionist. *"Bon. Merci, madame. Au revoir,"* she replied, with necessary courtesy.

"Au revoir, madame!" clipped the receptionist in return. Valé- rie gathered her grocery bags and stuffed the folded blank forms inside. They left the office and made their way back down the four winding flights of stairs.

Mathieu hung on her coat as they walked through the drizzling rain, dodging aggressive human and car traffic.

"Watch your step for dog poop, Mathieu," she instructed. They walked back down into the métro, where Mathieu's jacket pocket became snagged on the turnstile. He got stuck and began to wail. People behind him complained loudly and shoved their way through the next turnstiles. She unhooked his pocket and untangled him. They struggled through the crush of humanity on the platforms and trains, through six stops and two line changes. The air was stuffy and stale and the cars were crowded. Valérie fought her way to empty seats and plopped her son on them to keep him from whining for at least a few stops.

Then, back up the escalators and stairs from the métro to the street, where she tripped over the knee of a woman sitting on the pavement, begging for money. The woman yelled at Valérie, who decided this city was a horrid little piece of hell.

After walking the four blocks to their building, they wearily climbed their own three flights. Each step up drained energy from Valérie's body. Reaching the final landing, she felt as if all her vitality had been leeched out, bit by bit, by those nasty streets, regulated offices, irritating shops, stifling métro cars, and finally, their own never-ending stairs.

Back in the apartment, Philippe was already home from work, having picked up Mathieu's sister, Manon, from summer art camp. Though he looked wan and tired, he tried to summon a bit of enthusiasm as they pushed through the door.

Sweaty and fatigued, Valérie left her shoes, still stinking and dirty, outside the door, making a mental note to clean them after the kids were in bed. Mathieu sank onto the floor and began to cry.

Valérie dropped her bags, hung up her coat and walked directly to the bathroom. Maybe she would feel better after a hot shower, she thought. Before shutting the door, she said, "How about a nice glass of wine when I come out, dear?"

Then she closed it behind her and undressed, leaving her things on the floor. The building's ancient plumbing hammered and banged as she turned it on.

By the time she finished her shower, Mathieu's tears had tapered off. His attention was caught by a piece of a toy he'd found on the floor, and he was murmuring to himself. The shower did lift some of the stress of the day, and a moderately refreshed Valérie emerged from the steamy bathroom, wrapped in a robe and towel-drying her hair. She sat down at the kitchen table and smiled at Philippe. He gave her a tired smile and handed her a glass of Bordeaux. *"Santé,"* they both said joylessly in unison, clinking their glasses out of routine. *To better days,* they both thought to themselves.

Valérie took a big drink with one hand and continued toweling her damp hair with the other. She sighed deeply. "So, how was work?" she asked, instantly regretting having done so.

Philippe rolled his eyes upward and shook his head. "Politics, politics," he said wearily. She didn't ask for details, and he didn't offer them. As with so many married couples, this was a rerun of many similar conversations. They fell silent and sipped their wine.

The two had met while at university in Paris. She had grown up in the south, in Provence. He came from Bretagne, in the north. She was petite and olive-skinned, with a mass of dark, curly hair; he was blond, fair-skinned, tall and thin. She was emotional, effusive and Mediterranean, while he was cool and intellectual. Opposites attracted, and they had enjoyed the city together as a young, courting couple. They'd crossed the country together to meet and visit their respective families in the north and south. Their love was solidified in the shared fun of travel, and in the discoveries that new adventures brought. Valérie sometimes thought, lately, that their marriage felt so difficult now because those common joys had vanished with this new phase of their life.

After they married, Valérie worked as a city librarian, and Philippe secured a job in the Ministry of Foreign Affairs. He was smart and rose in the ranks, and within a year had won a junior posting in Copenhagen's French consulate. That began their international life, and two more foreign posts, in Los Angeles and Hong Kong, followed over the next several years. They enjoyed an exciting time abroad, where Valérie had little more to worry about than how they dressed and the appearance of their home. Their postings were politically calm spots, and their lives were easy. But new milestones brought new difficulties.

They started their family during their final post abroad, in the Canadian port city of Vancouver. They had both wanted children, but Valérie had difficult pregnancies and deliveries, and child rearing was a steep learning curve. She had always been emotionally and physically sensitive, and the twenty-four-hour days and mini-crises of minding babies and small children took a toll on her. Philippe was a caring husband and father, but he couldn't take the time away from work that Valérie's constitution seemed to require. He worked hard in his position, and at home felt put upon.

Philippe and Valérie had experienced a joyful bond as a childless couple, but found it difficult to make the transition to their new life with children. Their love and caring did not wane, but some of their happiness together did. Valérie often felt isolated, and those feelings only multiplied when Mathieu began showing odd behaviour as a toddler.

At the same time, Philippe was offered a desk position back in Paris. It was not a job he particularly wanted, and it paid less than the international posts did; but it was strategically important in the schema of his career. It was a stepping-stone position, so it was impossible to refuse. They left their life in green and airy Vancouver, and settled back into crowded Paris and its cramped apartment existence...this time with two young children, one of whom was showing developmental problems.

In this new life, Valérie shouldered the burden of the children's care. While their international positions had afforded a nanny and housekeeper, this Paris assignment didn't come with those luxuries. She was on her own. Philippe wasn't any help on the domestic scene, since his days were spent in a Machiavellian cauldron of colleagues jockeying for position. The couple missed the days of their foreign postings. CONSUL license-plated SUVs conferred special status, and cocktail parties were filled with easy, empty diplomatic conversation and the champagne that advertised France's good life to the world.

Valérie missed those parties and dinners. And she missed the stylish distinction of being a Frenchwoman abroad. Being French attracted an automatic cachet she had enjoyed. "Oh, Valérie," she would hear from a new friend in a foreign country, "I couldn't pull off that look with that scarf. Only a Frenchwoman can do that. You always look so elegant." And felt so lighthearted.

But the breezy confidence that foreigners gave her turned into yet another casualty of their move back to Paris. Now she was just another fortysomething wife and mom among a million stunning French girls. She tried to maintain her standards, but the demands of two children didn't leave her with the same motivation or time that she'd had before, when a nanny helped with child care and a housekeeper with the mundane tasks that were now hers alone.

The children's needs, plus her husband's new job, also took a toll on their romantic life. They were never alone together in the tiny apartment, and sex became perfunctory, if they weren't already too tired to bother. Their love and commitment was intact, but sexual heat had dissipated, at least in these days of grocery shopping, child rearing and career challenges.

"I'll get the kids dinner," Valérie said, pushing herself up from the table. She took her glass with her.

"I'll help. I'll make a salad," Philippe said, getting up, as well.

She boiled pasta for the children and recounted what had been accomplished that day along the lengthy progression of Mathieu's diagnosis and treatment. Life abroad had been deceptively easy, and they had taken it for granted. If they'd been less self-deluded in their former post, they would have noticed signs that their son wasn't developing normally, but the easy international scene had seduced them into thinking that their entire life was a carefree ride. Had they noticed, they would have sought help earlier and avoided the degree of difficulty they now faced.

The discovery that Mathieu sat somewhere on the ever-widening autism continuum brought with it despondency as they fought to regain their equilibrium as a couple, as parents and as a family. Valérie and Philippe both struggled to relegate Manon to last-in-line for care and attention as they tried not to grieve over the loss of a dream of having two perfect children. Life weighed heavily back here in Paris.

"One piece of good news," Philippe said as he drained the bottle into his wife's glass. "My parents called and said they'd like to have the kids for a few days. My vacation is already on the schedule at work, so I thought I'd take them up on the train on Wednesday and beat the rush out of the city."

They both knew that Valérie disliked his parents and wouldn't want to go, so he didn't even ask. "You can have a break from the kids and all the appointments and running around. You can stay in your pajamas all day and relax."

Valérie smiled at him, took his hand and squeezed it gently between hers, saying, "You're my angel." He leaned over and kissed her forehead.

Philippe was careful with Valérie ever since she had suffered a minor emotional breakdown in the midst of the move back to Paris and the shock of their troubles with Mathieu. Philippe made sure she took her anti-anxiety medication, and tried to ease some of her daily load.

"*Papa!* Mathieu ripped the head off Chloé!" Manon stomped into the kitchen and displayed the evidence in both hands.

"I didn't! I didn't! I didn't! I didn't…!" Mathieu yelled repeatedly from the other room. Valérie dropped her head. She so desperately needed respite from the chaos of…of just everything. She missed the big houses of international life. Here, space was a rare commodity, and although they had a roomy apartment by Paris standards, it was claustrophobic for a stressed family.

Philippe glanced at his wife, and when he saw her strained expression, jumped up and ushered Manon out in order to calm the waters.

PREPARATIONS AND DEPARTURES

The day before their departure, Valérie was packing Philippe's and the children's bags for their holiday in Bretagne. She was going through a mental checklist of what they would need for their beach days when the cell phone rang.

She walked into the hallway, found her bag and dug through it for her phone. "Yes, hello!"

"Valérie?"

"Yes?"

"You don't recognize my voice? Of course, it's been so long. It's Oscar from New York...."

"Oscar...Nathalie's friend? Yes, of course...Oscar, how are you? It's been a long time."

"Yes, it has, but I had such a nice time at that dinner, and I've never forgotten you both. How is your husband, your children?"

"Fine, fine. Are you here in France?"

"I am. That's why I'm calling. I'm in Paris for a few days. We had such a nice dinner in New York, so I got your number here from Nathalie. She told me you had moved back. I was going to ask if you and Philippe could meet me for supper while I'm in the city."

Valérie was stunned to be getting this call. Her heart began to pound and she started to sweat. Thank God this was over the telephone and not in person! She had to concentrate in order to keep her voice sounding offhanded and light. Oscar, of all people! During their Los Angeles posting a few years back, Philippe and Valérie had flown to New York to visit Valérie's sister. Nathalie had married a New Yorker, and worked as a private French tutor for firms that did business abroad. Oscar was a senior manager in an international sports federation, and needed to be multilingual, since their business was done around the world. He became one of her students, and eventually a friend, and had been a guest at the dinner party.

Valérie was instantly attracted to him. She had been seated across from him and they'd chatted throughout the meal, which his wife hadn't attended. Oscar was not a big man, maybe 5'6"—which accounted for his talent at soccer when he was young—but she liked his size, and beneath his sharp business suit his build seemed compact, lithe and muscular. She'd sensed a fierce sexuality under those executive clothes. He had light olive skin, and his face looked toned and angular. She even liked the shape of his neck, which made her wish he hadn't been wearing a tie, so that she could peek at his chest.

She loved a man's fit, lean torso, and how it made her eye travel down to his sex, and she still remembered that the lines of his shirt suggested he was strong and muscular. He sat comfortably, with his legs apart and his elbows resting on his thighs, and exuded the alpha confidence of an athlete. Philippe, though very attractive, was not particularly fit, and he held himself the way intellectuals and businessmen do, with their heads somehow disconnected from their bodies. But this man was different. She had felt that he was *in* his body, and that his mind and body were a powerful team. He had an aura that seemed to knock other men out of the room.

He was several years older than Valérie, and had beautifully graying hair and an appealing, virile five o'clock shadow that brought out his square jawline. His eyes, which had held her gaze longer than normal for a casual dinner gathering, were dark green. She'd found them captivating, and more than once had looked away when she felt the intimacy overwhelming.

She still remembered how, when he spoke, he'd rested his elbow on the table and lightly stroked his lips with his thumb while holding her glance. She'd found him sexy, and a little sly. For a diplomat's spouse, dinner parties were akin to a part-time job, and she met scores of good-looking men, married or not. Valérie had never imagined being involved with a man outside her marriage, and she and Philippe had been very happy together at that point. But Oscar had left an impression on her that hadn't disappeared.

All they'd shared that evening was common dinner party conversation, but underneath the banter she'd felt a current of heat between them. Had he shared her feeling? She had always thought so, because his eyes never left hers except when they perused her hair and her shirt front. She felt as if he was carefully checking her out, and was flattered, because she found him so attractive.

But she never found out one way or another. She and her sister didn't share intimacies, so Valérie had never mentioned him to Nathalie except in completely casual terms. She'd prayed that nobody at the party had noticed the heat she had felt between them.

At one point in the evening she had spied Philippe in a conversation with him, and when they were on their way home she learned her husband had exchanged phone numbers with Oscar, who apparently traveled widely for his job and sometimes found himself in Los Angeles. She had been nonchalant about it to Philippe, but was secretly thrilled. She was disappointed that they never heard from Oscar again, but had never quite forgotten him.

Clearly, the momentary attraction had not faded, because she was as excited as a schoolgirl to have him on the phone.

"Well, Philippe is taking the children to the north coast to his parents' for a few days, and I'll be on my own. We could get together for a coffee tomorrow. How's that?"

"Lovely. You're there in the sixteenth arrondissement, at the address your sister gave?"

"Yes, yes. And we have a good café at the corner, called Café Liberté. It has a blue awning—you'll see it. It's across from a little grocery with flowers in front."

"No problem. Is four o'clock fine for you?"

"Perfect. Tomorrow at four. See you then."

"I look forward to it! I'm so glad I'll have some company for a bit! Paris is a little harsh when you're alone."

"Oh, your wife didn't come with you?" she ventured. *What the hell am I thinking?* she wondered.

"No, no, I came for work in Madrid. She has work in New York."

"Oh, that's too bad," Valérie lied. "Well, anyway…till tomorrow then. Bye-bye."

"Tomorrow!"

They hung up simultaneously.

Valérie stood in the room with the phone in her hand. Then she sat on the bed, in the middle of the piles of clothes and toiletries and open suitcases. She dropped the cell back into her bag and took out a pack of cigarettes. Philippe disapproved of her smoking, but wasn't too angry if she did it only occasionally, and when she was alone.

She got back up, went to the window and opened it, then lit

up and took a deep drag. She looked mindlessly at the traffic below and the neighbors around her, and recalled her single meeting with Oscar. She remembered the color of his eyes and now, with the phone call, the calm of his smooth, sexy voice. She swallowed and took another drag of her cigarette, feeling something deep in her body that she hadn't felt in years. It was pure, sexual wanting. It was dormant sensation reawakened by the voice of this man she'd met for just a few hours years ago. She felt a flicker in her sex, as if it was being shaken awake, too.

She had never been unfaithful in her marriage, and had never shared more than an innocent flirtation with another man. But…then *what,* exactly? she asked herself. Things at home were so stressed, and sex was lukewarm at best. She didn't even wait for arousal anymore with her husband. She just wanted it to be done so that she could sleep. What a state!

Her discontent allowed a space to open within her. It did not open in her heart, but in her body, and she felt it through her nerve endings. She felt that a ray of daylight was piercing the dismal gray cloud of her life, and offering her something beyond her marriage. How could the timing be so *perfect?* she asked herself, careful to avoid the word *affair.* She didn't wish for any real distance from Philippe and her children; but while they were having *their* little holiday, might she have a "holiday" of her own…?

She was dying to know if Oscar was interested in her, and if he ever strayed outside his marriage; what man *wouldn't,* she wondered, if the opportunity presented itself? She felt the stirring storm of sexual anticipation that she had in New York. It had been *so* long since a man had moved her sexually. Physically, she lived in a dry desert of neutered sex, and had actually forgotten the earthquake of desire. Here it was, rumbling inside her.

She recalled the sizzling undercurrent she'd felt with Oscar, and her nerves jumped. Did he really just want a cup of coffee, or something more…? She would have to wait and see. And if *something more* meant something that could harm her marriage, the stability of the life she and Philippe had made together, or their children…these were issues too monumental for her to allow herself to consider.

Valérie wasn't a schemer or a planner, and wasn't deceptive by nature; but her circumstances and her own emotional weakness left her open to seizing a moment and hoping it would all turn out for the best. She felt such a great longing for respite from a difficult period in their lives. And unless she was very wrong, Oscar's sudden appearance felt ready-made: *prêt-à-porter!*

Looking out the window, she recalled Oscar and her sense of him. At the dinner she had imagined what he looked like under his sharp business suit—from the way his clothes fell she'd thought she could make out a taut, slim muscular build. She'd felt his raw sexuality. She remembered his green eyes gazing into hers like a cheeky dare…and she breathed hard. She put her cigarette out on the window ledge, closed the window, and turned back to packing for her family's trip.

The next day all the preparations were in place. The taxi was ordered, bags were packed and the grandparents were expecting them at the train station. They were leaving around lunchtime, so Valérie had prepared food for the trip.

"All ready to go?" Philippe asked the children. He looked at his wife. "This will be a good change of pace for everyone, don't you think?"

Valérie smiled warmly at him and hugged him around his waist. He reciprocated with his arm around her shoulder. They stood together, looking at the children, who were stuffing last-second treasures into their bags. The apartment buzzer rang, signaling the taxi. "Let's go! Taxi's here!" Philippe said.

Ding-dang-dong... The three-tone notices hummed continuously over the loudspeaker, announcing trains coming and going. Gare de l'Est was a loom in motion. Families, singles, couples, old people, children, backpackers—they walked and ran in every direction, their paths crisscrossing in a colorful weave.

"We'll miss you, my love," Philippe said. "Mathieu, you know *Maman* is staying home. She's not coming with us. It's just us three visiting *Mamie* and *Papie*."

Mathieu looked at his parents, then turned back to watch the crowd. He clung to his mother. "He's gonna throw a total fit the second we get on the train and he sees you're not coming," Manon said, matter-of-factly.

"Try and relax," Philippe directed, "and don't smoke too much. Remember to eat properly. I'll call you as soon as we're there."

"If I'm out, don't worry. I might go to a film or sit in a café. Just things to clear my head. Maybe I'll do some shopping for the kids. Make sure you all enjoy yourselves."

Ding-dang-dong...boarding train 631 in five minutes to Lorient on track 15...

CAFÉ LIBERTÉ

Back in the apartment in front of her bedroom mirror, Valérie thought that the pale green top gave her a flirty décolletage, but that maybe the black skirt wasn't so flattering. On the other hand, she thought as she tried on things from her closet, the pale pink linen dress showed off her waist and had décolleté, as well. She chose the pink dress and stepped into it.

She was in good shape for her age, despite having had a couple of kids. Her breasts hadn't bounced back to their former glory, but were still nicely shaped. Her olive skin tone was still pretty, and she had a slim waist and nice legs. She was a petite height, and had to watch what she ate to stay slim, now that she was nearly forty-three. She still cared about her figure, but had never anticipated being *naked with another man*. It had simply never occurred to her. She looked at her body and thought that her hair was still her best feature. She had wild, glossy black curls that fell below her shoulders.

Oh, maybe it's just a coffee, after all, she thought, hoping that it wasn't…but afraid that it was…! Conflicting notions pulled her one way and then another. On one hand she felt as if she had the right to a moment of pure joy with someone; yet on the other hand she knew she would be breaking a commitment she'd made to her husband. And then again, Oscar might be simply meeting an acquaintance for a coffee....

A police siren passing on a street snapped her out of her confused reverie. "Oh!" she said out loud to herself. She stood up straight and looked in the mirror. She glanced at the clock by the bed. She was meeting Oscar in just fifteen minutes. She fluffed out some of her curls, placing a thick mass just over one eyebrow. She tucked another clump behind one ear to reveal a dangly silver earring. She put on a bit of mascara and then sat back to look at her reflection. *Am I still pretty?* she wondered. She looked at the lines that had begun to appear around her dark, almond eyes, and at the circles underneath. *Just a coffee,* she repeated, dabbing on a bit more perfume and checking her lipstick in the mirror.

The café was half-filled. The right number of people: it was neither uncomfortably intimate, nor too busy and bustling. Oscar already had a table.

"Oscar!" She made her way through the tables. He stood.

"Valérie, my dear!" They brushed cheeks in a French greeting.

"Lovely to see you, my dear," Oscar said.

"Wonderful to see you again," Valérie said in return, instantly hoping that she wasn't giving herself away.

Oscar was exactly as she had remembered him. In a split second she sensed the same magnetic pull between them. He wore another smart business suit and looked as dashing as she'd recalled. Her stomach leaped, but she tried to act casual.

"Have you seen Nathalie recently?" she asked, starting the conversation with a subject they shared.

"Yes, a few months ago," he answered, "and I called her for your new phone number. Are you close with your sister?"

"No, not so much," Valérie admitted. "We've been in different places for so many years now."

The conversation was casual, but the air between them was not. His eyes locked on hers. While they mouthed pleasantries, she gazed back into the green eyes she recalled from the first time they had met. She felt drawn to him.

"And is your family well?"

"Everyone is fine. Our kids are happy at their schools, and I hope they're working hard. How is Philippe's new post? You must all be happy to be back in France."

"Yes, of course," Valérie said. "It's always easier in your own language. And the new posting is working well. It was a good move." She lied, feeling that the truth of her life was too heavy a burden for this lighthearted meeting.

"Well then, everything fine for all of us!" Oscar said brightly. He caught the eye of the passing waiter and turned to Valérie. "Listen, how about a nice glass of wine instead of coffee? I know it's a bit early, but it's so nice to be here. I'd like to take advantage of my few days in Paris...."

"Yes, yes, why not?" Valérie answered. "A glass would be nice." She knew that a glass of wine would loosen her up, but she felt as if every step forward led toward a precipice. The feeling both excited and scared her.

Oscar scanned the café blackboard menu and ordered wine for them both. His French was smooth and fluent. The waiter left.

"Your French is excellent, you know?" Valérie said, complimenting him.

"It's easy to learn with a good teacher like Nathalie! But I didn't have a choice—I had to learn for work. And you, are you working at all?"

"Me? Oh, no, I'm too busy with the children. When they're older I'll go back, but they're still small, you know."

The wine arrived and Oscar toasted to reacquaintances. *"Santé!"* they said together, touching glasses lightly. They both smiled, and their eyes met again. He gave a sly smile, and she felt a rush of warmth throughout her body. She had a fleeting image of the slim hips and tight muscles under that suit. She wanted to run her hand over a curving biceps, and suddenly thought, *I know how people do this.* She had an image of a grassy plain and a cliff's edge, and felt that a marriage was on that plain. At the cliff's edge was Oscar, and leaping off it together wourld be a daring, heart-pounding adventure. Looking into his eyes made her move closer to the cliff's edge.

"So," Valérie said, trying to be a bit flirtatious. It was a long time since she'd flirted with anyone, and she felt as if she was treading uneasily on unfamiliar, uneven ground. "How do you have time away from your work here to drink in the afternoon?"

"Oh, I don't have anything to do in Paris," Oscar answered, draining his glass. He stretched out his legs, crossed his arms and looked at her with a half smile. "I was working in Madrid and asked the company travel agent to arrange a layover. Just to relax, really. My wife is busy with work. And why didn't you go with Philippe and your children?"

Valérie rested her forearms on the table and leaned her chest toward Oscar provocatively. "Oh, Philippe had a chance to take the children to his parents', and we both agreed that it would be nice if I had the week to myself at home. I don't really get along with my in-laws, anyway." She cocked her head and answered his gaze with her eyes.

"Mmm." He nodded. "And me, I didn't want to waste all those French lessons on work! The Americans say 'All work makes Jack a dull boy.'" He laughed. Valérie laughed, too, and their smiles and their fast-disappearing wine both lightened and intensified the air between them. She felt as if a weight was lifting, and as if the cliff edge was fast approaching.

Oscar read her thoughts. "Listen, Valérie," he said, and when he leaned over the table he took her hand. He did it so swiftly and smoothly, without skipping a beat or breaking eye contact, that it took her breath away. Valérie felt her heart start to pound. *What daring!* she thought, truly shocked. *He knows I'm married!*

"Instead of another glass here, why don't you be my Paris guide and we'll have a walk along the Seine? I was going to ask you and Philippe for supper, but he's away. Maybe you'll join me for dinner tonight. Yes? No fun to eat alone, you know."

Before she could answer or remove her hand, which buzzed from his electric touch, he released it and signaled to the waiter for the check. *He's so cheeky,* she thought, attracted now not only to piercing green eyes, slim hips and strong hands, but by his daring. *He must want me, too,* she thought, feeling more confident than ever.

"I can't think of a reason to say no…." Valérie said, cocking her head slightly and holding his gaze for a few seconds. She twirled a lock of hair behind her ear and smiled at him.

"Well, there you go, then. It's decided," answered Oscar.

As they left the café and walked into the sunshine he subtly took her arm. In return, she moved closer to his body, feeling his strong, slim thigh beside her hip. She felt him beside her as they walked, and her nerves tingled. *When* was *the last time the sun shone?* she wondered.

DINNER OUT

Near evening, Oscar took Valérie to a restaurant he said he'd always wanted to try when in Paris, but hadn't had the chance. He said it was written up in the American food magazines, and its chef-owner won accolades for his North African-French fusion dishes. They drank a deep, bold Bourgogne, and toasted to "a little holiday together," as Oscar called it.

They tasted each other's adventurous plates, and at the end traded bold desserts where sweet and spicy flavors danced together. Fresh figs were gently enrobed in French *pâte feuilletée* and flavored with orange-water and cardamom. Spanish peaches were embedded in couscous spiced with vanilla and cinnamon.

"May I?" asked Oscar quietly.

Valérie put down her fork and looked at him inquisitively. She didn't know what he wanted. With his thumb and forefinger he picked up a warm, supple, deep amber fig, dripping with its honey-and-orange glaze, and lifted it to her mouth. She smiled and parted her lips. When he carefully slipped the slim brown tip inside, she closed her mouth around it and bit softly through it, its tiny seeds relenting to her teeth. Her cunt jumped with pleasure.

Oscar smiled with one corner of his mouth. He held the dripping fruit to his own lips, licked the part where her mouth had touched, and bit it off. Juice ran down his finger. They didn't speak. The intensity of their exchange blurred everything around them.

Valérie wanted him. The wine was erasing the edginess in her nerves, and she felt less confined to the imposed rules of marriage. She felt that the universe would let her love her husband and *make love* to Oscar. She *had* to feel his body around hers, she thought. But she just couldn't bring herself to tell him, to say it out loud. Would he say something? She fingered her long, silver chain and leaned toward him over the crisp linen tablecloth. She felt the wine in her body, felt her face flush and her vulva pulse.

Oscar's eyes met hers, and he finally said, quietly, "You're a beautiful woman, Valérie. You must know I think so. Is this a moment for us to share? If it isn't, maybe we should stop right here." He stroked her hand with the tips of his fingers and held her gaze. But before she could tell him how she felt, he said, "Don't answer now. I've had a wonderful time with you, but I'm going to put you in a taxi."

Valérie's eyes widened.

"Let's think about what we're doing," he added. "If we go any further, I'd like to feel that you're sure. We've got lots to protect, both of us. Listen, I'm going to sneak in a business call to New York before bed. It's still early there," he said.

She didn't know how to reply. She wanted to tell him that she wanted to feel his skin, to touch him, but she felt conflicted between desire and giving too much away.

"You're sure I can't offer you a cognac…?" she said, hoping it was the right thing to say in a situation where the lines between them were blurred. Now they were neither friends nor lovers.

He held her hand as they left the restaurant. The valet hailed a taxi, and before Valérie knew it, Oscar was holding the door open.

"I've had a wonderful afternoon with you, my dear," he said softly. "What a nice surprise. Thank you for sharing your day. And what are you doing tomorrow?"

"I have no plans, and I'd love to make plans with you...." A mental picture flashed through her mind of an embrace with him, of them standing against a wall and him pumping his ass against her, between her legs. She snapped out of the reverie. "Uhh, I have *nothing* to do. You know, if my family's away, then I'm on holiday, too. Why don't you call me in the morning? I haven't been to the Centre Pompidou in *years*...."

"Let's do it—let's be real tourists," Oscar said with a laugh. Then the mood shifted in an instant while they looked into each other's eyes. Oscar's hand swept into the back of her hair, and he leaned in and met her mouth with his with an urgency that sent a current of desire down her loins. The kiss was hot, deep and hungry. They both shuddered, and his hand palmed her body from between her legs, where he pressed against her, up to her breast, which he squeezed, kissing her even more passionately. Just as quickly, he let her go and held her by her shoulders, away from him. They looked at one another and breathed hard.

"I'll call you in the morning," Oscar said. He guided her into the taxi, announced Valérie's address to the cabbie and handed him some folded euros, then gestured warmly to her as the taxi moved into traffic. With the wine in her head, and the sensation of their kiss, and of their shared dessert...she simply remained in those moments. She felt the breeze from the open windows of the speeding taxi, and watched the glow of passing lights and fluorescent signs. His touch was branded on her senses, and their sexual energy hummed through her body until the taxi stopped at her building.

Valérie turned the key in the lock and entered a quiet, dark apartment. She kicked off her shoes and dropped onto a chair at the small kitchen table. She realized that she had never been in the apartment when it was empty. The silence pressed on her; she was unaccustomed to it. No din of the children. Nothing.

She turned the handle to open the window and let in the sounds of the Paris night. She looked out at the night sky and neighboring apartments. Her head spun with the excitement of being with Oscar, and it spun with the wine. She was still slightly startled that he was…well…*gone*. Not that she had expected otherwise, she reminded herself.…

She looked back into the dark apartment and noticed the red blinking light of the telephone answering machine. She sighed. She knew it was Philippe, but she wanted to remain in *this* moment.

Valérie got up, went to the bathroom, and then straight to bed. She couldn't remember when she had last felt that rush of electricity and anticipation. It was exciting and exhausting.

SIGHTSEEING

The morning was gray and rainy. She got up and showered, replaying the events of the evening with Oscar. She heaved a sigh out loud, knowing nobody could hear. After she dressed, Valérie dialed Philippe's cell phone.

"Philippe! How was the trip? How are the children?"

"We called but you weren't home! Where were you? Are you all right? Did you get the message?"

"Oh, I went out to a film and I had a sandwich in a café. I did a little shopping. And I didn't want to call and wake anyone." Her sense of guilt made her feel that even Oscar's presence in Paris was contraband, and she quickly decided to avoid his name altogether. She knew that they had crossed lines, no matter what happened now.

"Understood. We're all fine, and I think the sea air is good for the kids. After all the time at the beach and in the water, they slept like logs."

They covered the news of the trip and of the children, chatted and soon had nothing more to say. "I love you, my darling," Philippe said.

"I love you. Kisses to the kids," she answered. And they hung up.

The buzzer rang. Their next-door neighbor, Thérèse, came by most mornings to ask Valérie to watch her baby for a minute while she ran to the bakery for her morning baguette. "Yes, Thérèse!" she called as she walked to the door and automatically opened it.

"Am I bothering you...?"

"Oscar!"

Oscar let himself in, and closed the door. "You're so surprised! Should I leave?" He held up a bag. "You have a wonderful bakery just around the corner, and of course they make the best brioches and croissants. I just couldn't help myself. If you're busy, we'll just have a bite and I'll leave. Otherwise we can share a *petit déjeuner*."

"Oh, no, I'm not busy at all! Of course not! Come in, come in. I'll make coffee." She was grateful that she'd already dressed, but wondered at the state of her unmade face and hair. She brushed her fingers through some slept-on curls and hoped they would fall right. "I thought you'd call, but that's fine. You're a rascal, aren't you," she teased. She took the paper bag and started ahead of him toward the kitchen.

"I can be...." And she suddenly felt his hand on her arm. He took it firmly and pulled her back toward him, so she gasped in surprise. He turned her to face him and tugged her body to his. One hand moved up to her head, and he didn't hesitate before delivering a long, firm kiss. His fingers were entwined in her hair, and his other hand clasped her arm so that he held her close to him. His kiss was demanding, tantalizing and precise. She shivered. He smelled clean and yet musky. She drank him in. He stopped abruptly.

He held her shoulders and moved her away from him to look squarely in her eyes. "Let's make sure we know what

we're doing here…. I *want* you, but we've got families…."
He *knew* the significance of what they were heading toward,
and he wanted their intimacy acknowledged, permitted. He
gave her time to refuse, to have a second thought. One of his
hands left her shoulder and ran through her thick, wild hair.

She met his gaze, but didn't want to face real costs. Valérie didn't care about his wife or why he was doing this; and
she didn't care about her own life at this moment. She simply
felt intoxicated by him, and she *wanted* him. "Let's just call it
a holiday…." she whispered, putting an index finger to her
lips. "From everything…and no strings attached…" And she
moved swiftly to his mouth, kissing him and pulling him to
her. *Finally,* she thought, running her hand over his chest.

"Oh, yes!" she murmured aloud. Nerves shot up from her
deepest insides to the roof of her mouth. Her body remembered
these long-dormant carnal sensations. She swiftly undid his
shirt buttons and felt the hard curves of his chest muscles.
"I want you!" she whispered in his ear as she gently bit his
earlobe.

They connected with fierce energy. Their mouths played
together, lips and tongues in a wild little dance. His hands
began exploring her skin, and all roads of sensation led to her
pussy, which was pulsing and throbbing with the tension of
wanting. She felt his desire in the strength of his arms. His urgency, when he pressed her to him, made her gasp. His hard
cock pushed against her. Her heart pounded and the blood
rushed into her cunt.

Her moral compass spun with the gravity of what she was
doing, yet she lacked any motivation to stop it. She had been
drawn to Oscar from the beginning, and hadn't synchronicity
put them in the right place at the right time? She hadn't felt
such a pull to a man in decades. "I wanted this when I met you

in New York. I wanted to touch you as soon as you looked at me," she whispered.

The precipice they'd been on last night was crumbling beneath them. His hands were exploring her skin and she felt his mouth on her neck, then on her chest…and then his tongue on a nipple made her leap and gasp with delight. His hand kneaded her breasts and clutched her to him. "Ahh!" she sighed loudly. Her knees felt as if they would melt. She hadn't felt such abandon and joy in someone's body for so long!

"Let's get comfortable," he murmured in her ear. He looked up and saw the bedroom and led her to it—to Valérie and Philippe's marriage bed—where he both pulled and pushed her onto it. They fell together onto the still-unmade mattress. Every nerve exploded as her blouse was pushed up and away by Oscar's hands. He lightly skimmed her skin with the palm of his hand, and she strained and arched her back to meet his touch. She gasped. After so many years of lovemaking to the same man, her senses were in shock.

Oscar smelled different, a musky, sweaty scent coupled with a foreign cologne. He was firm and exigent, where Philippe was tender and tentative. Oscar *made love,* while Valérie's marriage bed had become a rote exercise. She reveled in his body as his mouth moved across her breasts and he sucked and bit her straining brown nipples. "Oh!" she cried without even realizing it.

"Baby…" he replied, pinching her other nipple between his thumb and forefinger.

For a single moment she felt a pang of self-consciousness about her body. How long had it been since a stranger felt her like this? The last time a stranger ravished her she'd had taut skin and the firm breasts and flesh of a young woman. But they were here, now, and Oscar showed no signs of stopping for dinner conversation. They explored each other like new lovers. He palmed the curves of her body everywhere; his hand slipped over her back and her ass. His fingertips trailed down the backs of her thighs and into crevices of olive flesh. She moaned with pleasure.

She pushed him away so that she could discover his sinewy form, which was as rippled and muscled as she had hoped. His cock was long and thick, and it strained while she ran her hands over his chest, down his slim hips and over his thighs. Then he growled from his throat and dragged her panties down, off her hips and down her legs. She helped by kicking them away. Finally, he flipped her over on the bed and opened her legs with his own. So fast, she felt his hands squeeze her ass, and then his finger search for her opening. She was wet and he slid his finger in.

"I've wanted to fuck you since I first saw you," he whispered in her ear, on top of her. He lifted himself and grunted with pleasure. He had his cock in his hand, and opened her legs wider to mount her. He dived deeply into her, and when he stopped for a second she felt as if his cock touched every nerve in her body. He began to rock and pump. She cried out, overtaken by waves of pleasure as he moved in and out, in and out.

"Baby, baby...I want to fuck you...." he murmured, lowering his head to nip at her earlobes and tongue her ear. His deep whispers made his fierceness even hotter. She had a fleeting reflection that she had taken someone into Philippe's bed, and struggled for a moment with the reality of it.

But Oscar interrupted those fleeting thoughts. "Do you have a vibrator, honey?" he asked, breathing hard.

"Uhh..." she stammered, lifting her eyebrows in shock. Talking to this man about intimate sex toys of her marriage...?

She stared blankly, and he whispered, "Married men know what works!" Valérie laughed and pointed to her bedside table.

He laughed, too, but he wasn't fooling around. He pulled out of her and went directly for the drawer, opening it so roughly that he brought the whole table crashing to the floor, with the lamp following. There, in the mess of spilled contents, was indeed her plastic, pink-hued vibrator. Oscar smirked, grabbed it and turned it on.

He flipped her onto her stomach and slid his straining cock back into her. "Honey…" he said, pumping again. He lifted her hips. He grabbed a pillow to make a cushion between her cunt and the vibrator head. Then he put the vibrating unit against her while he pumped his cock. She could feel all her nerve endings climbing. She felt her orgasm coming, and the sensation was that she was flying off that cliff that they had leaped from. The buzz of the vibrator registered like a plane engine.

And that was the end. She came with a crash that exploded deep inside, and her clit growled like a cat ready to pounce. When it did, she saw a kaleidoscope of colors so vivid that she gave an openmouthed cry. Did it last a second or an hour? She lost track of time, and came out of it sweating and heaving.

But Oscar wasn't done. He pulled out of her, sweet sex honey running everywhere, and turned her over. She had a chance to look at his cock. It was bigger and thicker than Philippe's, which accounted for its performance, she guessed. Oscar slid himself into her, face-forward, and devoured her with his mouth. His tongue explored every part of her tongue and, still pumping, he bent over to suck her nipples, first one, then the other. Finally, he emitted a grunt that began quietly, then grew to almost a shout. She felt as if she was fucking a tiger. She was thunderstruck.

It was over. His cream streamed out of her and onto the tangled mess of sheets. He flopped over onto his back and lay there, sweating and panting. Beads of sweat shone on his olive skin. She looked at him naked for the first time. His skin was darker than Philippe's, and he was hairier, but it suited him, since he was like a wild animal, she thought.

"I love your body..." she said quietly. His arms were muscular. He wasn't big, but she was right about the sexual power he held. He was hard and sinewy, his muscles taut. But she couldn't reconcile making love with him in Philippe's own bed, so she put it out of her mind.

"The timing was right," he said. "It was meant to be."

He circled the curves of her breasts with his fingers as they lay on the bed. "I forgot how lovely it is to lie together after making love," she said.

"Your hair is wild. It reminds me of an exotic queen," he replied, twirling a lock with his thumb.

She put thoughts of her husband out of her mind and instead chose to experience the moment, as if time was just stopping briefly. "I love your body...." she repeated, running her palm from his curved biceps, over his strong chest and down his stomach, where she stopped and kissed him.

"Maybe I'll make coffee...?" she asked, looking up from his chest.

He laughed and sat up, and grabbed a bedsheet to wipe some of the sweat from his brow and then his chest. "Yes, yes...and those croissants now. I'm famished. Can I jump into a shower?"

He came into the kitchen in his boxer shorts. He smelled faintly of her family soap, which confused her senses. He sat down at the kitchen table, where she had breakfast things laid out. "Please," she said, gesturing to the table.

He poured her espresso, then his own. "Sit down, sit down," he said, grabbing her hand as she moved back and forth in the small kitchen. "You're okay with this...?"

"I don't know. I've never done this before. I just wanted you...I wanted you ever since I saw you," she said, sitting down across from him. "Sometimes you meet someone, and then if you're lucky, you get a moment with them, I think… and this is my moment with *you*."

"That's how I feel," he said. "And wonderful things can happen even when you only have that moment."

He reached under the table and stroked her thigh. "No strings, just a…a short vacation from our lives? And nobody needs to know." He drank his espresso and tore a croissant.

"It's a deal. I never knew it could be so easy." They smiled at each other. "Have you done this before? Since you were married?"

"Maybe once or twice… I've been married a long time," he answered with a wink. "So it's a deal. It's between us." He extended his hand.

She took it and he pulled her toward him for a kiss. She laughed and drew away. "This won't get us far in Paris," she said.

"I don't care. *You're* what I want to see in Paris, baby," he answered, lifting her shirt to stroke her breast. "Come back to bed with me," he said, kissing her neck. He led her by the hand, and they fumbled their way back to the bedroom. They fell on the bed and he kissed her body, making his way down to her pussy.

Philippe hadn't bothered with oral sex for years. Now a soft stroke of Oscar's tongue on her inside lips made her quiver. His tongue found her clit and he sucked it gently. At the same time, he slid a finger in and out of her rhythmically, and in minutes her body rose in a tide of sensation.

Before she could come, he moved up and pushed his thick sex into her. Every nerve she possessed was now riding the white water of body bliss. "Taste your sweet honey," he whispered. "Give me your tongue." She parted her lips and he licked her tongue, and they exchanged her juices as they kissed again. He pumped her sopping wet cunt, and when she began to cry out, he let himself come, bursting into her with shivers of pleasure.

They lay together in a sticky mess of sweat and cum, and finally came apart. But it didn't last long. They began to kiss again, fondling and stroking each other's bodies.

"How about a shower...again?" Oscar suggested. "And this time you come with me. Then we'll get out and enjoy the city, like we planned."

"I *am* enjoying the city," Valérie said, "since *you're* in it."

He led her off the bed and into the shower. Water flowed and they soaped one another, sending bubbles running down and around and across hard and soft flesh, over breasts and taut muscles, soft curves and asses. Valérie soaped Oscar's soft penis, pumping it with her warm, wet hand, and it came to life again, hard and hungry.

"Turn around," he whispered in her ear. "I need to fuck you again...." She turned, and he entered her from behind, pumping hard while the warm water fell between them. He stroked her tits from behind and she caressed her own sex. "I want you to suck me before I come again," he urged. He pulled himself out, still hard and straining.

She went on her knees on the floor of the tub and took him in her mouth. He was bigger and wider than Philippe, and when she couldn't hold him in she sucked the purple tip of his cock, and licked it like candy. He moaned and grunted, spurting over her face. She caught some cum with her tongue and he groaned again. He dropped to his knees and kissed her deeply, tasting himself in her mouth.

"Okay," he laughed, when they had recovered from the moment. "Now let's really get out of here." They finally cleaned up, dressed and prepared to leave the apartment.

TOURISTS IN THE CITY

They decided to visit the Centre Pompidou. Valérie hadn't gone in years, and Oscar, always more interested in athletics, had toured few galleries. The diverse and modern collections gave them much to talk about, and they continued their conversation over lunch in a casual bistro where they ordered *steak frites* and a bottle of light rosé. They shared *clafoutis aux cerises* for dessert like lovers. They walked through the old neighborhoods and admired buildings that Valérie hadn't looked at in years. Who admired seventeenth-century architecture with two tired, arguing children in tow? she thought to herself. Who stopped to study the details of medieval gargoyles while hauling bags of groceries?

Oscar was a charmer, and he made her laugh with stories from his business travels in the world of pro sports. They held hands and shared ice cream. They kissed in the street. Oscar took her hand everywhere, and put his arm around her at every opportunity.

They ended the day with a stroll through the Jardin du Luxembourg, resplendent and majestic at the height of the season, topaz-toned sand and stone bright in the summer sun.

"I'd forgotten that Paris is such a fabulous city," she said, "or maybe *you* are what's fabulous?" She looked at him.

He smiled and winked. "It's the moment we have together, and it's *you*." He drew her to him and kissed her.

"There's a restaurant I want to take you to," Oscar said as they were leaving the gardens.

"You took me out last night. I'll make you something at home," Valérie replied.

"Didn't you say that this is a little holiday?" he said playfully. "And on holidays don't you eat in restaurants? Let me take you. My wife buys all those food magazines, but they just sit there, so I read them. I love to eat. I read about another new bistro." He took out his handheld and searched for the address. "Here it is. Let's go." He looked up and down the street, scouting for a taxi.

"Your wife…" Valérie started.

Oscar stopped her midsentence, putting his index finger to her lips. "'My wife,' 'your husband'—don't worry about anything. This is *our* little 'lost weekend' away from everyone. When it's over, we'll go back to our worries." He kissed her, and soon flagged a passing cab. She thought, in the taxi, as he held her hand, that he was right. There was no point in overthinking a little tryst, and she promised herself that she wouldn't mention it again. Reality, she knew, would return soon enough.

They ate in a stylish bistro that celebrated classic French cuisine done with global flavors. They fed each other grilled sardines dipped in miso-rosemary sauce from lacquered chopsticks. They drank a dry white wine, and ate French favorites—woodsy cèpes, aubergines and courgettes—in Sichuan spices. They nibbled and shared desserts of apples with burnt sugar, folded into layers of paper-thin Greek phyllo pastry. "I love to eat with you," Oscar said, brushing her cheek with his hand. "You enjoy food like you enjoy sex, and that's a very sexy thing." He reached underneath the table and caressed her thigh.

"Here's to us and our little holiday together," she replied, raising her glass. He raised his, but before they drank he took her other hand and brought it to his lips. She smiled and exclaimed, "I think I'd like a vacation in New York!"

"Why don't you come to my hotel tonight, and enjoy a four-star room? It's no fun for me all alone." He brushed a finger against her cheek again and smiled in turn. "Let's start walking, and if we get tired we can grab a cab."

They walked toward the river, stopping in front of small gallery windows to look at paintings. They passed a bookstore having an author's reading and stopped in the doorway to listen. They continued on, sharing favorite authors.

The only sour note in this symphony of romance was when Valérie realized she couldn't be away from the apartment for a night without an excuse for Philippe. She hated lying to him— hated the feeling of guilt in the pit of her stomach—but her desire for Oscar was greater than her wish to examine her life outside the confines of these few precious days.

"Listen," she said to Oscar, "I have to make a call...to Philippe.... I'll just step over there a moment," she said, gesturing to a large doorway entrance into a courtyard between two ancient buildings.

He nodded in agreement. "I'll wait here."

She flipped her cell phone open and speed-dialed. *"Mon amour!"* her husband answered brightly. "I left a message this morning. I didn't get you at home and I called your cell, but you didn't answer...."

"Oh, maybe I was in the métro and didn't hear it. I've been out a lot, just shopping and in the stores—it's so much easier without kids, you know."

"Of course," Philippe answered. "You should be having some fun."

"Well, I am…just meeting old girlfriends I haven't seen in so long. But listen, I have to go…. I just wanted to tell you that I plan to go to bed early and get a good night's sleep with no interruptions, you know? I'll probably turn off the phone tonight, so if I don't answer, I'm just at home asleep. Are the children fine?"

"Yes, they're having a wonderful time, and they miss you and love you, like I do. I won't call tonight, and you have a good, restful sleep. *Je t'aime, mon amour.*"

"You'll all be back soon—the day after tomorrow? *Je t'aime…*bye!" She hung up.

Valérie glanced up the street to find Oscar. He was standing in a doorway looking at his messages on his phone. He lifted his head and their eyes met. They both smiled. She walked to him.

"Everything fine?" he asked. "Fine. Let's go." He took her hand and they walked together. Afternoon turned into a warm evening. Streetlights blinked on and Oscar pointed to the sky. "Let's walk down to the Seine. Maybe we'll see a star or two."

At the bottom of the narrow street they arrived at Pont Neuf. They walked across and stopped to admire the Seine, its current glistening in the evening light. Boats moved along under them. Oscar tugged Valérie toward him and kissed her. He took her face in his hands and kissed her deeply and slowly. She heard other lovers whispering to each other as they crossed the bridge, and she heard bicycle wheels whirring past. She felt the night breeze brush past them, and the cool scent of the water wafted by. She felt the spirits of a thousand lovers on this ancient bridge, all having embraced and loved, as though it were a place where time stood still for passion and tenderness between souls.

"Come," Oscar said, after what felt like a kiss that flowed between time. "Let's find a taxi and go to the Tour Eiffel." They hailed a taxi and headed for the Jardin des Tuileries.

A NIGHT ON THE TOWN

Arriving close enough to the Eiffel Tower to have it looming skyward before them, Oscar said, "Let's take a detour. When was the last time you were on that big Ferris wheel?"

"La Grande Roue?" Valérie laughed, pointing to it. "You're crazy! It's been forever." In the park, tourists took photos of their children, tired from busy vacation days. The smell of popcorn filled the air around them, and they crunched kernels beneath their feet as they walked.

He took her waist and they approached the Ferris wheel, a perfect circle of twinkling lights by night. "Two, please," Oscar said to the ticket taker. They waited for the next turn, and were placed in a car. In others, young couples giggled and kissed.

Up, up, up moved the little car. The big wheel swept them up above the park trees, green in the city-lit night. Up, up and up, and they looked at the lights of Paris around them. Traffic circled endlessly around the Champs-Elysées. A thousand tiny lights glittered on the Eiffel Tower. And when Valérie looked up into the sky, she saw stars shining and planets blinking.

"The City of Lights. Beautiful, isn't it," Oscar said. At the top the Ferris wheel stopped for a few minutes, and they both registered their amazement.

"I forget that I live here...." Valérie sighed.

Oscar turned and brought her to him, and they kissed again. He stroked her cheek. "I want you," he said quietly.

When the ride ended, they made their way out of the park, hand in hand, and caught a cab to Oscar's hotel. "How is it that a lovely hotel makes you feel like you don't have a care in the world?" she said to him as they entered his room.

He drew her to him, and they fell on the bed together, their kisses a tango of tongues and eager lips. They shed each other's clothes, undoing buttons and zippers and unpeeling layers until they were naked and rolling together over crisp, white hotel linens.

He urged her head to his cock. After years spent making love to the same man, she wondered what Oscar liked. She licked the soft, purple head and heard him gasp. He held it at the base and moaned as she tongued its length. He stroked her hair while she pumped him with her wet mouth. It made her feel young and sexy and dirty, and she loved it.

She felt liberated from the dead air of her sex life. She pumped his cock and sucked hard. He gasped and groaned, shooting his white cum over her and the bed. He dropped onto the big pillows and exhaled deeply, exhausted. "Oh, baby," he said, lifting her to him to kiss her deeply. Their tongues collided passionately, and she felt a rush of not just her carnal high, but of happiness with this man and this moment.

Then he slid down her. His fingers parted the soft lips of her pussy and he carefully stroked her hard fuchsia clit with his tongue. It was confident and sure, not tentative like Philippe's. She cried out, and Oscar stroked it back the other way. He let his tongue travel outside and inside the plump, engorged lips of her vulva, and finally was too excited to continue. "I have to fuck you *now*," he growled, and mounted her in an instant like an animal. He drove his thick, rigid sex into her and they both panted like primal beasts. His hands were all over her hot flesh. She came with a cry, and he grunted, pushing himself into her harder and harder until he was empty.

They came apart, wet and sticky with sweat and cum. With his eyes closed, he left a hand roaming her skin, over her breasts and nipples. Finally, he turned toward her and kissed her. "A shower and room service? I'm famished again."

While Oscar showered, she wandered the hotel room, then stood at the window to watch the view. He came out in a thick hotel robe. "Your turn, my dear. What would you like?" he asked, picking up the room service menu. "I'm going to order a steak sandwich."

"Oh, I don't know. I'll have what you're having. And a glass of wine would be nice."

In the shower, among the little luxury hotel soaps and shampoos, Valérie looked forward to staying the night. The hotel made her feel as if her own world were truly on the other side of the globe, and with it her life of wife and mother. She showered a long time, running the hot water over herself like a summer rain. When she finally came out, body and hair swathed in thick, white hotel towels, the food had already arrived.

"I didn't want to bother you in the shower. I hope it's not rude that I started without you."

Valérie laughed. "You're kidding. Nothing could bother me right now. Restaurants, room service…" Then she lowered her voice, adding, "Making love with you…what could bother me now?" They toasted to the fun they were having together, ate and relaxed. Valérie stayed the night with him, made love and slept in the fantasy comforts of his hotel.

That night her dreams featured a whirlwind of movement. She dreamed of museums and taxis, and a place that looked like the Italian coastline where she'd once spent a week with a boyfriend when she was young. Always moving, never stopping, and making love in hotel rooms with open shutters that let in the summer air.

The next morning she and Oscar ate croissants and drank café au lait from room service. They sat in their plush white robes and looked at the newspaper together. "Well," Oscar began, "I have one more day here. What would you like to do? See some monuments? Go to one of those huge flea markets? Walk through the Marais?"

"A flea market...what a fun idea. I never go—it's impossible with the kids," she said.

They hopped in a taxi and spent the morning in one of the rambling, labyrinthine markets. They ambled through the alleyways and past the stalls. Oscar bargained with sellers just for fun, and they ate spicy little merguez sausages in baguettes for lunch, and washed them down with beer. "I don't know when I've had so much fun," Valérie told him, wrapping her arm around his waist.

Oscar said that he'd never been through any of the city's famed churches, and so they spent the afternoon exploring Notre Dame and Saint Germain des Prés. Standing on the street and looking at a map made her feel like a tourist. She felt above the bitter bustle of daily Parisian life, above it and apart from it, just like a *real* tourist.

"How about a glass of wine somewhere?" Oscar said as they left the cathedral. "Maybe we can find a nice bistro and have a bite for dinner. I don't want to be the first one to say it, but maybe this is our last evening together."

Valérie knew it, but had put it to the back of her mind. "Then let's go back to your hotel, so at least we can be alone." They flagged a cab and sat in the back with fingers entwined.

"I'm not looking forward to saying goodbye," she said.

He took her face in his hands and kissed her. "Don't talk about goodbyes. We still have a few hours...and who knows that we won't be together again sometime?"

"We'll have the Château Margaux 1983," Oscar ordered on the phone to room service once they reached the hotel. "A *confit foie gras de canard maison sauce poire* and an *escalope de veau*," he added, reading from the menu. "And a warm goat cheese on toasted brioches from the appetizers."

"Our last supper." Valérie smiled sadly, cocking her head.

"Listen," Oscar answered, "never say never. But let's just remind ourselves of the wonderful time we had…and let's make one more memory until we see each other again." He led her to the big bed they'd made love in. She slid out of her shoes and backed onto it as he kissed her, pulling her to him. They rolled on the bed, enjoying each other's bodies. "Were we meant to fit together so perfectly?" Oscar whispered.

Room service knocked. He signed for the food and closed the door again. "Let's go back to where we were," Valérie said, taking his hand and leading him back to the bed. There, they made love for the last time. They embraced tenderly and they embraced passionately. Oscar caressed Valérie's body, and tongued and sucked her nipples. When he thought she couldn't take any more, he drove his sex into her, and they rode a tide of pleasure together. They played together in bed like new lovers, enjoying and exploring, not knowing what the next moment would bring.

When it was over, Oscar opened the Château Margaux and brought glasses to the bed,where they lay naked in wildly rumpled sheets. "Here's to us," he said, pouring the wine. "Here's to us. Here's to little holidays from reality…and to little secrets." They put their glasses together and kissed.

EVERY VACATION ENDS

Philippe and the children came back without incident, and they were all happy to be together again. The children were tanned and rested, and Philippe seemed to have enjoyed himself despite spending a week with his parents. His family's happiness was his own. The children's tan faces reminded him of a week well spent, and he was grateful for the air of calm the week had brought to his wife.

She felt the letdown that came with the end of every vacation, but maybe it was also a small relief to return to her own surroundings. The children and their din, and Philippe, as he was, were those surroundings. She looked at his tall, thin frame and his slight paunch. She noticed that he was beginning to stoop slightly.

She didn't say much about how she had spent her days; she said that there wasn't much to tell. "Just rest and relaxation," she told Philippe. "I think the Americans call it R & R."

★ ★ ★ ★ ★

THE ENVELOPE INCIDENT
EMELIA ELMWOOD

My two best guy friends, Jake and Derek, came over that Saturday morning to cheer me up. I poured three cups of fresh coffee and set out a plate of danishes, a sinful treat in honor of my being dumped by Stephen, my boyfriend of three years.

Neither Jake nor Derek had the decency to look as if they felt bad for me.

"What you need," Jake said as he chewed on a cheese danish, "is to purge him from your system."

"I could start drinking," I said. "That oughtta flush him right out."

Derek shook his head. "No, something more…dramatic, I think."

"Take a trip?" I suggested. "Maybe some sort of spiritual journey? Or a weekend at a health spa?"

Jake and Derek were my very gay next-door neighbors who had adopted me minutes after I'd left Oklahoma for a job in Los Angeles. Jake was a lawyer at a nonprofit organization downtown. Derek was an amazing hair stylist at an upscale salon in Hollywood. The two of them had become the brothers I'd never had. Plus, I now had really great hair.

"I've been thinking about this for a while now," Jake said.

"I think that in order for you to find happiness in the next relationship, to rectify the karma, so to speak, you need to identify the single most problematic element of your relationship with Stephen and deal with it. Otherwise, you might just end up with another Stephen."

I sipped my coffee and thought about that for a moment. "Are you sure I only have to identify one problem? It seems like I could make a list."

Derek reached for a second danish. "If you really think about it, all of the other problems were just, I don't know, symptoms of the main one. Secondary problems."

I looked at Derek. "It sounds as though you've already identified the primary problem."

"Come on, Emma." Derek gave me a pleading look. "Think."

I didn't know where to start. Stephen and I seemed to be pretty matched personality-wise. We both loved movies, hiking, traveling, reading, Mexican food.

"This is just pathetic," Jake said. "Either you're absolutely clueless, or too embarrassed to admit the problem."

I looked up.

"Sex," Derek said. "You were sexually incompatible."

"I take offense to that," I said. "The sex was fine."

"Was it? He always looked a heck of a lot cheerier when he left in the morning than you did when you left in the morning."

I blushed. There was something weird about knowing your two gay brother stand-ins were tracking your sexual progress.

"Here's what I think," Jake said. "I think that Stephen pursued you because he saw you as a cute, all-American good girl from Oklahoma. Which isn't a bad thing." He held up a hand before I could protest. "But you also have a pretty serious inner tigress who likes adventure. And when you figured out that he might be scared off by the inner tigress, you caged her up."

"The problem, as I see it," Derek added, "is that Stephen picked up on the fact that you were holding something back from him, and that you weren't happy. And that's why he walked."

"And now you're worried that I'm going to keep my inner tigress locked up," I said, my eyebrows raised. "That's just weird, guys."

"Is it? What if, deep down, you're really worried that he picked up on that inner tigress? What if you think you just have to work harder to keep her caged up? You'll never be happy. The men you're with will never be happy. And then we'll never be happy," Jake said. "And you don't want us unhappy, right?"

I leaned back in my chair and nursed my coffee cup. This conversation was getting a little embarrassing for my all-American good-girl self. "So what's the cure?"

"A week of hot sexual escapades that will purge the lame missionary sex with Stephen right out of your soul," Derek said.

I burst into laughter.

"Uh, with whom?" I was laughing so hard that that my coffee was sloshing over the rim of my cup. "You guys?"

"I love you to bits, Emma, but you're just not my type," Jake said. "But we know a lot of guys—and a few girls, too—who would totally dig you."

I looked back and forth from Jake to Derek. "You're serious."

"Totally," Derek said.

"No fucking way," I said.

Jake pressed the back of his hand to his head in mock horror. "The inner tigress surfaced to utter a foul word, Derek."

"No," I said.

"You don't even know what we were going to say," Jake said.

"I don't have to. I don't think this is a good idea," I said.

"Besides, I don't need your opinion of me to sink. I feel low enough all on my own right now."

Derek leaned forward on his arms and gave me the most serious look I've ever seen from him. "Sweetheart, there is nothing that we'd like more than to see you be comfortable with yourself. How could we think less of you for that? Especially a couple of guys like us?"

Both Derek and Jake were estranged from their families because they were openly gay. Derek's father, a man who preached "love everyone" from the pulpit, had given Derek the boot when he'd turned eighteen. Jake's family had tried at first to be understanding, but when his nieces and nephews were born, Jake had grown tired of the way his sisters shielded their children from him. So he'd faded away.

I'd never really thought about how hard that must have been, leaving family and friends like that. Yet I couldn't imagine Derek and Jake happy had they not been true to themselves.

"You think it will take a whole week, huh?"

"Look," Jake said, "here's what I think you should do." He reached behind him to the kitchen counter, where I kept a pad of paper and pens near my cell-phone charger. "Ask your inner tigress to name the three most daring things she would like to try. Three things that she's almost too embarrassed to even tell you about. Write them down, one to each piece of paper. Put them in an envelope and slip them under our door. We'll make it happen for you."

I could only sit there and blink. "You've got to be kidding me," I said.

"Think about it," Derek said. He and Jake kissed my cheeks and headed out the door.

I refused to think about it. I cleaned my apartment. No, I scoured my apartment. I went for a walk. Then I tried jogging.

Then I rented a half-dozen movies. Two weeks passed, and I was restless, frustrated, embarrassed.

Then the dreams started. Very, very sexy dreams. I was tied up and naked and hands roamed my body. I was bent over a chair while being pounded by a giant cock. Mouths sucked on my nipples. Streams of cum shot across my chest.

For three nights in a row, I woke up hot, wet, sweating, needing. Pushing myself over the edge wasn't enough. I wanted more.

At three-thirty on a Wednesday morning, I sat at my kitchen table and picked up the pen and pad of paper with shaking hands.

Images of my dreams flashed through my mind. Even though I sat alone in my kitchen, my cheeks flushed with embarrassment. A good girl didn't have thoughts like this. A good girl didn't sit at her kitchen table, thinking about what kinds of crazy sex she secretly dreamed of having with people she didn't even know.

What the hell is the matter with me? I thought. *I'm just writing down thoughts. I don't even have to show them to anyone. I can have fantasies. I can write them down.*

I held my pen over the paper, poised to write.

It was four-fifteen, and I still hadn't written a single word. When did I become such a coward?

Or is the problem that I couldn't narrow my list down to three? I giggled. *Gee, Jake,* I could picture myself saying, *I hope you don't mind that I gave you thirty-five different pieces of paper. I hope you have that many friends.*

Just write something, I said to myself. *Anything. The first thing that comes to your mind.*

I took a deep breath and wrote in the most honest tone I could muster:

I want to be tied up, blindfolded and fucked by men I don't know and will never see.

My heart raced so hard I could feel the pulse in my throat.

With a shaky hand, I reached for a second piece of paper from the pad.

I want to taste pussy.

I couldn't believe I wrote that. I was so hot and so wet just thinking about it. I reached for a third piece of paper and thought about what my very last sexual fantasy might be.

I want two men at once. I want to ride a big cock while another cock is riding my ass.

I threw the pen on the table and jumped out of the chair. Tears of embarrassment streamed down my face, but I was so hot, so turned on, that I lay down on my living-room floor and fingered myself into three orgasms before I was calm enough to sleep.

I slipped the envelope under Jake and Derek's door, hoping no one saw me do it. During the entire six-mile drive to work, which took a solid forty-three minutes in Los Angeles traffic, emotions tumbled around in my head. I couldn't believe I had actually written down three fantasies. I couldn't believe I'd shared them with Jake and Derek. God, what were they going to think when they saw them? What were they going to do? What would my landlord think when a bunch of random people started visiting my apartment, and the oh-so-obvious sounds of wild sex could be heard through the walls?

I almost rear-ended the car in front of me twice.

And yet I was so, so very wet.

After work, I all but tiptoed back to my apartment. I just couldn't face Jake and Derek after what I was beginning to think of as The Envelope Incident. Relieved to go undetected, I locked the apartment's deadbolt and headed to the kitchen for a glass of water. My cell phone chimed its three-tone notice of a new text message. It was from Derek.

Biltmore downtown. 8 p.m. tonite. Rm 436.

Holy shit. That was only two hours from now.

Jake and Derek knew me well enough to know that I would

look for a chicken exit if they gave me time to find one. They weren't going to give me much of a chance to back out.

I showered and headed for the Biltmore.

I found the elevator and pressed Four. I stepped into the hallway and followed the arrows to 436. I stood in front of the door for what seemed like forever. I thought about walking away. I thought about running away. But then I thought about how one of my very own fantasies was supposed to be on the other side of that door. The hallway was empty. Who would know that I had been here? Who would know about this indulgence?

My inner tigress knocked on the door.

A tall, elegant woman with blue eyes and dark hair swept up into a knot answered the door. "I'm Evie," she said. "I'm here to help you get ready."

The room was actually a posh suite. We stood in the foyer, which lead to a large living room. Across the room were French doors, presumably leading to the bedroom.

Evie took my hand and lead me to the guest bathroom. She helped me undress and then gave me a lacy black robe to wear. I looked at myself in the mirror, my dark blond hair, my gray eyes, my pretty decent country-girl figure that was a little curvier and rounded than was preferred in Los Angeles. I felt self-conscious and insecure.

Evie ran her eyes over what she could see through the robe. I felt a flash of heat as the approval registered on her face. "Jake was right," she said. "Nate and Alex will love you."

She led me across the living room and opened one of the French doors to the bedroom. Two incredibly hot men were inside—one sitting on the giant California-King-size bed, the other sitting in an armchair. Both men wore black robes. The men stood as I entered the room.

"This is Emma," Evie said. She untied the sash of my robe and, stepping behind me, pulled it off. "She's all yours." Evie let the robe pool on the floor before stepping out of the room and closing the door behind her.

I stood there, naked and somewhat in shock, unsure of what to do. The blond man who had been sitting on the bed walked over to me and traced a finger from my chin down past my collar bone to the valley between my breasts. He was at least a foot taller than me, tanned, muscular and blue-eyed. I was wet just from looking at him.

"I'm Nate," he said. "Jake thought Alex and I could take extra special care of you."

Alex walked over to us and stood to my left. He traced my spine from my hairline down to my ass with the fingers of his right hand. Alex had an olive complexion, dark hair and dark eyes, and though he was a couple of inches shorter than Nate, he was just as muscular.

"So perfect," Alex murmured. "Just like Jake promised."

I looked each man in the eye. They were serious.

"So what do we do now?" I whispered.

"Now we satiate your tigress," Nate whispered back, and put his lips on mine. They were both soft and hard, and oh so perfect. I opened my mouth and let his tongue slide inside. I put one hand inside the opening of his robe, and he let go of me just long enough to shed it. His hands stroked my arms, and though my eyes were closed, I memorized the feel of his chest, his arms, followed the trail of hair down his chest, and brushed against his hot, velvety smooth cock.

I almost came on the spot.

Alex stood behind me, his teeth and tongue gliding and scraping along my neck. Shivers rippled over my skin. Nate fell to his knees before me and took my right nipple into his mouth. Alex held me up as I nearly crumpled with a moan.

I ran my hands through Nate's hair as he sucked and nibbled on my tits. *Yes, tits*, I thought. *This is just too hot to think good and proper words. Tonight is about getting fucked.*

My inner tigress growled with approval.

As he tugged on my left nipple with his teeth, his hand moved between my legs.

"God, you're ready," he said, almost in wonder. He rubbed his fingers over my clit, watched the syrupy wetness string from my pussy to his lips as he tasted his fingers. He pushed two fingers deep inside me. I was on the brink of an earth-shattering orgasm when I felt Alex gently spread my ass cheeks apart. Kneeling behind me, he ever-so-gently licked that most-delicate spot.

My control shattered and I came, holding on to Nate to keep from falling over.

"Now," Nate said. He stood and led me to the bed. He grabbed a condom off of the nightstand and rolled it down the length of his cock. He threw a second one to Alex, who did the same thing.

Nate lay down on the bed, his legs hanging over the end.

"Climb on top of me, Emma," he said. Mesmerized, I straddled him, facing him, my hands on his chest, my pussy rubbing over the head of his cock. He held it in place. "Now," he said, and I slid down the length of cock until my lips were pressed against his skin. He moaned as my muscles stroked and squeezed him.

"God, don't move," he said. "Just lean forward a little."

I tilted toward him, let him cup my tits in his hands. He tugged at my nipples. "Does that feel good, Emma?" he asked as I moaned. "Do you want me to play harder?" His cock inside me pulsed and I moaned again. "Tell me, Emma. Tell me what you want."

"Yes," I said. "I love it when you're rough with them." He squeezed my breasts and pulled harder on my nipples. Electricity shot from my tits to my clit.

Behind me, Alex was pouring lube over his fingers. "Just relax," he whispered, and gently rubbed my asshole with cool, wet strokes. My skin was on fire. I didn't know if I was going to last long enough to get to the final deed. Nate's cock pulsed inside me.

"Have you ever done this before?" Alex asked.

"Only myself, with a dildo," I admitted.

"Tell me what you liked about it," he told me, his fingers still feather-light, dancing around my still-tight sphincter.

I moaned.

"Tell me," he said again. "Tell me why you want a cock in your ass."

"God," I said, "it feels so good to be…full. It feels so good to be stretched to the point of it hurting. It turns me on to think about it being a cock, holding me open like that.…" I sobbed with pleasure as he slipped a finger into my ass. He worked it in and out. The walls of my pussy pulsed around Nate's cock, which pulsed in response.

"More," I said to Alex. "I want more." Doing my bidding, Alex slipped in another finger.

"I love the way you're opening up for me," he said, and slipped in a third finger.

"Please," I begged, "I can't wait anymore."

"Tell us what you want, Emma," Nate commanded from beneath me. "Tell us what you want us to do to you right now."

"God, Alex, please," I begged. "Please. I want your cock deep inside me. I want you moving in me. I want to ride Nate. I just want you both to fuck me. Now. Please!"

Alex stood between Nate's knees and pushed his long, hard cock into my ass. I stifled a scream as he invaded my ass, pushed deep inside me. I felt so hot, so full… Alex moved in long, steady strokes, which slid me up and down the length of Nate's cock. I was sure I would be torn to pieces.

Alex's hands roamed my back as Nate and I kissed. The blood roared in my head. I couldn't think. I could barely breathe. At any moment I was going to shatter—closer, closer, closer to the edge, until I finally let my body go, felt my ass and my pussy squeezing, gripping both cocks hard and fast as I thrashed with the most intense orgasm I'd ever had. Nate grabbed my hips and gave a hard thrust, and I felt his head spasm inside me. Then Alex gripped my hips hard and with three more quick strokes, shouted with his own orgasm.

I collapsed on top of Nate.

Alex collapsed on top of me.

For a moment, the only sound in the room was that of rapid breathing, slowly calming down.

"Ready?" Alex asked. I nodded. He slowly pulled himself out of my ass. I gasped at how empty I suddenly felt.

"Your turn," Nate said, and I lifted my body off Nate's cock.

I thought it would be awkward once we were finished. But it wasn't awkward. I felt strong and fulfilled and thrilled.

Nate wrapped my robe around me as he kissed me. "You're a treasure, Emma," he said. He turned me toward the double French doors. "Evie's waiting for you."

Two evenings later, I received another text message, this time from Jake.

Tigress—Omni downtown. Rm 1605. 9 p.m.

I wondered which of the two remaining fantasies it would be this time. I also wondered what I would owe Jake and Derek for their expensive taste in hotels. I took the elevator to the sixteenth floor, more excited than nervous this time, ready for my prize on the other side of the door to room 1605.

I knocked. Evie answered the door.

"The others will be here soon," Evie said. "I'll help you get ready."

Evie led the way to a luxurious bathroom complete with a sunken marble tub and shower with multiple showerheads.

Without asking, she pulled the zipper down the back of my dress, trailing her fingers down my back.

"Too bad I'm not your fantasy tonight," she murmured. The dress fell to the floor, and I unclasped my bra and pulled off my thong. Evie held up my attire for the night—a teddy with cutouts for the tits and an open crotch.

"Wow," I said as I stood in front of the mirror admiring the teddy. Hell, even I wanted to have sex with myself in that outfit.

I followed Evie to the giant four-poster bed. A black eye mask lay on a pillow, and sets of velvet cuffs were attached to the posts with long silky ropes. My heart pounded even faster.

"Why so many cuffs?" I asked Evie.

She smiled at me knowingly. "It depends on what they decide to do with you," she said. "But I have specific instructions regarding your first fuck of the night. Lie on your back across the bed."

Evie wrapped a cuff around each wrist and each ankle. I was spread-eagled across the width of the bed, my tits exposed, air swirling around my open crotch. Evie fitted the mask over my eyes, the elastic around my head. She ran a hand from my collarbone to my crotch. My nipples hardened and my pussy grew wet from her touch.

"I'll be back to get you ready for round two," she said, and quietly left the room.

A few minutes later, I heard the door open and close. Heavy footsteps approached the bed. There was a rustle of fabric— maybe a robe coming off?—and then I jerked against my restraints when large hands groped my tits.

"Perfect," a man said in a gruff voice. His hands were a worker's hands, coarse and rough and strong. He kneaded my tits deliciously hard, making them ache with need. I felt a heavy thigh on each side of my chest and realized he was straddling my body. Something hard, hot and velvety brushed my lips. His cock.

"Lick," he ordered in a rumbling bass. I licked and swirled my tongue over this cock I could not see. He rubbed his cock over the exposed parts of my face, my neck, my tits. He crawled down my body, his heavy meat searing my skin through the lace of the teddy as it rubbed over my chest, stomach and thighs. My legs were spread wide, and as my pussy grew wetter, I was increasingly aware of how exposed I was. I gasped when his rough, foreign fingers probed into my wet snatch.

Man Number One murmured his approval as he rubbed the head of his cock in my juices. He lifted my ass with his rough hands and thrust his cock into me in one hard stroke. I screamed from the invasion, the pure ecstasy of it. He moved in long, deliberate strokes, holding my hips up so that I could feel each deep thrust in my core. I could feel the orgasm coming, I wanted to squeeze him closer to me and control him, but the velvet cuffs held firm and all I could do was scream with the sensitivity following the orgasm as he continued to control the rhythm of our movements. I came again, and he pulled out.

I felt him climb up my body again, his thighs straddling my ribs, his knees in my armpits.

"Taste yourself," he ordered, and I licked my own juices off of his cock. Sweet and salty. Warm and wet.

"Open your mouth," he said, and he pushed part of his shaft and head into my mouth. I suckled and licked, and he moved his cock in and out of my mouth with a gentle but determined rhythm. His cock jerked out of my mouth, and streams of cum poured over my lips and down my neck. Man Number One climbed off me. I heard the rustle of fabric and the door opened and closed.

His cum was still warm on my neck when I heard Evie chuckling. I felt a warm, wet cloth pass over my neck and face and between my legs. Then Evie uncuffed me, and told me to lie on my stomach lengthwise on the bed. She recuffed me, one limb to each bedpost, and left the room.

Man Number Two entered the room, and I heard the familiar rustle of fabric. The room grew silent, and I felt nervous when I realized he was probably studying me from somewhere in the room. He must have been standing at the foot of the bed, because two large hands slipped under the back of my teddy and kneaded my ass.

"I have something special in mind for you," he said in a smooth, silky baritone. He pulled his hands away and I heard sounds I couldn't readily identify. Then I felt fingers prying the thin thong of the teddy away from my asshole. A cold, smooth and slippery object rubbed delicious circles over my puckered hole. My whole body coursed with excitement, my pussy wet, wondering what Man Number Two was going to do.

"Relax," he whispered. "I want to see your asshole swallow this butt plug."

I willed myself to open up to his toy, and was rewarded with the slurping sound of the smooth object being pulled into me. I sighed happily as my sphincter gripped the bottom around the base.

"Do you like it?" he asked me, and I moaned a yes.

He climbed off the bed, and then I heard him say from across the room, "Then you'll really like this."

The butt plug began to vibrate in my ass. I writhed against my cuffs as the pulsing moved through my body. My bare nipples ached and rubbed against the bedspread. I could tell that the crotch of my teddy was wet with pussy juice, and the vibrations pushed me closer and closer toward an orgasm. Suddenly, the vibrations stopped.

"No," I begged, "please. More."

"Not yet," he said. "We're not finished." He stood quietly across the room, not moving, not making a sound. I lay on my stomach, my face turned to the side, feeling my pussy lips tingle and ache with need. I tried to grind against the bed but the restraints held me in place. I waited and waited, feeling the near-orgasm subside. I jolted when the butt plug suddenly came to life. I moaned and screamed and nearly came, but just as the orgasm was in my grasp, Man Number Two killed the power again.

"NO!" I shouted, forcefully. "Please!"

More time passed, and tears of desperation streamed down my face. I heard Man Number Two approach the bed. He lifted my pelvis into the air a bit and thrust himself deep into my pussy—just one, long thrust. He didn't move, he didn't grind. He just filled my pussy with his cock.

"Please," I sobbed. "I need to come."

He turned on the vibrations again, this time set to a steady pulse that moved along the length of the butt plug. He didn't move, but I felt his cock pulsing, and he moaned as the vibrations grew stronger and stronger.

I couldn't hold on anymore. I squeezed down hard on his cock and the butt plug in my ass and bucked like a colt as the orgasm ripped through me. Then he came just as forcefully. Leaving the butt plug vibrating gently, he pulled himself out, and walked out of the room as I writhed with the pulsation deep in my ass.

"Are you sure you're ready for round three?" Evie asked me. I was breathing hard, but I nodded. She had pulled out the butt plug and was cleaning me with another warm, wet washcloth. She unfastened my cuffs and helped me off of the bed.

"Stand here for a moment," she said, and the door opened and closed. I knew Evie was not alone, but I didn't understand why I was standing by the bed.

"This guy has different ideas," Evie said. The mask still covered my eyes, but I could still hear someone settling on the bed, and the now unmistakable sound of the cuffs being secured. Evie led me to the bed. "He's all yours," she said, and closed the door behind her.

I blindly reached out and felt the warm skin in front of me.

I ran my fingers over the muscles in his chest, felt the pebbles of his nipples, the five o'clock shadow on his face. His cock was long and thick, velvety smooth, and pre-cum trickled from the tip.

"What do you want me to do?" I asked Man Number Three.

"Use me," he said. "Fuck me."

I started to remove the mask.

"No," Man Number Three said. "Leave the mask on."

His voice was familiar to me, but I couldn't place him. Did I know him? I felt a moment of terror at the idea of someone from my everyday life knowing my secret. I stood by the bed, unsure of what I wanted.

My tigress decided.

I climbed onto the bed, straddled his chest and thrust my tits in his face.

"Suck on my tits," I ordered Man Number Three. He latched on to my right nipple and heat shot through me. "Oh, suck harder. Pull with your teeth." I held myself over him, relishing the pleasurable pain, squeezing and pinching my other nipple while he worked.

"God, that feels good," I said, and shifted so his mouth could latch on the left one. I caught myself grinding my crotch against his chest, and knew it was time for more. I crawled up his body, grasped the headboard with my hands, and lowered my pussy to his lips.

"Eat me," I commanded, and his tongue slipped into the open crotch of my teddy. I held myself still, barely breathing, as his tongue stroked my clit, my lips, then delved into my wet hole. He licked and sucked until my thighs started to shake and I convulsed around his face.

Gasping for air, I turned myself around. "I want to suck your cock," I told him, and he moaned. "But you can't stop eating me out," I said, positioning my pussy over his face. "If you stop, I stop."

I swirled my tongue over his head, spreading his salty pre-cum over the velvet tip and around the ridge. Man Number Three bucked his hips and pressed his tongue into my pussy.

"Good boy," I murmured as I licked up and down the front of his shaft. I massaged his balls with my fingers and he gently sucked on my clit.

I could smell my spit mixing with the scent of his pre-cum. I licked my lips, relaxed my mouth and took his cock down my throat until my lips touched his body.

His hips jerked and he tore his mouth away from my snatch to shout. I pulled away from his cock.

Man Number Three whimpered. "Suck my clit," I said to him. "Make me come. And I'll give you the best head."

I leaned my pussy back into his face, and moaned when his tongue started stroking my clit. I took most of his cock back into my mouth, rubbing, stroking, massaging with my lips and tongue. The head oozed salty juice as his body came closer and closer to coming. His hips thrust upward into my mouth. My own body crashed with the waves of an orgasm, and still I rode his cock with my mouth, bobbing up and down, stroking his balls. I felt the maddening ripple just before his head jerked and he came explosively in my mouth. I let it run out of my mouth as I stroked his shaft until he begged me to stop.

I felt so powerful. So sexy. So deliciously used. Before he could protest, I tore the mask away and discovered Nate, who had helped me fulfill fantasy number one. I leaned over and kissed him, loving the way his cum and my pussy juice tasted together.

My friends at work commented on the "incredibly good mood" I had been in these past few days. I felt incredible. Powerful. Yet Jake and Derek had one piece of paper left in their possession, and I was more nervous about it than either of my other two fantasies.

I'd never even seen a naked woman in person before, much less had sex with one.

Two days went by, and I wondered how much longer Jake and Derek would keep me in suspense. Then, as I put away groceries that Friday evening, I received a text message from Jake.

Bonaventure. Suite 1725. 9 p.m.

Fantasy three was going to happen.

This time, Nate answered the door. I must have looked nervous because he stroked my hair away from my face and kissed me before whispering, "You will love her," into my ear.

"Are you going to dress me tonight?" I joked.

"She doesn't want you wearing anything," he said, and led me toward a giant marble tub in the master bathroom. Lighted candles surrounded the room, and scented water filled the tub. Nate pulled the T-shirt over my head and smiled at my cornflower-blue demibra. He unbuttoned my jeans and pushed them down around my ankles.

He stroked my pussy through my cornflower-blue boy shorts. "These are pretty sexy," he said, and he kneeled in front of me to push his tongue hard against the thin fabric covering my lips. Fire pumped through my body as he stroked me with his tongue and hot breath.

"Too bad it's not my turn tonight," he said. He unhooked the bra and tossed it on the counter. He slowly pulled the boy shorts down to my ankles and helped me step out of them.

I stepped into the hot, fragrant water and gloried in Nate gently rubbing a washcloth all over my body. Then he offered me a hand out of the giant tub and dried me off.

My body hummed as Nate led me back to the bedroom.

Evie stood in front of the bed. "It's finally my turn," she murmured, and untied the single knot that held her robe in place. The silk robe fell to her feet.

I'd never unabashedly stared at a naked woman standing in front of me before. I'd never visually caressed her from her dark, shiny tresses down to her toes. I'd never really looked at another woman's tits, watched the nipples pucker and traced the carefully maintained curls to her lips.

But I wanted to now.

"I want to watch you touch her," Nate said in my ear. Obediently, I stepped in front of Evie and looked into her blue eyes.

"I want to touch you," I said, and I stroked her face, her lips, her shoulders and arms. Evie guided my shaking hands to her tits, and for the first time in my life, I was relishing the heavy weight, the soft skin, the texture of another woman's body.

Evie moaned and leaned toward me for a kiss. There was no doubt I was kissing a woman. Her lips were so soft and gentle but no less demanding. Her tongue slipped into my mouth.

Tears burned my cheeks as I admitted to myself how wonderful it was to be kissing this woman.

She pulled away from me for a moment. "Tell me what you want, Emma," she said. I swallowed hard. Did I really want to do this? Yes, I did.

"I want to touch you," I said. "Everywhere. I want to suck on your tits. I want to feel your fingers spreading my pussy open. I want to taste your cunt. I want you to bury your face in mine." Tears streamed down my face as I realized how badly I wanted it all, and how scared I was to actually do it.

Evie stroked my face, silently reassuring me. She then looked over my shoulder to Nate, who silently moved to stand right behind me.

"I want to watch you suck on her tits, Em," he said to me. I bent in front of Evie and cupped her right breast in my hand. Her nipple puckered into a pebble, the areola around it tight with anticipation. I latched my mouth on to her breast and stroked her nipple with my tongue. Evie arched toward me and moaned. I suckled a little harder, and Evie grabbed my shoulders as she whimpered. I stroked her other breast with my fingers as I gently grazed my teeth over the nipple in my mouth.

"The other one now," she pleaded, and I moved my mouth and attached it to her other nipple.

My own tits felt painfully heavy with the need to be touched. My nipples ached. I knew my lips were slick with pussy juice. I wondered if Evie's were, too. Without moving my mouth, I ran my hands down her sides, over her hips. Sensing what I wanted, Evie stepped her legs apart, and I stroked the insides of her thighs. My left hand moved up, up her soft skin, toward the radiant heat. I stroked the curls until my fingers found that extremely feminine slit. I traced her lips and then parted them.

My God.

So slick. So smooth. So wet. So hot.

I felt, for the first time, the nub of another woman's clit, and gently stroked it with my fingers. Over and over, I stroked the insides of her flesh, and, feeling brave, I slipped one finger deep inside her.

Evie gasped. "Bed," she panted, and stretched out on her back, her long legs bent at the knee.

I spread her legs apart with the palms of my hands and looked at her pussy. Her lips glimmered with wetness. I spread them with my fingers and watched the smooth, wet juice pool out of the very core of her. I slid two fingers inside her and marveled at the texture, the strength of her muscles.

Leaving my fingers inside, I dipped my head forward and smelled her salty, earthy scent. I felt her eyes on me as I gently licked her clit. I thought about how I liked to be handled, and stroked her clit along the sides, gently up and down, building the intensity, and then pulled away for a moment. I focused on moving my fingers in and out, in and out. Just as she started to sink back down, I wrapped my lips around her clit and sucked. I sucked and licked. Her thighs squeezed against my head. She panted, she begged. I pushed a third finger into her cunt and sucked harder.

She clenched around my fingers.

Her thighs tightened around my head.

She thrust her hips up off of the bed and into my face. I gentled my mouth on her, but didn't stop until she begged me to.

I pulled away, aware of her juice all over my face, her sweat on my skin.

I'd almost forgotten Nate was in the room until he said, "Your turn, Emma. On your back."

Evie sat up as I lay on my back. She smiled at me. "You were incredible for a first-timer," she said.

Evie straddled my hips and leaned forward so she could knead my tits. "Such a handful," she whispered, and tugged at my nipples. I bucked my hips and thrust my chest into her hands.

"You can be rough with them," I said, and cried out when she squeezed harder. She bent her head over my nipple. I couldn't take my eyes off of her as she took it into her mouth and sucked hard.

Evie held herself up on her right forearm. Her left hand stroked my stomach, down my pelvis, and moved between my thighs. My heart fluttered when her fingers dipped into my snatch, stroking, rubbing, knowing just where and how to touch.

"Hold her open for me, Nate," Evie said. Nate leaned against the bed, holding my knees apart. I could hear the wet sound of my lips being spread open by her fingers. I watched her face dip toward my cunt.

She thrust her tongue inside me. I bucked against Nate's hands.

Evie's mouth moved to my clit, her tongue stroking, licking, bringing me closer and closer to a screaming orgasm. She pushed two fingers inside me a few times, and then traced them from my pussy toward the back. Evie stroked my clit while tracing circles around my other puckered hole.

My pussy grew wetter. My asshole quivered.

Evie pushed a finger inside. I moaned.

"Yes, I know how much you like this," she said. She pushed in a second finger and roughly tongued my clit.

My asshole impaled on her fingers, my clit in her mouth, I couldn't hold on anymore. I screamed, bucking my hips, trying to close my legs, only to be held down by Nate's strong hands. My clit grew more sensitive, but Evie wouldn't let go. Instead, she pushed a third finger deep into my ass and her thumb into my pussy. Real tears of sensitive pain and pleasure poured out of my eyes.

"Hold her down, Nate," Evie said. "There is something I really want to do." She pulled her fingers out of my body and stood. She picked up a bottle of lube from the side table and flipped open the cap. Nate and I watched as she spilled lube over the fingers, palm and knuckles of her right hand.

Excitement and fear swept through me.

Nate was so hard he was going to burst out of his pants.

Evie closed her mouth over my clit again. I moaned.

She slipped one finger into my puckered hole. Then a second. Then a third.

I felt hot and tight. Juice dripped out of my pussy toward her hand. Her fingers held tightly together, Evie pulled them out for a moment and then pushed in a fourth. One knuckle in. Then two. Then the knuckles of her hand. My asshole stretched wide open as her hand moved inside, all but the thumb, which imbedded into my pussy.

I screamed, writhing, bucking, burning with pain and heat and ecstasy. I could see in my mind the erotic image of her hand holding me open. I came hard, hard, hard, squeezing her hand, her thumb, my thigh muscles aching as they fought against Nate's firm grasp.

Evie licked me gently a few more times and lifted her face.

Her eyes focused on mine as she pulled her hand away. The slick, wet sound of her fingers leaving my body filled the room. I panted, stunned by the intensity, yet frustrated by how incomplete it felt.

Evie gave me a knowing smile as she headed for the bathroom.

"I think she could use some cock, Nate," she said as she closed the door.

"Do you need some cock, Emma?" Nate asked.

"I need your cock, Nate," I said. "Please."

I opened the door for Jake and Derek, who came over that morning for breakfast. Nate was in the kitchen, making French toast. Jake gleefully opened up the business journal to show me an article about my ex-boyfriend, Stephen.

I choked on my coffee as I read the headline: Exec Arrested for Fraud.

"That's just perfect," I said.

"You're looking well," Derek said, and Jake snickered into his coffee cup.

I patted Nate's hand, which was resting on my shoulder. "Life is good," I said.

And I let Nate bend me over the dining table right after Jake and Derek left.

★ ★ ★ ★ ★

THE CHALLENGE
MEGAN HART

"You're late. Again." Katie Donato barely glanced away from her laptop as Dean Manion slipped the nonfat, sugar-free white chocolate latte onto her desk and his lean, long body into the chair next to hers.

"But I brought lattes."

She glanced at him then, taking in the smug grin, the artfully careless hair, the slightly loosened tie. "You know, traffic is a good excuse for being late. Lost car keys. Forgetting you had to pick up your favorite suit from the dry cleaner's, even. But not last-minute blow jobs from the dude at the Copy Cabana."

Dean laughed and sipped from his own cup. "Not last-minute, not Copy Cabana."

At this, she swiveled in her chair to study him. "Don't tell me you had a sleepover last night?"

Dean grinned in answer and drank deeply. "Ahhh, sweet caffeine. I'm going to need it."

"Is that your subtle way of saying you were up all night fucking?" Katie lifted a brow and sipped at the drink, then tipped the cup toward him. "This is a peace offering but it still doesn't let you off the hook. We have a meeting with

Smith and Simon in half an hour and I've been here since eight putting this proposal together."

"Sorry." Dean's brows knitted and he leaned forward to rub his knees against hers, but Katie pushed him away with a laugh.

"Stop. I'm not some eighteen-year-old, just-out-of-the-closet emo-banged pretty boy. I'm immune to your wiles."

"Bullshit." Dean said this with the utter and absolute confidence of a man who oozes sensual appeal and knows it. He leaned back and propped his feet, shod in expensive Italian leather, on her desk.

Katie shoved them off. "It's not bullshit. I know you too well, Dean. You're like a Lladró figurine. Pretty to look at but too expensive to be practical and not at all useful."

"Hey." He frowned at this and set his cup on the desk to lean toward her again. He touched her knee. "The fuck's that supposed to mean?"

Katie, spreadsheet completed, hit the print button and stood to smooth the wrinkles in her skirt. "It means you should've been here at eight this morning to do your part of this project and you weren't, because you were too busy getting your dick sucked."

She wasn't angry—not really. Annoyed but not furious. She'd worked with Dean long enough to understand him, so when he sidled in late to work with a latte for her, she knew better than to be surprised. Didn't mean he was free of blame, though.

"I said I'm sorry."

She knew he meant it, even as she knew without even looking at him he was giving her a patented Dean sexy stare guaranteed to bring most anyone to their figurative knees. She pulled the papers from her printer and stapled them, then slipped them into the presentation folder she'd carefully prepared. She gathered the rest of her materials while he watched in silence, but damn it, lost it all when she could no longer stifle the yawn that had been doing its best to sneak out of her.

"Ha!" Dean stood, looming. "What's that?"

Katie feigned innocence and swigged coffee. "What?"

"You yawned." Dean had no problems invading anyone's personal space if it benefited him, but he was one of the few who could get away with such a thing with Katie. Now he sidled up close, blocking her retreat by pressing a thigh against hers to keep her pinned with the desk at her back. "Up late?"

Katie bit hard on the inside of her cheek to keep from giving in to a grin. "None of your business."

"Katie," Dean said in a low, sultry tone. "Of course it's my business. Who was he? Guy from the dry cleaners? The gym? Don't tell me he's that loser from college who looked you up on Connex."

"Time for the meeting."

It was useless, and Katie should've known better. Dean put out one long arm and kept her from moving past him. "Spill it."

She sighed. "Fine. You don't know him because I've never mentioned him before. I met him in a coffee shop a few months ago."

"The Green Bean? Which guy?"

"No. The Morningstar Mocha. And you wouldn't know him, he's straight." At least she thought Jimmy was straight. She hoped he was.

"A few months ago? You've been holding out on me?" Dean frowned. "Damn."

"Not holding out." Katie rested her butt on the desk, an eye on the clock, and drank her coffee. "There isn't anything to tell you. Unlike you, I don't bang just any guy who comes along."

Dean put a hand over his heart. "That hurts. You act like I don't have standards."

It was nice to have a friend good enough to understand that a single raised brow meant so much. "Uh-huh."

He leaned against the filing cabinet across from her. "He kept you up late. That's something."

"We weren't fucking, Dean."

He made a face. "Why the hell not?"

"I don't know," Katie teased. "Maybe I'm wrong and he is gay."

Dean snorted into his coffee and tilted his head to study her. "You like him?"

"You like the guy you were with this morning?" She deflected the question easily enough.

"I like all the guys I'm with, at least at the time."

Katie ticked off the list on her fingers. "You let him sleep over and were late to work because of him. Granted, that doesn't mean much, but add to that the fact you haven't been describing every inch of his cock to me in precious, explicit detail, and I'm pretty sure that means you like him."

Dean's gaze shifted. Ah, she was spot-on. Wow.

"Dunno what you mean."

"You only keep quiet about the dudes you like, which are few and far between lately." Actually, there hadn't been any. Katie kept the tone light, not wanting to bring up old flames just for the sake of needling her friend—there was plenty to tease Dean about without bringing Ethan into it.

"Sure, I like him. I like lots of stuff."

Katie laughed. "I know you do."

With this laid out between them, Dean seemed satisfied. "So long as he's not that douche from Connex. That guy was bad news."

Katie laughed at the way Dean bristled on her behalf. "Umm…no. I wouldn't even fuck him with your dick. C'mon, move that pretty ass. Time to shine."

"We have a few minutes."

Katie sighed again. An old argument. She liked to be prompt, even early. Dean preferred to make a grand entrance. She eyed his practiced pout. "I told you, that doesn't work on me."

"It works on everyone."

This was very close to true. "Only because everyone else doesn't know you like I do. All promise, no delivery."

Dean leered, once more leaning so close Katie could get a full whiff of his delicious cologne. "Shut your mouth! The fuck you mean, no delivery? I deliver."

Katie leaned, too, so her breath would tickle his earlobe. "No, babe. That ass and that smile promise a lot but Dean Manion only delivers to addresses on Penis Avenue. Vagina Street's out of your delivery zone, remember?"

He turned his face half an inch so his lips brushed her neck. "Just because I don't doesn't mean I couldn't."

At this boast, so typical, Katie burst into laughter loud enough to make her happy she had her own office with a closed door. She pushed at his chest. "Please. You've never fucked a woman. Have you ever even *kissed* a woman?"

"I've kissed you," he reminded her, letting her push him away but not making it easy.

"A New Year's Eve kiss under mistletoe. Besides," Katie said as she gave his tie a fond yank, "there was no tongue. Doesn't count."

"Doesn't mean I couldn't," Dean repeated stubbornly.

Katie cast another glance at the clock. Fifteen minutes to make it from her office, down the hall, up three floors in the notoriously slow elevator, down another two corridors to get to the meeting room. "Look, your reputation as a sex bomb is safe with me. I swear I will never reveal to all the women crushing on you that you'd rather get a paper cut on your tongue than eat pussy."

She laughed again at his outraged expression. "Don't act

like it's not true. I've seen you with the girls in reception, the ones who always give you doughnuts. You can whore yourself for a bear claw all you want, but when it comes right down to it, you won't put out."

Dean was the part of their team who came up with the brilliant ideas; Katie figured out how to put them into action. Dean orchestrated the flash and bang while Katie made sure all the pieces fit into place. Yet it was Dean who fought the hardest to win the accounts, even when Katie's careful financial summaries determined the risk wasn't worth the effort. Dean who worked long hours ripping apart campaigns and sewing them back together until nobody could possibly offer something better. The same competitive edge that made him killer at racquetball drove him in his work, too, just as Katie's intrinsically neat and tidy personality did in hers.

She'd just tapped Dean's warrior nature. She saw it in his eyes and stance, so briefly fierce she'd have stepped back from it if the desk hadn't already been under her butt. Any other man in the office—hell, anywhere—who gripped her hips and pulled her close up on his crotch that way, who ran his mouth along the curve of her neck to find her ear and breathe heat into it—any other man would've earned a knee to the nuts and possibly the heel of her hand into his Adam's apple.

Instead, Katie tensed under Dean's practiced touch, head tipping to give him greater access. There was no denying he was scrumptious. Probably more so because they were such good friends, and she knew his quirks. Most definitely because he was gay and triggered the "never gonna get it" hormone. Now she closed her eyes while he ran his lips lightly over her skin.

"This is so out of the boundaries of appropriate workplace behavior it's not even funny," she murmured.

He moved away, not quite enough. "Since when have I ever been appropriate?"

"This is true," Katie said, amused to hear the sex-syrup tone of her own voice. God, it had been too long since a man had put his hands on her. "However, it doesn't mean you could make me come."

Disgruntled, Dean stepped back. "You think it would be so easy to get me off?"

"I do, actually. Now c'mon, shake that oh-so-fine ass, please. We really have to move."

Dean crossed his arms, still looming over her. "What makes you think that?"

"Because I'm looking at the clock."

"No." Dean shook his head. "That I'd be so easy to get off, but you wouldn't. What makes you so sure?"

He was, Katie saw with genuine surprise, seriously wounded. She tugged his tie gently. "Because you have a penis, sweetie, and penises are notoriously easy to please. And I like sucking cock. I'm sure if you closed your eyes, you'd never know my mouth was attached to a set of breasts and a cunt. On the other hand, the fact you've never made love to a woman and aren't turned on by women, would probably mean that providing me with the same favors wouldn't be as successful."

She paused, deciding to go for the truth simply because Dean was a friend and a good one, at that. "And because I have a hard time getting off with straight men who are into me. I think managing an orgasm with a guy I knew was cringing the whole time would really be impossible."

"Is that a challenge?"

"Oh, for Pete's sake. No."

Dean gave her the full force of his flirting grin, the one she'd seen slay the girl who brought around the bagels, random guys on the street and everyone in between. "You're afraid to take me up on it?"

"Are you suggesting I...fuck you?" Katie didn't even look at the clock this time. The idea was intriguing. Tempting, even. It wasn't like she'd never wondered what it was like to get in Dean's pants. And to be the first woman to ever have him?

Fucking delicious.

"I'm saying we should fuck each other. We'll see who gets who off first." Dean ran a hand through his hair, pushing it away from his eyes. "And fastest."

"Sex is always such a game to you."

"And that's wrong…because…?"

"Because we're late, for one thing," she said sternly. "For real, this time. Let's go. If you want this account—"

"Say yes, Katie."

She looked him up and down, taking in every detail. She knew every inch of Dean already, having spent so many hours with him, and suspected he was probably as familiar with her. She looked at him with new eyes now. She'd gone to bed with men she was less attracted to than she was to Dean, so really, where was the issue? Sex with him was unlikely to lead to one of those three-in-the-morning talks about what it all meant, and if it did, both of them would be fools. At the very worst, she'd be proven right, and even with that, how could getting a full serving of the delicious, deep-dish pie of gorgeous that was Dean be wrong?

"You're on," Katie said.

"You did what?" Jacob, standing at the sink and rinsing a pot of steaming hot pasta, turned so fast a few strands of limpid spaghetti slopped over the sides.

Dean leaned against the counter, bottle of beer he hadn't yet tasted in one hand. "You heard me."

"Oh, I heard you." Jacob turned back to the sink and ran cool water over the pasta before dumping it all into the bowl. "I just can't believe it. You're going to have sex with a woman?"

Now Dean drank. "Yeah."

He watched Jacob's shrug, wondering whether that meant the other man was dismissing the possibility or expressing jealousy. Or maybe Jacob didn't give a shit, Dean thought, tasting the richness of the beer. Would he have cared if Jacob had told him the same thing? What would Dean have said?

Jacob turned again and brought both Dean's bottle and Dean's hand to his mouth to drink. He licked his lips, then mirrored Dean's stance against the counter, both hands gripping the marble at his sides. "And she agreed to it?"

"Of course she did." Dean drank again and set the bottle on the counter to grab Jacob's wrist and pull him closer. Jacob stood just an inch shorter, his sandy hair cropped in a buzz cut shorter than Dean usually liked. Eyes bluer, ass just a little too flat. But a mouth made of perfect, one Dean had no trouble kissing or fucking.

Jacob opened his mouth when Dean kissed him. Their tongues teased languidly until Dean slid a hand down to cup Jacob's crotch. Then Jacob drew in a hitching breath and pulled away enough to center his gaze on Dean's.

"I can figure out why *she* agreed to it, but why did you?"

Dean tasted Jacob on his lips but didn't go in for another kiss. He shrugged. "Because she thought I couldn't."

"Ah." Jacob tilted his head. "Well, I guess you can't let her get away with assuming that just because you like cock that makes you, oh, I dunno, GAY or anything."

"Hey!" Dean didn't like the insinuation, especially since Jacob didn't know him well enough to judge him that way. "She knows I'm queer. I never pretended otherwise."

Jacob gave an exaggerated shrug and made a face. "You don't have to prove anything to me, sugar. Just wondering if you need to prove it to yourself or something."

"I've known I was queer since the eighth grade," Dean said flatly.

Jacob's gaze dropped to Dean's crotch. "Uh–huh. Like I said. You don't have to prove it to me. I had your dick in my mouth this morning, remember? Then again..."

"Then again, what?" Dean looked at the door, thinking how he should've walked out on this conversation ten minutes ago but hadn't, and not quite willing to ponder why.

"Even straight guys can be convinced getting head from another dude isn't gay." Jacob grinned, showing white teeth just a tiny bit too crooked.

Dean snorted lightly. "Yeah? The fuck you getting at, Jacob? You want me to suck your cock?"

Jacob rubbed at his crotch without breaking the gaze. He knew just how to work this, that little bastard. He'd known Dean all of two weeks and already had his number. Not that Dean was going to admit it, hell no. No guy got under his skin, not that he'd let on. Ever.

"Sure," Jacob said with a raised brow.

In answer, Dean grabbed Jacob's belt. Undid the buckle. Then the zipper. He freed Jacob's dick, stroking it from half–hard to full–on wood in half a minute after that. Jacob swallowed hard, eyes getting heavy-lidded.

"You think I don't suck cock?" Dean breathed, voice husky in anticipation.

"Well," Jacob said, feigning a nonchalance made obviously false by the tremor in his tone, "you haven't sucked mine."

Dean laughed at that, still stroking until Jacob pushed his hips forward. "Your spaghetti's going to get cold."

"I...like...cold spaghetti." Jacob's voice broke on a gasp, and that was all the impetus Dean needed.

He went to his knees and yanked down Jacob's jeans at the same time, baring the other man's body and gripping his tight ass. Jacob's cock was thick and hard, bobbing upward at the release from tight denim. Dean captured it at the base with one fist. His mouth found it next, and he slid Jacob's cock deep into the back of his throat.

Dean closed his eyes.

Not because he didn't want to see what he was doing. He liked watching, as a matter of fucking fact, but this was different. On his knees, giving head, was different than looking down at someone in the same place. On his knees, Dean liked to lose himself in the smells and sounds, the taste of whoever he was fucking. He let go of Jacob's ass to put Jacob's hand on the back of his head, curling Jacob's fingers into his hair. Urging him to guide the pace, if he wanted.

Yeah, Dean liked being on top. Fucking. But he wasn't averse to giving pleasure, either, and it was always, always better when the other person felt comfortable enough to say what they liked. Or show him. Dean wasn't above admitting he could be an asshole, but never let it be said he was a selfish lover.

"Fuck." Jacob's fingers tightened in Dean's hair and his hips pumped. "Fuck, baby, that's so fucking good."

Baby?

Dean paused at the endearment, his fist sliding up to meet his lips as his mouth came down. Jacob didn't stop moving, fucking into Dean's hand and mouth. And after the barest moment, Dean went on. Sex talk didn't mean anything.

Then it didn't matter what Jacob said, because Dean unzipped his own jeans and pulled his cock free. Now came the complicated dance of hands and mouth, stroking and sucking at the same time. He had to catch up—Jacob was already making the low sound in the back of his throat Dean had come to recognize as his prelude to coming.

"Wait, wait." Jacob tugged harder on Dean's hair until Dean looked up.

It took Dean a second to understand Jacob wanted him to stop. Who the fuck ever wanted him to stop when he was blowing him? Dean looked up, one fist still pumping Jacob's dick, the other his own. "What?"

"I just...want..." Jacob licked his lips and swallowed, then cupped Dean's cheek. "Stand up."

Dean did with a quizzical laugh. Two men, pants around their ankles, cocks hard. His laugh slid into a groan when Jacob pulled him by the back of the neck to kiss him. It was a hard kiss, but not punishing. Jacob sucked Dean's tongue as his hand curled around Dean's dick.

"Use your hand on me," Jacob said as he stroked. "I want to make you come. I want your mouth on mine when you come all over my hand."

This was not what Dean had expected but fuck, Jacob was jerking him just right and the kiss went on and on, getting hotter by the second. Nothing to do but stroke Jacob's cock, too. They fell into mutual rhythm.

His balls got heavy, his cock impossibly harder. The kiss stuttered and broke as Jacob gasped. Dean didn't have the breath to gasp. He was going to come....

Jacob came first. Heat and slickness filled Dean's palm. Pleasure exploded out of him. He found the breath to groan.

Panting, Jacob kissed him again. Soft, this time. He still cupped Dean's cock, but his other hand came up to hold the back of Dean's neck. Forehead to forehead, he smiled.

"Hey."

"Hey," Dean said.

Jacob looked between them. "That was hot."

Dean laughed, shaking his head. "It was definitely not what I was expecting when you told me you wanted me to suck you off."

Jacob reached behind him to grab up a dish towel, wiping his hands and handing it to Dean. "Baby, I am *not* what you are expecting."

Dean wiped his hands and put himself back in his jeans before stepping back. "Is that so?"

Jacob licked his forefinger and drew a "one" in the air. "That. Is so."

It was a good cue to leave. After all, they'd both already gotten off. Dean's stomach was rumbling, but dinner was cold and he could pick up something on the way home. He'd already spent last night with this guy. And the morning.

Jacob looked over his shoulder at the sink and the pot with the now-cold pasta. "This will only take a minute to warm up. You staying?"

Dean leaned to kiss him, relishing the taste of salt and beer on Jacob's mouth. "Sure."

Late-night conversations. Katie loved them. Darkness and distance provided by the phone made intimacy, and she loved that, too.

Jimmy was good at late-night talk. Jimmy had a voice like melting butter, all warm and soft and sweet. Rich. It didn't matter what he was saying, really. He told stories like some men built houses, layer by layer and piece by piece, until Katie realized hours had passed and dawn was breaking.

He'd make love like that, too.

Katie wondered if she'd ever find out. She'd met Jimmy weeks ago. He'd flirted with her right away. Asked for her number. He'd actually called, too, something that had surprised her since guys like Jimmy always said they'd call but never did.

Katie wasn't sure just how they'd fallen into late-night discussions about old movies, art, books, music. About their favorite colors and foods. All she knew was that she told Jimmy things she hadn't told any guy in a long time, and nothing she said ever seemed to put him off or be too much.

Katie had spilled her guts about a lot of things from her most embarrassing moment to her secret fetish for knitted slippers.

They had become friends, and that was great, but Katie was beginning to wonder if that's all it would ever be.

"You stand in front of three doors," Jimmy said. "What color are they, what is behind each and which do you pick?"

Katie laughed. "Where do you come up with these?"

"I have a book. Two hundred and seven of the most obscure questions to ask a beautiful woman."

At least he'd said she was beautiful. Katie cleared her throat. "Let me think about it. You go first."

"That's not fair. I've had time to think about it longer than you have."

"Tell me, anyway," Katie told him and settled deeper into the blankets.

"The doors are red, blue and purple. I pick the blue one."

"Why?"

"Because," Jimmy said, "blue's your favorite color and I bet you're behind it."

Heat twisted through her. "And what about the other doors?"

"I don't open them," Jimmy told her, "so I have no idea what's behind them."

"Good answer."

"Your turn."

Katie couldn't begin to think about doors and colors and what was behind them. Or rather, she could think, but every door she imagined was glass, each had Jimmy behind it, and no matter how hard she tried, she could open none of them. She sighed. "Tell me something else, Jimmy."

"Like what?"

"What's your favorite poem? Do you have one?"

Jimmy laughed softly, and Katie imagined the brush of his

breath against her neck. "Unless you count Jim Morrison lyrics as a poem, no, I guess I don't. What's yours?"

"I like e.e. cummings. My favorite starts off 'the boys I mean are not refined.'" Katie thought of the girls who bucked and bite, the boys who shake the mountains when they dance. She recited it to him from memory, and Jimmy was quiet for a moment after that.

"I never liked poetry," he said. "I had a...teacher...in school who made me recite lots of poetry. It was a way to...well, it doesn't matter why. I hated poetry because of that teacher. I never thought I could actually like a poem. But I like that one."

She heard him yawn and frowned, safe in knowing he couldn't see her. She was already making a face in anticipation of him ending the conversation, but her voice was neutral in reply when he told her he had to hang up.

"Yeah," Katie said. "It's late."

The invitation was on the tip of her tongue, but she bit it back. She didn't want to invite him out, not even to the coffee shop where they'd first met. He might say no. Worse, he might stop calling her.

"Night, Katie. Sleep tight."

"You, too," Katie said and clutched the phone tight in her fingers after he'd disconnected before she did, too.

She was still thinking of that conversation when she got home with Dean in tow.

"Maybe that's your problem," Dean said as he flipped through a magazine she'd left on her coffee table. He tossed it down and looked at her. "What? Maybe he knows too much about you already. Destroyed the mystery."

"So then why does he keep calling me?" Katie nudged off one shoe with a sigh and then the other before flopping onto her couch. "Do men often call women late at night just to chat because they long to hear the sound of another voice? I think not."

"You're asking the wrong guy about that."

"Do you ever call *someone* late at night just to hear them talk?"

"Only if I'm jerking off at the same time," Dean said.

Katie made a face and wriggled her toes, free of the high-heeled pumps. "Maybe he's jerking off."

Dean shot her a grin. "Do you?"

"That," Katie said, "is none of your business."

Dean slid onto the couch beside her. "You do."

"Maybe. Once or twice." Katie curled her feet underneath her, looking at him. "He has a very sexy voice."

"So why not invite him over? Put on some soft music, make him dinner. Guys love that sort of shit." Dean tweaked her knee through her soft skirt. "Make the first move."

Katie shrugged. "I don't know. I like him. Maybe too much. I don't want to fuck it up, Dean. If he was into me like that, don't you think he'd have asked me on a real date or something instead of just calling me and talking for hours?"

"Maybe he's afraid, too. Guys can be afraid," Dean said.

"Are you?" She tilted her head to study him.

"I'm not afraid of anything." Dean frowned.

She let it go. She knew him better than that. After Ethan left, Dean hadn't said his name again. He'd erased Ethan from his life as thoroughly as though his lover had never existed as part of it. In some ways Katie admired that about Dean, his commitment to forgetting the past. On the other hand, she knew there had to be fond memories among the bad ones. She never regretted remembering relationships, even ones that ended.

So why was she so afraid to take a chance on one with Jimmy? Even if it didn't work out, she wouldn't have lost anything and might be missing something great. Katie sighed.

"Hey." Dean squeezed her again. "You're not having second thoughts, are you?"

"Huh? About Jimmy?"

"Focus," Dean said. He pulled out a strip of condoms from his back pocket and unfurled them, dangling, before tossing them onto the coffee table. "About us. This."

"Oh, the challenge." Katie drew out the word, then smiled. "No. I'm up for it."

Dean smiled, too. "Good."

Katie was used to Dean encroaching on her personal space. He was a hugger, a toucher, a stroker. Working together on projects, bent over a computer screen, it wasn't uncommon for him to stand behind her with his chin on her shoulder to see what she was doing, or to put an arm over her shoulders while they walked someplace. Dean's physical affection was constant and casual.

This was going to be something totally different.

She wasn't sure what to expect when Dean kissed her. It was nothing like the New Year's Eve smooch. That had been rough and teasing, both of them a little drunk and laughing. Not serious.

She should've known better than to think her experience with that kiss could've prepared her for the sensation of Dean's mouth for real. He slanted his lips over hers as his hand came up to cup the back of her neck. The couch gave as he moved, dipping under his weight as he braced his hand on the back of it. His knee moved between hers. His mouth opened. He tasted of mint.

She'd closed her eyes automatically when he kissed her and opened them when he pulled back. Dean blinked, eyes heavy-lidded, mouth wet. He slid his tongue over his lips.

"That's a start," Katie said.

Dean laughed, low. "You're not going to give me one fucking inch, are you?"

"No. You're going to have to work for this, Dean." She moved closer and brushed his lips with hers back and forth before pausing a breath away. "I told you it wasn't going to be easy."

His fingers tightened at the base of her skull. When he licked his mouth again, his tongue teased her lips. They kissed again, deeper this time. Longer. When they pulled apart this time, Katie's heart had started up a determined thunder-thump she felt in all her pulse points.

"Your mouth," Dean murmured, "is so soft."

She laughed and tipped her head back when he moved to kiss her jaw and throat. "All of me is soft."

Dean pressed his teeth to her skin and in the next moment, Katie felt sharp suction. His hands shifted, sliding down her body to her hips. She was on Dean's lap a moment after that, straddling him with her knees pressing the couch's soft cushions and her hands on his shoulders.

The kiss got harder still. Tongues tangling, teeth clashing, lips nipping. Dean gripped her hips. Katie pressed herself against him.

This was definitely working for her, but for Dean? Not so much, at least so far as Katie could tell from the lack of stiff, hard cock pressing against her. She broke the kiss and cupped his face in her hands.

"Close your eyes."

He narrowed them, but didn't close them. "Huh?"

She took his hand from her hip and put it to her breast, shifting his thumb to rub over her tightening nipple. "These are distracting you."

Dean looked at his palm full of breast and gave her a rueful grin. "Naw."

Katie laughed softly. "Close your eyes. Wait. I have a better idea."

She'd tied her hair back this morning with a soft vintage

scarf. Now she pulled it off and unwound it, letting the silky fabric slide over her fingers. She folded it in half as Dean watching, eyes still narrowed.

"I didn't know you were kinky, Katie."

"Shh." She tied the scarf over his eyes and smoothed the fabric, letting her fingers trace his cheekbones and chin before running a fingertip over his lips. He tried to bite her finger but she pulled away before he could.

Then she kissed him again. They kissed for a long time without a break. Katie unbuttoned Dean's shirt and put her hand inside, flat on his bare chest. His heart had begun thumping, too. His cock had also gone satisfyingly hard against her crotch.

Still kissing him, she moved off his lap and unzipped his fly. Dean lifted his hips to help her push his pants over his hips. He wore navy boxer briefs, the front tenting impressively. Katie took his prick in her hand through the soft material of the briefs and stroked.

Dean groaned into her mouth.

If she spoke, it might spoil the illusion for him, whatever that might be. Whoever he was imagining. So Katie kept silent. Instead, she kissed and stroked him, eventually freeing him from the confines of his briefs. She couldn't help the small groan of her own when at last she held Dean's silky hot cock against her bare skin.

Katie'd been serious when she told Dean she had no doubts she could make him come. Now, with his prick in her hand and his mouth open beneath hers, begging, Katie was determined to enjoy it. And not just because it would mean she'd win this challenge.

She moved her mouth down his body, kissing and sucking gently on his smooth, warm skin. Sucking harder when Dean's breath caught and the tight muscles of his belly jumped beneath her lips. A great hand-job wasn't about showing off, in Katie's opinion. It was about paying attention.

It was also about being smart. With a quick glance at Dean, Katie reached for the bottle of lube she kept in the drawer of the end table. She filled her palm with thick, slippery fluid. This time when she stroked him, Dean muttered a low curse.

With this beautiful body in front of her, Katie wanted to worship it. Take hours kissing and sucking and licking every curve and line. Her cunt ached, sweetly aroused at the erotic fantasies stroking Dean gave her. She'd never been a fan of denial, either, saw no point in it, so as she stroked Dean's cock a little faster, she also slid her hand into her panties and gently squeezed her clit between her thumb and forefinger.

She moved from Dean's lap to the couch without letting go of his erection. She leaned to kiss him and his greedy mouth took hers in a kiss deep and long and fierce. Her fingers in her panties moved faster as she jerked him off.

When Dean put his hand on hers, changing the pace, the pleasure building in her clit leaped up a notch. This was everything she loved about sex—a little fast, a little rough, a little furtive and dirty. Yet safe, too. Nothing would change between them because of this. Nothing really could.

"Fuck," Dean muttered as his hand gripped hers, moving it faster. "I'm gonna come...."

"Me, too," Katie murmured as her fingers circled her clit faster.

Dean let out a short, startled gasp. Maybe at the sound of her voice, maybe at his orgasm. His cock throbbed in her fist and he shuddered. Heat spilled over her fingers and the scent of him, along with his low, desperate growl, sent Katie tipping over the edge right along with him.

His hand kept hers from moving more. Panting, Katie fell back against the couch cushions and took her hand out of her panties. Then she laughed, soft at first before getting slowly louder.

Dean hooked the scarf from his eyes and tossed it at her. "You cheated."

"I didn't cheat," she protested. "I told you I could get you off. I did."

Dean glanced at her lap, her skirt rucked up around her waist, and gave her a smug grin. "So did you."

"Ah," Katie said, leaning in to brush a sweet kiss against his mouth, "but you didn't do it for me. I did it myself. So it doesn't count, does it?"

"Cheater," Dean murmured against her mouth, but didn't pull away.

The kiss lingered. She was surprised. Surprised more by the look on his face when she finally pulled away to rearrange her clothes.

"What?" Katie asked. "Like I was going to leave myself high and dry?"

Dean reached for a handful of tissues from the box on the end table, and took care of cleanup before tucking himself back into his pants. "I call do-over."

"Do over?" Katie guffawed and got up, letting her skirt fall back down around her ankles as she headed for the kitchen. "You want something to drink?"

Dean caught up to her in the kitchen. He trapped her between his body and the counter as she reached for a glass. "I mean it, Katie."

She paused. "Dean, it's no big deal. Really."

"It's a big deal to me."

Before she could answer or protest, her cell rang. She recognized the ring tone. "That's Jimmy."

Dean frowned and stepped back. "Guess you'd better answer, then."

"Is this going to make trouble between us? Because I'd

never have agreed to it if I knew that." Katie grabbed her phone but didn't answer it. The call went to voice mail and beeped while she waited for Dean's answer.

"No trouble. I'll see you at work tomorrow, okay?"

"Dean—"

"Hey," he said, frown erased by a classic, sunny Dean grin. "This isn't over, Katie. Don't worry, I'll let myself out. See you tomorrow."

Her phone beeped with a text message. Also from Jimmy. Katie looked at it, then at Dean, who was already waving goodbye as he ducked out the door. "Dean!"

But he was already gone.

It hadn't been the best hand-job he'd ever had, so why the hell couldn't he stop thinking about it? Her hands had been small and soft, her mouth soft and sweet, her curves sweet and lush. Katie was a gorgeous woman and he liked her. Being queer didn't mean he couldn't appreciate her attributes, but until she put the blindfold on, he hadn't been able to really get into what they were doing.

He was more determined than ever to prove her wrong.

"Your face is going to stay that way," Katie said serenely from behind him.

She was the one who'd brought the coffee today, two paper cups of it bearing the familiar logo of The Green Bean from down the street. She handed him one and sipped from her own. She looked fresh and bright-eyed, a habit that annoyed him most days but particularly on this one.

"You couldn't even see my face. My face is fucking fabulous," Dean said.

"Your eyes are squinty," she said in a low voice as she passed him, like she was sharing a secret though there was nobody around to hear them. She bumped him with her hip.

He followed her into her office and closed the door. She looked up with a sigh and set her cup down. Dean didn't sit.

"We didn't even fuck," he told her.

"Oh, for heaven's sake. Are you still on that?" Katie flipped her fingers at him and leaned back in her chair.

"We *said* we were going to have sex."

"We did have sex. Sort of." Katie crossed her legs and her skirt rode up, giving him a flash of thigh and something that looked suspiciously like pink satin panties.

"I want to try again," he said.

He'd known Katie for a long time. She often had a witty comeback or a response as subtle and effective as a raised brow. He got her, that was the thing, and knew she understood him, too. It was what made them great partners and better friends. Now, though, he could read nothing on her face, nothing in her eyes.

"I don't think that's a good idea," Katie said after a minute.

"What? Why not?" He wasn't used to this, someone turning him down. That was a cliché and arrogant, but true. Mostly because Dean had a finely honed sense of who to hit on, not necessarily, as Katie had so often said, that nobody ever wanted to refuse him.

Dean had been refused before, all right. He knew how it felt. It sucked.

"Because we're friends, Dean, and I don't want to mess that up."

"You agreed to it before."

"That was before," Katie said calmly enough, but he didn't have to hear a tremor in her voice to see she was sort of upset. He could tell by the way she didn't drink her coffee.

"Hey. What's going on?" Dean slid into the chair across from her and moved forward, forcing her to uncross her legs so his knees could press hers. "Something up with that douchebag Jimmy or whatever the hell his name is?"

"Nothing's up with Jimmy. That's the problem."

"Forget him," Dean said. "If he can't see what's right in front of him..."

She laughed at that. "Right. Because you're the expert on seeing what's right in front of you?"

Dean frowned and stood. "The fuck's that supposed to mean?"

Katie shrugged and swiveled her chair back and forth. "Maybe I want more than a quick fuck from him, that's all."

"Isn't the problem you're not getting *any* sort of fuck?"

She sighed, her shoulders lifting and dropping with the force of it. "Forget it. You wouldn't understand."

"So...the challenge is off?"

Katie eyed him, one eye squinting and her head tilted as though she were seriously studying him as something foreign. Incomprehensible. "Why do you have such a bug up your ass about this sex thing?"

"You said I couldn't," Dean told her.

And that was the truth, mostly.

His phone rang, the ring tone a snippet of classical music he'd assigned to Jacob. His fingers slipped a little on the phone's glass face as he looked, anyway, to make sure that was the number. He didn't answer it.

Katie was smiling at him when he looked up, her smile half-quirked. "Was that him?"

"There is no *him*," Dean said.

Her grin got a little broader. "Right."

She swiveled again, kicking her foot up and down, showing off an expanse of shapely thigh he knew she'd never have revealed to anyone else in the office. Katie didn't do shit like that, use her tits and ass to get attention, even though she could. She was always more comfortable with him than with the other men in the office, and for the first time, this stung a little.

"Is it because you don't think I'm manly enough?"

Her grin wavered, her brow furrowed. "What?"

"You don't think I'm manly enough," Dean said, convinced.

"Oh, Dean. Really? C'mon. You should know better than that."

Her scoffing didn't make him feel better, especially when she turned her chair to face the computer, dismissing him. Dean spun her around to face him again. Katie looked as surprised as he felt.

"I want to do it," Dean said in a low voice.

Katie drew in a breath. She smelled good. She always did, but today he seemed to notice it more. He seemed to notice everything about her more than usual today, most of it accompanied by the memory of her hand on his cock.

"Would it change your mind," Katie murmured, her gaze bright, her voice throaty, "if I told you I absolutely believed you could make me come?"

"I'll prove it to you."

Her laugh this time snagged, rough and sultry. He'd never heard her sound that way before. "Fine. Prove it to me if it's so important to you."

"Done," Dean said as his phone rang again, the same bit of classical music. "When?"

"Tonight? There's no point in waiting."

"Your place?"

"Be there at eight," Katie said. "I don't want to be up all night."

"Oh, you'll be up all right," Dean said. "Maybe until tomorrow morning."

It was no big thing, Katie told herself. It wasn't like she'd never thought about what Dean would be like in bed, or that she'd never gone to bed with a friend before. As a matter of fact, a few years ago she'd had quite a successful "friends-with-benefits" experience with a man she still kept in touch with, unlike many of her friends who'd tried that sexual experiment and had it end badly. So it was no big thing, but she couldn't stop thinking about it. How he'd smell and taste and feel, if he could indeed get her off the way he promised.

Katie was sure hoping he could.

Distracted by thoughts of Dean's hard cock, she nearly got hit in the face by the door to the coffee shop as she was heading in and someone was heading out. An old woman, layered in scarves and carrying a monstrously large cup of coffee, barely even looked Katie's way as she pushed through the door, but fortunately instead of clipping her face on the glass, Katie only banged her elbow.

"Excuse you," she muttered, turning to watch the woman pass.

It was the only reason she looked to the street corner and saw Jimmy, wearing familiar and delectable denim jeans, his longish hair tousled, his face scruffy. He was leaning against the street sign talking on a cell phone. If it had been anyone else, even an ex-boyfriend, Katie would've had not even a second's hesitation in approaching him. But this was Jimmy, master of the late-night phone call. Things were always different in daylight.

She didn't have time to scoot inside the coffee shop before Jimmy looked up, still talking, eyes getting bright. He smiled and said something that must've been goodbye, because he slipped the phone into his front pocket and headed toward her.

"Katie."

"Hi, Jimmy." She sounded too breathy, too gooey, too junior high. Katie tried again. "How's it going?"

"Good, good." He nodded. The breeze moved his shaggy hair, and the sunlight lit up his face. He had eyes the color of caramel, something she hadn't remembered. "You going in?"

She glanced over her shoulder. "Oh. Yes."

"Good." Jimmy grinned again and held open the door, then followed her.

It was the same coffee shop where they'd met, but this time, Jimmy bought her latte and brownies for both of them. He pulled out her chair, too, something no man had done for Katie in a long time. Sitting across from him, their knees bumping every so often, Katie tried hard not to think of this as anything romantic.

It was hard, though, with Jimmy keeping eye contact and laughing at her jokes. Or at the way he casually brushed past her on the way to get more napkins, some cream for his coffee, a fork. He touched her, hand flat on her back between her shoulder blades as he passed. And on the upper arm, and on the shoulder when he got up to greet another friend who'd come into the shop.

He touched her seven times, never in any way that could've been construed as anything more than casual, but Katie counted each time, her nerves tingling more with every press of his palm against her. By the time she'd finished her coffee, the brownie not even touched as she'd lost the capability to eat anything while Jimmy flirted with her, Katie thought if he touched her again she was going to melt into a puddle right then and there.

"Well, hey, it's been great," Jimmy said suddenly with a glance at the clock on the wall behind her, "but I have to scram."

He stood, leaving Katie blinking and thinking of something witty to say, but he'd already squeezed her shoulder again and was pushing in his chair.

Damn.

He'd reduced her to speechlessness, which was not her normal state at all. She really hated not being herself around him, that somehow he'd made her the sort of woman who got all giddy and dumbstruck with a crush. More than that, though, she hated that Jimmy seemed either oblivious to his effect on her, or so used to creating that response in women that he took it for granted.

"Thanks for the coffee." Katie stood, too.

"Anytime. I'll call you," Jimmy promised and shot her a grin.

Katie watched him go, wishing she could believe his offer was real and for her, instead of just his standard response to every female in the world.

Jacob hadn't been too happy that Dean was going to Katie's tonight. If any other man had snapped at Dean like that, told him off, said he'd better get his priorities straight instead of fucking around just because he "could" and not because he "should," well, Dean would've told him to fuck off. It had come close to that, actually.

"You want me to cancel?" he'd asked, still tasting garlic and red sauce and wishing Jacob had brought all this up before they'd started eating.

Jacob had cocked his head and looked Dean up and down with a flat, cold gaze. "Would you, if I asked?"

"No."

Jacob had shrugged. "Then do whatever the hell you want to, Dean. I won't be that guy."

"What guy?" Dean had asked, though he was pretty sure he knew.

"The one," Jacob said as he got up and took his plate, food uneaten, to the garbage can to scrape it, "who waits around for you to figure everything you want and need is right in front of you, while you just keep walking away."

"Is that a threat?"

Jacob had shrugged and given him another long look. "No, baby. It's a fact."

Then he'd pointed at the door, and Dean had gone with

his tail between his legs, a fact that pissed him off so much he thought he might just delete that little prick from his phone entirely. But he didn't. Sitting here in the car in front of Katie's house, Dean held the phone and waited for it to ring.

But it didn't.

The last guy he'd wanted and needed had cheated on him, lied to him and finally, left him. What still hurt wasn't that Ethan had fucked around and been dishonest about it, but that in the end Dean had forgiven him and Ethan had still walked away.

The one who waits around for you to figure everything you want and need is right in front of you, while you just keep walking away.

"Fuck that," Dean said aloud and tossed the phone into his glove compartment so he wouldn't hear it not ringing. He looked at the house and wet his lips with his tongue.

He was going to do this, all right. The reasons had gone blurry—he was sure Katie would be okay if he cancelled, but then she'd always look at him when she thought he wasn't looking and think about how he'd been a pussy. Hell, did that even matter? Why had this become so important? Why couldn't he just let it go?

The porch light blinked twice. Katie. He probably looked like the biggest douche ever, sitting here in the car like he couldn't make up his mind. Dean drew in a breath. In, out. Game time.

She greeted him at the door with a smile that didn't quite reach her eyes. "Hey. I thought you weren't going to make it."

"No. I'm here." He paused, suddenly feeling like maybe he should've brought flowers or something like that. Feeling lame. This was Katie, for fuck's sake, his friend. He could've at least brought a bottle of wine.

"C'mon in." She stepped aside and closed the door behind him.

They stood in the entryway, more awkward than they'd

ever been with each other. Dean remembered his senior prom, standing with his date and feeling the same way. Feeling like he was putting on a show that wasn't fooling anyone.

Should he kiss her? He'd have kissed her on the cheek or hugged her, at least, if they hadn't agreed to fuck. He'd have at least slipped an arm around her waist as he followed her to the living room to give her a squeeze as he asked about her day. All things he'd done before but now couldn't quite manage.

"Something to drink? I have some of that wine you like," Katie offered. "Actually, I already poured it, so you'd better be having some. I can't finish the bottle myself."

She pointed to the coffee table. Bottle, two glasses. It was his favorite.

"Yeah." Dean sat, took a glass, looked at her. "Do you need this?"

Katie looked a little surprised as she sat next to him, reaching for her own glass. "You mean…for tonight?"

"Yeah." Dean cleared his throat. "You want to back out? Or you need to be a little drunk?"

Katie laughed and shook her head. "No, sweetie, I totally do not need to be a little drunk to fuck you. Unless…you don't want to?"

She looked wary and hesitant, an expression Dean felt on his own face and didn't like. "No. I mean…unless *you* don't want to."

Katie sighed heavily and sank into the couch cushions while sipping the wine. "Oh, Dean. Listen, this was your idea, so if you don't want to, I totally get it. We don't have to have sex. Believe me," she added somewhat sourly, "you won't be the first man today who didn't want to make love to me."

That sounded bad. Maybe even worse than his own trials with Jacob. Dean turned to face her. "That fucker Jimmy?"

She shrugged and ran a fingertip around the top of the

wineglass, making it sing. "I saw him today. I mean actually saw, not talked to on the phone."

She detailed how they'd met by accident. The coffee, the touching. It pissed Dean off to hear how sad she sounded about it.

"He's a fucking moron," Dean said flatly. "A foron. Really, babe."

Katie's sigh was shaky as she put her glass on the table. "I should just forget him."

To his alarm, because Katie wasn't a wilting flower at all, Dean saw she was on the verge of tears. "Hey. C'mere."

He pulled her close so she could snuggle in at his side, her cheek to his chest. She fit just right in the curve of his arm, his chin against her hair. She sighed heavily again and put her arms around him.

"I'll be fine," she assured him, voice muffled.

He stroked a hand down her hair and they sat that way in silence for a few minutes. The words that came out of him next surprised him, quiet though he said them. "He wants to be in a real relationship with me."

"Of course he does," Katie said, brushing her cheek against his chest again. "You're fabulous."

"…no. I mean…yes," Dean said. "But that's not what I mean."

More silence.

"You're afraid," Katie said softly. "I get it. I know about you and Ethan, remember?"

For the first time in a long time, Dean didn't stiffen at the other man's name. For the first time, Ethan's face had faded enough another face could replace it. "I don't want to be like him, Katie, and that's what Jacob said I was like."

She looked up at him, her eyes wet though her cheeks were dry. "He said that?"

"Not exactly," Dean admitted. "I mean, fuck, he doesn't

know about Ethan. Not like you do. But he said he wasn't going to wait around while I just keep walking away."

"Ah." She didn't move away from him. "Well, sweetie, maybe he has a point, you know?"

"I don't want him to have a point," Dean said.

She smiled sadly, her mouth quivering. "We're a pair, aren't we? You've got someone you're not sure you want, I have someone who doesn't seem to want me."

To her chagrin, because Dean didn't want to be the reason Katie cried, her tears spilled over her lower lids and traced their way down her face.

"Hey," he said. "Don't, okay?"

He swiped the tear with the pad of his thumb and Katie shuddered, turning her face to press her mouth to his palm, holding his hand close to her face for a moment before looking up at him with still-sad eyes. A lot of women had cried on Dean's shoulder over the years, but Katie never had. Looking at her now, all he could think was how good a friend she'd always been, and how much he didn't want her to be unhappy.

She murmured against his mouth when he kissed her but made no protest. Her mouth opened. She tasted sweet, the way she had the other day. His hand went naturally around the back of her neck to cup it, her hair a soft, thick weight on his fingers. Somehow she ended up on his lap, straddling him, their kisses turning from soft and slow to hard and demanding.

She'd tricked him before, with the blindfold, but he didn't need it this time. His mind put together the taste and smell of her with the memory of pleasure, and his cock responded. He pulled her closer, kissed her deeper, put a hand on the small of her back to grind her down a little harder against his dick.

"Dean," she murmured into his mouth, but his kiss stopped her.

Dean favored men close to his size and build. Compared to that, Katie was so much smaller and softer, he had no trouble putting his hands under her ass and lifting her. She let out a small, strangled gasp but didn't stop kissing him. Their tongues twisted, tangling, and fuck, it felt good. Really good.

He didn't try to make it to the stairs, much less up them. Her rug was soft and thick and deep, and he laid her down on it, settling between her thighs as he closed his eyes and sank into the sensations. The semi-desperate surge of pleasure coiling in his gut surprised him, making him think his cock really did have a mind of its own.

Somehow she got him undressed, a feat he could only admire since they never stopped kissing and he was fumble-fingered about her clothes. In her bra and panties beneath him, Katie laughed softly as he tried to figure out how to unhook her bra and got it off herself.

"You really never have done this," she said.

"Of course not." Dean slid his hands up her sides but stopped just below her breasts to look into her eyes. "Did you think otherwise?"

She got up on her elbows to look at him. "I guess maybe I thought I wasn't that special."

"Shut your fucking mouth," Dean told her before kissing her again and saying against her lips, "you're special."

She laughed again into his kiss, and that was better than her tears had been. She lay back with him between her legs. Her hand found his dick and stroked it from half-hard to fully erect, and Dean shuddered at how good it felt. When she stroked her fingertips over his balls, he drew in a breath, holding it for a moment, before opening his eyes to look at her.

"Oh, no," he said. "The challenge was to get you off."

"Sweetie, seeing you enjoy yourself goes a long way toward that."

Dean couldn't argue with that, since he was a fan of such tactics himself, but he shook his head. "I'm going to make you forget anyone else tonight, Katie. I promised."

"Already done," she breathed, eyes gleaming, and ran her hands up over his thighs. "Touch me."

He slid his hands up her sides again to cup her breasts. Her nipples tightened against his palms and she drew her lower lip between her teeth. She liked that, he thought, trying to imagine what a woman would like. The same things as a guy, probably, if only he could figure out the right parts to focus on. If only he could find them, he thought as Katie parted her legs a little and arched her back.

Fuck, this might be harder than he'd thought.

He bent his mouth to a nipple, sucking gently. Not flat like a man's, Katie's nipple peaked and grew as he stroked it with his tongue. And wow, she bucked her hips up against his belly. Dean did the other nipple, too, until both of them were rosy-red and hard.

Dean had seen plenty of hetero porn—his college roommate had been addicted to the stuff, leaving skin mags around and playing a nonstop collection of VHS tapes he rented from the video store. It had all seemed sort of vague and mysterious, unlike gay porn in which everyone had erections and came in great, spurting jets of jizz, on camera. Katie wasn't acting like a woman in a porn video. Aside from the lack of Lucite platform shoes, she was squirming only a little when he touched her.

Kissing her, though, was getting better and hotter. She pulled him to her mouth, her soft body wriggling under his. She was an amazing kisser, knowing when to pull back and when to suck his tongue just hard enough to get him moaning.

She shifted against his cock, hard on her belly, and ran a hand down his bare chest to tweak one of his nipples before pushing her panties down and wriggling until she got them off. She lay back, naked, her gaze bold but her chin lifted a little.

Dean wasn't stupid. "You're beautiful," he assured her.

She raised a brow.

He kissed her, hands stroking over her sides and hips, over her belly, then up again to cup her breasts so he could use his mouth on her nipples again. "You are."

"That feels good," Katie murmured, laying back onto the rug and running her hands through his hair.

It wasn't going to give her an orgasm, he knew that much. Dean might not like pussy, but he wasn't ignorant about anatomy. All those hours of trying to study while porn ran in the background might pay off now—at least he had an inkling of where to find her clit, something his college roommate never seemed to have managed if the sounds his girlfriends made in their bunk after lights-out were any indication.

He rolled onto his side, kissing her mouth again, as his hand slid down her soft belly and through the tangle of curls covering her pussy. His fingers stroked down. This was utterly foreign, completely unexpected...and absolutely erotic for all that. She was soft and hot and wet, and when he found a small, hard bud with his fingertips, she cried out.

Bingo.

Katie opened her eyes. "Right there. That's good."

She put her hand on his wrist, shifting him a little, slowing his pace, but letting go as soon as he adjusted. Fascinated, Dean watched her sink back against the rug, her cheeks flushing as she closed her eyes. She bit her lower lip again before breathing in, lips parted.

This was so unlike anything he'd ever done. Cocks came in a lot of sizes, but they were all big enough to grip. To stroke. Beneath his fingertips was the one small spot he had to keep his attention on. This was the real challenge, and Dean wasn't going to fuck it up.

His cock ached, his balls heavy, as he stroked her, but he didn't move to do anything about it. He couldn't afford to lose track of what he was doing. Female orgasms, to his knowledge, could be tenuous and easily lost.

They kissed forever, and he didn't care. The longer they went, the better it got. He found a rhythm that turned out not to be so different than what he was used to, and the way Katie reacted—moaning softly, rocking her hips, he thought she was enjoying it.

She stiffened, her hand going to his wrist again, her mouth open beneath his but no longer kissing. "Oh…"

Dean paused, fearing he'd somehow done something wrong. "Katie?"

"Oh, god, so close," she whispered, and looked at him. "Just…slow down a little. Make it last."

Dean grinned, slowing his circling finger. "Like this?"

Her eyelids fluttered. "Oh, god…"

The sound of pleasure suffusing her voice sent a throb from the root of his cock all the way through it. She moved against his hand. The flush on her cheeks had spread down her throat, across her breasts, and without thinking too much about it, Dean bent to suck gently at her nipple again.

Katie cried out, something wordless and ecstatic. The feeling of her moving, the sound of her—fuck—the smell of her arousal sent slickness oozing from the head of his prick. His balls tightened. When she kissed him, he felt her clit pulse under his fingertips. She moaned into his mouth.

"Fuck me," Katie said, not like a command but more like a plea.

He wanted to, but there was the matter of logistics. Katie blinked again, her gaze clearing for a minute, and she pushed at him to roll him off her as she reached into the drawer of her end table to pull out a box of condoms. Just as she'd figured out how to get them both naked before he could, now she pushed him to sit up as she opened the box, tore open the package and sheathed him in latex before he could do more than shift his hips. Straddling him, her thighs gripping his,

Katie put her hands on his shoulders. His cock rubbed at her belly and then lower as she looked at him.

"You sure about this, sweetie?"

"Did you come yet?" Dean asked, voice hoarse at the pressure of her cunt pushing his cock against his stomach. Her ass was smooth under his palms.

Katie smiled and reached between them to grip his dick at the base. She bit her lower lip, looking down, as she shifted and then...oh, fuck.

"Oh, fuck," Dean said aloud. "You're so hot. And tight."

Blinking, surprised, he let the pleasure wash over him as she sank onto his cock all the way. She was tight, and hot, and slick, too. Her cunt gripped him better than any fist ever had, and he had to breathe out, slowly, to keep himself from shooting off like a kid with his first strokebook.

Katie pressed her forehead to his shoulder for a second. "Oh. God."

He'd never fucked in this position before, but it didn't take him more than a second to figure out how to shift and thrust upward. His cock slid inside her without effort, and she bit down, hard, on his shoulder. Dean had never been one for painplay but that was too fucking much. His cock throbbed and he made a low, grinding noise.

"Yes," Katie breathed into his ear. "Fuck me. Just like that."

Soft, low, distinctly feminine, her voice was in no way like a man's. Her body, soft and curved, not like a man's. Nothing about this was like anything he'd ever even fantasized about, but Dean discovered it didn't fucking matter, not then, not with her cunt wrapped around his cock like that. Not with her tongue licking at the sore spot her teeth had left. Not with her moving on him, riding him. Fucking him as pleasure built and built and built.

"Touch me," Katie said into his ear. She took his hand,

slid it between them, pressed his thumb to her clit. "Oh, yes. Right there. Like that, just like that... Oh, god, Dean. Yes!"

Until this point, everything he'd promised her had been all talk. Until he felt her shudder and heard the soft sighing gasp of her breath as orgasm swept over her, Dean hadn't really been sure he could make her come. But now Katie rocked against him and his own climax shuddered through him. Perfect timing.

She blinked rapidly and looked at him, then laughed. "Wow. Well, I guess I'd say you won. Very well done, sir."

Dean blew out a breath, fingers tightening on her hips as his breathing slowed. "Saying I told you so would make me sort of an asshole, wouldn't it?"

Katie kissed him lightly on the cheek and eased herself off him, stretching as she reached to snag up her panties and T-shirt. "Sort of."

He watched as she got dressed without appearing to be the least bit embarrassed. He admired that about her. Not that he was embarrassed, exactly. Just more like wondering what the hell he'd just done.

Katie looked over her shoulder at him as she pulled on her clothes, then frowned. "You all right?"

Dean nodded, sitting there on the floor with a condom on his getting-limp dick, after having fucked one of his best friends. A woman, at that. It wasn't his most shining moment.

But Katie, still frowning, crouched next to him and pulled over a small garbage can and handed him a box of tissues, then his clothes. "I didn't think you'd be the one to get all emo, afterward."

"I'm not emo." Dean frowned and took care of cleaning up, then pulled on his briefs and jeans.

Katie studied him. "Uh-huh."

"I'm not."

She smiled and stood on tiptoe to kiss his cheek again.

"We fucked, Dean. And it was good. For me, anyway, and I'm pretty sure you enjoyed it. It doesn't make you straight. Just...open-minded."

Her smile urged his, even though none of this was as gratifying as he'd expected it to be. He'd thought it would feel like a conquest. Instead, he found himself hoping Jacob would forgive him.

"Damn it," he said, suddenly miserable. "Remind me that I like sort of being an asshole?"

"Why? Are you going to say you told me so?"

"No. Not about that."

She knew him too well, Katie did. "Ah. It's him, huh?"

"Jacob."

"*Him* has a name?" She looked impressed. "Wow, Dean. Wow."

"Fuck." He sank onto the couch and cradled his head in his hands. "Fuck, Katie, what did I just do?"

"Hey." She sat beside him and took his hand, linking their fingers. "Seriously, you're going to give me a complex, here. What happened...do you really think it was all just that stupid challenge? I mean, I know you don't do pussy as a general rule, but...maybe that's why you did it. Not why you suggested it, sweetie—that was all your huge ego. But...maybe it's why you actually went through with it."

He wasn't getting it, and she could tell.

"What I mean is, being with him scares you. I know why. But being with me isn't scary. Right?"

"No. Of course not."

She smiled. "Because you and I both know that no matter how stellar that living room rug fuck just was, and it was pretty delicious, it's not going to lead to anything. Right?"

He gave her a cautious nod. "Well...right."

"And for me," Katie said, "I really just needed someone who was into me. Even if only for an hour."

"I'm into you for longer than that," Dean told her and squeezed her hand.

She laughed, sounding better than she had earlier, which made Dean feel better. "You know what I mean."

"Yeah. I do." He leaned back against the couch cushions and stared at the ceiling. "He makes it all seem so easy."

"It's not how he makes it seem," she said. "It's how he makes it feel."

Jacob made it all feel easy, too. Dean frowned as Katie's cell phone rang, vibrating the coffee table. She looked at it and sighed, but didn't pick it up.

"It's Jimmy."

"Douchebag," Dean said and picked it up. "Hello?"

"...Katie?"

"She's busy," Dean told the guy.

"Oh. Um, can I leave a message?"

"No," Dean said, and hung up.

"Dean!" Katie looked shocked, but was laughing.

Dean shrugged. "Maybe he'll think better of jerking you around."

"Maybe he'll never call me again!"

"Would that be a bad thing?" Dean asked. "For real?"

Katie frowned without answering, and Dean pulled her close to hug her. They sat like that for a while without speaking. Then she sighed and pushed away from him.

"Go to him," Katie said.

Dean nodded and stood, then handed her the cell phone. "Call him back."

Katie almost bailed.

She'd waited until the morning to call Jimmy, not sure if she wanted to go down that road, maybe waiting to see if he'd call her first. He didn't. She wasn't sure how she felt about that. It didn't matter how she felt now, though, since she'd already called him and asked him to meet her for coffee. He'd hesitated before saying yes, a pause that had lasted a thousand years while she forgot to breathe. She wasn't, in fact, sure she remembered to now when he walked through the door.

He looked too damned good, she thought. It wasn't fair.

"Hey," Jimmy said as he slid into the chair across from her with a cup of coffee he put on the table. He shook his shaggy hair out of his face and shrugged out of his coat. His grin was at half-wattage.

"Hi, Jimmy." Katie had a mug of coffee in front of her, but she hadn't even sipped it. It was cold now, but she clutched it, anyway, as though the porcelain would warm her hands.

"This is nice. Meeting like this. Thanks for asking me." Jimmy sounded hesitant, uncertain. Not his usual self at all.

But what was his usual self? Did Katie even know? She had to admit she probably didn't. Everything about Jimmy was late-night conversation, and just because she'd bared her soul to him didn't mean he'd done the same.

"Thanks for coming. It's nice to see you."

They never talked like this. Even the first time he'd called her, they'd slipped into a loose back-and-forth that had only gotten easier over time. Now it was as though they'd only just met and had no reason to get to know each other better.

Jimmy's smile amped up a notch, still far from his usual bright grin, but noticeable. "Yeah. Two times in one week, that's some kind of crazy, huh?"

Katie had always believed honesty to be the best approach, but facing Jimmy across the tiny café table, all she could think of was how she wanted to make up some lame excuse for why she wanted to see him instead of just telling him the truth. "Yeah. Super crazy."

Jimmy seemed to relax a little bit, his long fingers turning his cup around and around on the table. His knee nudged hers. "Sorry."

"It's okay."

This was going nowhere. Katie hated it. She wanted to ask him if he liked her, or if she was just some myth, a story he liked to tell over the phone. She wanted to tell him about how she smiled at the sound of his voice. Of how she wanted more.

Jimmy glanced over her shoulder toward the counter. "I'm going to grab a refill. You want one?"

Katie shook her head. "No, I'm fine, thanks."

He touched her again as he passed. A hand on her shoulder, fingers curving and squeezing just momentarily. It was too much, the final straw, that casual touch that felt too good.

She got up without thinking, without looking back, heading out of the coffee shop and down the street. The wind burned her eyes, not tears, she told herself as her heels click-clacked on the sidewalk.

She was almost to the alley before he caught up to her.

"Katie!" Jimmy hooked her elbow, turning her as she stiffened at the sound of her name. He didn't let go. "Hey. Wait."

Katie opened her mouth to protest or maybe just to walk away without a word, she wasn't sure and had no time to decide before Jimmy was kissing her. Openmouthed and hungry, his hands on her hips pulling her close up against him. He tasted better than she'd imagined, his kiss deeper, his body harder.

He pulled away, shoulders rising and falling with his breath. His gaze searched hers. "I didn't... Was that..."

Katie kissed him. Softer than he'd done, her tongue stroking his as her fingers wound in the hair at the back of his neck. She pulled a little as his hands gripped tighter on her hips. She felt the bulge of his crotch through denim against her belly, and she pulled away, her own breath coming fast and sharp.

Jimmy smiled, his lips wet. "I should've done this a long time ago."

"Why didn't you?"

"I wasn't sure you wanted something like this," he said. "With me, I mean."

People passed them on the street, some giving them curious glances but most ignoring them. He stepped her backward into the relative privacy of the alley and leaned against the brick wall of the storefront without letting her go. Katie pressed against him, noticing he'd run out after her without a coat.

"Why on earth not?" she cried, pushing at him with her fists but not too hard. "God, Jimmy. We've been talking for weeks. You know the color of my favorite panties and the name of my first dog!"

"I know, I know, but…hell, I'm better on the phone than in person," he said.

Katie frowned and swiped her tongue over the taste of him lingering on her lips. "That sounds like a very bad excuse."

He sighed, looking serious. "I know. B-but…" Jimmy paused, drew a breath. "Well, I'll tell you. Until I was about fifteen, I stuttered."

Katie raised a brow.

"I grew out of it, or taught myself not to, whatever," Jimmy said slowly. "But by then I'd already found out I was better on the phone than talking to someone face-to-face. On the phone I could take my time or something, I don't know. It became a habit."

She shook her head. "I don't care if you stutter. You could've told me."

Jimmy nudged her just a bit closer into the space between one cocked leg and the opposite thigh. "I liked you the first time I met you, Katie. But then we started talking…"

"And you didn't like me anymore?"

"No." He laughed. "I liked you more. A lot more. I didn't want to ruin it."

She made a disgruntled noise, already forgiving him because to do anything else would only spite herself. "You almost did."

"I know. I'm sorry." Jimmy kissed her again, lingering this time. "Do you think we could start over?"

"Hell no," Katie told him, wrapping her arms around him and getting up on her toes to return the kiss. "Start at the beginning? No way. Let's go straight to third base. Unless," she paused meaningfully, "you really are better on the phone."

Jimmy grinned, eyes gleaming, and leaned in close to whisper in her ear. "Why don't we go to my place and you can decide for yourself?"

"That," Katie said, "sounds like an excellent idea."

Dean had brought flowers.

He didn't even know if Jacob liked flowers.

Dean liked flowers, purple and red and yellow, tied with a green ribbon. He liked them in vases around his house. Dean liked flowers because they were pretty and they didn't last long, and he didn't have to take care of them the way he'd have had to be responsible for a potted plant.

Maybe it was time he stopped being so afraid of taking care of things.

He'd just tossed them into the bushes by Jacob's front door when he was caught by the door opening. Jacob looked at the bushes. Then at Dean.

"Why are you throwing flowers into my bushes?"

Dean tried to look innocent and knew he failed by the way Jacob's eyebrows rose. "Uh…"

Jacob peered behind the bushes, then put a hand on his hip. "Did you bring me flowers and then throw them away?"

"Yes." Dean's jaw tensed.

Jacob smiled.

When Dean kissed him, it felt right. Like coming home. When Jacob kissed him back, it felt even better.

"I like flowers," Jacob said against Dean's mouth. "Thank you."

Dean pulled away just enough to look into Jacob's eyes. There was probably more to say but nothing came to him just then. He spoke with his body, his mouth using kisses instead of words to express what he wasn't sure he should say aloud. Jacob seemed to understand, though.

He smiled against Dean's mouth. "Come inside."

Dean nodded. Then he smiled, too, as he followed Jacob through the doorway, walking behind him.

Not walking away.

★ ★ ★ ★ ★

TASTE OF PLEASURE
LISA RENEE JONES

PROLOGUE

"Silk" was the name swirled in fancy, curly writing on the edged-glass, double doors of the entrance to the club. Inside, skin, sin and satisfaction dominated more than the menu—it dominated private cubbyholes with sheer curtains, the open areas as their centerpieces. Velvety couches sat in these showcased areas, all well adorned with naked bodies indulging in sublime delights.

This was a place Sarah Michaels would never in a million years have dared to enter had she known what to expect. Her close friend Carrie had dared her to be "wild and crazy," in celebration of her acceptance into UCLA's law school. And since lately, "wild and crazy" meant a burger and fries without the take-out bag and library decor, the idea held appeal. She yearned to let her long raven hair out of its tightly braided confines as much as she hungered for a little male companionship. She'd worked hard these past few years to build a future outside her family's business, to create her own identity. To stand on her own. She deserved some fun, to play a little.

But the bodies melting into bodies, the sighs and moans,

were far more than she had bargained for. Sex surrounded her. Disturbingly, despite the illicitness of it all, a part of her that she didn't recognize as herself was aroused, excited. She felt young, inexperienced, afraid, but yet she was effortlessly *seduced*. Deny it as she might wish to, she reveled, with an uncomfortable certainty, in the hedonistic indulgence of watching. This was not her—she was prim, proper, all about business. The dampness clinging to her panties defiantly contradicted her silent claim.

Sarah crossed her arms in front of her body and clung to any form of cover, a shell to hide beneath. She found it in her slinky black dress and a silent vow that it would not be removed despite everyone else's state of undress.

Everyone included Carrie, who she'd just left in a private room attended by the companionship of two other females. The facade of sweet, little-girl and Goldilocks innocence that often clung to Carrie had vanished almost instantly upon entering the club. From Sarah's witness, Carrie was more like the wolf with her prey—in control, hungry for respect and pleasure.

Unwilling to consider how easily her study buddy might have become something far different and irreversible, Sarah had quickly left Carrie's presence. She had no idea where she was going, but she didn't want, nor did she need, to face her own potential actions tomorrow through Carrie's eyes. Deep down, she recognized a desperate craving for anonymity, for the freedom it offered.

Sarah inhaled, finding herself at the bottom of a winding metal stairwell. Hesitating a mere moment, she raced upward, away from her friend but not from this place—reluctantly admitting her attraction to its forbidden allure. Had Carrie seen this side of her? Seen things Sarah wasn't willing to see in herself?

At the top of the stairs she found more couches, more curtains. A heavily shadowed corner offered the impression of invisibility, and Sarah pressed tightly into its hollow. It somehow granted her permission to remain. To allow the music, soft and sultry, to ripple through her body as surely as did the lusty heat of arousal as she watched one sensual act after another.

How long she stood there, she did not know. How long until *he* appeared—far too long. Tall, powerfully muscled, with longish, light blond hair, he stood before a half-moon-shaped couch, a light spraying him in a dim glow, as if he commanded its attention. Certainly, he commanded hers, and that of the two voluptuous, naked females who stood before him, offering their bodies for his enjoyment, receiving a noncommittal inspection in return. He was arrogant, dominant in his demand for attention by way of sheer existence. She was instantly submissive to that demand, instantly seduced. He wasn't even naked, but then, he didn't have to be—he was that ruggedly beautiful. His presence exuded an elixir of leather-clad man rippling with delicious muscle and erotic promises.

Heaviness expanded in her chest, her nipples tingled and tightened. Her eyes traveled his body with frenzied hunger. Never before had she drunk of a man's presence as she did this one. Never before had every pore of her body cried out in explosion at the mere sight of masculinity. She wanted to know why, wanted to know "more."

She studied him, inspected his physique with the thoroughness of an artist inspecting a masterpiece. She blinked as he removed his shirt. Wet her lips at the sight of his bare chest, his skin glistening golden-brown beneath the glowing lights. Broad shoulders complemented a defined chest sprinkled with just the right amount of hair. Her eyes dropped to his ripped abdominals where a tattoo circled his belly button. She couldn't make it out, wanted to make it out, wanted to see it up close, touch it...lick it. Her hand went to her stomach. God. What was this man doing to her?

Suddenly, his chin snapped upward, attention diverted from the females at his feet, gaze snapping to Sarah's corner. She froze, heart skipping a beat. Could he see her? Panicked for reasons she couldn't explain, she searched his face. But that question was shoved aside as her stomach fluttered violently. She knew him. She knew those eyes, knew them well enough to know what she could not see at this distance—that they were baby-blue, sparked with flecks of amber that made them look like ocean water twinkling at sunrise. Knew him because their families were enemies, a friendship flawed through the corporate anger that had arced between two fathers—his and her own.

Seconds passed, pregnant silence surrounding her, blocking out the music, the surroundings. There was just her and him. Tension stretched, and so did the warmth in her body, so did the arousal heavy in her limbs. His lips twitched, lifted—a smile but not a smile. Awareness. That word came to mind. He knew she was there, that she watched, that she longed to do more than watch. Perhaps he knew who she was. Perhaps he did not. If he did, he gave no indication of that knowledge. His eyes lingered, held her paralyzed. An invisible hand seemed to stretch across that couch, across the space, and caress her with promises of forbidden pleasures she would not soon forget.

She should have moved. She should have left. She felt traitorous to her family, to her roots and to herself. Rebellion and desire flared out of nowhere and pressed her against the corner wall, not away from it. Sarah wasn't going anywhere, she realized. She was staying. She was watching. She was celebrating.

CHAPTER ONE

Eight years later

If not for the weight of the four long weeks as interim CEO at Chocolate Delights, Sarah suspected she would have known he was there. Suspected she would have recognized the tingling awareness trickling down her spine as more than the warm splash of water in the Olympic-size pool of the Houston, Texas, country club. Instead, she dismissed the sensation as the edginess created from hours of boardroom brawls, an edginess she'd hoped to dispose of in a dozen laps. And since her swim appeared to be failing miserably, she had every intention of pulling out the big gun—a pint of Ben & Jerry's cookie dough ice cream. Of course, she'd have to run by the store. Unlike her Austin home, her corporate apartment wasn't well stocked with critical necessities like her favorite frozen treat.

Her mouth was watering with anticipation of the cookie dough flavor she adored when she brought herself upright, her fingers curling around the concrete ledge of the pool, and blinked a pair of dusty cowboy boots into view. Boots that could have belonged to any one of the hundreds of club members, but the late hour, near nine o'clock in the evening, coupled with the instinctive thunder of her heart, said they did not. Those boots were going to be trouble, like everything else that had been thrown her way since her father's diagnosis a month before.

Slowly, Sarah's gaze lifted, taking in long, muscular, jean-clad thighs and lean hips before jerking to his face—Ryan White, aka the CEO of Delights's rival, Deluxe Sweets, for the past five, highly successful years. Ryan White, who was also the star of most of her midnight fantasies. She didn't think for a minute that his appearance poolside was a coincidence. Nor was his choice of faded jeans, rather than one of those designer suits he'd worn to grace the covers of numerous business magazines.

Deceptively casual. Calculated. As was his showing up when she was darn near naked. Well, she wasn't a young college kid anymore, easily intimidated. She was a corporate attorney with years of experience. Granted, only a few of those years were actually with Delights before she and her father bumped heads over the direction of the company's future and she'd departed. But that made no difference. She'd met plenty of men like Ryan White, men who were after success at all costs. Okay, maybe not *exactly* like him. A flash of him standing over those naked women in that club years before had her swallowing hard. Regardless, he was after something—and she knew what. She knew all too well. And he could forget it.

"You heard about my father," she said flatly, not playing the game of unnecessary introductions any more than she would play cat-and-mouse.

He bent down, light blond hair framing a handsome face. "How is he?" Ryan asked, his voice, his expression, actually sounding concerned.

Emotion welled in her chest, defensiveness rising in her chest. "He has cancer," she said. "Other than that, he's great."

And he's ready to quit fighting, she added silently. The certainty that he would lose the company was eating him alive as rapidly as his cancer. And with good reason. It was in financial ruin. No doubt, Ryan thought to take advantage of the weakness. He could think again.

Sarah lifted herself out of the pool and directly into his path, giving him no chance to avoid the splash of water. She expected him to back away. He didn't. His hands went to her waist, over the simple, navy, one-piece suit that had felt conservative before it was wet and clinging to her every curve. Sarah froze, heat rushing over her, awareness like she hadn't felt, well...ever.

"Hello to you, too, Sarah," he said, his eyes latching on to hers, simmering with heat, his voice a confident, sexy drawl that dripped arrogance and sex. His gaze melted into hers a moment, and then, with intentional directness, he let his eyes slide downward, over her nipples pebbling through the material. Lingering, touching her without touching her.

How long had she wanted this with this man? How long had she known what she knew now? That he was the definition of forbidden fruit. She wanted to shove him away; she wanted to stay close. But she held her ground, refusing to be intimidated. Seconds ticked by like hours, before crystal-blue eyes the color of the pool lifted back to hers, heat simmering in their depths. Then he said, "It's been a long time."

A long time. In three words, the intimidation rolled through her. In three words, he had successfully zapped her customary control—hit her with the dreaded memory, too soon after the wave of emotion over her father—and melted her into a rare moment of weakness. Heat and embarrassment flooded her system, weakening her knees. They had not seen each other since they were children except once in that club so many years before. The idea of him using that night against her to gain an upper hand didn't sit well. Not well at all.

Her teeth ground together, her words intentionally prim and perfect. Controlled. Something she had mastered in the courtroom. In her life. "Please let go of me." She smiled. "Or you might slip and fall into the pool. In some mysterious way I'd have nothing to do with, of course."

His lips hinted at a smile, and his light blond hair accented the baby-blue eyes, alight with mischief. "You should remember our childhood games enough to know I never back down."

Their childhood. He'd been talking about their childhood. Not the club. Relief washed over her, and so did the recovery of her courtroom-honed sparring skills. "Because back then," she said, "I wouldn't have made you back down. But this is now, not then." She lifted her chin. "I've changed."

He chuckled and stepped backward, hands up in mock surrender. "You wouldn't have won so many cases in the courtroom if that wasn't true." And before she could process his admission that he'd followed her legal career, he added, "Other things can change, too, Sarah. Family feuds begin and they end. We could start that ball rolling with a cup of coffee."

Or with a bedroom brawl. She shoved aside the naughty thought with a sharp reply. Too sharp, she realized too late. It showed her hand, showed he'd gotten to her. "Save your dollar and your sweet-talking conversation." She hugged the small towel around her a bit tighter, discreetly, not about to let him see her squirm. "Chocolate Delights isn't for sale."

His eyes narrowed almost imperceptibly so that only her practiced courtroom skill allowed her to notice. "You intend to try and turn the company around then," he said. "Good." He smiled. "And you aren't about to have coffee with me, are you?"

"Not a chance," she agreed quickly.

He smiled. "Not even if I promise not to talk business?"

"Not even."

"I've done the whole take-over-for-my-father bit," he said. "You might be surprised at what I could do to help."

"Me or you?" she asked tightly, convinced he was a problem, no, more than a problem—dangerous, lethal—because she actually wanted to say yes to coffee. Yes to a "bedroom brawl." Yes to anything that involved this man.

"If I say both?" he asked. "Will I be sent for execution?"

"Both would indicate you have a self-serving purpose in mind, thus making a date with Ben & Jerry's cookie dough ice cream my best offer of the night." The flippant retort held a well-intended bite. Ben & Jerry's competed with the new ice cream line he'd just released at Deluxe. And it was darn good ice cream. Better than her previous favourite, but she'd never admit that to anyone. Ever. Especially not to Ryan. Nor would she admit she occasionally sneaked a pint of Deluxe's bestselling Cake Batter Deluxe ice cream into her freezer.

Unexpectedly, Ryan laughed, a deep, throaty masculine sound that rumbled in her ears and shimmered across her skin with electric delight. "Damn, Ben & Jerry's are always keeping me on my toes." He took a step backward. "I'll leave you to them then." He winked. "For now." He started to turn and stopped, his tone shifting to solemn, his expression with it. "Delights has been in trouble a long time, Sarah. If your father could have fixed what's broken, he would have. If you want to save it, don't question yourself. Don't worry about what your father will think when he returns. Own your role." His tone softened. "And if you change your mind about that coffee, you know where to find me."

He turned and sauntered away, a sexy swagger to his hips, her heart racing with his every step. He reached for the door, and glanced over at her. "You should live a little dangerously tonight," he said. "Try the Cake Batter Deluxe."

And then he was gone, tempting her in all kinds of dangerous ways.

CHAPTER TWO

It was Saturday, nearly a week after her Ryan encounter, and Sarah was at her home away from home—her father's desk at the Delights's corporate office. Long hours were necessary if she intended to turn the company around. She wasn't going to let a week of discouraging financial reports get her down. Though the fantasies of Ryan, which were hot, wet, melting fantasies she could conjure both in her bedroom and in the boardroom, were becoming a serious problem. The company was in trouble and she, its only hope of survival, kept fantasizing about her biggest competitor. Naked. She kept imagining Ryan naked. With her. But then, her fantasies of Ryan were easier to forgive than her inability to change the reality of a company that needed a miracle. No amount of spending limits, staff cuts she didn't want to make, or creative cash flow would change that fact.

The company had needed a good makeover a long time ago—new product lines, creative distribution, things she'd brought up even before she'd left the company years before. Ice cream shops in the airports and malls to promote their brand and bring in new users. Movie theater distribution for packaged candies. These things could work. They *would have* worked. But now...now, good ideas weren't enough. She'd need cash. "He should have sold out years ago," Sarah mumbled, tapping her pencil on the desk. Now she wasn't sure that was an option. The minute she opened the books for review, a buyer—even Ryan, especially Ryan—would run for the hills.

Sarah's chest tightened, her eyes prickling. "Damn it," she mumbled, and tossed the latest financial reports on her fancy mahogany desk, or rather her father's fancy mahogany desk, in his fancy corner office in downtown Austin. "Crying won't get you anywhere, Sarah." The problem was, she'd seen her father that morning, seen how frail and weak he was, and worst of all, she'd seen the light in his eyes when she'd vowed the company would survive. A vow she feared she couldn't keep.

The phone rang and she jumped, her hand going to the navy silk blouse she'd paired with navy pants. Dressing like a CEO on the weekend had been a last-minute choice springing from a need to feel in control. A refined, prepared executive-in-charge, in case she ran into anyone. She felt she had to be ready, yet she so wasn't ready. The company was crumbling and even the phone set her on edge.

Her gaze touched the console and the blinking private line that said she was about to speak to her father. She drew a calming breath and grabbed the receiver, forcing a smile and praying it reached to her voice. She didn't have time to test the strategy. Before she could speak, a deep, familiar voice resonated through the phone. "The ever dedicated CEO working through her weekend."

Ryan. Momentarily stunned, the name vibrated through her body. It was like a cool blast of air on a hot Texas day, chillingly unexpected, pleasurable, and oh, so powerful. "How did you get this number?"

"I'm resourceful," he assured her, and then, with a rasp of seduction lacing his voice, added, "In all kinds of ways."

She didn't miss the innuendo. Of course, he didn't mean for her to. Which wasn't the problem. That she *liked* it was. "I assume," she said drily, sounding remarkably unaffected by him, considering she was anything but, "that since you put those resources to use to get my direct line, you have a reason."

"Come downstairs and I'll tell you," he said.

She blinked and shook her head a little. She was tired, clearly not hearing well. "Downstairs? What?"

"I'd come to you," he said. "But Big Mike didn't think that was a good idea."

Big Mike. The security guard. In *her* building. Ryan was in the building. Heart racing, Sarah slammed the phone down, pushed to her feet and charged toward the elevator. If people saw Ryan in her building they'd think…well, most likely that she was selling the company, or merging it with the competition. People would fear the future, fear for their jobs. Assume the worse. Jump ship. She'd never hold things together then.

In a mad dash, she was in the hallway repeatedly punching the elevator button, as if that would actually make it appear on the twentieth floor faster. The ride was slow, the fluttering of her pulse erratic. Big Mike had been working his post for ten years. He knew everyone. He'd talk. *People talked.* It was human. But Mike did his job and did it by the book. How Ryan had managed to get Big Mike to let him call her private line, she didn't know. At six-four, with broad shoulders and an expressionless face, Mike was the biggest, baddest, most intimidating black man in the building, and probably all of downtown—at least to newcomers who didn't know his teddy bear side.

The difference between Ryan and Mike was physical versus intellectual muscle. Big Mike intimidated by size alone. Ryan was calculating, a man with a cobra-sharp tongue he used proficiently with acid, wit or charm, or any combination of the three.

The minute Sarah exited the elevator into the lobby, she heard the rumble of Ryan's voice saying something about a quarterback who'd been sacked three times in his last game. She rolled her eyes and had her answer as to how he'd managed to wrangle her private line from Mike. Ryan must have done his homework, and known that Mike was a former University of Texas linebacker, which, regardless of the past tense or the Houston location, made him a local celebrity. Ryan had reeled Mike in, hook, line and sinker, with football talk. An assessment validated when she rounded the corner and rolled her eyes at what she found. Ryan was standing across from Big Mike, who sat behind the extra long, black-glass security desk, dressed in a burnt-orange University of Texas football T-shirt.

Stiffening her spine, she marched forward, her heels clicking on the glossy twelve-by-twelve white tiles of the lobby. Both men glanced in her direction, and Ryan leaned an elbow on the desk, watching her approach, deceptively casual, like a tiger lying in wait for his prey. A rush of awareness, spun with a mixture of heat and arousal, pulsed through her limbs at the idea of being that man's prey. It also ticked her off. She *would not* be aroused by her competitor.

Upon arriving at the desk, she stopped at a respectable distance from Ryan and, with an intentional snub, settled her attention on Big Mike. "I see you share a love of orange with Mr. White."

"Seems that way, Ms. Michaels," he said. She glanced at Ryan, intending to offer a cordial greeting, but noting the sparkle in his sea-blue eyes, she forgot what she'd intended to say. "Funny that," she said. "Since you went to UCLA."

"I regret that choice," he said. "Which is why that was the last time I ever allowed my father to tell me what to do."

He arched a challenging brow with the silent question— *Can you say the same?*—that was too damn clear with Mike standing there.

"Can we talk?" she asked tightly. "In *private?*"

He pushed off the desk. "Sure," he said, motioning toward the elevator. "Lead the way."

She countered with a wave in the direction of the exit door. "Let's step outside."

His lips twitched and he eyed Mike. Mike grinned. "Told you she'd never let you upstairs."

Sarah's gaze flashed approvingly to Mike. "Good work, Mike."

Instantly, Mike straightened, his shoulders broadened in a prideful gesture. "Never let the offense get to the quarterback, which is you, Ms. Michaels."

Though his remark was meant to be supportive, Sarah's stomach fell to her toes, because even Mike, who knew nothing of the inner workings of the company, understood that Ryan was in offensive mode with a touchdown in sight, while she was playing a poor version of defense, with a loss in sight. She couldn't afford to have anyone believing the doom and gloom of certain failure. Not her staff, not Mike and especially not Ryan.

Resolve stiffened her spine, and this time Sarah pulled *her* shoulders back. "Give me a few more weeks," she said, her gaze shifting to Ryan. "Ryan will be the one on the defense, not me. You can take that to Vegas and bet on it."

Sarah started walking to the exit, her intention to force Ryan to follow. His deep, sexy taunt of laughter followed in her wake.

"I do believe I just got a smack-down, Mike," Ryan said, his voice steady, unmoving. He wasn't following.

"Actually, sir," Mike replied, "that's what we call an interception."

"And my chances of getting the ball back?" Ryan asked coolly, amusement lacing his tone.

Too coolly to suit Sarah. She whirled around to face Ryan to find him, once again, leaning on the security desk, even as Mike replied, "About as good as making it through a tornado without a basement." His eyes widened on Sarah, and he rephrased, "Correction. You're a broken-down Volkswagen driving straight into that tornado and you're about to be crushed."

Ryan laughed and pushed off the counter. "I've never been compared to a Volkswagen before, but somehow I bet Ms. Michaels has been called a tornado." He sauntered toward Sarah, all loose-legged and confident, faded denim hugging powerful thighs.

Sarah wanted to smack him. Or get naked with him. Or both. In that order. Or maybe the order didn't matter at all. Years of fantasizing about this man were clearly having an inconvenient impact, because now was not the time to be thinking of sex, most certainly not with Ryan. She told herself to play this cool, regardless of how hot he made her feel. She knew how to do that. She'd done so in the courtroom plenty of times, under turbulent, uncomfortable circumstances. And the dull throb of awareness settling in the lower region of her body was most definitely uncomfortable.

Calling on her inner Ice Princess persona, which she'd used for certain "uncomfortable" legal battles, she prepared for confrontation. But when Ryan stopped in front of her, toe to toe, close enough to be considered intimate, close enough to smell the spicy male scent of man, and his undoubtedly expensive, delicious cologne, her wall of ice melted under the scorching heat of his presence. Good Lord, she could feel the heat radiating off his big, gorgeous body. She blinked into the predatory gleam alight in his blue eyes that said he wanted to gobble her up. When she might have turned into one big puddle of melting female, she reminded herself, he'd gobble Chocolate Delights up right along with her.

Her chin lifted, her gaze narrowed. "I know what you're trying to do, and I won't let you. You can't have Delights."

Seconds ticked by at a crawl, his expression unreadable, his body too near. "I didn't come here today for Delights," he said, his voice low, sandpaper-rough. "I came for you, Sarah."

CHAPTER THREE

Ryan watched the flicker of uncertainty touch Sarah's naturally warm amber gaze, before she quickly masked it behind anger. "I don't know what game you're playing."

"No game," he said. "Just here to collect that coffee date."

She stepped closer, lowering her voice. "I'm not buying you being so calculated for a cup of coffee."

He laughed, amusement impossible to contain. "Did you really just accuse me of seducing your security guard?"

With a sharp nod, she crossed her arms in front of her chest, glaring up at him without any inkling of intimidation and seemingly oblivious to how, at six foot two, he towered over her a good eight inches.

"If the shoe fits, buddy," she said. "And I'd say it's just the right size."

His lips twitched, his zipper expanded. "What happens at six tonight, Mike?" he called over his shoulder.

"UT kicks the Aggies' butts, sir."

Ryan arched a brow. "Satisfied?"

"Like I said, you had a plan, which I assume is to start

rumors about my private meetings with the competition, and shake up my staff."

"If I wanted Delights," he said, lowering his voice, "I'd go after Delights in a far more aggressive way than starting a few rumors. And just so we get this behind us once and for all, I couldn't buy Delights even if I did want it, not with its present balance sheet, and not without my stockholders having me shot."

Her eyes widened. "What do you know about our balance sheet?"

Compliments of their many legal issues with unpaid vendors—plenty. "This isn't a conversation for the lobby," he said. "Invite me upstairs."

She inhaled a sharp breath, her gaze probing, assessing his resolve, before she accurately determined that he wasn't going away without some one-on-one time. "Not upstairs," she said. "Outside." She turned on her heels and marched toward the door.

Holding his ground, he tracked her retreat with what he knew was a hot, hungry gaze, enjoying the sway of her hips and picturing the moment he'd hold that tight little swimmers butt in his hands. It was true there was a business element to his visiting Sarah, but not one she would ever expect, and not one he'd even determined he was willing to pursue. But he'd been curious about the little girl who'd become a beautiful woman with erotic tastes. Curious if she'd ever pursued those tastes beyond a secret corner. The answer was no, she had not. He could see it in her eyes, feel it in her presence.

And so he let her run for now, let her have a few seconds to compose herself, knowing he had her on edge, when his real intention was to *take her to the edge.* That meant being gentle, giving her the safety and security to explore and let go, with him, through trust. And she *was* most definitely *running*—

from him, from what she was going to have to do to save her family business, and from the secret they'd shared so many years ago. But most of all, she was running from herself, and while he'd be easy with her, while he'd protect her, he wasn't going to let her hide.

When he finally joined her outside, as expected, she'd recovered any lost composure, and her gaze flashed hotter than the high Texas sun. He'd already surmised her anger and sharp wit were her shields, her protective walls, and they would have to go, quickly.

"I've told you," she said. "Chocolate Delights—"

"Isn't for sale," he said. "I know." He stepped toward her and gently but forcefully guided her by the elbow. "Over here." He maneuvered them inside the intimate enclave created by the side of the entryway and a large round pillar, and he settled her against the wall, cornering her with his big body, but dropped his hand, didn't touch her. Anticipation had value—it excited and intensified pleasure. "I also know how protective you feel about the company and your father right now. But we are not our fathers. And I'm not your enemy. Even if Delights was thriving right now, it's gone a different direction than Deluxe. We aren't even direct competitors anymore."

Her eyes flashed. "And if I change that?"

"I hope you do," he teased. "Then I really could buy you out."

"Maybe I'll buy *you* out."

"Let the challenge begin," he said, smiling, and then sobered quickly. "Sarah. I saw my father's face when he heard about your father's cancer. He cares about him. I'm not even sure either of them really even remembers why they're fighting. If mine does, he refuses to talk about it. They're just old and stubborn, and just won't get over it, whatever *it* may be."

"They fought about how fast to grow the company," she said.

"Did they?" he asked. "I'm not sure my father would be so secretive if that were all there was to it. But either way, you're in the same boat I was. And let me tell you, taking over for my hardheaded father was no walk in the park." Ryan hadn't had the guilt of a cancer diagnosis either, like she did now. "I bet you didn't know we were near bankruptcy when I took the reins, now did you?"

Her eyes went wide. "No. You... I had no idea."

He nodded. "My father was a great visionary, not a great leader. So when I said I know what you're going through with the company, I do. You can talk to me, Sarah."

"I can't talk to you, Ryan," she said. "I can't just forget who you are."

"Why?"

"Because," she said. "I just...can't."

"Even though you know you want to?" A welcome cool breeze slipped past the pillar, and a wayward strand of Sarah's rich brunette hair fell over her brow. Ryan reached up and brushed it from her eyes, the touch hissing with an instant, intense charge of electricity. Her eyes were warm with awareness, and he wondered what they'd looked like when she'd watched him in the shadows of that club. "Do you ever secretly wish you could let go of control, Sarah?"

"Never," she said, her mouth a lush pink, her eyes telling a different story.

"Liar," he accused, letting his hand drop.

"Do you?"

"Pleasure is my form of control," he said. "I do believe it's your personal hell."

"You couldn't be more wrong." She laughed, but there was an edge of bitterness to it, an edge of discomfort. "Not having control is my hell."

"You're afraid of thinking you have control and then finding out you don't."

"Which never happens to you, I assume, oh, master of the great balance sheets?"

"Master, Sarah?" he asked softly. "I wonder what made you choose that specific title?"

Her eyes went wide, her face paling with the realization of what she'd said, of what he'd said, of what they now had out in the open. "I'm done talking." She tried to sidestep him.

He maneuvered slightly, so she'd have to touch him to pass, successfully stalling her retreat. "What we shared that night is nothing to be ashamed of."

Her eyes widened farther, her cheeks flushed. "We didn't share anything."

"Didn't we?"

Panic flared in her eyes. "Let me pass."

"I give the orders," he said. "That's how it works."

"Not with me." Yet she held her ground, didn't try to pass again. She wanted to know more of what he could show her, and he was frankly shocked that she'd clearly never explored the world she'd visited inside Silk beyond that one night. Shocked that she'd suppressed her obvious desires so completely, yet he was undeniably pleased she could be his to teach, his to pleasure.

"You're afraid."

"I'm not afraid."

"Then why did you hide from me that night in Silk? Why not walk right up to me and take part in the experience?"

"I was dragged there by a friend," she said. "I didn't even want to be there. And we weren't exactly friendly. The strife between our fathers was at its worst back then."

"Which would have added a sense of the forbidden we would have enjoyed," he said. "Knowing yourself, Sarah, facing your fears, knowing what pleases you, what *controls you,* what turns you inside out, makes you stronger. Gives you control. And you will have control. We set boundaries and limits. You do nothing you don't want to do. But you need to know that neither do you get to hide from what you want to do. I won't let you."

Desire and fear, a hint of panic, flickered in her eyes. "I don't want— I can't... No."

"You can," he said. "And you want to." He studied her a moment and then stepped backward. "But obviously you aren't ready. When you are—and I believe you will be—you know where I am." He said nothing more, leaving her there to face the decision, and herself, alone. Until the time when she faced it with him.

CHAPTER FOUR

At nearly nine o'clock, a month after her encounter with Ryan, Sarah sat at her desk, her fourteen-hour workday still well under way. She had a million plates spinning in the air, and she was terrified one of them was going to tumble and break, with devastating results. She reached in her drawer and pulled out the note Ryan had sent her the morning after his visit. *When you're ready—Ryan,* the plain white note read, along with several phone numbers.

Sarah stared at it, as she had innumerable times, as she'd tried to deny she wanted what Ryan offered her, that she, the ultimate control freak, could actually want to be controlled. But the fantasies of Ryan doing just that were far too many and far too frequent. Still so very easily, the image of him at that nightclub so many years ago—naked, powerful, commanding and wholly masculine. The ring of her cell phone had her setting the note back in the drawer, and cringing at the caller ID. It was her mother, again. This made three times in the past hour, and from the prior two messages, Sarah was well aware of why she was calling. Despite Sarah's best efforts to keep it from happening, her mother had found out about one of the toughest changes Sarah had made at Delights these past few weeks.

With a sigh, she knew she had to answer. Sarah grabbed the phone and punched the send button. "Hi, Mom."

"You can't stop production of the Delights Peppermint Patties," she said, not bothering with hello. "Do you know what your father will do when he finds out? That's his favorite product, our first product. It's the staple of the company."

"It doesn't sell, Mom," she said. "It's—"

"Your father's favorite product. Don't take *that* from him. He's lost his hair, his health. Let him keep his damn Peppermint Patties."

Sarah squeezed her eyes shut, aware of the fear and grief motivating her mother's illogical demand. "Mom," she said softly, "I know this is hard. It's hard for me, too, but I made Dad a promise I'd save the company. And I'm going to save it. I have to attract investors to the company, and that means making tough choices."

"What am I supposed to tell your father?"

"Tell him I'm not going to let him down, and I love him." She hesitated, dreading what she had to confess, but knowing it would avoid another panicked phone call. "I'm shutting a dozen retail stores, too. I'm making the announcement Monday." And considering it was Friday, it was going to be a long weekend. And a long phone call. It took thirty minutes for Sarah to calm her mother down, to explain some of the innovative partnerships she was pitching, to assure her things would be better. When Sarah finally hung up, ending the call with a heartfelt promise to visit her father the next day, she had to check and see if her hands were shaking. Who was she kidding? She was barely hanging on to control.

She yanked open her desk, grabbed the note from Ryan

and, before she could stop herself, dialed. He answered on the second ring. "Hello."

His voice was deep and sexy, and...

"Sarah?"

"Yes," she said, leaning back in her chair. "It's me."

"How's your father?"

It wasn't what she expected, though she wasn't sure what she'd expected. "The doctor says he's where he should be at this stage of treatment, but he's having a tough time."

"And you?" he asked. "How are you?"

"I just hung up with my mother," she said. "She found out I killed the Peppermint Patti product line, and she was upset."

"We had a Peppermint Patti line, you know," he said. "I killed it, too. They don't sell. You did the right thing."

"I know," she said, "but hearing you say it is comforting. Though it shouldn't be. I mean, you're—"

"A friend, Sarah," he said softly. "Let me come and pick you up. We can—"

"No," she said quickly, her heart exploding in her chest. "No. I have work to do. I just, well, I needed to talk to someone who understands."

Silence lingered a moment before he said, "Nothing happens that you don't want to have happen with me, Sarah. If we never do more than talk—"

"I know," she said. "Honestly, I really do know. And thank you, Ryan, for being a friend. And if you really aren't a friend and I find out I am the biggest fool on the planet...I'm going to kick your butt."

He laughed. "I'm not using you. In fact, I believe I've invited you to use *me*."

A flutter of butterflies touched her stomach, heat rushing through her limbs, before she dared to say, "Right now, I'm not prepared to reach beyond my own imagination."

"Are you telling me you've been fantasizing about me, Sarah?" he asked, his voice low and whiskey-rough.

"Maybe it's that forbidden-fruit appeal you mentioned the other day," she said, barely believing what was coming out of her mouth. "Or maybe I want..."

"Want what, Sarah?"

To be brave enough to act on those fantasies. But instead, she said, "I remember that night in Silk like it was yesterday. It was my first time, my only time, in a place like that. Is that the kind of place you frequent?"

"My tastes are far more refined and exclusive now than they were then," he said softly. "I'm a member of a highly elite club, where discretion is as valued as pleasure."

"I see."

"What else do you want to know, Sarah?"

"You don't mind me asking questions?"

"You *should* ask questions," he said. "Choices should be educated."

She liked that answer. "Okay then. What if I didn't want to go to this club you are a part of?"

"Then we wouldn't go," he said. "But just so you know, we would have a private suite for play, where it's just you and me."

For play. Her stomach fluttered again at what that might mean.

"We don't venture beyond that room unless I know you're in your comfort zone," he continued, "I push you, yes, but I protect you, too, Sarah."

She absorbed it all, aroused, interested—terrified—needing to back away to think. A sense of desperateness rose inside her, and she quickly and without any semblance of smoothness changed the subject. "I'm closing twelve stores Monday."

And to her utter shock, he shifted right along with her, asking all the right questions and offering some solid advice.

Lisa Renee Jones

They ended the call a quick hour later, and Sarah sat at her desk with his parting words replaying in her head.

When you're ready, Sarah.

But she wasn't sure she'd ever be ready to give up control, especially not to a man like Ryan, who might not ever give it back.

CHAPTER FIVE

By the time Thursday evening rolled around, Delights's first ever layoff had become a special news report on a local station. Sarah's staff had panicked. Then, her mother had panicked. In turn, Sarah had rushed from work to the hospital, where her father was staying for several intense treatments. She hadn't even taken time to change from her black suit dress and high heels. And now, sitting in the recliner beside his bed, she watched him staring at the late edition of the news, certain he'd be the next to panic.

Instead, when it was over, he hit the remote button to turn off the television with a grimace on his pale, thin face. Sarah held her breath, waiting for the explosion that didn't come. Instead, he set the remote on the nightstand. "These news people will do anything for a story, honey. Don't let them get to you. Once you land these big new accounts you're working on, we'll rattle cages until they tell the good news just as vividly as the bad. I have faith in you."

Sarah blinked in surprise. "I'm sorry, am I in the wrong room? Because my father is the man with a stubborn side who loves to argue with me and curse out those who tick him off, even if they are on the television."

He smiled weakly, looking far older than the fifty-two years he'd always appeared to be, and running a hand that shook ever so slightly over his head. "Your father also used to have thick brown hair that wasn't falling out or turning gray. Things change. I've read over your marketing plans and your bank proposal, and I already know the dismal truth about our bottom line. I should have listened to you years ago."

"Dad," she said, taking his hand, her heart in her throat.

He squeezed her fingers. "Cancer has made me see the light. I've spent too much time blinded by what is familiar rather than seeing what there is to learn. I just hope I survive it long enough to show you. I meant what I said. I believe in you. I know you have things under control."

Fighting the pinch in the back of her eyes, Sarah smiled at him. "I'll welcome the day you are back at the office giving me attitude and making me fight you tooth and nail to prove my decisions are sound."

Sarah spent the next hour with her father, trying to forget the cancer, the work on her desk, and the fear of letting him down. She just wanted to be with him, to enjoy every second with him. They were watching *Indiana Jones* when her mother arrived with the doctor in tow. There was good news. Sarah listened to what sounded like the first real breakthrough in her father's treatment, and felt the doctor's words like a cool breeze on a hot day, washing her with relief. They weren't out of the darkness yet, but they had a night-light, and it was a beacon of hope.

The doctor left and her mother flipped the television back to *Indiana Jones,* settling into the chair beside the bed in Sarah's place. Despite it being nearly eight o'clock, Sarah was invigorated, ready to head back to the office and get to work.

"Everyone says your father looks like Harrison Ford," her mother said, looking tired but at peace for the first time since Sarah's return home.

"But better-looking," her father joked.

Sarah smiled at their familiar, loving banter, and said her goodbyes for the evening, leaving her parents alone. But as she walked down the hall, her black high heels clicking on the tiled floor, her mood grew heavier with each step, her father's words playing in her head. *I believe in you. You have things under control.* What if she didn't have things under control? *I do,* she told herself. *I have a brilliant marketing plan. I have a great staff, ready to take things to a new level.* Right. She had things under control.

Forcing herself to repeat those words the rest of the way to the parking lot, but breaking her mantra when she neared her car, Sarah dug in her purse for her keys and couldn't find them. She dug harder, deeper. She emptied her purse on the hood, thankful for the parking spot near the door and the streetlight. With a bad feeling in her stomach, she pressed her face to the tinted window and squinted. Sure enough, her keys were on the seat. She closed her eyes in complete frustration, hearing her father's words. *I believe in you. You have things under control.* And what did she do? She lost control of the most basic of life's responsibilities. She'd locked her keys in her car.

She didn't know how much time had passed when she finally lifted her head, but there were tears on her cheeks and she swiped at them angrily. She hadn't cried before now, not with the cancer diagnosis, not with the grim news week after week and not through the upheaval of racing home to take over the company. She was too tired, both mentally and physically, and she knew this. She was scared of failing. Of making wrong choices. But none of this was a good enough excuse. She didn't have cancer. She wasn't dying. It was time to get a grip on herself and do something other than sit here and act like a wimp.

She snatched her phone from her purse and tried to figure out who to call, because she wasn't going inside and upsetting her parents. Calling for roadside service seemed logical. That made sense. Instead, without consciously doing so, she thumbed through her numbers and stared at Ryan's number. She punched the recall button and dialed Ryan. "I can't believe I'm doing this," she whispered.

"Hello," his deep, sexy, deliciously male voice said after only one ring, and absolutely no time to change her mind and back out.

Sarah sucked in a breath. He could be at work, or with a woman, at his club. She had to hang up.

"Sarah?"

Damn. Of course, he had caller ID. "Yes... I... My car." She swallowed hard. "I lost my keys and—"

"Where are you?" he asked, not seeming to need more than her cryptic nonsense, also as out of character as locking her keys in her car and then dialing his number.

"The hospital," she said, and glanced around. "Row One-A at the front, by the door."

"I'll be there in a few minutes."

He hung up. Sarah sank against her car and waited for her own panic rather than her father's, panic created by what she'd just done. But instead, she replayed, not her father's words this time, but Ryan's. *By facing your fears, you grow stronger. It gives you control.*

And when Ryan's sleek 911 black Porsche pulled up beside her, and the passenger door popped open, Sarah wasted no time climbing inside. She pulled the door shut, closing herself inside the intimacy of the sports cars, the masculine, spicy, powerful scent of him insinuated into her nostrils, into her bloodstream. The car idled as they stared at each other, shadows wrapping them in intimacy but not invisibility. She could see he was dressed in a dark suit, a light shirt, his tie still in place. She could see the light stubble of a newly formed beard. "I hope I didn't interrupt anything," she finally said.

"I would have come even if you had," he said. "Do you have extra keys somewhere we can pick them up?"

He'd come here fully prepared to offer her aid without any physical connection. Knowing this made her more certain than ever she wanted him. "I don't really care about my keys right now."

He put the car in Park and turned to her, his eyes dark, lost in the shadows. "What does that mean, Sarah?"

She wanted him to touch her, but he did not. She wanted to touch him, but somehow, she knew she should not. "You know what it means."

"Say it," he ordered.

Anything to get him to touch her, anything to finally know the escape this man could give her. Yes, she wanted the escape. She wanted it with him. "I'm ready, Ryan."

CHAPTER SIX

The car was dark, the engine all but silent as it idled in place, the air heavy with anticipation, with a sexual charge. Ryan had never wanted a woman's submission the way he wanted Sarah's, but true submission was given freely. It was a choice, not a reaction.

"What makes tonight the night?" Ryan asked. "What happened in the hospital?"

She stared at him a moment and then started to turn away. He captured her hand, held her in place. "Talk to me, Sarah. Is something wrong with your father?"

"No," she said. "I mean yes, but not his health. He had good news on his treatments. But he's changed. He's not questioning my decisions. He's not yelling about what went right or wrong. I know how to deal with my father who rants and yells and demands. But he said he believes in me. He said he should have listened to me sooner. Ryan, he said I have things *under control*."

He narrowed his gaze. "And you're afraid you don't."

"No," she said. "I know I have control now...it's more the pressure to stay in control I'm suddenly feeling more than ever, and it's freaking me out. It's just...it's intense." She sighed. "Tonight...I don't want that pressure. I don't want to make the decisions. I don't want to be the one in charge." This was the answer he wanted, the right answer. Ryan studied her a long moment, the pulse of arousal pumping through his veins, into his cock. He slid his hand up her arm, over her shoulder, and gently let his fingers settle on the delicate skin of her neck. He could feel the quickening of her pulse beneath them, almost taste her as his lips lowered a breath from hers, and lingered.

He inhaled the scent of her, vanilla, honeysuckle and innocence, the kind of innocence a woman had when she hadn't discovered her true self, her true desires. His lips brushed hers, his teeth nipping roughly, before he licked the delicate flesh. "Take off your panties, Sarah."

Her lips parted in shock, a delicate sound, as delicate as her sensibilities appeared to all those who didn't know her secret desires. Proved to him by the way she showed no other resistance until voices sounded nearby, and she feared discovery, and that someone but he would know those secrets. She jerked back as if to pull away, to look for the visitors' location. He held her steady. He'd known they were there. He was testing her limits, testing her trust in him.

"You let me worry about the rest of the world." He made the statement an order. "You focus on what I tell you to do." He leaned back, studied her, allowed his hand to fall from her neck when he really wanted to drag her to his lap and fuck her right here. But that was too much for her now, too much too soon, so instead he said, "Unless you want to stop here, stop now?"

Seconds ticked by, the voices growing closer, her teeth worrying her bottom lip. "No," she whispered. "No, I don't want to stop." She turned and eased her skirt upward, flashing the lacy trim of her thigh-highs as she lifted her hips and tugged a strip of black lace down her thighs and over her high heels.

She turned back to him and dangled them off one finger. "Do they please you, *Master?*"

The words rolled off her lips, as if practiced in those fantasies she'd shared with him, and his cock thickened in response, his zipper stretched. A slow smile slid to his mouth before one of his hands closed around the panties and the other wove into her hair and pulled her mouth to his. Sliding his tongue past her lips, he kissed her deeply, passionately, drinking the sweet nectar that was Sarah—a forbidden fruit for far too long. "Yes, Sarah," he said when he tore his lips from hers. "You please me very much." Pleased him in ways unique to her.

Thirty minutes later, Ryan pulled the car to a halt inside the security gates of the sprawling, three-story, twelve-thousand-square-foot white mansion that sat on twenty acres and was their destination. He'd tried to take Sarah to his home, where they could be alone, intending to slowly ease her into his world. Sarah had quickly rejected his well-intended plan, though, insisting that "ready" meant "ready," which had spoken volumes as far as Ryan was concerned. It had told him that, indeed, she *was* ready—and not just ready, but also that she wouldn't give herself an escape from facing her most intimate fears and desires. Ready to discover what she was capable of by allowing herself the freedom of destroying boundaries, ready to take on the new challenges in her life. And so Ryan had brought her here, to the society, where a night of discovery and pleasure awaited them both.

"So this is the Alexander Quarters you spoke of?" she asked.

"Named for the owner, and the society's president, Marcus Alexander," he confirmed, having encouraged her to ask questions on the ride here, knowing trust between them would soon be paramount.

"It's magnificent," she said, her voice quavering slightly in what seemed to be a combination of awe and nerves.

He followed her gaze, seeing what she was seeing. The mansion was alight with delicate spotlights, and framed by a massive green lawn and a circular driveway leading to a mountainous ivory stairwell with huge white pillars. Inside the curve of the driveway, a rock waterfall was aglow in a pale blue haze. Various structures, all fetish fantasylands, sat at locations spread across the property.

Ryan hit the remote control on his visor, and a garage door off the side of the house, used exclusively by the six Round Table Masters in the society, began a slow upward glide. The Round Table was a group of six masters who were the elite of the elite, a court of law for the society, with Marcus as judge. Ryan was one of those six.

By the time the garage was resealed with them inside the building, he was already opening Sarah's door, watching as her skirt rode high on her long legs, a sight all the more tantalizing with the absence of her panties. Seeming to understand where his thoughts were, she stood, her gaze avoiding his, then quickly, primly inched her skirt downward, as if he wasn't about to take it off her anyway. "You're nervous," he observed.

She glanced at him from under long, dark lashes. "I... It's just..."

He shut the door and pulled her close to him. "If you're nervous, say you're nervous."

She blinked up at him, the surprise in her expression at the sudden contact turning to warmth as she melted into him, all soft, willing woman, her fingers tentatively spraying across his chest. She was petite, delicate, a sweet flower with an exotic undertone that was part innocence, part princess and part wanton concubine. His cock thickened, tension coiling in his gut, hot tension, born of desire. The kind of tension and arousal that a recent bout of boredom had declared unattainable, with no solution to be found, no matter how daring the society game he'd tried. Yet, this inexperienced, sensual woman had him on the edge, had him hungry. He wanted her more than he remembered wanting anyone in a very long time, which only made the urgency to set the parameters for the night more imperative. Once the play began, it was critical he know where their boundaries were, and how far he could push them.

"Are you nervous, Sarah?" he repeated, when she still hadn't replied.

"Yes," she admitted. "But—"

"No buts," he said. "If I ask you what you feel, you tell me. You don't own your inhibitions tonight, Sarah—I do. Just like I own your pleasure." His hand slid over her backside, and he began inching her skirt upward. "Nervous can be good, even arousing, when it's created by the anticipation and excitement of what's to come next." The hemline rose higher, exposing her backside, and he watched her swallow hard, knew she was feeling some of that anticipation now. He palmed her cheek and caressed downward, lifting her leg to his waist. "Are you still nervous?"

She gasped, her fingers curling around his shirt, and he slid his fingers up her thigh, where she was bare to him, no panties to stop him from sliding right into all the wet heat of her arousal.

She laughed, and those nerves of hers were etched in the sound. Then she buried her face in his shoulder, her spine arched. She whispered, "I can't believe I'm doing this."

"Don't hide from me, Sarah," he ordered, still teasing her intimately, sliding a finger over the slick, wet folds of her core that told him above all else how much she wanted this. He heard her intake of breath as he slid a finger inside her, felt her shiver, but still she didn't look at him. "Sarah. Look. At. Me."

Slowly, she lifted her head, focusing a heavy-lidded, aroused stare at him. "I'm trying, Ryan."

"Do you like what I'm doing to you?" he demanded, knowing she did but needing to hear it. There were rules and boundaries that had to be set before they were inside the society.

"Yes," she whispered.

"But yet you hid your face from me, and you claim you can't believe you are doing this," he stated. "That doesn't sound like a woman who's ready to go inside the society."

Her fingers tightened on his shirt. "No... I mean, yes, I am... I..."

Her hesitation set off alarm bells, telling him she was either having cold feet or too shy to tell him what she wanted or didn't want. Whichever it was, he needed to know, and he needed it remedied if they were going further into sexual exploration.

He lowered her leg, dragged the material of her dress down her legs, and then trapped her body against the car. He broke their physical connection, his hands on the roof, body framing but not touching her. "We're going to keep this simple, since this is your first, and perhaps, only time inside the society," he said. "If you don't like something, you simply say 'stop,' and I'll stop. If I ask you if you want me to keep doing something or if you like something, and you don't answer, I will stop, as well. Understood?"

She blinked at him. "Yes." Her chin lifted. "And I'm not afraid to say what I want or don't want. I'm just new at this. I...I didn't want you to stop what you were doing, but I need to make sure we have one thing clear. Tonight, I'm yours.

Tomorrow, I belong to myself. And I'm darn sure no one's submissive in the boardroom. This changes none of that."

"We have an agreement," he said, and he meant it. Her ability to be both submissive and dominant drew him to her. Not that she was the first woman he'd known with such a trait, but the first who had held his interest. Sarah appealed to him in all kinds of colorful, arousing ways that few others ever had. "That is, as long as you, Sarah, know that tonight, I own more than your pleasure. I own *you*."

CHAPTER SEVEN

Ryan had been right when he'd said anticipation equaled arousal, because as Sarah followed him out of the garage and into the house, with her hand tucked into his, her pulse was jumping, and her body was wet and hot in all the right places. Her high heels clicked on expensive tiles, and her gaze brushed even more expensive paintings on the walls. But her surroundings were mere decoration since it was the man who captivated her.

Sarah watched Ryan as he walked, claiming every molecule of the room with his presence, her gaze riveted on the confident way he carried himself, on the killer way his custom suit was molded to his broad shoulders, accenting his athletic build. He was a gorgeous man who exuded power and masculinity in ways few others did. Sarah wanted the fantasy she'd lived all these years since her visit to Silk. The fantasy wasn't just about being a submissive; it was about being a submissive to Ryan. Yes. Ryan was her fantasy.

Though admittedly, she'd endured a moment of panic back by the car with the first moment of feeling out of control—sleeping with the enemy wasn't what most people would consider smart, while willingly playing sex games with said enemy, which required her to be submissive, would most likely be called borderline insane. And perhaps, the illicit, forbidden aspect of being with Ryan was all a part of the enticement. All her life she'd been good, she'd been in control. Tonight, she wanted to escape.

They paused in a foyer, where a winding stairwell, covered in red carpet, led to a high balcony and made her think of old elegance, *Gone with the Wind* style.

"Where is everyone?" she asked, realizing that this place was nothing like Silk. They were alone, not a voice to be heard or a person to be seen. There was no music, no moaning, no naked bodies. Somehow, the calmness, the lack of what she'd assumed would be an obvious display of sex and seduction, as had been the case in Silk so many years before, set her on edge. There was no place to hide here, no place to disappear in the midst of everyone else's pleasure.

"The mansion is the master's quarters I mentioned in the car," Ryan explained. "It's an exclusive section of the society that isn't open to the general membership, just as a nonmember isn't allowed inside the society domains without formal application for membership."

She remembered what he'd said, yes, but hadn't computed then, as she did now, that Ryan was one of the controlling masters of the society. The realization sent a wild flutter through her stomach, and a rush of heat across her skin. Of course, he was a controlling master. He was a leader in everything he did, dominant in every way, in control. Soon to be in control of her, too. Their eyes locked and held, electricity crackling in the air, and she knew he was thinking the same thing.

"Welcome to my world, Sarah," he said softly. He started to walk backward, leading her by the hand he still held, toward a double door to the left of the stairwell, when a male voice called out from the stairwell.

"Ryan."

Sarah and Ryan turned toward the unexpected voice, and Sarah found a tall, dark-haired man in his mid-thirties, headed their way, a man who could be described as nothing shy of magnificent.

"I wasn't aware we had a guest tonight," the man said, nearly at the bottom of the stairs now, and Sarah noted that his black slacks and black button-down shirt were tailored to perfection, and clung to the long, lean lines of a body honed to magnificence. This was the kind of man who made the clothes, not the opposite. The kind of man who claimed everything he touched.

Ryan's hand slid to Sarah's back, closing the distance between them, as if *he* were claiming her, as if he sensed what she was feeling. She could feel the heat of his hand, the possessiveness burning through her thin dress. And she liked it. She liked it probably far more than she should. What was it about Ryan that made an independent businesswoman want to be possessed? She didn't know. No other man had evoked such primitive arousal in her.

The newcomer cleared the stairwell and stopped in front of Sarah and Ryan, towering above her, but eye level with Ryan. The men shook hands before Ryan did the introductions.

"Sarah," he said. "This is Marcus Alexander, the controlling partner in the society and the owner of the property." He glanced at Marcus. "And Marcus, this is Sarah Michaels. The acting CEO of Chocolate Delights."

Marcus arched a dark brow, a pair of piercing blue eyes registering understanding and interest. "An interesting pairing if I ever saw one." He offered her his hand. "Nice to meet you, Sarah."

Sarah accepted his hand, and she felt the touch clear to her toes, as if she was ultrasensitized, as if he oozed sex and it was seeping clear to her bones. She actually felt her cheeks warm, not to mention her thighs burn. Good gosh, she was an attorney, a CEO now, too, and she was blushing. *In a sex club.* Something she was pretty sure was a sign she was in over her head here. "Nice to meet you, as well," she managed to choke out, thinking how insane the formality was under the circumstances. Actually, the formality was etched into the very walls of this place. No. It wasn't formality, she realized. It was ultimate, complete control, that one could not, would not, be allowed to hide from.

As if driving her thoughts home, letting her know he did, indeed, believe he owned her while she was in his home, Marcus held her hand several drawn-out seconds, his stare resting on her face, assessing, probing, like an attorney with a witness on the stand, before finally he released her, his gaze lifting to Ryan's. "We have a new membership test beginning at the top of the hour. I'll arrange to have Sarah included."

Sarah's heart jumped right into her throat. New membership test? Oh, no. She didn't like the sound of that one bit, but before she could fully reach the point of panic all over again, Ryan said, "Not tonight."

It was all Sarah could do to contain a sigh of relief, which she construed as yet another indicator that she was in over her head with this society. So *very* over her head. Part of her screamed with the loss of her fantasy, wanted to cling to it, while another part just wanted to run—and run fast and far.

Marcus considered Ryan a moment longer, with what appeared to be a hint of surprise, before he gave a short nod. "Understood." He then shifted his dark, heavy gaze to Sarah. "I hope to see more of you very soon, Sarah." He turned and headed to the front door.

Sarah stared after him, repeating his words in her head, no doubt the meaning meant *naked* and *at his mercy*. No. No. No. Not happening. This man might be sexy, but he had a ruthless quality to him. He'd take her control and never give it back. And it was then she realized that her ability to explore herself, her wants, desires, her fears, was only possible because of the unexplainable trust she had in Ryan, something that remarkably defied their families' rivalry.

"Sarah," Ryan said, urging her to turn to him.

Sarah whirled around. "Ryan—"

"I have no intention of sharing you, Sarah," he said, his hands settling warmly, firmly on her arms. His touch sent a deep shiver down her spine, searing her with possessiveness, with command, which somehow managed to comfort and arouse rather than intimidate as Marcus had done. "I never intended to share you," he continued. "You're off-limits and Marcus knows that now. You don't belong to him, or the society. Any play we take part in tonight will be behind closed doors. Exactly why we're going to my private chambers now where we will be alone. Where you can watch and explore, under the safety of seclusion."

Seclusion. Yes. She wanted seclusion. She'd thought the society would be like Silk, a wild festival of sex games, where she'd simply blend in, where the sheer volume of sex acts would consume her inhibitions. Maybe even, if she was honest, a way to hide from what Ryan made her feel. She wanted to keep this about sex, when she feared she was starting to feel more for him. But it was clear now that this place wouldn't let her hide. Ryan wouldn't let her hide. But he'd also promised her protection, and he'd given it to her with the offer of privacy. He'd known what she needed more than she did. Maybe she'd sensed that, maybe that was why he was safe.

His hand slid down her arm, goose bumps gathering in

its wake, her nipples pebbling and aching, until he drew her fingers inside his. Again, he walked backward, holding her stare even as he led her toward those same double mahogany doors they'd been approaching before Marcus appeared, where she assumed his private quarters were. And she followed willingly, watching him with more of that nervous anticipation, as he punched a security code into a panel, shoved a door open and turned to face her again. He stepped close, his big body touching her, claiming her.

"Before you go inside," he said, his hands framing her face, "let's be one hundred percent clear about something, Sarah. Tonight has nothing to do with Delights or Deluxe or any family dispute or competition created by that dispute. This is about you and me. You do this for you, no other reason. You have nothing to prove to me."

"I know," she agreed, surprised yet pleased with both his declaration, and the gentleness of his touch, knowing the primal male beneath such tenderness. It stroked her confidence, stroked the ache between her thighs to create a thrumming need. "But you have something to prove to me."

His lips lifted, his eyes alight with a hint of amusement. "I have something to prove to you?"

"That's right," she assured him. "You said giving away control would give me control." Though right now she was thinking more about him giving her pleasure than about control. "Prove it."

She watched his expression instantly darken, his eyes heat, before he maneuvered her to stand in front of him, her back to his chest. His hands once again settled on her shoulders, his hips framed her backside, and her body tingled everywhere he touched, everywhere she *wanted him to touch*.

"All you have to do now is step past the threshold, and I'll show you what you want to know. You will be mine for the night. I will be *your master.*"

Sarah felt his words in the wet heat between her thighs, in the pebbling ache of her nipples, in the nervous anticipation that, most definitely, was arousal. She wanted this, she wanted him. She entered his private chambers, and his world became hers.

CHAPTER EIGHT

The door shut softly behind Sarah as she entered Ryan's private chambers, a moment before dim lighting illuminated the ceiling, leaving the rest of the room, and the erotic secrets it might hold, in the cover of shadows. A large room with several doors, a living area and a bedroom, she thought, as she tried to gain some sense of location, of control. Or perhaps distract herself from the uncertainty of what was to come.

Ryan stepped behind her, his arms closing around her, his lips brushing her ear. His breath trickled seductively along her neck. "Finally alone," he whispered, one of his hands flattening intimately on her stomach. "Are you scared, Sarah?"

Oh, yeah, she thought. And excited, and aroused, and impossibly turned-on. "A little," she replied, and then barely contained a moan as he molded his hands to her breasts.

"Tell me what scares you," he replied, his thumbs stroking her nipples, kneading her with a hard, erotic touch. She bit her lip, holding back the need to moan again. Already he commanded her body; already she was embarrassingly wet, embarrassingly capable of orgasm.

"You," she replied, her head falling back to his shoulders,

the pleasure of having this man finally touching her almost too much to bear. How long had she wanted this? How long had she been tantalizingly aware of the dark desires this man awakened in her? How long had she blamed him for those desires, and avoided him, avoided those temptations, when the truth was, she was doing exactly what he said he wouldn't let her do—hide from herself.

"I don't scare you," he said, as if reading her mind. He tugged her dress up her hips as he had in the garage and then pressed her bare bottom against the thick bulge of his erection. Acting on instinct, she arched into him, even as he squeezed her breasts and rolled her nipples with a tight pinch of each that she felt all the way to the ache in between her thighs.

"I own you during our play session, Sarah," he said, turning her to face him, his hand sliding to her face. "And if I want to know what scares you, you tell me what scares you." His tone was demanding, his touch firm as his palm slid to her backside. "There is a price for disobedience." He caressed one cheek of her backside, and then lightly but solidly smacked her there.

Sarah sucked in a breath, feeling no pain, but plenty of surprise and, yes, pleasure. A thrilling sting that started at the spot of the connection and traveled like a flame along a fuse, spread through every inch of her body.

"What scares you, Sarah?" he demanded, sliding his hand over her backside with the promise that he would spank her again, harder this time. And Lord help her, she actually wanted him to. Adrenaline set her blood coursing, her heart racing. This was a side of herself she'd never seen, never known, a side Ryan brought out in her.

"You do—you scare me," Sarah hissed.

"Wrong answer," he said, a sharp note of disapproval in his voice. "We both know I'm not what scares you. The first rule of play, Sarah, is trust, and there is a price for violating that trust." He released her, leaving her skirt at her hips. "Take everything off but your shoes."

Stunned by both the absence of his touch, and the order, Sarah stood immobile a moment. Undress. He wanted her to undress while he watched, while he judged her and her body. While he remained fully clothed. Of course, she was standing there with her skirt at her waist anyway, which had to look ridiculous.

"Undress, Sarah," he repeated, his voice low with warning yet somehow gently prodding.

It was the way he managed to both soothe and demand, she realized, that had drawn her to him, drawn her here tonight. Made her feel safe to explore this side of herself, a side she knew existed but had for so long suppressed. With a deeply inhaled breath, Sarah slid her skirt into place down her hips, then tugged the zipper at her side down, as well. She shrugged the material off her shoulders. Her dress fell to her feet, and she stepped away from it, her gaze riveted to Ryan, looking for some reaction.

He stared at her, his gaze hooded, his arms crossed, his jaw set. "All but the shoes," he reminded her.

Sarah reached behind her, nervous and fumbling with the bra hook, then helplessly glanced in his direction. He moved around her, unhooking the bra and caressing it off her shoulders. His touch was again gentle, yet the crackle in the air still sang with the promise of something darker, of reprimand.

She tossed the bra aside, not sure what to expect now, anticipation thrumming through her veins, sensitizing her body.

"Put your hands on the door," he ordered.

"What?" She started to turn, but his hands settled on her waist and stopped the action.

"You heard me," he said. "Put your hands on the door."

Sarah's lashes lowered, her breath lodged in her throat. She was really going to do this. She needed to do this, could feel her body hum just thinking about fully submitting her will to him. Sarah took the short steps forward that allowed her to press her hands to the doorway, could feel his attention on her, goose bumps rising all over her flesh with his hot stare scorching her.

"Spread your legs wider," he said, still not touching her. Why wasn't he touching her?

Sarah tried to look over her shoulder. "Ryan?"

His hands came down on her hips, his body framing hers, his cheek pressed to hers. "I'm here," he said, his hands sliding to her breasts, caressing and teasing. "Does that feel good, Sarah?"

"Yes," she murmured, and tried to cover his hands with hers.

He pressed them back against the wall. "Leave them." His hands covered hers, his body stretched over hers. "Do I feel good, Sarah?"

"Yes," she said. So good. Too good.

He slid his hands over her arms, over her back, over her hips, and then inched her legs apart, spreading her wide. His finger slid along the crevice of her backside, even as his other hand slid low on her stomach.

Sarah gasped as both of his hands pressed into the aching sensitive heat of her core, an assault of pleasure from both front and rear, even as his teeth nipped her shoulder. "So wet and hot," he murmured, nipping again, one of his fingers penetrating her. "Do you want me to keep touching you?"

"Yes."

"Do you want me inside you?"

"Yes."

His hands moved to her hips. "Then tell me what scares you, Sarah."

She squeezed her eyes shut, wanting to beg him to touch her again, to stop pushing for an answer she didn't want to give. Because he scared her, and she knew he didn't like that answer. She didn't know what to say. "Ryan—"

His hand slid into her hair and gently but firmly pulled her head back to his shoulder, her lips an inch from his. "I don't scare you or you wouldn't be here." He kissed her, a long, deep, hot kiss that had her panting with need, and when he released her mouth, he said, "You don't kiss me like I scare you." He released her hair, slid one hand down to her backside. "What scares you, Sarah?"

"You do," she said. "Damn it, you do, Ryan."

He smacked her backside, a short stingy slap that had her gasping for air, and her sex clenching with ache. And then he smacked her again, and once more. She was panting when he finished, preparing for another smack, wanting another connection. His hand slid to her breast, fingers tugging roughly at her nipples. "You like being spanked," he said. "You like the idea of me controlling you, and that's what scares you. You're afraid of yourself, of what you want...what you need."

Her head fell forward as she struggled with an admission that made her feel vulnerable. "Yes."

"Do you want more?"

"Yes."

"Yes what?"

Yes what? "Please."

He smacked her backside three times, not hard, just stingingly erotic and oh, so pleasurable, then he turned her to face him, pressed her against the door, his hands doing delicious things to her body—touching her breast, sliding to her sex, fingers pressing inside her until she was riding his

"I told them I'd sign a note if I had to," he said. "And I will. I also know you won't let me, but then you won't have to. You'll use my connection for leverage, as you should, and you'll get your credit line."

"And you get?"

"You, Sarah," he said thickly. "I get you."

The possessiveness lacing the words sent a rush of heat through Sarah's body, and a rush of erotic memories with it. Memories that reminded her just how delicious being possessed by this man really was.

"Open the second envelope, Sarah."

Sarah crossed her legs, amazed at how a phone conversation with Ryan, especially minutes before her big meeting, could have her aching with need. She tore open the flap to the envelope and pulled out a delicately taped square of tissue, which she opened. Her heart squeezed when she saw the heart-shaped necklace with a shackle attached.

"The story of O," she whispered, recognizing the BDSM emblem he'd shown her on a previous occasion, and its relevance.

"Symbolic of your journey into submissiveness with me, and me alone, Sarah. A journey that has only just begun, if you choose to wear that necklace. It's easily tucked into your blouse and hidden. We wouldn't want anyone to know you're sleeping with the enemy."

She smiled into the phone. "I stopped thinking of you as the enemy sometime…oh, maybe a week ago."

He chuckled. "That's not what you said last night."

"Ah, well," she said. "You were making me mad and words were all I had to fight back with." Because he'd had her tied to the bedpost.

"Because I wouldn't let you come," he supplied.

"Exactly," she said, laughing then quickly turning somber,

hand like a wanton wench, and spasming in release. She was panting and, at the beginning of embarrassment creeping over her, he said, "Don't. Don't even think about regretting what just happened. I forbid it. And I am the one in control here."

"I wish it were that easy."

He gently stroked her hair from her face. "It *is* that easy. While you're here with me, you just let me make all the decisions. The weight of making them yourself lies just outside that door. And you're beautiful and sexy when you let yourself go, Sarah." She warmed at the words as he added, "And I will never do anything to hurt you."

"I know," she said, meaning it. "I know or I wouldn't be here. And I…want to be here." Nerves fluttered in her stomach, but they were good nerves, so good. The kind that were accompanied by yearning for what came next, knowing it would be unexpected and perfect, in the same moment. "What's my next lesson, *Master?* And please tell me it includes you naked or I'm going to leave really disappointed."

"Naked and buried deep inside you," he assured her, and picked her up, carrying her toward a massive, four-poster bed, which he proceeded to show her he owned as much as he did her pleasure.

CHAPTER NINE

Six weeks after the first of many "play" dates with Ryan, Sarah sat at her desk, chatting with her father on the phone. "I'm thinking I'll retire," he said, "let you run the company."

"Retire," Sarah repeated, certain she'd heard him wrong. "You live for the company."

"I used to live for the company," he said. "But you've proved you're the one who can give it life."

She knew he meant the huge new contract Delights had managed to land with a bookstore to provide various products in a large test region. "The contract only matters if I get our credit line extended at the bank, to manufacture and distribute the product. The meeting is this afternoon."

"You will," he said. "I have complete faith in you, Sarah. You have more of a vision for Delights than I have had for years. I was just too stubborn to see it. I am so very proud of you, Sarah."

"Dad," she said softly, her heart squeezing with the pride in his voice. "Thank you."

They chatted a few more minutes before Sarah hung up

the phone. Almost instantly the warmth of the call turned to a knot in her stomach. She *had* to get the credit line approved.

Her mind went to Ryan, to the escape he gave her, to how addictive that escape had become. Though he'd yet to introduce her to the society, assuring her that day would only come *when she was ready*. But they'd watched the play in the club, exploring her limits, exploring each other.

The jangle of her phone jerked Sarah into a frenzy of disaster fighting, a frenzy that ended not long before she had to leave for her meeting at the bank. She was packing up when the call came in and, without looking at the ID, she quickly answered.

"Are you alone?" Ryan asked.

A shiver raced down her spine at his deep baritone voice, her gaze flickering to the closed door. "I am," she said. "I'm about to leave for my meeting."

"Look inside your briefcase," he said. "Side pocket."

She reached down to where it sat by her feet and opened the side pocket where he'd apparently stuffed two envelopes, one white and one red, sometime the night before when they'd been together.

"Open the white one first," he instructed.

She did as he said and found a business card. "The President of National Bank?" she asked, reading it.

"He's my banker and a close personal friend," Ryan said. "Someone very eager to keep my business. In other words, he'll give you your credit line."

She sucked in a breath, her mind racing with the pros and cons of this offer. Ryan owning her in play was one thing, but owning her in business was another.

"Use this," he said. "Tell your banker if he won't extend your credit line, National Bank is willing to step forward."

"They haven't seen my financial reports," she said. "So how can they—?"

remembering Ryan talking about the BDSM jewelry, how some took it lightly, how he did not. He was a society master, a rule maker, a protector of those in the community. His chosen submissive was a reflection on the entire community, and no one had ever been worthy. The necklace said she was, though. It said he was reaching out to her, claiming her in a way that reached beyond a few erotic encounters. And he'd given it to her now, as a show of support before her meeting. Her fingers closed around the necklace. She had no idea where their relationship was going, how it could work out with the rivalry between families and companies, but she knew she had to find out. "The next time you see me, I'll be wearing the necklace."

"Tonight," he said. "After you go get that credit line."

"Yes," she agreed, with a smile. "Tonight."

★ ★ ★ ★ ★

NIGHT MOVES
EDEN BRADLEY

Kate leaned into the hard edge of the metal-framed window as the train pulled out of the station. Klamath Falls, Oregon. The least exciting town in existence. But her pulse was thrumming, anyway.

She always felt that lovely anticipation, that thrill, when she was on a train. But the biggest thrill lay ahead, after the other passengers had fallen asleep. She could hardly wait.

Her gaze caught the flash of lights on the slowly retreating platform, then there was nothing but the velvet night. Nothing to see in this part of the country. No scenery, no city lights. Didn't matter. What mattered was being there, feeling that motion, that sense of possibility, of *going*.

It was nearly midnight: far too late for the dining car. The train had been delayed, leaving her sitting in the quiet, small-town station for hours. Good thing she'd stopped to eat as soon as she'd arrived from Ashland. Klamath Falls shut down early, and there was nothing but an old candy machine wedged between the ancient rows of wooden benches inside the station.

But that part was over now. Now there was just the luxurious idea of the long, slow ride ahead.

Something sexy about trains. She wasn't sure what it was. But she always swore she could feel that rocking motion hum through her entire body like one enormous vibrator. She was beginning to melt a little all over at the thought.

Have to be alone soon.

Thank God it was late. The lights were kept low, and most of the other passengers would be asleep soon.

She leaned back in her seat, allowed the rolling sensation to lull her, felt it pulse between her thighs.

This part was almost as good as the rest, the anticipation of her little adventures. She'd done this on trains all over the country; she never tired of it. Didn't even matter too much where she was going. *Going* was the important thing. The motion, the smooth, forward thrust of iron.

She stayed in her seat for another half hour, absorbing the hard whisper of tons of metal moving beneath her. Finally, she couldn't stay still any longer.

It's time.

She got up, hefted her overnight bag over her shoulder and moved silently down the center aisle, passing between row after row of passengers nested in for the night. But for her, the night was just beginning.

She pulled open the door, stepped onto the noisy platform between cars, opened the next door and slipped inside as quietly as she could, kept going until she reached the sleeper compartments.

She took a deep breath before opening that last door. Then she moved through, easy as water, sliding the heavy door shut behind her.

She stood in the hallway, getting her sea legs, listening, her heart a loud thrumming in her own ears. And the longer she stood there, the more the heat built between her thighs, the seam of her worn jeans rubbing there as she swayed with the motion of the train.

Soon...

The car was empty. She moved down the row, quietly trying the first doorknob. Locked. Damn.

She moved on, tried the next one. Locked. One by one, she made her way down to the other end of the car, slipped out with a sigh of frustration and went on to the next car.

Just as quiet. Her head was filled with the gentle roar of the engines, the *snick* of the wheels on the tracks. She stood a moment, savoring the sound, the sensation, before moving on. The first door was locked. But the second turned under the gentle pressure of her hand.

Ah-ha!

She pulled the door back, peered into the small, darkened compartment, her pulse hammering in triumph and the flickering idea of getting caught. There was nothing on the floor or the padded bench seat, no luggage, nothing to indicate anyone was in there. She stopped anyway, listening, but all she heard was the night rushing by outside the window. She slipped inside, closing the door behind her.

Her skin was heating all over now, her body humming with need. Dropping her bag onto the bench seat, she moved to the window, leaning her weight against the cold glass so she could really feel the motion. She stayed there for several moments, perfectly still, absorbing it all: the rumbling of the train, the vibration of it moving through her body. She pressed her breasts against the glass, the cold of the hard, sleek surface bringing her nipples up through the cotton of her T-shirt.

She was wet already. Had been for the past half hour.

With a quiet sigh, she unzipped her jeans, slipped one hand down between her thighs, beneath the lace of her panties.

Oh, yes.

She brushed at her mound, but the ache was too strong, too insistent. Like an eager lover, she pressed on her clitoris, the nub of it hard against her palm. Leaning harder into the window, she let the motion of the train move through the back of her hand. Pleasure swam in her system, hot, insistent. And when she slid two fingers into her soaking wet slit, between the swollen folds, she gasped.

Then it was too late for any show of teasing, any restraint. She plunged her fingers in deeper, rubbed the heel of her hand hard against her clit, the train moving beneath her like some monolithic lover. Pleasure rammed into her, even as her fingers did, deep, deeper.

Yes...

She rubbed harder, her body arcing into her hand, into the side of the car. She was hot all over, melting, her legs weak. And still she worked herself mercilessly, her hand and the rocking of the train drawing her climax into her. Pleasure rose, crested, and she pressed hard onto her clit, thrust her fingers in deep, and came into her hand. Moaning, gasping, as sensation overwhelmed her.

So good, always, her secret perversion. She smiled to herself.

A quiet voice came out of the dark. "Nice. Beautiful."

"Jesus!" She yanked her hand out of her pants, nearly fell onto the vinyl-covered bench.

"I'm sorry. But you came in here while I was sleeping, and I woke up...and then I couldn't interrupt you."

Her face was burning. With embarrassment, with anger, with fear. And her heart was racing at a thousand miles an hour.

"You scared the shit out of me!" She zipped her jeans with clumsy fingers. "Look, I'm...I'm going. Okay? I'll just... disappear."

"I wish you wouldn't." The voice was calm, soothing. "I'm going to turn on the light. Don't be scared, okay?"

Kate grabbed her big bag, was backing up to the door.

"I'm going to go. You…you don't need to tell anyone I was here, all right?"

God, what if this guy was some sort of pervert? But what was she, then?

The light flicked on; just a small amber glow lighting up the sleeping bunk. She blinked.

He was sitting on the edge of the bunk, all classic California surfer guy, his tousled, dirty-blond hair sweeping the top of his shoulders, his neatly trimmed goatee a few shades darker. He was wearing a pair of wrinkled cargo pants and nothing else. And he was beautiful.

She couldn't move.

"Wow," he said.

"What?"

He smiled at her, blinking his eyes. They were pale, but there wasn't enough light for her to make out the shade. Gray? Green?

"What?" she repeated, her hand tightening on the strap of her heavy bag.

Why didn't she just get the hell out of there?

"You're pretty."

She laughed. "You sound surprised. But I'm not pretty."

"You are. And I guess I didn't expect you to be when it was dark and I was…watching you. Except that I could see the silhouette of your hair."

She reached a self-conscious hand to her long, unruly blond curls. "What about my hair?"

"It's beautiful." His voice was deep and husky with sleep. Sexy. Or maybe it was just her body still simmering with the last threads of her orgasm. Or his beautiful face, his hard body…

"You must be blind."

"No, I saw everything."

"Shit. Look, I'm going to go."

She reached for the doorknob, pulled on it.

"I liked it."

Why did that stop her cold?

He pushed off from the bunk, the tiny train cabin too small for him to do anything but stand right behind her. She swore she could feel the heat emanating from his body, carrying his scent. Patchouli. Classic surfer scent. It made her shiver.

"Don't go," he said again. "My name's Ian."

She turned her head, looking over her shoulder at him, and he was right *there*. Too close. This wasn't the way it was supposed to go. It was all about her and the train. And he'd ruined it.

Hadn't he?

But her body was still loose and warm from her climax, and Ian was making her heat up all over again.

"Tell me your name," he said quietly. Gently.

"You're not going to report me?"

"I'd be an idiot if I did."

He was grinning at her now, but even though his eyes glittering in the half dark were all heat, there was nothing leering in his gaze.

She smiled back at him. "So, have you always been a voyeur?"

"Not until tonight. Have you always been an exhibitionist?"

"Yes. Always."

"I think I've just discovered that I like that in a girl."

They stood for a moment, silent, smiling, while desire

hummed in the air between them like piano wire strung tight, sending out one long, lovely note.

I want you.

Oh, yes, she wanted him. Wanted him, and wanted it to be on the train. Too perfect. Too strange.

She wasn't usually one for casual sex. Not that it had never happened. She'd met a few guys in her travels. But it had only been five months since she'd broken things off with Dominic, and she'd sworn off men since then.

Now might be a good time to break her vow.

"So, you're staying?"

"I'm thinking about it," she admitted.

I must be losing my mind.

"Tell me your name," he asked her again.

"Kate."

"Kate. Nice." He put a hand on her bag. "Why don't you put this down?"

She nodded, let him take the heavy bag from her and set it on the bench. Watched as he straightened up. He wasn't quite six feet tall, maybe five foot ten, five-eleven, but since she was five-four, it didn't matter. She didn't like a guy to be too tall. And he had one of those surfer bodies, all long, lean muscle, heavier around the chest and shoulders. On his left forearm was a tattoo. She reached out, ran one fingertip over the design.

"What's this?"

"A motherboard. I'm a computer tech."

"Really?"

"Really. Why? What did you expect?"

"Hmm, I'm not sure. You look a lot like one of the guys who works at this little coffee place by my house."

He took a step closer. "And do you like the guy at your coffee place?"

"Sure." She could smell him again, could almost feel his

tan skin beneath her hands. She flexed her fingers. "But not as much as I think I could like you."

"Really? How much is that?"

"Enough that I'm not running out of here the way I should."

"Yeah, this is kinda crazy. Meeting like this."

"It is."

Insane, really, that she wasn't running out the door. But she wasn't the kind of girl who played it safe. That had been one of Dominic's complaints: she was too spontaneous, he couldn't ever pin her down. Not that she wanted anyone to do that. But this…this was a little extreme, even for her. Which made being here with Ian all the more appealing.

"Kate…" He stopped, shook his head.

"What?"

"I really want to kiss you."

He was looking right at her, his gaze steady. His eyes were green, she was almost positive now. Beautiful against his tan skin.

"I really want you to."

"You don't know me."

"It doesn't matter. I don't know why, but it doesn't. There's even sort of something…great about that. Mysterious. Do you know what I mean?"

"Yeah, I do."

"So, are you going to kiss me, Ian?"

"Yeah, I am."

He lowered his head. Yes, she must have lost her mind, to be here with this stranger. But she didn't want to think about that now. No, all she wanted to think about was how lush his mouth was up close, how good his skin smelled. She reached up, slid her hand around the back of his neck, under his long hair, and pulled him down to her.

His lips met hers, soft at first. So soft. She went warm all over, just heating up like crazy even before he slid his tongue into her mouth. And then there was nothing soft about what was happening between them. It was all need, hunger. He pressed his mouth to hers, hard, bruising, but it was exactly what she needed. Even better when he slid his arm around her and pulled her in close, until she could feel his erection through the fabric of his clothes and hers.

His mouth was so sweet. The guy could kiss, that was for damn sure. Her breath was just going out of her body.

He pulled back, whispered, "Damn, girl. I need to touch you. Okay?"

"Yes. Please."

He pulled her T-shirt over her head, then stood and stared. "Perfect," he whispered. Reaching out, he stroked her stomach with one finger, making her pulse flutter, sending heat like warm, wet lightning to her sex. Sharp. Electric. And the train rumbling beneath them, carrying them through the night, a heavy undercurrent of tension, of pure sex.

"Come on, Ian," she pleaded.

"Come on, what?"

"Let's get naked. It's too good to wait."

He nodded, his face tight with need. He slipped one of her bra straps down, then the other, before stepping back in close to her. Reaching behind her, he rested his head on her shoulder, his goatee a little rough against her skin as he unsnapped her bra. It fell away, and he pressed closer, bare skin to bare skin.

"Yes, just like that," she breathed.

He pressed harder, crushing her breasts against the solid wall of his chest, moving her body until her back was up against the cool metal of the door. He was kissing her again, his mouth on hers, his tongue slipping between her lips, thrusting into her mouth in some primal rhythm, his hips grinding into hers in the same tempo. And the hushed roar of the train like music. Like sex itself.

She groaned. Let her hands wander, smoothing over his skin, feeling the rise and curve of muscle in his shoulders, his back. Even the sensation of his skin under her hands was erotic to her.

He moved back then, just an inch or two, enough to get his hands in between them, to cup her breasts, teasing her nipples immediately with his thumbs into two hard, aching points.

"Ah, you like that."

"Yes."

He took her nipples between his thumbs and his forefingers, pinched a little, drew them out.

"And that?"

"Yes. Oh…"

"You're so hot, Kate," he said, his voice low, nearly a whisper. "Your skin, your breasts, your mouth." He squeezed her nipples, hard, and she moaned softly. "So hot. So responsive. I can barely stand it. I'm so damn hard. Feel me, Kate."

He pushed against her, the hard ridge of his cock pressing into her belly.

"Ian…come on."

"Yeah…"

He worked quickly, slipping out of his cargo shorts, then a pair of dark boxers. His cock was fully erect, thick. Beautiful. She felt her mouth water. Felt her pussy go tight.

Need it. Need him. Yes…

And the fact that this was happening here, on the train. Like every fantasy she'd ever had, all of those nights getting herself off while a train going somewhere, anywhere, moved beneath her. Drove her. Made her come as much as her hand moving frantically between her thighs.

Ian went down on his knees, slipping her jeans off, then

her panties. Still on his knees before her, just breathing on the narrow strip of hair between her thighs. Warm. Excruciating, to make her wait.

She buried her fingers in his hair, pulled a little, spread her thighs, inviting him. And gasped when he planted a single, small kiss there.

"Don't tease me, Ian. I can't take it right now."

"Yes, you can. I'm going to enjoy this."

"Fuck, Ian."

"Yeah, we'll get to that. But you're too good to rush through."

She groaned, forcing herself to still while he used his fingers to hold her pussy lips apart. While he held her open like that and just breathed on her.

God…

She waited, her juices trickling down the inside of one thigh. The sight of his beautiful body bent before her, his silky blond hair tickling her skin, was almost too much for her. That and the lovely, smooth motion of the wheels against the tracks.

Finally, he moved his fingers, massaging her nether lips. Slowly, slowly, working one finger toward her waiting hole, and then, dipping inside.

"Oh!"

"Yeah, girl. It's good, isn't it?" he murmured. "I want to see you squirm before I make you come."

"Yes, Ian…"

He leaned in, and she could feel his warm breath on her again, before he flicked his tongue at her clit.

She arced her hips.

He did it again, and again, his tongue like some tiny, wet lance, driving pleasure deep into her body. And his fingers still holding her apart, one buried deeper inside her.

Her legs were shaking, need like some sort of drug coursing

through her veins. And when he took her clit into his hot, wet mouth and sucked, she exploded.

Pleasure shafted into her, deep, deeper, leaving her shuddering.

"Fuck, Ian!"

He worked her hard with his fingers, his mouth, until she was breathless, spent. Then he pulled away.

"Oh, yeah, I'm going to fuck you."

Before the last waves of her climax had faded, he had her on the edge of the small bunk.

"Wait here."

He fumbled in a backpack on the bed, pulled out a small foil pouch, and she watched as he sheathed himself.

"Spread for me, beautiful girl. Yeah, that's it."

Her thighs fell open wide, and as he stood before her, she reached for him, pulling his hips into hers. He stopped at the entrance to her sex. She could feel the tip against her wet opening.

"Come on, Ian. Come on and fuck me."

He let out a long breath. Slid in an inch. Pleasure pulsed in her blood, in her sex.

"Deeper."

Another inch, and his cock was already beginning to fill her up. She surged against him.

"You want it all?"

"Oh, yes."

He reached out a hand, caught her hair up in his fingers, twined them there, pulling tight, and plunged deep, burying himself inside her.

"Oh!"

"Jesus, you feel good," he murmured, before he began to move.

Her fingers dug into the flesh of his hips as he drove into

her, over and over, pleasure burrowing into her with every sharp thrust. Her legs were wrapped around his narrow waist, holding him tight against her. And when she looked up at him, his face, drawn in ecstasy, was one of the most beautiful things she'd ever seen.

"I just need to fuck you, Kate. Just fuck you."

"Yes, do it. Do it hard."

He slammed into her, the wool blanket on the bunk scratching her skin, the metal frame below the thin mattress biting into her spine. She didn't care. All she knew was she had never felt so taken over, never been fucked so hard in her life. Never been fucked to the rhythm of the train that was pure sex to her. And she loved every minute of it.

She rocked against him, rocked with the turning of heavy iron wheels over solid iron tracks. Something so primal, so basic. And the scent of sex was all around her. The scent of sex, of Ian's skin, of her own juices.

"Fuck me harder, Ian. Come on, you can do it."

He drove into her, pummeling her, his pubic bone crashing into hers, and she was coming again, panting, her pussy clenching in pleasure. It spread, deep into her body, into her mind, while a thousand stars went off in her head. Blinding. Beautiful.

He was still fucking her, his body going hard all over. Then he tensed, shuddered, muttered, "Jesus, girl, have to fuck you, fuck you, yeah..."

The train kept moving, sliding over the rails, while they breathed together, the air pungent with their sweat, with the tangy scent of sex, the earthier scent of come as he pulled the condom off.

He pulled her with him onto the narrow bunk while they caught their breath. His body was warm, felt good against hers. One arm was looped beneath her shoulder, and he idly played with her hair.

"That was perfect," she told him.

"Yeah, it was."

"Ian…"

"Hmm?"

"I want to tell you something. It's easier because I don't know you."

He laughed softly, a deep chuckle. "You know me now, girl."

"Maybe. But I still want to tell you."

"Okay."

"I have a…fetish. It's about the trains."

"Ah, so that's what it was all about earlier, you making yourself come like that."

"Yes. I've done it before. As often as I can. I love to ride the train, but even more, I love to wait until it's night, then find an unlocked compartment, and bring myself off."

He was quiet a moment, then, "And? Is that all?"

"Yes. No. Part of it is sneaking in here like this, you know? Doing something I'm not supposed to do. It's fucking thrilling as hell, if you want to know the truth. I've done it a few times now. And it gets better every time. It starts sooner each time. I was wet the moment I got on the train tonight. I had to find a place to be alone, had to get myself off."

He groaned. "I'm getting hard again just hearing you tell me these things. But that's not the only reason why I'm glad you told me."

They were both quiet for a while. Then she said, "This is… almost magical for me. Like something I made up."

"Maybe you did."

"Maybe. But you're real. You're experiencing this, too. My fantasy."

"Yeah. But it's mine, too. Meeting a beautiful girl on the train in the middle of the night. How often does that happen to anyone?"

"I'm not beautiful."

"It's true. I don't know why you don't think so."

"I'm too skinny and my hair is totally out of control."

"That's what I like about it. It's wild. Like you. And your skin is like fucking silk. Like pale silk."

"You don't have to say that."

"Yeah, and you didn't have to stay here. Didn't have to sleep with me. But you did."

"Because I wanted to."

"That's right."

She was quiet a moment. "Okay."

She smiled to herself, and he pulled her chin up, kissed her, his tongue slipping between her lips. She was hot all over again immediately.

"Kiss me like that and I'll believe anything you say," she told him when he pulled away. "I'll do anything you say."

"That's very tempting."

"I mean it."

And she did. Maybe it was the train. Maybe it was something about him. She didn't even know him. But it didn't matter. All that mattered was how much she wanted him, craved his touch. His mouth, his hands on her flesh.

"Why do you trust me so much?" he asked her.

"I don't know. But I do."

"You don't know anything about me."

"Sure I do. I know you're a tech geek."

He laughed. "Yeah. Do you want to know more? Or do you want to just be strangers who fucked on a train?" There was nothing bitter in his question. He was simply asking her.

"Yes. I want to know more." She did, she realized. "Tell me where you're from. Are you going home?"

"Yeah, heading home from Bend, to Huntington Beach."

"Ah, do you surf?"

"Everyone in Huntington surfs."

"And what were you doing in a nowhere town like Bend, Oregon?"

"I went to my uncle's funeral."

"Shit. I'm sorry."

"No, it's okay. I never liked him much. I went because I thought I should. Because my family expected it."

"Do you always do what other people expect of you?"

"Almost never. But this time… I don't know. I knew it'd make my mother happy. And no, I'm not a mama's boy."

"I don't think mama's boys can fuck like that."

He laughed. "So, what about you? Where are you off to? Did you get on in Klamath Falls, or were you already on the train?"

"Yes, I got on in Klamath. I was in Ashland for a week with some friends at the Shakespeare Festival. Have you ever been?"

"No. But I've heard about it."

"It's a pretty amazing thing, if you like theater. Do you?"

"Yeah, I do. I um…I played Puck in my high school production of *A Midsummer Night's Dream*."

"Really?"

"Yeah, really."

"I like that. A guy who knows Shakespeare."

"We're not all football-playing jarheads."

"Maybe not all of you."

He grinned at her, smoothed her hair from her face.

"So, where's home? And what do you do there besides read Shakespeare?"

"San Francisco. I'm a graphic artist. I work freelance. It lets me travel."

"I love San Francisco. Love the food there. And they have some of the best beer bars."

"Have you ever been to Zeitgeist?"

"Yeah, that biker bar? The best ale anywhere."

She nodded. "I love living in San Francisco. I have a place down by the ocean. I love the fog, the loneliness of it. The grayness." She stopped, laughed. "You probably think that's strange."

"No, not at all. I like to go out surfing in the morning, and I mean really early. 5:00, 6:00 a.m. It's always foggy that early. Peaceful. Like it's just me and the ocean out there. And the ocean is endless and powerful. It wipes everything else away. Whatever is on my mind. Job stress, whatever. I take my dog with me, and he just sits on the sand and watches me."

"I like dogs. What's his name?"

"Petey. Do you know the dog in that old show, *The Little Rascals?* He's a pit bull and he looks just like that—white with a black ring around one eye."

"Yes, of course I know that show. I love old black-and-white television. All those shows from the fifties and sixties. *I Love Lucy. The Honeymooners.* Everything was so simple. These days, everyone wants everything at once."

He was watching her again, his pale eyes all dark pupil now, glittering. "All I want right now is to kiss you. To make you come again."

She smiled as he rolled her onto her back, laid his long body on top of hers. Straddling her, he bent so he didn't hit his head on the top bunk. He started by running his hands over her skin: her stomach, her throat, her shoulders, making her nipples peak hard, wanting to be touched.

"Come in, Ian," she said quietly.

He laughed. "You're impatient, girl."

"I am. You said you'd make me come."

"Oh, I will."

He took both nipples in his fingers and pinched hard, making her gasp.

"Good?" His eyes were gleaming in the half dark.

"Oh, yes."

He pushed her breasts together, leaned in and traced his tongue over one hard tip. She moaned, pleasure filling her up, spreading into her arms, her legs, her sex.

"Oh, I like that. Don't stop." It came out a quiet, breathless whisper.

He paused, looked up at her, his lush mouth crooked in a half smile. "I won't. Not since you asked so nicely." He bent his head once more, his hair falling onto her chest, stroking her skin as his tongue went back to work, lapping, licking.

He went from one nipple to the other, his hands hot on her skin, his tongue wet, unbelievable. Desire ran like a current through her body, lighting up her sex with need. She arced her hips, but he stayed focused on her breasts, his tongue like some lovely sort of torture.

"God, Ian."

He pulled one nipple into his mouth, just letting it rest against the softness of his tongue, not moving.

"Ian. I need…I need more."

But he held still, the wet texture of his mouth on her making her crazy with need, lust pulsing between her thighs, aching.

"Ian…suck, please."

He took the hard nub between his teeth, grazing the surface, and even that brought a sharp twinge of pleasure. He moved to the other breast, took her nipple between his teeth, this time biting into the flesh a little.

"Oh, yes…"

Then he went still again. She was panting, her breath coming in short, sharp gasps. She couldn't believe what he was doing to her. Her pussy was drenched, hurting, hungry. She almost felt as though she could come like this: just his hands, his mouth, on her breasts.

Her hips arced, and she wanted to squeeze her thighs together, but Ian's body was in between them. If only he'd shift the tiniest bit, just press on her mound with one strong thigh. With his hard, lovely cock.

He lifted his head. "Patience, Kate." He laughed a little, a husky sound low in his throat. "I've got you. Don't worry."

She groaned as he squeezed both nipples in his fingers.

"You like that."

"Yes!"

He was watching her, his gaze on hers as he squeezed again.

"Oh!"

"So beautiful…"

He kept twisting, tugging, pulling on the pink flesh, and she felt her nipples swell impossibly. Her sex pulsed, hot and wet. And his face over her, his teeth coming down on his lush lower lip, concentrated lust making his features soft.

Too good…

She was going to come.

"Yeah, that's it. I can feel it, girl. Your body going tight. I bet if I slipped my hand between your thighs your pussy would be so damn wet, I could slide right in. Like silk."

"Yes…please, Ian."

"But I'm not going to do it. I'm going to make you come, just like this. I know you can do it."

"Yes… Oh, God…"

He twisted again, pain and pleasure mingling in some unfathomable way, making her shiver, making her sex clench. So close…

"Come on, girl, you can do it. Come for me."

He tugged hard, her nipples stinging in pain. But the pleasure was so intense, surging into her body, shafting deep inside her sex, like his cock, like his fingers inside her, like his mouth sucking, sucking. Except it was only his clever hands, every sensation carrying from her tortured nipples, screaming through her system, until...

"Oh! Fuck, Ian!"

Her climax ripped through her, shuddering, explosive. And she shook all over with it, hardly believing it was happening in some dark corner of her mind. Then she was just melting, her muscles going lax, pleasure still humming through her like the thundering motion of the train beneath them.

She squeezed her eyes shut, fought to catch her breath.

"That was good," he murmured. "So damn good, just watching your face. Fucking beautiful."

He let her lay there for a few minutes, quiet. Then he lifted her chin. "Hey, girl."

"Hmm, what?" She let her eyes flutter open.

"I need to fuck you. Now."

Before she could answer he was lifting her, his hands circling her waist. He pulled her upright, off the bunk and onto her feet, pushed her up against the window so she could see the velvet sky racing by, a sliver of moon shining through the clouds. He was right up against her, his warm body pressed against her spine. Using his thigh, he made her spread her legs, pulled her hips back toward his until she felt the swollen head of his cock against her buttocks, then between her thighs.

She was still drenched from her orgasm, but the lips of her sex were swelling with need already.

"Yes, do it, Ian."

"I will, girl."

She heard the small, metallic rip of a condom packet, waited while he pulled away to sheath himself. Then his big body was up against her once more, and he slid into her, hard and sleek, filling her.

God, she needed this. Needed it rough and hard, with no time to catch her breath as he began to pump into her right away. He used his body to press her up against the side of the train, her bare breasts on the icy glass of the window. It felt good on her sore nipples. It all felt good. Unbelievable.

"You love the feel of the train, don't you? The vibration."

"Yes..." Even hearing him say it sent a shiver of pleasure through her, beating hot and urgent in her thready pulse.

He slipped one hand around her waist, dipped down until the heel of his hand was flat against her mound. He found her clit, pressed there.

"Yes, just like that."

He pushed her with his hips, until her body was hard against the side of the train, the metal wall pressing against the back of his hand. And that vibration carried through his hand to her clit, like the enormous vibrator she'd imagined earlier. Only so much better this time, with his cock thrusting in and out of her.

"Ah, Ian, it's almost too much," she panted.

"You can take it, girl."

His voice was rough with pleasure, and she loved hearing it; loved to hear him on that brink, where control was so easily lost. Lovely. Intense.

"Fuck me harder, Ian."

"Yeah..."

He drove into her, his cock shafting deep, pushing pleasure through her sex and deep into her body, like something heavy and liquid. Pleasure like lava, flowing, spreading. In moments she was coming again, falling over that lovely, keen edge, pleasure a dazzling flash of light. Blinding. Stark.

He tensed, rammed harder into her, called out, even as she shook with her own climax still. He was holding her so tightly, his fingers digging into her skin. Didn't matter. Nothing mattered but his cock inside her, his hand, the rocking of the train.

Iron and come and flesh.

Her legs were weak, and his thighs trembled behind her. But he held her up. As her eyes refocused, she saw a moonlit field flash by in a dark watercolor stream, the silhouette of mountains in the distance. Beautiful.

His body was so warm against hers. And the train seemed almost like a living beast, like some creature that was part of the sex, or maybe some driving force behind it. She couldn't seem to separate it all, somehow. Not now; she was too dazed.

"Come on, Kate."

He took her with him as he rolled onto the bunk, held her against his side. He was all heat and smooth, bare skin. He smelled like sex.

She curled into his heat, his half-hard cock pressed against the small of her back. He felt good. She was relaxed, loose. More comfortable than she'd been in a long time.

She'd never been this comfortable with Dominic. Never been so unself-conscious, so much *herself* with him. Maybe it was something about not really knowing Ian? About understanding that she'd get off this train and never see him again.

It seemed important to her suddenly, being who she was, finally. Maybe the universe had conspired to put her here with Ian for this purpose? Or was she being melodramatic, reading more into the situation than was really there?

But she was too tired to think about it. She inhaled deeply, pulling in the scent of Ian's skin, that dark patchouli, along with the distant scent of the countryside rushing past the windows. Soon, she slept.

★ ★ ★

Early sunlight behind her closed eyelids, invading her easy sleep. She stretched, felt the solid weight and heat of Ian's body still lying beside her.

Nice.

His voice was rough with too little sleep. "Hey, morning, girl." He ran a hand through her tangled hair, tugging on it.

Smiling, she turned to him. "Hey."

He kissed her then, a light brush of lips against hers, his goatee soft on her skin. Sweet. Romantic.

Don't start thinking this is a romance.

No, but whatever it was, it was lovely.

"Kate, we'll be at the Oakland station in a little over an hour. That's where you get off, right?"

"Oh." She looked at her watch. "Yes."

He raised himself on one arm, looked down at her, and she saw for the first time the pure, pale green of his eyes, like a calm summertime sea. His face was too serious, making her heart pound.

"We don't have much time," he said.

She swallowed. She didn't want it to matter so much.

Pulling him to her, she kissed him hard. In moments he was on top of her, grinding his hips against hers, and they panted together, breathed each other in. He found another condom in his backpack. And then he didn't stop kissing her, even as he drove into her body, as she wrapped her legs around his waist, pulling him deeper into her.

The sex was hard and fast. Desperate. Was she the only one feeling like this? But he thrust harder, fucking her, fucking her, fucking all thought from her mind. And pleasure was like the train itself, like moving iron pounding through her system; that heavy, that powerful.

When she came this time she just broke, shattered, her body

shaking hard all over. And the train rumbling away on its tracks, the churning motion of the wheels, blurred, dimmed, until there was only Ian, his cock, what he was making her feel.

Soon he tensed, shivered as he came into her body, his mouth still hard on hers. Wet, demanding, pulling pleasure from her even as her climax faded away.

He took her with him as he rolled off her, pulling her body on top of his in the narrow bunk.

"Jesus, Kate. Jesus, girl."

"Yeah."

He looked up at her, his eyes glassy with pleasure, his lush mouth slack, his lips swollen. His dirty-blond hair was wild. She wanted to kiss him all day, wanted to just eat him up. Wanted to remember him exactly like this.

"You are so damn beautiful," she whispered to him.

He smiled at her. Dazzling. When he reached up and stroked a lock of hair from her face, his fingertips lingering to brush her cheek, her heart thudded in her chest.

No, don't do this....

She looked away. "Are you hungry? I'm starving."

"Yeah, I could eat. Uh, I think the dining car opens at six."

She nodded, got up and found her clothes, fumbled her way into them.

He got dressed, and they stopped to use the restrooms before wandering down the long aisles until they reached the dining car. It had just opened, and there were only a few other people there. He insisted on buying breakfast: coffee and blueberry muffins. They sat at a table, the morning light making her feel raw, vulnerable, highlighting the hair on his arms, his goatee, his eyelashes, in gold and red.

"Hey, what's up with you this morning?" he asked her. "Do you regret last night? Do you regret meeting me?"

"What? No. Of course not."

"What is it, then? You've been so…wide open with me. And now you're all closed up."

"Shit. I'm sorry. I'm just… You know, I was thinking at some point in the night how easy I feel with you. And I liked it. I don't feel like I have to pretend to be anything I'm not. But this morning…"

"What is it?"

What was there to say but the truth? There was no point in doing anything else, not with Ian.

She shrugged. "I'm getting off the train in Oakland and taking BART back to San Francisco. And you're going on to Huntington. Going home."

"Yeah."

"I mean, your dog is waiting for you. Your life."

He nodded his head.

"I just wish…"

"Yeah. Me, too."

He reached out, took her hand across the table. "But do you regret it, Kate?"

"No. I don't."

It was true.

"Look, we don't live that far apart," he said. "I could make the drive in six hours."

"That long-distance stuff, it's so hard."

"It's not impossible."

"I don't know. Maybe it is. Everyone has this dreamlike expectation of what things will be like, but then stuff comes up and someone always ends up disappointed. It's silly for us to make each other any promises after one night. You can't base anything on that."

"Maybe."

"Ian, I really like you. I love what's happened between us.

And I don't want to fuck that up. This has been...beautiful, if you want to know the truth. Maybe we should just leave it that way."

He was quiet a moment, his eyes going dark. Then, "Yeah, okay. Whatever you want, Kate."

He looked too damn serious. Then he reached out, stroked her cheek with one fingertip, smiled at her, those dazzling white teeth, and everything seemed okay again. Everything seemed right.

"Come on—we'd better go get your bag. We're almost there."

She let him lead her back through the train, the sound of the wheels on the tracks seeming too loud in her ears, the morning light too bright, making her wince.

They reached his compartment, and the conductor announced her stop over the loudspeaker.

Ian grabbed her hand. "Let me help you off."

She shook her head, the train screeching a little as it pulled into the station. She could see it from the corner of her eye through the window, could see the cold concrete of the city in the distance.

"I'm just going to go. Okay?"

He paused, his eyes locking on hers. She waited, thinking he was going to say something, but he just shook his head. "Yeah, okay."

She squeezed his hand tight. Then he pulled her into his arms, kissed her, his mouth coming down hard on hers, his coffee-scented lips, his tongue, so damn sweet. She let herself melt into him because that was exactly what she wanted to do.

Be myself.

He let her go, took a step back. "Better get going."

He smiled at her, and she nodded, heaved her bag onto her shoulder, turned and walked through the door.

"Fuck, fuck, fuck," she muttered under her breath as she made her way to the next car, went down the stairs, stepped onto the quiet platform. All around her the city was gray, bleak. Lonely. But she couldn't move, couldn't go until the damn train pulled away.

She waited while a handful of new passengers boarded, waited while the train idled, then lurched forward, iron wheels grating on iron tracks. Frantic suddenly, she tried to find the window of Ian's compartment, but the windows all looked the same.

"Fuck."

She hadn't even gotten his last name, his phone number, email.

She ran a hand through the wild tangle of her hair, pulled tight.

If she was really going to be herself, be true to herself, she would have stayed on the train, asked Ian if she could go to L.A. with him, spend some time with him, get to know him. Take that chance. Wasn't part of being yourself living without regrets?

The train was gaining speed, wind rushing past her, pushing her hair into her eyes. She wiped it away, her vision clearing as the last of the train left the station.

Ian stood on the other side of the tracks.

He was smiling, looking a little unsure. She grinned back, her heart pounding a lovely rhythm in her body. And his smile broke, lighting up his face. Dazzling. Brilliant.

Without taking his eyes off her, he stepped onto the tracks, crossed over and took her in his arms.

★ ★ ★ ★ ★

CUFFING KATE
ALISON TYLER

"I can't fucking believe it!"

A debate is a game. There is always a winner and a loser. This is why I don't debate. Sonia sees things differently. She never loses.

"What's up?"

My roommate slammed into my bedroom so hard that the door hit the wall. Another ding in the plaster. I shoved the dirty book I was reading under my pillow, but Sonia didn't even look my way. She was already pacing. I kept quiet about the fact that she'd entered my room without knocking. Sonia loves to make an entrance, which means that she rarely ever knocks.

"The fucking bastard."

I stared at her, curious. I'd never seen her like this before. Well, that's not entirely true. Sonia's hot-tempered. She gets all riled up during debates about war in the Middle East or why *tofurkey* is the wonder food. But this was different. Her cheeks were flushed a bright fuchsia and her dark espresso-hued eyes looked huge and wild.

"Did you have a fight?" I asked tentatively.

"A fight? No, not a fight." She bit off each word as if chewing on a piece of that nasty papaya fruit leather she buys at the local health food store. I watched her stomp out of my room, heard her clomping toward the kitchen in her vegan no-cows-were-killed boots. Silently I trailed behind her, dumbfounded as she pulled a Guinness from the fridge—one of *my* beers. I'd never seen Sonia drink an alcoholic beverage.

"Then what happened?"

"The bastard. He actually tried to…"

She swallowed a huge gulp of the brew and leaned against our fridge. The Well-behaved Women Rarely Make History magnet was poised over her head on the freezer. It read like a caption. I waited, but she didn't continue.

"Tried to…" I prompted.

"He really thought I would let him…"

"Let him…" I echoed, faux helpfully.

"Never mind. Chalk the experience up to a bad fucking date."

"What did he try to do?" And why did I care so much?

Sonia strode into the living room, threw herself onto our thrift-store sofa and grabbed the ugly comforter her great-aunt had crocheted. She was calming down. I could tell. Maybe she wouldn't tell me the rest. Sometimes she kept things from me. This is why I read her diary on a daily basis.

"He was kinky," she said with finality.

Sonia was decidedly *not* kinky. That's mostly what I'd discovered by reading the tightly cramped handwritten pages in her recycled-paper journal. She wasn't kinky, and she wasn't that into sex, and she wasn't that into men. But she didn't seem to realize this last fact yet. Maybe when she discovered the latter the former would change.

"What do you mean, 'kinky'?"

She shrugged and turned on Bill Maher, dismissing me by

not responding. I thought of pushing the issue, of trying to take our roommate status to a higher level. Sonia considered us good friends, but we weren't. She never shared her feelings with me, and she didn't seem to care about my own. Mostly she preached her beliefs in my general direction—trying to guilt me into giving up things that she thought I shouldn't do, or eat, or drink, or think.

I went to my room, consumed by visions of the man she'd been out with. Jules Rodriguez. I knew him from school. Senior. Handsome. Of course, I understood perfectly why he'd asked Sonia on a date. She looked as if she'd be hellfire in bed. Anyone with an ounce of imagination could envision her in the heat of the moment—long twists of black curls spiraling as she moved, huge eyes glazed with lust. Aside from that, she dressed like sex on wheels: tight clothes in electric colors, earrings that jangled when she walked. Men were drawn to her. She baited them, and then dismissed them. Over and over and over.

I thought again about the recent one. Jules. What naughty thing had he suggested to Sonia? And why did I so desperately want him to try that same thing out on me, whatever the trick might have been?

My mind made an instant laundry list of deviant possibilities: *Spanking? Anal? Sex toys?*

For a moment, I considered returning to the living room. Sonia *was* drinking her first beer, after all. Maybe she would have looser lips than usual. But I didn't feel up to listening to a full-on rant. Hopefully she would write about the situation in her diary. Tomorrow when she went to class, I could sneak in and read every filthy little detail.

Except maybe I couldn't wait that long.

Jules lived in an apartment down the hill from campus. I knew because I'd known him before Sonia. We'd shared one class together—a cozy little 500-student Art History class. I also served him his daily caffeine infusion as barista at the central campus coffee bar. From my vantage point, I could spy him often in the quad. I hate to admit that I followed him, so let's just say that one day our paths crossed in town, and I watched as he entered a retro white stucco apartment with wrought-iron railings on the balconies.

Sonia may look like she'd be a good lay—but I thought Jules looked like he knew how to get inside a woman's head. He was tall and lean, given to dressing simply in battered blue jeans and a khaki jacket. In between serving up shots of espresso, I'd drawn pictures of the two of us entwined. My canvas: white paper napkins. To my dismay, he simply hadn't chosen the right woman.

What had he asked her for? What had he wanted to do?

"I'm going out," I told Sonia as I passed behind the sofa to the door.

"Where?"

"A walk."

"If you go by Juiceeze, pick me up a smoothie," she said. "Carrot and ginger, please. That beer was foul. You shouldn't drink those."

I didn't answer. I worship Guinness.

"And you don't need any more coffee," she added as I began to shut the door. "Putting caffeine in your body is like depositing counterfeit money in your bank account." These were the pearls of wisdom Sonia tossed out every day. I let them roll under the dresser like dust bunnies on roller skates.

Without a plan, I walked by Jules's apartment. Then I stopped and looked at the shades on the windows. What if I went up and knocked on his door? What if I forced him to tell me exactly what had happened? I could imagine the way he would look at me. Every day, he bought java from the coffee bar, but we'd never actually spoken more than the most casual chitchat. What kind of crazy person confronts a virtual stranger about his sex life?

I took a step. I spun around. I went home.

Patience is one of my only virtues. This strength comes with the fact that I have had to wait for nearly everything I've ever wanted. I'm not complaining. This is my truth. But is this also why I envy Sonia? Men fall into her lap. Instructors trip over themselves to hear what tidbit of wisdom she has to offer. This time, all I had to do was bide my time until she left for class.

Her diary was exactly where she always kept it. Sonia would never think of me as a snoop. She lives so much on the surface, she never stirs her unvarnished toenails in the water to see if there's depth.

I sat on the edge of her bed, my hands shaking as I found the latest entry. Jules had asked her to dinner, but not at a restaurant, at his house. That was smart of him. Sonia has such restrictive eating habits. There are few decent vegan hotspots in the vicinity. He'd poured wine, which she accepted, even if she didn't take a sip. Why had she gone to his place? From all the previous entries I'd read, Sonia had never gone home with a man.

Her own words answered the question for me.

He was a gentleman, and I loved the way he spoke. His words were eloquent as he described the text we're reading.

So what had happened? Sonia bored me for two paragraphs as she described her own feelings about the text then wrote a bit about how Jules had offered to coach her before her next debate. Finally there it was. A word leaped out at me, big and bold and black: *handcuffs.*

He said I was beautiful, but out of control. The way I had to ges-ture when I spoke, pacing, like an animal. He said he wanted to bind

*me down, so that I couldn't move, and then he would see—we would
see—what I had to say.*

I put the book down. I knew the ending already. She hadn't
let him bind her down. But I was aflutter at the thought that
this man was so attractive, so intelligent, so kinky, and yet
so unable to read the fact that Sonia was not the type of girl
he was after.

All year, I'd watched different men discover this fact for a
variety of reasons. Sonia was like a coveted chocolate from
the center of a scarlet, heart-shaped box—once you bit in, you
found you'd made a disappointing choice. Too much nougat.
Too many nuts.

I'm the opposite. My coworker, Dan, described me as
WYSIWYG: what you see is what you get. Simple attire: well-
worn Levi's and an oxford button-down. Simple hairstyle:
long and straight to the middle of my back. No frills, maybe,
but simplicity can be sexy, too. Calvin Klein built his empire
on clean-cut lines, didn't he? Not that I could compare myself
with the models in CK ads, but I have always striven for that
sharp elegance. Black and white. No gray.

I reread the part about being bound again. And again.
Reluctantly I put her book back, exactly where she kept the
journal, and went to my own room to touch myself. This
was a skill I excelled at. In seconds, my hands were in routine
motion—one stroking my breasts, the other making lazy
circles over my clit through my panties—slow, languorous
circles that had my breathing quickening immediately. But
what to think about? What fairy tale to display today? I stared
up at the ceiling, mentally tracing a tiny crack in the biscuit-
hued plaster. Not sexy. I turned my head and took in the
posters on my wall: black-and-white photos of lovers kissing
on the subway, kissing in a way I've never been kissed. Sexy,
but distant. I'd never experienced passion like that before.

I turned my head the other way, confronted by my own image in the mirror over my dresser. Damn. Shy girl, with straight red hair, freckles, a lost look on her face.

I shut my eyes. It was safer this way.

There is a specific routine that always gets me off. I stroke myself gently at first, always through the barrier of whatever undergarments I have on.

Oh, like that. Yes, like that.

Only as the pleasure begins to build do I give in to touching myself skin to skin, fingers slipping underneath the waistband to taunt and tease. Why? I need to make myself yearn for release. See, when I'm by myself I have to play both Dom and sub.

But did I?

Suddenly I thought of Jules. He wouldn't want me to touch myself, would he? He'd want my hands tied, so that I couldn't move, so that we could see what would happen. Nice thought. But that presented an urgent problem: Could I actually come without any touching at all? Was that possible? I'd read about a porn star who could do this—a male, who would focus until he reached that pinnacle of pleasure all by himself. But, then again, he was a pro.

With my hands at my sides, I spread my legs wide on my mattress. I thought of Jules, conjuring him up in my mind.

When I draw, the pictures appear without thoughts. My hand works almost independently from my brain. I fall into the zone. That's the easiest way for me to describe the sensation. Sometimes, when a picture is complete, I have no true recollection of having put pen to paper—or in my case, pencil to napkin. That's where most of my art takes place. I draw all the time, quick sketches or "doodles" as my coworker, Dan, says, a hint of a feature here, a line of an emotion there.

Coming is like that for me. I lose myself in my fantasies. When I emerge, I am dazed.

This was different.

At first, I felt nothing. I was aroused, but I couldn't imagine climaxing without actually touching myself, physically sliding one hand down my body, pushing my fingers under my white cotton boy shorts, finding my clit and pinching tight. I tend to tease myself—throwing in firm strokes in between the sweet caresses. This was frustrating. My legs were spread, my heart was racing, but nothing happened.

I almost gave up right at the start, almost said, "fuck this" and went with the normal dog-and-pony show: round and round, in and out, round and round. A pinch, a spiral, a pinch. My hand was actually in motion, on the way back to the split of my body. But then I thought of what Sonia had written about Jules: *He said he wanted to bind me down, so that I couldn't move, and then he would see—we would see—what I had to say.*

Oh, I liked that. No man had ever spoken to me in that way. I had to steal Sonia's sex life for my own form of foreplay, but I had no shame. I stole away. What if Jules had said those words to me? How might I have responded? I definitely wouldn't have left the building. I would have desperately soaked up every last moment Jules was willing to give. So why not pretend?

My pussy began to grow wetter. I could feel my juices flowing. Slowly the heat built between my thighs. I imagined Jules watching me. I envisioned him standing at the foot of my bed, staring down at me with those dark blue eyes of his, daring me to come without any additional stimulation.

"You can do this," his eyes seemed to say.

"No, I need you. I need you to touch me," I responded, lips moving, with no sound, like a TV show on Mute.

"Come on, Kate. All you have to do is try."

"I am trying." And I was. Really.

"Try harder. Do this for me."

I'd drawn his face often enough to imagine his expression. The challenge in the tilt of his chin. The dare in his eyes.

But something was wrong. I recalled what Sonia had written in her diary, and then I brought my hands over my head and clung to the curlicues of brass that make up my headboard, pretending that I was cuffed. The metal was cold against my skin, and I shivered but didn't let go.

How could she *not* have given in to him? How could she not have said, "Yes, please"? Nothing like this had ever happened to me before.

Don't get me wrong. I'm no virgin. Maybe that's difficult to believe. Someone as shy as I am doesn't seem like a person who could land a date, much less a lay. But that's the thing. You don't need a lot of bells and whistles to find a man. I simply hadn't found the man I needed. My freshman year, I'd hooked up with a partner in my science class—but we had no true chemistry. My sophomore year, there'd been a writer I liked from my journalism class—but ultimately he was yesterday's news. Jules had always looked to me like someone I could whisper my fantasies to. The ones that kept me up after normal people went to sleep.

When you work at a café—when caffeine is freely accessible—there is no such thing as a normal time to sleep. I've grown accustomed to quietly roaming the apartment late at night, to sitting up in my window overlooking the lights of the city, to fucking myself with my vibrator while praying that one day I will find a lover who won't take my quiet surface as the end result. Who will understand sometimes the best prizes are the ones you dig to the bottom of the Cracker Jacks for.

I raised my hips. I let go of the headboard.

"Giving up so soon, Red?" Jules was displeased that I had broken the rules. His thumb stroked his belt buckle.

Resigned, I reached for the brass once more. My body was begging for release. I didn't know how much longer I could hold out. The imaginary Jules chided me. "Don't even think about letting go," he said. "I want you immobile. I want your pleasure to come at my speed. Don't make me have to punish you, Kate."

Oh, God.

"You know what I mean when I say that word, don't you?"

A shiver. A tremor.

"I can be nice and sweet, Kate. Or I can make all your filthiest dreams come true."

I let go of the headboard once more. The fantasy Jules couldn't stop me this time. *Punish.* That word always gets me off. My fingers slipped underneath the waistband of my knickers. I began to make those circles that flow as naturally from my fingertips as pictures emerge from my pencil. My hips beat against my black-and-white comforter. I shivered as the pleasure began to work through me. Hot, and wet, and stealthy.

This was ideal. The only problem was that I was all by myself. I twisted on the mattress. My fingers worked harder, faster. I bit my lip to keep from moaning, even though I was alone in an empty apartment. I felt as if Jules was really there, watching me.

You cheated, Kate, the dream Jules chided me.

Yeah, but I came, I replied, as I rolled over on the bed.

Sonia arrived home that night repeating the rules for the debate team. She entered my bedroom without knocking, as usual, and she proceeded to practice for me.

She was one of the all-star players. Sonia knew how to capture the audience's focus. I'd seen her in action often enough. She understood all the tricks. A good introduction is key. You have to grab the attention and interest of the audience from the very first line. This comes naturally to Sonia. She's a gifted debater. She knows how to state her opinion in a way that makes you think it's fact. But ultimately, it's not fact. Proof? She gave me the rundown on her vegan diet with such conviction that I tried my best to follow her rules—until the tofurkey episode. That ended my vegan lifestyle with a bang.

This is what I've learned from her: a debate is a game.

There are always two different sides.

"A shot in the dark."

When Jules ordered his coffee the next morning, my hands were trembling slightly. I wondered if he noticed. Luckily I didn't spill any of the precious dark liquid, but I came close. Could he tell that I'd come the previous night while thinking of him? Jules put money down on the counter, and then he reached for a napkin. Not a fresh one from the stack, but the one I'd been drawing on. I hadn't realized he'd noticed.

"Nice cuffs, Red."

There were handcuffs in the picture.

Dan stopped going through the tip jar looking for wheat-back pennies. (He was on a quest for the 1909 S-VDB—I've heard about the penny often enough to have those numbers and letters embroiled in my brain. This particular wheat-back is worth an astonishing $550. "It would make the fact that some schmuck put a penny into the tip jar so much more satisfying," he was fond of saying.) But the word *cuffs* clearly caught his interest. My picture had both wrists and cuffs. *My* wrists and cuffs.

"But you got one thing wrong," Jules said softly, eyebrows uplifted as he regarded the picture, and then looked at me. "You forgot the keyholes."

I stared down at the sketch, embarrassed, realizing he was right.

He leaned across the counter. I could feel how close we were. "How will anyone set you free if there aren't any holes for the keys?"

I blushed hot. Dan snickered behind me. I'd never seen a pair of handcuffs up close before.

Jules left a five-dollar tip in the jar, and he took the napkin with him. "Do a little research," he said over his shoulder.

I knew where the store was, a dark hole-in-the-wall type of place. These stores are never well-lit on the outside. You have to push through the dimness to find the glitter, the neon, the glow. How do I know? I had to buy my trusty vibrator somewhere. I couldn't risk having my roommate opening a delivery box from a kinky specialty catalog. I didn't know where Sonia stood on sex toys, but the thought of receiving a lecture on my pleasure wasn't something I ever hoped to experience.

Now, I wanted handcuffs. At least, I thought I did.

The shop clerk glanced up at me, gave me a quick once-over with obvious disinterest then returned to his book. He was reading at the counter, surrounded by some of the largest dildos I'd ever seen. I stared at him, the blue spiky hair, inky ribbons of tribal tattoos on his biceps. I tried to look nonchalant, but there was no way I could pull off a jaded expression. I wanted to explore everything. I wanted to touch all the toys. I wanted Jules.

"Do you have cuffs?" I asked, working for blasé, but channeling Minnie Mouse—squeaky instead. Minnie Mouse on helium. Only dogs could hear me.

"Fur-lined? Regulation? Solo use?" He might have been

ticking off different brands of laundry detergent. He sounded so indifferent.

I had no idea handcuffs came in multiple styles. I wished I'd paid more attention to Sonia's diary. Had she spelled out what Jules had wanted to do to her? No, she'd only said "handcuffs."

"What does 'solo use' mean?"

There was suddenly a hint of curiosity in the clerk's eyes and he closed his book. His eyes were ringed by dark kohl outlines, smudged and blurred. "You can't figure that out for yourself?" He nodded to my sweatshirt with the University logo on the center. "College girl like you?"

"I mean, how do they work?" I tried to sound like an investigative reporter. This information wasn't for me. I was simply gathering up the facts for a paper on...on...

"Ice in the lock. When the ice melts, the lock opens. You can be bound down for one hour, two, three. Depending on how much water you add to the lock, and how long you want to be immobilized." He appraised me for a moment. "But I don't believe you really can't find anyone to bind you to a bed." His apparent attraction was growing by the second.

"How do you know the cuffs are for me?" Could I trot out the line about the research paper now? Maybe I was doing a term paper on bondage devices in the twenty-first century. Or on kinky coeds. Or on sneaky coffee vixens who read their roommates' diaries.

He smirked.

"I mean, why wouldn't you think I wanted to bind someone else down?" Right, because I have pro-domme written all over my face. Where was this coming from? Why was I even talking to the guy?

"You have a look," he said. I thought of Sonia. Men seemed to think that *she* had a look. What kind of look did I have?

"Novice, neophyte, ingénue," he continued, as if reading my mind.

"What's that you're reading?" I asked, feeling sarcastic. "Roget's Thesaurus?"

"You don't have to be a college boy to have a big *dick*-tionary."

"Give me all of them," I said, feeling anger rise inside of me. "Fur, regulation, solo. I want them all."

Did I? No. But I didn't want to walk out of the place empty-handed, either. The smug expression didn't leave the clerk's face as he rang up my purchases. When he handed me my change, he also handed me a card from the store. "If you can't find anyone to do the tying, angel, give me a call."

I didn't make it home before I had to come. I pulled over to the rear of a generic grocery store parking lot and shoved one hand down the front of my jeans. The need was so intense I didn't even worry about being caught. Fuck the foreplay, I crushed my fingers against my clit and rocked my hips. The pleasure was instant. I felt the wetness all over my fingertips. I took a deep breath and pressed harder still.

So I had the look of a novice. That wasn't an insult. It was the truth. But I could learn. I could be taught. I could walk up to Jules with the handcuffs in the glistening black Mylar bag and say, "Use these on me. Bind *me* down. Find out what *I* have to say."

What would I have to say?

I couldn't be sure, but I had a few ideas. I thought I might say, "Fuck me, Jules. Please fuck me." Or maybe, "Do me, baby. Oil me up and take me. Anyway you want. Anyway you like." I'd never talked like that in my life, but the thought of the cuffs unlocked a new wave of passion inside me.

A battered blue station wagon pulled next to mine, and I stopped what I was doing, frozen. Should I pull my hand out of my jeans or stay still and pretend I didn't exist? I removed my hand and reached for my satchel, rummaging through the bag as if looking for something. Something like my sanity.

What sort of rabbit hole had I fallen down? I'd walked into a sex toy store and been offered bondage. I was now in a very public location fantasizing to images of myself being cuffed by my roommate's date. A date she'd classified as *too kinky*. I had to stop. I had to get myself under control. I had to…

The middle-aged blonde driver of the car in the next spot locked her car. She had a bad dye job, I thought meanly. And her acid-washed jeans were too tight. She would never go to a sex toy store and buy three sets of handcuffs, would she? But was that an insult or praise? I watched in my rearview mirror as the woman walked toward the grocery store. I relaxed and immediately slid my hand back down my jeans. I didn't care if I was stroking myself to fantasies about Sonia's sex life. She didn't deserve a man as hot as Jules.

I squeezed my eyes shut tight and thought about the handcuffs. Thought about Jules. Wondered what he'd say if I showed up at his apartment with all three sets in the bag and asked, "Which one is right? Which one do you want?"

The problem with my fantasies was that I didn't know Jules's dialogue. I had to put words in his mouth. But I could do that.

"Let's try each one," the fantasy Jules said. "We'll start with the steel. Cold metal on your skin. We'll bind you down, and then we'll see. I want to watch you come, Kate. I want to see your body change."

Oh, fuck, I wanted that, too.

"And then we'll try the ice lock," he continued. "I'll do my work in the other room, leave you all by yourself with your own dirty fantasies. And when I come back, you'll have to tell me each naughty one. If you don't, I'll have to punish you."

A laugh. I'd heard him laugh before. But this was different. Darker. "And maybe I'll punish you anyway."

What would that mean for him? I knew what the word meant for me.

"I'll put you over my lap," Jules promised. "I'll spank you on the bare. I'm sure a spanking will make you wet. Am I right, Kate? Am I right?"

Yes. Yes, he was right.

"I'll use my hand first, and then my belt. I'll make you cry hot tears, and then I'll fuck you so hard, so fast."

My head back against the seat, my body trembling, I let the wave of pleasure slam through me and recede before I even thought about turning on the car once more.

At home, I spread out my new prizes on the bed. I started to manhandle each one, to stroke my fingers around the curves of the steel, to pet the fabric of the faux-fur-lined set, to investigate the ice lock. Jules had wanted to handcuff Sonia. I wanted Jules to handcuff me. But I wanted to know what handcuffs would feel like first. What if I couldn't stand the sensation of being bound down? Or what if I loved the feeling so much I never wanted any other kind of sex again?

Either way, I didn't need three pairs of cuffs. Did I?

Slowly I ran my hands over the pink, leopard-print set. These were silly—a gag gift for a bachelorette party. I would feel ridiculous wearing them. I held the steel ones. They had a good, solid weight. The keys were sweet and small. I wished I could put the cuffs on, but I was scared. What if I couldn't make the key work while my hands were bound? I put on one cuff and let the other hang loose. I liked the weight.

God, why had Jules asked Sonia out? Why hadn't he asked me?

The sound of the front door opening made me start.

Quickly I tried to undo the cuff with the key, but my fingers were slippery. I climbed off my bed and kicked the door closed, the sound of soldiers marching in my head. Leaning my body weight against the door, I fumbled with the key some more. My breathing was ragged, as if I'd been running. What if Sonia came in? What if she figured out that I'd read her diary and that I wanted what she didn't want? Finally I got the key in the hole, turned the right way, released myself.

Jesus.

I shoved all the cuffs and the packaging into the bottom drawer of my battered dresser and then went out to greet Sonia. She was on the sofa, reading the rules for her next debate. "Seven minutes. First affirmative construction..."

"A shot in the dark."

When Jules bought his coffee the next day, he put his hand out.

I'd already given him his change.

"Sketch?" he asked.

Blush was apparently the new hue for me. I handed him the napkin. The cuffs had keyholes now.

"Good girl," he said before walking away. If my coworker, Dan, hadn't been standing behind me, I would have sunk to the floor in a puddle of arousal and shame. As it was, I stared after him, hearing the words reverberate in my mind: *good girl, good girl, good girl.*

When Sonia went out the next night, I locked myself up once more. I'd been impatiently waiting for her departure for hours. In fact, I'd been so nervous and jumpy that she'd given me two separate lectures on the poison of caffeine. How could I tell her that coffee wasn't to blame for my excitable state— her diary was the culprit?

The clerk had said the ice lock would take an hour to three hours to melt depending on how much water you'd frozen. I'd gone with one hour—hiding the cuffs in the freezer behind a bag of frozen peas. I hoped I'd gone with one hour. I couldn't be entirely sure. As soon as Sonia left, I stripped off my clothes and climbed onto my bed. I fastened one cuff easily on my left wrist, and through some fairly simple maneuvers, threaded the chain through the brass curls on my headboard before attaching the other cuff to my right. Why did I get naked? Because Jules would have wanted me like that. Why did I bind myself to the headboard? That seemed the appropriately kinky thing to do. I craved knowing how this would feel— every second, every sensation. Could I come while my wrists were like this? I didn't know. So far, every time I'd tried, I'd cheated. This would keep me from giving in.

Sonia was supposed to be at a debate club meeting. I ought to have the apartment all to myself until at least midnight.

That was the plan, anyway. But plans often go astray, especially when you are totally nude, in your bedroom, cuffed to your bed, and your roommate enters your apartment with a guest four freaking hours before you expect her home.

Holy fuck. Holy fucking fuck.

For a second, I think my heart actually stopped. Then my brain began to race with questions. Well, with the same question over and over: *What to do? What to do? What to do?* Deep down, I knew that there was nothing to do. I was cuffed— *naked* and cuffed. The chain ran through the curlicues of brass of my headboard. My heart pounded so hard I was sure Sonia could hear the throb in the living room. "What's that drum beat?" she might be asking her friend. "Is someone playing Led Zeppelin on eleven?"

Maybe she had forgotten something. She and whoever she was with would simply grab the missing item—jacket, or purse, or note cards, or Wesson Oil, whatever the fuck they'd forgotten—and be on their way. But if that was the case, then what was that sound? I didn't have to be a rocket scientist to recognize the echo of footsteps approaching down the hall, growing closer by the second.

Oh, God, why had I done this? Why hadn't I been comfortable enough with putting a single cuff on my wrist? Why had I needed to try something different?

Desperately I attempted to get free. I rattled the chain, to no avail. Maybe the heat of my cheeks would melt the ice quicker than the expected time. Nope. I bucked against the mattress.

My mind exploded with dirty words.

Sonia never knocked. Not ever. How could I not have locked the door? Simple. This was my maybe not-so-bright backup plan. I had worried that I might need assistance. What if I'd done something wrong? What if the lock got stuck? The firemen could easily open the door and find me. They wouldn't have to break down the door.

So what could I do now? Could I somehow drag the whole fucking bed through the room so I could block the door? Not likely.

The voices grew louder.

No hunky firemen were in my future. Right when I realized that I ought to simply shout out, "Don't come in!" Sonia and Eleanor, a friend of hers from the debate team, entered my bedroom. They were talking to each other, so they did not notice me right away. That is, they didn't notice what I looked like. Then Sonia sucked in her breath, her friend looked aghast, and I bit my lip and tried hard not to cry.

The other woman politely backed out of the room—I'm sure Emily Post would have approved—but Sonia stood in the doorway, staring. Another person than I am might have been indignant. A different kind of girl might have appropri-

ated a *what the fuck do you think you're looking at?* attitude. But
that chick wasn't me.

"Are you okay?" she finally asked, her voice trembling.

"Well..." I said, thinking, "Hell, I've been better."

"Did someone do this to you?"

Sigh. *Yeah. I did. I did because I read your fucking diary, you
nitwit. I did because I wanted to know what it would feel like to be
handcuffed, without having to go through the whole thing of finding
a boyfriend and begging him to use bondage tools on me. Men don't
offer things up like this to me every day. I'm not you.*

I shook my head.

"Do you want me to unlock you or leave you alone?"

Did I really have to explain to her about the ice lock? I
took a deep breath. "Don't worry about me," I said, before
adding, "but maybe you could cover me up." She looked as
if she didn't want to step too close to me. I wanted to tell her
that I wouldn't bite, and she didn't have to worry anyway, not
with me bound down. Reluctantly she came close enough to
spread the quilt over my body. Then she sat at the foot of my
bed and stared at me. I saw confusion in her eyes. At least,
that was better than pity.

"I wanted to know," I said, as she seemed to expect some
type of explanation.

"Know what?"

"What being bound would feel like."

Had she made the mathematical mental connection? Her
diary plus my fantasies equaled intense orgasms.

"Well, what does it feel like?"

Wow, for once Sonia wasn't spouting platitudes at me. She
wasn't telling me I should get in my light and do my work.
She wasn't explaining the dangers of kinky sex. Instead she
looked truly interested in what I had to say.

I stammered, "I l–like the sensation." I'd have liked it a whole lot better if Jules had been between my thighs, but I kept that part to myself.

Nothing happened after that. I waited until I could free myself, and then I freed myself. There was no way I was going to get off tonight. I was so mortified that I didn't even leave my bedroom until I was sure that Sonia's guest had departed and Sonia had gone to sleep. Except, as I was brushing my teeth, I thought I heard soft noises from Sonia's room. Noises I'd never heard before. These weren't the sounds of a heated debate.

Not unless a heated debate sounds a lot like fucking.

"Oh, God," I heard in a stagelike whisper, then louder, "Oh, my, God!"

I paused, and then realized my electric toothbrush was still running. Quickly I pressed the button to turn off the brush. I wanted to hear everything I possibly could. Sonia's normally recognizable voice sounded extremely unrecognizable. There was lust, passion, arousal in her moans.

Should I come closer? Press myself up to her door and try to peek? No. I'd been caught by her already today. I didn't want to flip the situation and catch her. Still, I couldn't wait to read her diary the next day.

But when I went to look in the morning, the book wasn't there.

Jules strolled up to the coffee bar as usual. I started trembling when he approached the counter to order. "Shot in the dark, right?"

He reached out and put a hand on top of mine, holding me still, calming me down. Was he going to ask to see more of

my sketches? I had a stack behind the counter. Was he going
to tell me he'd only threatened Sonia with cuffs as a joke?

"Everyone knows she's a lesbian," Jules said, smiling.

I couldn't believe what he was saying. "Break," I told Dan,
"be right back." Dan gave me the evil eye before stepping up
to the counter. He liked making money, but he hated having
to work. I walked out of the small structure to find Jules
waiting for me at the back.

"What did you say?"

He took my hand again. I was extremely aware of his skin
against my skin. I wanted to tell him that usually, I touch
myself through a barrier. Only when the heat arises do I try
skin on skin. To mimic this in real life, we ought to have
been wearing gloves. Those were the nervous, crazy thoughts
jangling through my brain. Luckily I was wise enough to keep
my lips sealed as he led me away from the coffee bar, down
a little hill, to a concrete planter. We sat together under a
jacaranda tree. All around us were the pale, purple blossoms,
the honeyed scent in the air. Maybe this was a dream. I
couldn't, for the life of me, understand what was happening.

"Sonia's a lesbian. You know that. I know that."

"She doesn't know that," I said. Then I backtracked. "Well,
I mean, I don't think she did until last night."

"What happened last night, Red?" He stroked my hair out
of my eyes, and a fresh tremor ran through me. He was gazing
at me in a way that men generally admired Sonia. Which
reminded me in a heartbeat that he'd asked her out first.

"I think she hooked up with Eleanor. But why on earth did
you ask her out if you think she's into women?"

He stared at me with the same expression I'd seen on his
face in class, a look that said he knew something more than
the instructor did, had a concept that had yet to be explained.

"You really can't guess?"

I shook my head.

"You can, but you want me to say the words. That's fine. I can say the words. I asked her out because I wanted you…"

"But…" I wanted to believe him. My heart felt too big in my chest. He had his hands on my wrists now. I gave a test tug, pulling. He held on tight. *Handcuffs.* I saw that word again— this time written in my mind instead of in Sonia's notebook.

"But why didn't I ask you out from the start?"

I swallowed hard and nodded.

"I wanted you to *want* what I was going to give you. I wanted you to be consumed with need. There are rules in a debate," he said, "but there are always people who cheat."

Oh, Christ. He'd played me so well. Knowing how jealous I was of how men responded to her, knowing somehow that I was kinky. How had he known that? How had he known I wanted someone to tie me up?

"But what if she'd said yes?" I needed to know the answer to this.

"She wasn't going to say yes."

"What if she had?"

He shrugged. The lady or the tiger? I would have to choose the decision for myself. Would he have postponed the encounter, or tied her up and fucked her? Did either answer make me want to run? No.

I stopped tugging. His grip did not relax. He squeezed even tighter, before finally releasing me.

"Do you know where I live?" he asked.

I nodded without telling him I'd stood outside his apartment before, staring up at his windows. Considering begging him to handcuff me.

"Come to my place after work," he said.

He would have no debate from me.

★ ★ ★

I burned myself twice in the next two hours. Exasperated, Dan finally told me to call it a day. I must really have been driving him nuts if he were willing to man the coffee shack by himself. I untied the apron and grabbed up my battered messenger bag. I knew I ought to go home and change clothes—the aroma of coffee permeated my whole being. I could go and snag one of Sonia's little dresses from her closet, put some emphasis on my figure, something different from my standard uniform of faded jeans and a plain white button-down.

But when I went to her room and looked in her closet, I was at a loss. How could I put on a costume when all I really wanted was for Jules to see me naked? I headed back to my room. At the very least, I could capture my hair in a flirty ponytail. I might even slick on my one shade of lip gloss, if I could find the tube.

On my bed sat a book—a book I recognized immediately. Sonia's diary. That's why I hadn't found the journal in the morning. She'd cottoned on to the fact that I was a snoop. Guilt flickered through my body. That didn't stop me from perching on the edge of my mattress and cracking the spine once more. Her latest entry was written differently this time. It was written directly to me.

When I saw you on your bed like that, I couldn't get the image out of my mind. I went and told Eleanor what you'd said, and Eleanor spoke to me differently than anyone ever had. Do you want that? she asked me. Want... She hesitated.

To be tied down, or tied up?

It's no coincidence, is it? You read my diary. You saw what he said. You knew what he did.

The guilt was back. I was shivering all over.

But I'm not angry, Kate. Because last night with Eleanor was the best fucking night I ever had. The best night fucking, too.

Now, I smiled.

Oh, yeah. And do you think we could borrow your cuffs sometime?

I put down Sonia's diary and grabbed the pretty faux-fur, leopard-print cuffs from my bottom drawer. She'd like these best, I thought. They went with her style. I set both the cuffs and key and diary on Sonia's bed. Then I looked at my clock. Jules had said to meet him after work. Maybe I ought to have changed—turned myself into someone else. Like in one of those fairy tales I used to read when I was a kid. But I didn't have a godmother.

Instead I went as myself.

Jules was waiting for me on his front porch, beer in hand.

I could hardly speak English when he opened the front door for me. I might have said hello but the word was erased by the sound of a truck rumbling by on the road, and I didn't try again. Jules waited like a gentleman for me to step inside and came in after me. Was I really here? Was this really happening? I turned to look at Jules. He smiled, as if he could read all the thoughts that were in my head. But he couldn't possibly. There was no way that he could know how often I'd thought about him, and the dirty things I'd imagined him doing to me.

He set his beer down on the table in the entryway. I set my satchel down on the floor. We stared at each other for a moment, and I wondered if this was going to be easy or awkward or...

"This way."

Easy. I let him lead me once more, this time to the bedroom. I thought of Sonia, thought of her hot-tempered reaction to his initial suggestion. How different I was, meek and willing, desperate.

"You look in the mirror," he said when we got to his room, "but you don't see the truth."

"What do you mean?" His room was all white. White walls, white furniture. But the bed had a black spread on the mattress, and there were framed black-and-white posters on the walls. I was secretly thrilled to see several that I owned, as well.

"You don't see. You can't possibly. Or you wouldn't behave the way you do." As if to prove his point, he spun me around, so I was facing a gilded oval mirror hanging above his bed. I looked down. He tilted my chin up. I shut my eyes. He brought his mouth to my ear and said, "Don't disobey me. If I want your eyes closed, I'll use a blindfold."

His words made me instantly wet. Did he know? Could he tell?

I sucked my lower lip between my teeth and bit hard. I wished I could be eloquent with words the way Sonia was, able to put arguments into clean, precise phrases. Able to fight when someone tried to dispute me. Not that I wanted to fight Jules, but I wanted to understand, and I wanted to be able to voice my…my…fears.

"I watched you in class. You soak up everything, but you don't respond. And then I realized, it's all in there. You keep you emotions within, sublime and tight. You don't know how to let things out."

"So you're going to tie me down to teach me how to let go?" There. That was a little voice, right? Jules smiled again. God, he had a nice smile.

"She's learning. Quick, too. That's not all I'm going to do, Kate."

Had he said my name before? Like that? Outside of my fantasies? I didn't think so. He'd always called me Red. I wanted to hear him say it again. *Please, say Kate again,* I silently willed.

"What else are you going to do?" And how had I gotten myself backed into a corner like this? Somehow, I had managed to wedge myself completely into one corner of Jules's bedroom. My arms were crossed over my chest, and my hands rested on my shoulders as if I were trying to mimic a mummy in a sarcophagus.

"What do you want me to do, Kate?"

Oh, like that. The way he said my name struck a chord within me. I wanted him to press his lips to my ear and whisper my name over and over. Instead of telling him this, I shrugged, feeling the walls on both sides. He was waiting. Clearly waiting. Finally I whispered, "I want you to do what you said."

"What I said to who?"

I sucked in my breath. "I read Sonia's diary," I confessed. "I want you to do to me what you said you'd do to her."

I didn't have to ask him twice.

He had cuffs like the second pair I'd purchased: regulation, steel handcuffs with a silver gleam. I knew what they were going to feel like. I'd held them. Cradled them. Caressed them. None of that prepared me for the sensation of having Jules strip me of my clothes and position me in the center of his bed. I thought I'd been so smart doing the research, buying the toys. Turned out, I hadn't learned a fucking thing.

"Arms over your head." I was naked on his mattress, and I felt his warm hands on my wrists before the cold steel closed tight.

I took a breath. I could come from this alone, I thought. Why had I needed to cheat every other night? Simple. Because Jules hadn't been in the room.

He stared down and me, and his face looked different than

all of my sketches. "You bought the cuffs when I told you to do research, didn't you, Kate?"

"Yes."

What had been missing from my drawings? The warmth in his eyes that I saw now. He was handsome, yes, but he was more than that. He looked pleased with me, as if I'd risen to some challenge.

"And you tried them out?"

I thought of the fiasco with Sonia walking in, and I turned my head away from his. He gripped my chin and forced me to meet his gaze. "When I want you to look away from me, I'll tell you," he said. There was a beat of menace to his voice. But that made me wetter still.

"Yeah, I tried them," I admitted.

"That's what she told me."

"She?" The words weren't making sense.

"I was helping her prepare for her debate. She told me that she'd found you."

"I thought she was never going to talk to you again."

He shrugged. "There's *never* and then there's *never*. After she got together with Eleanor, she called and wanted to talk."

"So she told you…" He'd known the answer before he'd asked the question.

He grinned. "I would have liked to have found you like that. Walked in. Discovered you bound to your bed all by yourself. The games I could have played with you."

I would have turned my head away, but he'd told me not to. I would have shut my eyes, tried to hide by embarrassment, but he'd already warned me. Instead I simply stared back at him, forced to face my fears. My stomach tightened. This was much more difficult than I'd expected.

"Good girl," he said, just as he had before, words that

warmed me inside as if he'd banked my internal furnace. "Don't turn away from me. Don't ever turn away from me."

Then it was like every fantasy I've ever had and ones I never thought of before. He started by kissing me, his lips on mine, kissing hard. I'd been kissed by other men—but maybe what I'd felt previously should be given a different name from kissing. Those were pecks. Smooches. This was real. This was what kissing is all about, a definition from a dirty dictionary. I felt his lips part against mine. I felt our tongues meet. I wanted this to go on forever, at least until he slid one hand along my body and began to stroke my pussy.

"You're wet," he said.

"I know."

That changed everything. Now, I wanted something else, something new, something more. Jules began to kiss his way down my body. He didn't leave any part untouched. If his mouth was caressing my nipples—one, then the other—then his hands were busy stroking and fondling every inch of my skin. I felt beloved, admired, adored.

And still I wanted more.

Greedy. That's what I was. Jules didn't seem to mind.

Finally he slid between my legs and parted my pussy lips. "Oh, God." I sighed, unable to keep quiet.

"Go on," he said, "make noise. Let it out. When I want you quiet, I'll use a gag."

I hadn't gone there mentally before. A gag. A ball gag? A leather strip? Would I have to make another trip to the sex toy store? Maybe. But I had the feeling I wouldn't have to go there alone. I imagined what the tattooed, wise-ass clerk would think if I walked into the place with Jules at my side, and then I fell back into reality as he started to lick my clit. For once reality was better than my fantasies. Jules knew exactly

how to work me. He seemed to understand how sensitive I was, and he began slowly. But he didn't stay slow for long.

"You like that?"

I looked down at him. His lips were glossy with my own juices. That realization brought a fresh tremor of excitement throughout me, and I bucked on the bed as a way of answering. Jules was having none of that. "Answer me when I ask you a question," he murmured.

"Yes," I told him. "Yes, I like that."

He made sensuous circles with the point of his tongue. Then, "Tell me. Tell me what you like."

I couldn't believe it. He actually wanted me to speak at a moment like this?

"Tell me, Kate."

"Everything," I said, hoping that would satisfy him, but knowing somehow that it wouldn't.

"Tell me exactly."

"What you're d-doing," I stammered. "The way you're making those circles."

Oh, it felt so good. He spiraled his tongue in circles that grew smaller and smaller until he was focused right on my clit. The pleasure and the pressure were intense. I would have pulled away, but I couldn't. Not handcuffed like that. Was that the point? I'd always thought of bondage as something you did in a dungeon—an atmosphere of darkness and chill pervading. But this was all heat and wet. I rattled the chain. He licked me harder.

Fuck, that felt good. As soon as I thought the words, I said them out loud. "Fuck, that feels good." My voice had become the blending of a moan and a sigh. Jules continued, bringing me higher and higher until I could almost taste the bliss of the impending climax.

Then he stopped.

I would have done anything, said anything, promised anything for him to continue. But he backed off the bed and went to his desk. He returned with a stack of white paper squares, paper I recognized, napkins I'd drawn on. He showed me the pictures, one by one, and I felt my cheeks burn. Now I did look away. Jules's tone made me turn back to him.

"You told me what you wanted," he said, "without ever saying a word."

"But why...?" I was in that hazy state of almost coming, yet I still needed to ask. "Why?"

"I told you before. If I'd just asked you out, you'd have been nervous and jittery. Unsure. You might have run away when I told you the things I hoped to do to you. Instead you came looking. You came to me."

"Where'd you get the napkins?"

"Dan."

I thought about my mercenary coworker. Before I could ask the next question, Jules said, "A dollar a napkin. He's been saving them for me."

He stripped off his own clothes and then crawled back on the mattress. We were surrounded by my pictures, drawings of people fucking, of couples overlapping, of handcuffs and blindfolds and toys. There was him. There was me.

Jules moved up my body and parted my legs. I could not wait for him to thrust inside me. My whole being was poised on the edge of that precipice. Was he going to tease me some more? Make me beg? Demand I tell him exactly what was running through my mind? Thankfully, no. He slid the head of his cock inside me, and I sighed and relaxed. Oh, this was sweetness. This was heaven and light. And then he started to move, pounding into me, thrusting hard. I had never felt anything like this. I was captured by the cuffs, but my body could still respond, my hips raised to meet his, my thighs spread apart. He used one hand to touch me, running his palm over my ribs, over the flat of my belly, then down to my pussy.

"Oh, yes," I hissed. "Just like that."

Lust bloomed bright within me.

As he fucked me, he stroked my clit, light and easy at first, then rougher as the passion built between us. I shut my eyes tight, but he said, "No, Kate, look at me." And then, "Please, Kate. For me." Surprising me because he sounded almost as if he were the one begging.

I opened my eyes. I stared at him.

We were connected, bound together somehow, even as I was the one bound down. The handcuffs rattled as he thrust inside of me, reminding me with every beat that I was his captive. And yet somehow, somehow, I felt as if we'd set each other free.

How neatly our bodies fit together. I'd never paused to wonder, to worry, whether we'd be compatible. If his parts would interlock with my parts. Thankfully they did. Perfectly. His cock seemed made for my body. Each time he drove forward, I felt my muscles contract, as if wanting to hold him to me forever. My hands were useless, but I possessed plenty of other powers. My legs around his body, pulled him to me.

Jules used his thumb right against my clit as he fucked me, finding a rhythm that made sense—the rhythm of my blood, of my heart, or maybe of our hearts beating together. We were in complete sync. He worked me steadily, and I kept our connection solid, gazing into his deep blue eyes—the color of cobalt, rich and dark. Even as I wanted to hide, even as the pleasure became almost insurmountable, I kept staring into his eyes. Seeing him. Really seeing him. How was he doing this? How did he know?

"I'm going to…" I gasped, teetering right on the cusp.

"Yes, yes," he said. "Come for me, Kate. Come *with* me."

The climax was different from any I'd ever had. Better. Beautiful. I felt electrified, as if every single part of my body was coming at the same time, as if I were all lit up with fairy lights. Jules bucked hard inside me, fucking me so hard I felt the bed shake. Then he stilled, his strong arms coming tight around my body, his cheek pressed to my cheek.

"I found you," he said. "You showed me the keyholes. I had the key."

I realized he was right. He'd played me.

And we'd won.

★ ★ ★ ★ ★

GOING DOWN
SASKIA WALKER

"Just as well I like a good challenge," I murmured to myself as I assessed the antique elevator shaft in my new abode. The ostentatious wrought–iron affair was the most complicated contraption I'd ever seen.

When I'd arrived at the apartment block the evening before I'd used the stairs, allowing the concierge to take my luggage in the elevator. I wanted to get my bearings, and as I climbed the stairs to the fourth floor I took in the elegance of the beautiful building, a nineteenth-century block in the 15th arrondissement of Paris. I'd been allocated a small apartment there for my six-month stint working in the city.

The elevator ran up the center of the building. The much more solid–looking marble staircase wound around it, and I'd peered in at the elevator shaft as I worked my way up to the fourth floor. Although daunting, it was a beautiful thing, all black metal and designed in the Art Nouveau style. The frenzy of decorative metalwork did not distract me from the fact that the floor appeared to be scarcely more than a metal grid and one could see the cables and the whole shaft from inside and out.

This morning I had my smartest outfit and heels on and I figured I'd better try it out. The question was how to operate it. I leaned into the metal gates and peered down the shaft. The elevator was stationary, two floors below.

"Going down?"

I jolted upright, startled to find I was no longer alone.

Turning on my heels I faced the man who had spoken.

I don't know what surprised me the most, that he had approached me without me realizing, or that he knew I was English and had spoken to me in my own language. He was obviously French.

French and gorgeous.

Dressed entirely in black—open-neck shirt and jeans, with a tailored leather jacket—he observed me with blue eyes that contrasted starkly with his swarthy skin. His black hair was cropped close, the square line of his jaw, angled cheekbones and strong forehead giving him a distinctive look. Even though I wore my highest heels, he towered over me. He had to be a neighbor. Perhaps he'd been on his way down the stairs when he'd caught sight of me. I straightened my skirt, aware that I'd probably just given him an eyeful as I peered down the shaft.

He gestured at the elevator gates. "It bothers you, the cage?"

The cage. What an intriguing moniker, and so appropriate. "Not at all," I fibbed. "I think it's beautiful, I just wasn't quite sure how to operate it."

"Allow me to demonstrate."

He rested his hand against my back briefly, encouraging me. The momentary contact made me sizzle. He pressed the call button. It was round, ivory and encased in gleaming brass. The elevator cable tightened with a loud creak, then the mechanism whirred into action and the cage loomed up from below.

"Some of the tenants in this building won't use it, but it is quite safe and an object of some beauty." The seductive allure in his voice had my attention well and truly hooked.

"Absolutely, it's a work of art in itself."

There was an approving expression in his eyes.

Once the elevator shunted into position, he unlatched the gates, internal and external, and rolled them apart. I stepped into the cage, as he called it, and he closed the gates behind us. The shunting of metal and wheels, and the resolute sound of the internal latch did make it feel cagelike, and yet light shone through here and there beneath our feet. He pressed the button for the ground floor and the elevator jolted into action. Adrenaline pumped through my veins and I staggered slightly on my heels.

My companion turned to face me and his mouth moved in sensual appreciation as his gaze made a slow circuit of my body. I felt stripped to the bone. I'd never felt such intense scrutiny. It wasn't staring, exactly. It was as if he could gain the measure of me by looking at me that way. He stood with one hand around a decorative metal coil, the other rested on his hip. His posture was so self-assured, appearing languid but as if he could pounce at any moment. What was more unnerving, the way he made me feel, or the fact I could see the elevator shaft between the metal fretwork beneath my feet? As we descended I felt as if I was on a dangerous precipice, in every way.

When his gaze returned to meet mine, his mouth lifted at the corners. Had I met with his approval? Moving my laptop case from one hand to the other, I tried not to feel quite so self-aware. It was hard not to, and my outfit—which had seemed businesslike and professional—now seemed far too tight-fitting and alluring. It was the way he admired the curve of my body at breast and hips that made me feel that way. Almost as if I'd been touched. What would it be like, I wondered, to really be touched by him? The man exuded sex appeal. *Get a grip,* I told myself, embarrassed. I'd only been with the man a few seconds, and now my face was growing hot and I was in danger of making a fool of myself. The liberation of being in a strange, exciting city, perhaps. Or maybe it was all down to my companion.

"Is it the original elevator?" I asked, in an effort to break the tension I felt building inside me.

"Yes, it was built in 1899. Apparently it was almost ripped out in the 1970s. There was talk of replacing it with a modern box, but luckily it did not go ahead. It would have been a tragedy to lose it."

A man who appreciated the fine things in life. I wondered what else there was to discover about my charming neighbor. Despite the fact I worked with diplomats and government officials, it was rare that I met someone quite so intriguing.

When the elevator came to a halt on the ground floor, he put his hand on the latch but paused. He was close to me, dangerously close. I could smell his cologne, sharp and musky, and it invaded my senses, making me ache for contact.

"You live underneath me," he stated.

Underneath him. Why did that make me think of sex? Because he was so damn sexy.

"If I play my music too loud," he continued, "you must please inform me." He opened the gates.

I recalled hearing the faint strains of classical music the night before as I fell asleep, but it hadn't bothered me—quite the contrary. So, it had come from his apartment. "I liked what I heard last night," I responded as I stepped out into the reception area.

"I'm glad to hear it. I'm a producer. I work in a studio in the daytime but sometimes I bring samples home to listen to in a different environment." He closed the gates securely behind us. "The gates must be closed properly, or it will not be able to collect anyone else who calls it."

We walked across the checkerboard-tiled hallway together, heading for the glass entrance doors.

"So, will you choose to enter *La Cage* again?"

A smile hovered around his handsome mouth, and his eyes glinted. That sounded like a loaded question. He knew how it came across, I was sure of it. Anticipation built at my center, my blood rushing in my veins. "Oh, yes, I enjoyed the ride immensely. Thank you."

I met his gaze, my smile lingering. I wanted him to know I was interested. I was single and in Paris, of course I'd thought about the possibility of meeting new people. Mostly I thought the opportunity would come my way through my job.

As we left the building the concierge saluted us from his reception post, a polished-oak-and-glass office at one side of the hallway.

"May I offer you a drive to your workplace?" My companion nodded at a sleek black Mercedes parked on the opposite side of the street.

"Thank you, but a colleague is meeting me at the métro station." Would I have accepted if I'd been able to? Of course I would. Looking up into his sharp blue eyes I wondered what that sensuous mouth would feel like covering mine, and I couldn't deny it.

"*Au revoir,* Jennifer."

My breath caught. Warning signals sounded in my mind. "How did you know my name?"

"I am your landlord, as well as your neighbor." He offered his hand. "Armand Lazare."

The strength of his handshake made me feel as if it was holding me up. Or maybe it was because my legs turned weak under me when he touched me. Then he took my hand to

his lips, and kissed the back of it. When he released me, I had
to reach out for the marble pillar at the bottom of the steps
to steady myself. My stay in Paris had launched in the most
delectable way.

"Au revoir," I whispered as I watched him dart across the
road toward his car. I couldn't help admiring the view. His tall
frame was limber and fit, broad at the shoulder and narrow
at the hips. Gathering myself as quickly as I could, I headed
off toward the métro station before he could look back and
see my gawking.

The encounter kept flitting through my mind over the
course of that day, my moments in *La Cage* with my upstairs
neighbor haunting me in the most intimate way—keeping me
simmering and alert.

That night as I lay in my bed listening to the faint strains of
his music, I stroked my body to a delicious peak as I thought
about him. The underlying rock beat to the classical score
seemed to get under my skin, fueling my lascivious thoughts. I
saw myself in the cage, back to the metal struts, with his hands
on me. *Going down?* The way he'd said that made me picture
myself on my knees in *La Cage,* my hands on his belt, opening it while he stared at me with those intense eyes. When
he'd spoken to me, before he let me free from the cage, he'd
been so close I could smell his cologne. I wanted him closer
still. I stared up at the ceiling, imagining him over me in a
different way, naked and eager and thrusting.

In time to the music, I ran my fingers back and forth over
my swollen clit, following the rhythm of the music, letting
my fantasies run wild, letting Armand Lazare fill my senses
until I found my release.

The following morning Armand ran down the steps as I
locked my door.

"Good morning, Jennie."

"*Bonjour,* Armand." Was it obvious that I was grinning because we had coincided again? I didn't care.

He gestured at the elevator. "Shall we?"

As he latched the doors closed and turned to face me I took a deep breath and savored the feeling of being alone with him in that confined space. Although he did not move, he seemed always to be prowling. It was his nature, I realized.

We began our slow descent.

"Are you enjoying your work at the embassy?"

His question leveled me, momentarily. He knew what I did. The embassy probably had to tell him who was moving into the apartment they'd rented. I imagined what they might have said—single female, conference and events organizer. Was he single? I hadn't seen him with anyone, but that didn't prove a thing.

"It's going well, thank you. I'm settling in and finding my way around. Their elevator is not as beautiful as yours, though."

I wanted to talk about him, not me. Was I being obvious?

"There aren't many quite so beautiful." He stroked one of the metal struts as he spoke, and the action did bad things to me, making the heat between my thighs build, fast.

"I heard your music last night, while I was in bed. It was beautiful."

He inclined his head, accepting the compliment gracefully. Humor lit his eyes. I felt as if he knew what I'd done while listening to that music. Why did I think that? Because I wanted him to know? Something about the man made me feel decadent and wanton. I wanted the space between us to disappear and for him to touch me.

"Do you live alone?" I asked.

"Yes." No hesitation.

I nodded. His gaze held mine. We were circling each other,

the mutual interest overtly reciprocated. When the elevator jolted to a halt I gasped aloud. I'd been taken unawares, my attention fixed on him as it was. He stepped over to me and steadied me with one hand beneath my elbow.

"Thank you," I whispered breathlessly.

There was some kind of commotion in the reception, a delivery.

"May I offer you a drive?" he asked, before he even broke contact with me.

Once again I had to refuse. My colleague was determined to guide me through the métro for the rest of that week.

By Monday, however, I wanted to be able to say yes.

The following day was Friday, and as I left my apartment I figured I could ask Armand what I should do during my first weekend of free time in Paris.

Alas, there was no sign of him. I waited by my door, lingering while I put my keys into my shoulder bag. He did not appear. I checked my watch. It was a quarter to eight, exactly the same time I had left my apartment on the previous days.

I hovered expectantly by the elevator but he still didn't appear. Then I noticed that the elevator was there on my floor, as if it had been left there specifically for me. I shook the odd notion off and flicked the latch up, heaving the metal gates open. It was about time I tried it out for myself. In the evenings I'd jogged up the stairs to shake off the workday, but I didn't want to take on the stairs now.

The gates were heavier than I'd expected but once they got going the oiled wheels sped them on. Of course Armand was so much stronger than I, he made it look easy. As I locked the internal gate I realized I'd also missed the chance to ask his advice about my free time. Perhaps he'd gone away for the weekend. The thought made me realize just how much

I'd enjoyed meeting him. It was such a good start to the day, being confined in *La Cage* with my sexy landlord.

As the elevator made its slow descent I felt almost forlorn, not having seen him. Silly, really, but I couldn't help it. He was such a thrilling man to be around. Why was that? I wondered. His sexual magnetism, yes, but there was something else. As I stood in the metal cage, alone, it occurred to me that it was his air of utter self-control. He was a confident man, subtly commanding, too.

A shiver ran through me; a shiver of arousal. Would he be like that as a lover?

Yes, I just knew it. He'd be masterful.

I reached for a metal strut and held on, my senses running amok, my body stimulated by wild thoughts alone. I glanced at the staircase as the elevator passed through its spiral, imagining him walking down the steps, looking in at me as he did so. Even though he wasn't there, his presence haunted me.

When I retuned to the apartments that evening I noticed that Armand's Mercedes was parked opposite, and the window was wound down. As I got closer my breath caught, because I saw his reflection in the wing mirror. He climbed out of the car, tossing a pair of sunglasses onto the seat before closing the door.

As I glanced his way he smiled and waved, then stepped across the road, joining me as I arrived at the steps up to the apartments. Had he been waiting, hoping to catch me? If it was a coincidence, it was uncanny.

"Good evening, fourth-floor neighbor," he said.

"Good evening, fifth-floor neighbor."

While we walked across the black-and-white checkered hall, side by side, it occurred to me that this was so much better than having seen him this morning, and I could ask him about the weekend after all.

"Shall we climb into *La Cage* together?"

Was it just his delicious French accent that made that sound so damn sexy, or did he mean it to sound like an overture to something entirely different than riding in the elevator with him? The suggestive undertow in his statements kept me on edge whenever we spent those precious few minutes together.

I nodded. "Although I'll have you know I managed it alone."

He paused before he closed the gates. "You in the cage, alone. How beautiful you must have looked, like an exotic bird." His eyes burned with his intensity. "I'm sorry I did not catch sight of you."

I could only stare at him, startled as I was by his comment. He really did think of this as a beautiful cage, and I was in it. The slow metal clanking sound as he hauled the gates together seemed to catch my very nerve endings, stringing them out with tension.

He took his time, controlling the complicated contraption, as ever. When the doors were secured he put his hand to the fifth-floor button and pressed it. Then he rested back against the metal struts and folded his arms loosely across his chest. He looked at me, watchful as ever, if not more so.

He hadn't pressed the button for the fourth floor, my floor. Had he forgotten, or had he left me to do it on purpose, so that I'd have to reach over to his side of the space? He didn't seem the sort of person to forget, but maybe he had something else on his mind? My heart raced.

The cable mechanism whirred and after the longest moment, jolted into action. The elevator began its slow ascent. Still he didn't press the button. The only one lit up was for his floor. If he'd just forgotten, I'd look a twit when we shot past my floor.

The tension escalated.

"Oh," I said, as if I'd just remembered. I reached over, but before I could press the button his hand covered it, stopping me.

"I thought you might like to come up to my apartment, share a bottle of wine and listen to some of the music you liked." He kept his hand over the button. The look in his eyes was so suggestive that there was no mistaking his intention. This wasn't just a casual neighborly invite.

So much for asking for his advice about what to do with my spare time. He'd derailed me, but onto a much faster track. My hand dropped to my side. I nodded. "I'd like that."

The way he had taken charge aroused me immensely.

We rode the rest of the way in silence. That prowling aura surrounded him again. Expectation built steadily inside me.

"Yours is the only apartment up here?" I asked as we stepped onto the landing. There was only one door. It bore no number or name, unlike all the others in the block.

"Yes. The building belonged to my grandmother and when I inherited it I added this space, to make the most of the view, and the light."

As soon as he unlocked the door I saw what he meant. Despite the fact we were in a long hallway, a glass wall at the far end filled the space with amber light as the sun lowered over the city skyline.

"Come in, please."

I hadn't realized that I'd hesitated by the door, but I had. Nerves gathered in my belly. I'd stepped into his cage, and now I was going into his lair. I wanted to do it, but fear of the unknown had me in its grip.

When he led me into the lounge I found myself mesmerized by the massive space, and the view. Once again, tinted ceiling-to-floor glass gave way to a superb view across the rooftops of the city. Stepping through the room—which was furnished with black lacquered cabinets and low leather sofas—I put my laptop case and shoulder bag down and gazed out at the sight.

It was only when I heard the chink of glasses in the background I realized that he'd been busy. I heard wine sloshing into glasses, and then he switched on the stereo. Fusion music filtered up all around me, orchestral but with a samba beat. I turned back to him, ready to comment on the amazing view, but my words slipped away into nothing as I caught sight of the massive framed photographic print on the wall.

"Wow." My eyebrows lifted. Frozen to the spot, I stared at the blatantly sexual image. It depicted a naked woman, starkly lit so that her body faded into darkness on one side. She was tethered by rope from above. The rope twined around her wrists, then back and forth across her torso, waist and hips. The way the rope was arranged seemed to emphasize her bared breasts and shaved pussy. She stared out of the image with fiery, accusing eyes. Thick, blunt-cut, bleached hair gave her a punky look

Armand watched on, as if waiting for me to say something. He'd removed his jacket. "Shibari, do you know it?"

I shook my head.

"It is the art of sensual rope work. Does it offend you?"

There was humor in his eyes.

He knew I wasn't offended. He knew exactly what I was. Horny, and getting hornier by the moment. It was as if he'd led me in here and stood me in front of this picture to get a reaction out of me, and he certainly had. Between my thighs I was hot and damp, my body bristling with uncertainty and expectation. I thought we were going to sip wine, chat and listen to the music, some kind of slow lead-in. Instead I felt confronted—raw and edgy because I'd been thrust into a situation that both aroused and unnerved me.

When I didn't speak, he stepped closer to me. He put his finger under my chin and lifted my face, staring into my eyes as if examining my soul.

I swallowed, willing myself to act appropriately. "Is it your girlfriend?"

Was it an impertinent question? Maybe, but I didn't think so until it was out. I'd exposed my concern about territory and what was going on here.

"I like your directness, Jennie," he replied.

My directness was more blundering than intentional, but I wasn't about to tell him that.

"It's a friend," he continued. "We were lovers for a while, not anymore. She moved to the States. We shared the same interests, as you see." His gaze flickered to the image and back to me.

That was to the point. His interests included rope, and cages. I forced myself to look at the image again. Armand bound and displayed her that way. That much was obvious.

"It is art." His sensual mouth moved in a provocative smile.

It was art, yes. It was also blatantly kinky and erotic, but I wasn't going to be pedantic about it, not while he was touching me that way. Besides, the image thrilled and fascinated me.

Still he studied me, his fingers moving down the length of my throat. "Human nature intrigues me. We are greedy sometimes, we like to keep beautiful things as possessions, so that we can admire them, caged even."

He was so close I was sure he was about to kiss me.

"From the prettiest birds to rare, wild creatures...other people."

His knuckles moved around the curve of my breast, his touch all too vague and tantalizing through my clothing. "The urge to possess the thing we desire, even for a fleeting time, is great."

With his fingertips exploring me and his philosophical meandering about cages and possession, I was awash with desire. Over his shoulder, the blonde punk stared at me with those accusing eyes. I wanted to be displayed that way, naked and lewd and helpless—and so obviously his plaything. All the things he said to me about being caged, and the sound of the metal doors shunting together and apart as he handled them, filled my mind.

I thought he was going to kiss me, but although he looked at my lips, he didn't. Instead he asked me another question, one that I wasn't expecting.

"Why did you come up here, Jennie?" His tone was serious.

My heart raced erratically. "Because you invited me."

He shook his head, and his eyes bored into mine. "The real reason?"

Heat flared in my face. Unnerved by his serious tone, I squirmed, my weight shifting from left foot to right. I couldn't believe he was pushing me to say it aloud. The attraction had been there between us, but his sudden interrogation made me feel awkward and obvious.

"You are so beautiful when you blush." His expression softened. "The real reason you came up here is because there is curiosity between us, *n'est-ce pas?*"

"Yes, there is." It was hard to voice my thoughts so blatantly and so soon, but the rush I experienced having said it aloud was astonishing. It was liberating, and now that it was out I felt as if we'd been shunted up to the next level.

"Have you seen anything that surprised you? The photograph, perhaps?" He'd reached inside my jacket and was running the back of his knuckles over the buttons on my shirt, as if he was readying to undo them.

"It did surprise me."

"It has that effect, but she was a willing submissive, believe me."

I bet she was. My eyelids flickered down, because I was unable to meet his bold stare a moment longer. I could scarcely believe it. He was touching me, questioning me provocatively while we stood there in his black lacquered bachelor pad, with its bleached bondage queen looking on, making me feel as if I couldn't ever be as good as her. A willing submissive. I could see why. The man made me melt just by looking at me. His touch would have me in a puddle of lust at his feet. But I also felt horribly inadequate and gauche.

"Perhaps I should go." I turned away, breaking the contact.

Armand put his hand on my shoulder, halting me. With the other he reached around and stroked my torso from collarbone to waist. The brusque, demanding nature of his touch stole my breath away. My eyes closed. When I moaned aloud, he eased me back to him. My upper body rested against the wall of his chest.

"Do you really want to go now, Jennie?" His fingers moved inside the collar of my shirt, pushing it aside. His mouth was on my neck, then my collarbone, his kisses making me sizzle. "If you want to leave I'll let you go, but I don't think that's what you really want."

I could have stopped him then, he was making that obvious, but I didn't want to. His hips moved from side to side, slow and seductive, taking mine with them.

"No," I said, breathlessly. "I don't want to go, I'm just..." *Overwhelmed.*

It felt good, though, and I didn't want to be afraid to explore this. I wanted to know this masterful man who had shocked me several times over within the space of a few minutes.

With his hands locked on my shoulders, he turned me

around and his mouth covered mine. Finally. His kiss melted me. My lips gave and his tongue moved between them. He devoured me, his tongue tasting my lips before thrusting into the damp cave of my mouth. I clutched at his shirt. My center ached, my clit throbbing wildly.

"I wanted you the moment I saw you," he whispered as he drew back. His voice was husky. He removed my jacket as he spoke, then his fingers went to my hair, easing it free of the clips that held it up. As it fell to my shoulders he murmured something in French.

I nodded. "It was the same for me."

My words seemed to act like a trigger on him, because he cursed in French. His eyes turned dark and his hands moved to my skirt. Without further ado he tugged it up, handling it roughly, until it was bunched at my waist. With his hands around my bottom he lifted me, wrapping my legs around his hips. I was so astonished that I clung to him, arms twined around his neck. One of my shoes fell to the floor. A moment later the other followed. The position he had put me in splayed my pussy against his hard erection. Unable to stifle my response, I gripped his shoulders and rocked my hips, rubbing against the hard, bulky protrusion.

His jaw clenched. He carried me easily, walking over to the long dining table that ran down the far side of the massive lounge. Resting me down on it, he eased my upper body flat to the table with his hand against my chest. "I think that first we must fuck, then we can play."

My body arched on the table. *Overwhelmed.*

I covered my eyes with the back of my wrist, moaning aloud at his blatant statement. He was going to have me on his dining table, right now.

"Unbutton your shirt." He stared at my stocking tops and

his eyes flickered mischievously as if they were giving him ideas.

As I undid the buttons with trembling hands, he stripped off his own shirt and I had my first look at his body. I already knew from the way he'd lifted me so easily that he was strong, but his muscles were hard and defined, solid. He stared down at my groin and shook his head. "This must be done."

As soon as I got my shirt open, he bent to kiss me in the dip of my cleavage. My head rolled against the hard surface of the table. The way he took control made my pulse race and the damp heat between my thighs became sweltering. He tugged at the cups of my bra, pushing my breasts free of the fabric. He tongued one nipple, then the other, and the stiff points stung, making my hips squirm.

Armand lifted his head, put his hand between my thighs and cupped my pussy through my lace panties. Direct and demanding, it triggered a heightened need for release. The firm squeeze he gave me there at my pussy made me gasp aloud.

He trailed his fingers over my bare abdomen, which made me shiver. When I glanced down I saw a damp smudge on the front of the fabric. Pressing my lips together tightly, I moaned softly. Meanwhile Armand's eyebrows lowered, and his expression was brooding. When I glanced lower—and I couldn't help myself—I saw the bulge of his erection beneath the zipper on his jeans and my eyes flashed closed.

He ran his fingers beneath the band of my panties, then tugged at them, pulling them down. I wriggled my bottom and lifted it to assist. When I was entirely naked, I squeezed my thighs together, suddenly aware that he had only removed his shirt. I felt so exposed.

"Open your legs," he instructed.

The way he said it made something hot coil and flex deep in my womb.

"Show me." He reached into his pocket, pulled out a condom packet and put it on the table.

I wanted to see him rip it open and roll it on. I wanted his hard cock ready to be inside me. It was the urgent sense of need that made me braver. I parted my thighs a couple of inches, exposing myself to him.

It was enough. Armand acted on it. First he inserted his fingers between my thighs and stroked them up and down over the soft, sensitive skin there. I began to pant, my hips rolling against the hard surface of the table. Still he stroked me. When the muscles in my thighs began to relax, he lifted my stockinged feet and put them flat to the table, forcing me to plant them wide apart, exposing my pussy fully. The sound of my blood rushing thundered in my ears. For several long moments that and the music were the only sounds in the room. Armand stood between my open legs in silence, apparently admiring me while I was so thoroughly debauched and displayed.

"Beautiful." He stroked his fingers up and down my damp folds.

I cried out, the tantalizing touch like torture when he made contact with my swollen clit. My hips rocked again. I wanted to rub myself against his hand, desperate for release.

"Easy." He arrested my jaw in one strong hand, making me meet his gaze. "I'm going to prepare you now," he whispered, "then I will fuck you, and I will need to do it hard."

The statement left me speechless, but I didn't need to respond because he ducked down and dipped his tongue into the damp groove of my pussy, rolling it back and forth over my swollen clit. The rush, the relief, the pleasure—for a moment I couldn't catch my breath. Then the lap of his tongue forced me to pant aloud. He had his hands planted either side of my hips on the table, his shoulders gleaming while his mouth engulfed my swollen clit—eating me from his dining table as if I was a delicious meal and he was a starving man.

His cologne and the scent of his body danced through my senses, making me want him even more. His hands were now wrapped around my buttocks as he lifted me to his mouth. The muscles in his shoulders rippled. All the while his words repeated in my mind, his promise to fuck me hard making me wilder still. My breasts ached, the nipples needling with sensation. My clit felt unbearably tight and hot, but his rapid tongue movements were pushing me ever closer. Then he grazed my tender flesh with his teeth and the release barreled through me. He pushed his tongue inside me, collecting my copious juices.

I was still gasping for breath when I heard him rip open the condom packet. I glanced down in time to see him rolling it onto the length of his erection, which arched up from his hips. My sex, still in spasm, clutched in anticipation. A moment later he hauled my hips closer to the edge of the table, moving me bodily across the surface so that I was positioned right at the edge and my legs dangled free. Never had I been so thoroughly manhandled, and never had I felt so deliriously high on something that I might consider base and primal if I was asked to think about it for too long.

When I felt the blunt head of his cock pushing at my slippery opening, my fingers curled into my palms. I remembered his warning. I wasn't ready. I felt too vulnerable—too exposed and sensitive, with my sex awash and swollen. But Armand had warned me, and he moved into position quickly, thrusting the hard length of his cock into me in one swift maneuver, stretching me, filling me and possessing me to the core.

"Armand!"

The pressure of his crown against my center sent an aftershock through my entire body. My torso lifted from the table, my hands latching on to his shoulders.

He scarcely gave me a moment before he had me flat to the table again, my legs over his shoulders while he worked his length in and out of my sensitized sex, his hands on the table for purchase while he drove himself into me, relentlessly.

I was back at the precipice in moments, my groin alive with sensation.

The table was strong but shifted under us as he banged into me. His forehead gleamed, the depth and rhythm he maintained pushing us both closer. I could hear the slick pull of my wet pussy as he worked his cock in and out. My sex was sensitive to the point of being in pain, and yet it felt glorious. I was so close to coming again that my back arched and my fingernails bit into my palms.

Armand leaned closer still, bending my legs under him, his weight against my pussy. Again I flooded. The release was so great that I felt dizzy even though I was flat on my back, but the hard rod of his cock inside and the pressure of his body against my clit kept me there.

The muscles in his shoulders and neck stood out, his eyes closing.

His cock stiffened, stilled and jerked repeatedly. Another wave hit, my thighs shuddering as my every nerve ending was strung out with the raw pleasure of multiple orgasms brought on by this man.

He took me out to eat.

"You need sustenance," he said. "I will take good care of you, if you spend the weekend with me."

Sustenance for what? I wondered, remembering his comment about playing later. And now I was spending the weekend, not just the evening. Both fear and desire flared in my gut, making me tremble. I felt shell-shocked. He wasn't done with me yet. That certain knowledge was exhilarating. When we stepped out of the apartment block, the noise and lights of the city street seemed even more dazzling and exciting than they already were. I was high on the afterglow, and let him lead and guide me.

He took me to a small bistro two minutes' walk away from the apartments. It was simple, and busy. As if aware of my heightened senses, he asked for a secluded booth at the back. There he sat alongside me, closing me into a world of our own. He ordered for us both and fed me delicacies with his fingers, while I sat looking at him in awe, accepting whatever he gave me. A couple of hours in his company, not much longer, and he'd mastered me so thoroughly.

The claret he ordered was good, and it made my muscles relax. Was that his intention? "The woman in the photograph…"

"Yes." He sat back and studied me as I spoke.

"She was a girlfriend?"

"Yes." He put his head on one side. "It bothers you?"

"No." It did. Of course it did. What woman likes to see the gorgeous ex, even if this was only a one-night stand or a wild weekend or whatever it was. "I have no right, we're just…"

I looked away from our booth.

"Your hair is the color of honey," he said, drawing my attention back. He eased his finger through my thick mop, admiration shining in his eyes. When I met his gaze he shook his head. "You are what I want."

The simple statement did exactly what he meant it to.

It pushed away my doubts.

"I mean to enjoy you, thoroughly," he added. "If you are willing?"

The doubts had gone, but the nerves hadn't. Not completely. Taking a deep breath, I nodded.

"Strip for me," he said when we went back to his apartment. I glanced at the glass walls. "Can people see us?"

I'd been so caught up in the heat of the moment during our previous tryst that it hadn't even occurred to me. But now that we were back and he stood me deliberately at the center of the room, I felt very much on display. The lights were on and the city sky was dark above the rooftops.

"No. Only me."

My hands shook as I reached for the zipper on my skirt. I wanted to do it, but the concept of following a man's instructions regarding getting undressed was something I never thought I would ever do. It felt so good, though. At that moment I was under his command and loving it for as long as it lasted.

What did he intend to do with me? The question kept running back and forth through my mind, keeping me on edge and nervy. I took off my shirt. Kicking off my heels, I shuffled my skirt off, then ran my thumb under the band on my lace undies, pausing.

He lifted one eyebrow.

"Will you... Are you going to use the rope on me?"

"No." There was no hesitation in his voice. "Maybe another time," he added, and smiled indulgently. Perhaps it had pleased him that I was curious about it. "I have something else in mind for you, something that will perhaps help you overcome your shyness about displaying yourself to me."

My attention was locked.

"Do you trust me to take care of you? That is very important."

Instinct led my judgment. "Yes, yes, I do."

"I am only interested in pleasure.... Extreme pleasure, yes, but I don't wish to hurt you. If I do, you must say so."

I swallowed my nerves. "I understand."

He studied me a moment longer. "It is your submission, your pleasure at my hands, that pleases me. I need to push your boundaries, in order to test my own."

My thumb was still caught in the band of my panties, and my fingers plucked at the fabric restlessly. "What do you have in mind?"

My voice was scarcely above a whisper.

"You will find out, when you strip for me." Humor lit his expression, warming me right through.

I reached around and undid my bra, peeling it off. When I cast it aside, he gestured again at my panties.

He wanted me there in that room again. Naked. Why in here? I was about to find out.

When I shoved my underwear down the length of my legs and stepped out of the abandoned lace, he nodded. I went for my lace stocking top and rolled the stocking down my leg. When I changed to the other leg he strolled behind me and stroked his fingers along the underside of my exposed buttock. The brief, provocative touch sent my nerve endings crazy. It was hard to keep undressing, but I had to.

Once entirely naked, I dropped the second stocking and presented myself.

Armand opened a drawer in one of his cabinets, and lifted out a slender stainless-steel bar. Cuffs hung at either end of it. He held the slim metal bar out in front of me, his fist wrapped around it at the center point. "Offer me your wrists."

I did as instructed.

He did up the metal buckles that held the soft leather in place. I found my arms pushed apart by the object. I'd never seen anything like it and as I observed I realized I was now helpless. I couldn't move my hands unless he allowed me to.

When it was in place, he wrapped his fist around the middle between my hands, and lifted it, stretching my arms over my head. The movement was so sudden and so unexpected that I gasped aloud. My shoulders rolled and locked, my breasts lifting and then pushing together with the movement. Tension beaded down my spine.

He stared at me, then ran his free hand around my breasts.

My face heated. Unbearably self-conscious, I turned my head to one side.

"You flush so beautifully, because your skin is so pale."

I squirmed. No longer sure I could do this—even though I wanted to—I had to bite my tongue to stop from replying. Then his fingers locked on my uptilted nipple, and he fondled the stiff peak. Pain rang through me, delicious pain, like a heady intoxicant that made my groin heavy with longing. If I thought I'd been his plaything before, it had been nothing on this. He had complete control of me now. My head dropped back and I cried out.

His gaze drifted down my body and back up. "I intend to explore every part of you."

My skin was damp, everywhere, heat breaking out on the surface of my body. I lifted one foot, shifting my weight. I knew the look in my eyes was pleading, I meant it to be. "Please, Armand."

When I begged, he lowered his arm, tugged me right against him with the bar and kissed me. Hard. Each time I felt the thrust of his tongue in my mouth my center ached for him to thrust there, too. The heat between my thighs had built, and I could feel the sticky tracts of my juices marking my inner thighs. My heart soared, the rush of raw emotion I felt for the way he handled me entwined with the real physical desire I felt. Breaking the kiss, he led me with the bar, taking me to one corner of the room. There he lifted my arms above my head again, and latched the bar onto a hook that I had not previously noticed. I was at full stretch, my spine straight.

The room was his arena, his play den. The solid table, the cabinets and their contents, the hook. What else hadn't I noticed—what else was there to explore?

Armand stroked my body, taking full advantage of my helpless state to explore me. My skin was tingling wildly, everywhere, my nerve endings ragged. Then he lowered to a squat in front of me, ran his thumbs down my pussy, opening me up. Inside a heartbeat, his mouth had covered my clit. The metal restraint creaked when my body jerked. He stroked his tongue up and down over my clit. I was so sensitive from his earlier ministrations that I felt sure I would have pushed him away with my hands on his shoulders, had I been free. It was almost too much, and when his tongue rode back up, there was nothing I could do but submit.

"So sensitive! Armand...please..."

Back and forth his tongue went. It was as if he loved oral sex and couldn't get enough of me—either that or he wanted to drive me insane. My clit thrummed, and a wave of release hit me. I'd barely inhaled, and his fingers were thrusting into my sex. One of my legs lifted as I tried to pull away from the intense stimulation, my knee against the side of his head. When I glanced down I found him looking up at me with dark eyes, possessive eyes.

My legs shuddered. For a moment I hung limp in the restraint, allowing the hook to hold me up. I didn't care how I looked.

"Oh, yes, you're ready to offer yourself now."

Ready? Apparently he'd only just got started. How much more could I take? I'd never experienced such an intense barrage of stimulation, from pleasure to pain, desperation and embarrassment; it all hit me, tearing down my defenses and making me powerless and malleable in his hands.

He rose to his feet and held my waist. He kissed me and the pungent taste of my own arousal in his mouth made me aware of just how horny I was. How had this happened? I wondered vaguely as I let him possess me. Sex had never been like this before.

"The shame will soon be gone, all of it. Then you will only beg for the pleasure."

"Is that a threat or a promise?" I seriously wasn't sure. My current state was a combination of bliss, acute arousal and humiliation, the latter because his mouth was so heavy with my musk.

He gave a husky laugh. "A promise." He ran his thumb over my cheek. "Freedom from shame is a wonderful gift, you will know this soon."

Leaving me with that thought, he strolled off to his cabinet. When he came back he had a second slim bar in his hands.

What the hell was he going to do with that?

He unhooked me, lowering my arms. My shoulder ached, but it felt good, like a long workout or a sports massage.

Armand gestured at the floor. "On your hands and knees."

Swallowing my nerves, I lowered to my knees. The carpet was thick under my bare knees. I put my hands out to balance myself, moving awkwardly within the restraint.

I saw his shirt drop to the floor. Then he squatted in front of me, and lifted my chin with one finger. With a swift move he brought a glass to my lips. I looked into his eyes as I sipped gratefully at the cold water he offered.

"Enough?"

I nodded. He took the glass away. When he returned he'd

shed the rest of his clothing. My breath caught in my throat as I looked up at his magnificent body.

A moment later he stepped behind me and his hands enclosed my ankles, hauling them apart. I felt him move the cold metal under my feet. He moved my legs farther apart before he tied my ankles in place.

I muttered incoherently when I realized how exposed my rear end was, every part of it on display to him. Squirming—with my head hanging down and my hair obscuring my face—my body reacted, my sex tightening. When it did, moisture ran down between my folds, which only made my situation worse. I tried to move forward to gain my equilibrium, but the friction of the carpet on my knees made me realize just how useless my attempts were. I swayed, my breasts dangling lewdly.

"Please," I begged, desperate for him to take control of me and bring me release.

He walked around me, surveying the scene. At first I cared about how I must look, but then his gaze on me while I was so vulnerable and helpless made me burn up with longing, and I didn't care anymore. I thrust my pussy out between my open legs, lifting my hips in the air, needful and restless and apparently now shameless.

Armand whispered words of approval in French. I could scarcely breathe. When he circuited me again his cock was at full stretch, its crown gleaming. He seemed able to ignore it, while he took his time studying my body. Wasn't that what I had wished for, though, to be lewdly displayed just like the bondage queen in the photo? Well, she'd got off lightly. He'd pushed me in a different direction altogether. Confronting my shyness about my body, he'd put me in this position, arms and legs apart, every part of me exposed and vulnerable.

He paused in front of me and when I looked up at him,

curious, he rode his fist up and down his hard cock. His jaw was tight, his eyes narrowed. The tight muscles of his abs were standing out, his belly a hard rock of tension.

My mouth watered for a taste of him. "May I...may I taste you?"

His eyes glittered, his eyebrows drawn down as he concentrated. His only response was to direct his cock head to me. Rising up on my knees, I first rested my cheek against the hot surface of his shaft, moving my face against him adoringly. Then I licked him, eagerly absorbing the fecund taste of his cock. When I ran my tongue up and down the shaft, he growled in his throat. Taking the swollen head into my mouth, I closed my eyes and sucked, my tongue lapping around the head before I shifted and took as much length into my mouth as I could.

"Enough." He pulled free.

I felt his hand on my back, directing me to my former position, on hands and knees. I wavered, panting for breath, but lit up with the knowledge that he was going to mount me now. At my back, I heard him rip open a condom packet. All of it impacted on my senses, making me restless as an animal in my restraints, my body undulating, pussy pushed back and out expectantly.

"You want this?" He let me feel the weight of his cock against my hot niche.

"Please," I begged. "Desperate for you." I hung my head.

He entered me, giving me a couple of inches, then held back.

Tears smarted in my eyes.

"What do you need?"

"You," I whimpered, moving my hands uselessly within the restraints.

He gave me another inch. "What do you really want...? What is your most basic need at this moment?"

"But..."

"Say it, admit it."

"I need to come," I blurted. "But only because you put me in this state!" I shot that over my shoulder. I had to say it, to blame him, because it was true.

Armand laughed softly. He stroked me at the base of my spine, soothing me. I felt affection in his touch. Then he held my hips, and—mercifully—gave me his full length.

He drove into me with more caution than before, seemingly aware of how sensitive I would be, but once his cock was bedded deep within me his hands roved over my buttocks and he pulled them apart, his thumbs stroking over my exposed seam.

It drove me wild.

Earlier on I'd reflected that I'd never been handled this way. Now I realized I'd never been treated this way, forced to address my animal need for pleasure—and Armand was right. It did feel good, desperately good.

Armand was gentler with me. This time it was me who couldn't hold back—it was me who worked him. He stroked my body, caressing my spine while I took what I needed, driving back on to his hard shaft. He reached around and fondled my dangling breasts, then tugged on my nipples.

All the while I chased the prize, riding the long slick erection that he offered, working myself with the restraints to use it well. I wriggled and squirmed, my hips moving back and forth against him, mewling loudly as my sensitive flesh milked him off in rhythmic clutches.

"Oh, yes, Jennie, it's good, very good," he said, his cock jerking.

I'd made him come, and I'd reached the point of sheer

ecstasy. My sex clenched over and over. My body was free from decorum, unleashed, until finally it was a blur of sensation and nothing more.

I didn't leave Armand's apartment again that weekend. He told me I didn't need to because the weekend was "ours." He had food delivered, and he cooked for me. It was as if he was happy to keep me as his private plaything, and I was thrilled to be that. Paris could wait until another weekend.

He went to my apartment to collect my toiletries, refusing to let me fetch them myself. While he left me alone, he handcuffed me to the wrought-iron headboard of his bed. It should have felt wrong, but it didn't. The way he cherished me overruled any possibility of that. When he returned he claimed me back by kissing me, everywhere.

The weekend passed in a glorious haze of sensory overload.

On Monday morning, at seven, reality forced its way back in. I had forty-five minutes until I had to be on my way to the embassy. With regret I kissed him and climbed out of his bed, running around in my shirt and panties, barefoot, trying to find my belongings. I needed to get back to my own apartment and prepare for the working day ahead.

When I darted into the lounge, however, I was once again frozen to the spot.

My shoulder bag dropped from my hand as I stared at the blank place on the wall where the image of the blonde bondage queen had been. It was no longer there. I glanced around, but couldn't see it standing anywhere. Armand must have taken it down when I was asleep.

My heart fluttered. Why had he done that?

He followed me in a moment later, still heavy with sleep. He wore his nakedness with complete nonchalance, prowling over to me. He arrested me in a lazy but possessive embrace, covering my face with hungry kisses.

His large hands on my bottom pressed my hips to his, and I felt the bough of his erection against my belly.

"Armand, please. I must go and prepare for work."

"You will come back to me tonight?"

"If you want me to." I couldn't keep the smile from my face.

He returned it, then nodded his head back in the direction of the space on the wall where the photograph had been. "I need your help to select some new art."

He had taken it down for me. It was a significant gesture.

I laced my fingers around his neck, brimming with happiness, suddenly willing to let another few moments slide away in order to give this the attention it deserved.

"I'd love to," I responded, and then lifted my eyebrows. "Or perhaps we could make some art of our own…?"

Armand growled as he ducked to kiss my jaw.

Over his shoulder, I looked at the blank space on the wall and my mind ran wild with ideas. My six months in Paris promised to be a voyage of discovery, and with Armand as my master, I was ready and willing for every moment of it.

★ ★ ★ ★ ★

TAKING HER BOSS
ALEGRA VERDE

My boss, Bruce Davies, CEO of Davies and Birch Advertising, stood there in the doorway with his mouth open in surprise. I didn't say anything. I couldn't. Alex had me bent over my desk, my short black pencil skirt shoved up to my waist, my breasts spilling out of its matching jacket, nipples trailing against the desk blotter, and his big cock shoved so far up my cunt that I felt like singing opera. Alex was breathing hard behind me, a death grip on my hips. "Don't move," he barked as he increased his speed. My ass twitched against his groin as he filled me again. His shirttails tickled my lower back. "Oh, Glory." His voice was a harsh whisper as his cock grew and hardened inside me. I squirmed to get closer, feel more of him. "I can't stop, babe. I can't." I flexed my muscles, stroking his cock to let him know it was okay to keep going, that I wanted him to continue, that I was feeling him. His hands, slippery now, slid along my ass as he tried to maintain his grip. And then he was coming, his body jerking against my ass as he spewed his seed. I was glad I'd remembered to make him wear the condom. It felt like he had uncapped a fire hydrant and couldn't get the cover back on. Finally, he trembled a bit and went still, his hands coming to rest on my waist and lower back.

"When you're done here, Ms. James, I'd like to see you in my office," Mr. Davies said before he backed out of the doorway and pulled the door closed.

"Sorry about that," Alex said as he pulled out, tugged my skirt over my exposed ass, and set about repairing his clothing.

"Hey, what can you say?" I said, not just to soothe him, but because there wasn't anything to say. I'm Glory James, Junior Account Rep, but mostly I am, or was, assistant to Mr. Davies. I don't file or type his correspondence or anything like that. He has another assistant for those things. I handle the things he doesn't have time for like preliminary research, clients' backgrounds and sales or production figures that he needs right away, or tweak contracts before Legal finalizes them. Sometimes I pick a client up from the airport and make sure he or she is settled in, and occasionally I take them to dinner or for drinks when Mr. Davies has an emergency. That was the case with Alex here. Alex and his ex-wife design and manufacture shoes mostly, but they do fashion and have recently developed a line of furniture. They've been scouting ad agencies. That's where I come in. There's a pun in there somewhere, but fucking Alex was not intentional. I mean, it isn't in my job description. I just liked him. He's a big man who takes care of his body and he's smart, reads books, not just trade magazines and newspapers.

"Will you be okay?" he asked after we'd both straightened our clothes and exhausted the container of wet wipes I kept in my desk drawer. "Do you want me to talk to him?"

"No, I'm good," I said, smiling at him 'cause what the fuck. I've been working for Davies for two years with no complaint. I've always done everything he asked and he has continued to give me more responsibility. That must mean he likes the way

I do things. If he can't forgive this one indiscretion then he's in the wrong business. Besides, it's after hours, and the client is none the worse for wear.

Alex pulled me close, offering me comfort. He kissed the top of my head. "I don't think he will, but if he fires you, you can come work for me and I'll take my business elsewhere."

I leaned my face into the crisp baby-blue of his shirt, taking in his masculine scent and the heat that radiated from his chest.

"And don't let him bully you into doing anything you don't want to do." He pulled me back a bit from his chest so that he could see my face, and I could see the meaning in his eyes. I nodded.

"I'll wait here," he said, turning me toward the door.

"No," I said. "You go on back to the hotel. I'll call you later."

He stood there, unmoving.

"Really," I assured him, "I can handle this."

"Glory," he began.

"I got this, Alex, really," I said, and picked up the file we'd come up here for. "And take this with you. Read it over and tell me what you think. I'll call you. Tomorrow midmorning at the latest." I was shoving him and the folder out the door.

"I can wait, and you could come back to the hotel with me," he coaxed.

I laughed. "Thanks, but really, I need to deal with this and I need a minute. I *want* you to go, okay?" You have to be firm and clear with some guys. Alex is nice, but I wasn't looking for a relationship. You have to give him credit, though. He isn't like some of these jerks who get theirs then skitter off like the rats they are at the first sign of difficulty.

I stood on my tiptoes and pressed my lips against his. I could feel his soften and meld with mine. "It was good," I said against his lips, and it was, too, even though I didn't come.

That probably had more to do with being interrupted by Davies. "*You* are good," I said, and slid the tip of my tongue between his lips. He cupped my ass and squeezed.

"Now go," I said firmly, and pushed him out the door.

I watched for a minute to make sure he headed to the elevators and didn't detour to Davies's office. When I heard the ding of the elevator, I closed the door to my office and leaned against its hard surface to catch my breath and steel my nerves. Then I headed to the side door of my office, the one that led directly into Davies's.

I knocked once. "Come in." He voice was muffled by the closed door, but it was clear. Uncertain how these matters were usually handled, I stood in the doorway contemplating my next move. "Sit," he said and waved toward one of the three leather armchairs positioned in a half circle in front of his desk. I took the center one, seating myself directly in front of him as he sat behind his massive desk leaning forward, his elbows just at the edge supporting his weight. He studied me for a minute letting the silence speak as he clasped his hands together. One finger strayed from the steeple to toy with his lips.

"Alex Rodriquez?" he said, or was it a question.

"Sir?" Mine was a question.

"Why?"

"I like him." The bare truth. He nodded.

"Why here?"

"It just happened. We came back here for the prospectus. He didn't want to wait until tomorrow."

"Is he the only one?"

"Sir?" What was he asking?

"Of our clients?"

"Yes."

"I must say—" he leaned back in his chair "—I was surprised by your...actions."

I waited.

"Of course, I've always known that you were a very sexual person. Anyone can see that, but you've always been so...so... well behaved."

I couldn't help it. I laughed at that. *Well behaved,* where did that come from?

"No." He reddened a bit. "I mean, you've always been businesslike in your dealings with me."

What does one say to that? I nodded, and I'm sure my eyebrows rose and furrowed like they do sometimes when someone says something obvious or irritating.

"I mean, I've always found you appealing." His fingers were rubbing his chin thoughtfully like he does when we brainstorm about clients and contracts and plot the best strategies to lure and secure them.

Oh, no, I thought, *and I really liked this job.* I liked Davies. He was a good boss, good at what he did and he trusted me to do my job, no second-guessing. He seemed to know my strengths and made sure that I had input on the accounts that could benefit by them. Further, he kept his hands to himself. We'd been out drinking with clients many a late night and he'd never even allowed a hand to accidentally brush my breast, and if a client got too friendly, he never failed to divert the client's attention, and on one memorable occasion let the client know in bold words that my favors were not on the menu. I respected Bruce Davies. The little girl in me wanted to cover her ears and click her heels.

"And you're quite capable," he went on.

Of what, I wanted to ask.

"I like a capable woman," he said.

My eyebrows did their thing. *Two years,* I was thinking,

two years of prepping, planning and hard work. I thought that I could make a home here, that I could grow. I sat up and scooted to the edge of the chair, preparing to leave. I'm good at my job; I do not have to fuck the boss or anyone else to keep a job.

He tensed. "Wait," he said, holding a hand out as if he could hold me in place with the gesture.

"Glory, I'm not making any demands on you. We can continue on as we have been. It's just that when I saw you with Rodriquez..."

"You figured I was fair game," I finished for him.

"No," he said, and looked directly at me, as if he wanted me to see the truth, "I realized how much I wanted you."

The baldness of his statement stopped me for a moment.

"Do you have someone special?" he asked.

I shook my head. It was difficult to look at him because his eyes were searing into me.

"Me, neither," he said. "Since the divorce, there has been no one I can trust. And without trust, I'd rather go without."

I looked at him now, trying to understand.

"I like to be told what to do," he said simply.

I nodded as though I understood, but I didn't really, not entirely. I was seeing another side of this man, a side that he rarely shared with others. He sat there in his dark, immaculately tailored suit, the tie a little loose, but still in place. His hair was thinning slightly, but his close cut made no excuses and gave the impression that he was solid, reliable. The cut was flattering because its sparseness gave full reign to his sharp cheekbones and gray eyes. At fortysomething to my twenty-seven, he could have been...well, at least an uncle, but there was still a draw there. I could feel the pull. He was telling me that he needed me, but he didn't move. He sat and waited silently for me to issue a verdict.

"I'll think about it," I said finally.

He nodded, his finger rubbing his lower lip as he studied me.

I stood up.

"Glory," he said my name softly, "only if you want to. No strings."

"See you tomorrow," I said as I made my way back through the door to my office.

After a few days, everything went back to normal, more or less. Alex signed with us. He called a couple of times and I went out with him, usually to dinner with dessert in his hotel room, but I was glad when he went home. Nice guy, but I knew he had a girlfriend back home in Madison, Wisconsin, and I wasn't interested in taking her place. Mr. Davies was the same. He didn't look at me strangely and he didn't slack up on the work. He had a smile for me when I greeted him in the morning, and treated me with the usual courtesy when we lunched with a client or if we were having a bite alone in his office while discussing a campaign. That's why I was so surprised when one evening about three weeks later, I turned to see him standing in the doorway that connected our offices. For one, he never used that entrance, and for another, he looked uncertain, almost pained.

"Did you think about it, Glory?" he asked.

I wanted to say, "What?" A part of me wanted to pretend I didn't know what he was talking about, because things had been going along so nicely.

"Yes," I said because he wanted me to, and I had been thinking about it. I had been thinking more about what he might want. I got that he wanted me to make demands, *to tell him what to do,* but I was afraid of how far it could go. How-

ever, if I were being truthful with myself, I'd have to admit
the prospect was both frightening and alluring.

"What would you do?" I asked.

"Anything," he said. His voice was a whisper, confiding.

"What are your limits?" I needed more information.

He thought a moment. "I won't hurt anyone. I wouldn't
hurt you." He stopped, and then added, "You may...hurt me,
punish me if I misbehave."

I nodded.

"It must be between us," he reminded me.

"I know," I said. "You can trust me, Bruce."

He smiled, a brilliant one, one that I had never seen before.

I went to the door of my office and turned the lock. He
waited, hands at his sides, loose.

"What I'd like," I said as I stood behind my desk and eased
my bottom onto the smooth surface of the blotter, "is you, on
your knees before me."

He moved woodenly at first. "Close the door," I said as he
neared. "Lock it," I ordered. He did as he was told and then
he was kneeling before me, still in his jacket and tie. A hot
hand grazed my thigh, a nose pressed close to my sex, rubbed
against the moisture on my panties.

"No," I said. "Not yet."

He stopped and sat back on his knees.

"Remove my panties."

His hands slid under my skirt, up my thighs, and pulled
at the elastic band, drawing the bit of silk along my legs and
off. Then he sat back on his legs, head bowed, my panties
scrunched up in his hands.

"I want your mouth on me, your tongue sliding over my
clitoris, slipping between the lips of my sex," I said as I sat
back on the desk.

He, with the utmost care and gentleness, pushed my skirt

farther up around my hips, rested my legs on his shoulders, and pressed his mouth to my center. I was glad that I had gotten a wax this morning, and that Bruce was faced with a thin, pleasing line rather than the sometimes-unruly bush.

Pressing his nose through the slit, he held it there, breathing in as though it truly was a rose, all soft petals and sweet scent. And then he lapped along the slit, nipped, bit and nuzzled until I was pulling his hair and pushing at his forehead. But he kept at it until I was trembling, batting myself against his mouth, and biting my lip to keep from keening.

He pressed his face into my inner thigh, and then held his cheek there until the trembling subsided. "May I…"

"No," I said.

"I just want to feel you."

"No." I don't know where it came from, but I suddenly needed to get away. I lifted my leg over his head and slid off the desk. "I have to go." I fixed my skirt, picked up my purse, and without another word, I walked around him. He fell back onto his bottom, sending my chair skating back against the wall. He was looking down at his hands and the bit of pink silk that they held as I walked through the door.

The next morning, it was as though nothing had happened between us. There was a general staff meeting with breakfast in the boardroom. Trays of hot buttered croissants, iced Danish, spiced as well as regular coffee, cranberry and orange juice, and slices of mango, pineapple, melon and fat strawberries.

"Somebody's upgraded the fare," one of the account execs said to a colleague as he loaded his plate. "Where'd they bury the doughnuts and bagels?" The statement elicited a burst of chuckles from the growing crowd.

"You lot deserve the upgrade," Bruce said as he came into

the room. "Two new clients, and the Blake cereal campaign is performing well in the test markets."

He cast me a generic smile, the same one he'd given everyone else in the room. I had expected him to be angry or sullen, but he wasn't. He was jovial, spirited even as he took his seat at the head of the table. I sat in a corner to his right, nibbling at a piece of melon and sipping coffee. I figured it was a good place because I was nearby if he needed me, but out of his immediate vision. The table filled quickly followed by the seats that lined the walls. By the time the graphics guys made it up from the basement, there was standing room only and the fruit was running thin. They stocked up on coffee, rolls, iced Danish, and found spaces to lean on the wall.

Davies was in rare form. He listened intently to reports, offered suggestions and praise where warranted, solved disputes with the Wisdom of Solomon and delivered quips like a seasoned stand-up comic. Birch, who sat at the other end of the table, chimed in only occasionally. He, too, recognized the high that Davies was on and was more than willing to take full advantage of it. Everyone filed out of the meeting full and happy, and when they were all nearly gone, he turned to me with a beatific smile before gathering his notepad and file folder and following the crowd.

I stood there stunned for a full five minutes before I found my way back to my office. Our little interlude the night before had pleased him. I had to think what to do with this revelation. I had to think whether or not I would proceed. It was clear that he saw it as a beginning, but I wasn't sure it was something I could do or even wanted to do. I got my purse and told Claire, Davies's assistant cum secretary, that I wasn't feeling well and was going home for the afternoon.

Davies called, but I didn't answer the phone so he left a message on my machine expressing his concern and wishing me well. The next morning I'd made up my mind. I handed Bruce a key card to a room I'd rented at a Super 8 off I-75 south. It was clean and catered to families on road trips to Six Flags or Disneyland. I'd stayed there the night before and watched the mothers sit under umbrella-covered tables and sip soda from cans while their kids splashed around in the tiny kidney-shaped pool just off the parking lot. The fathers spent their time loading and unloading SUVs and Volvo station wagons.

He held the key in the palm of his hand as though he wasn't sure what it was. The hooded look he cast me seemed uncertain for a moment, but it disappeared quickly and turned blank. I told him to go there at nine, to shower well and wear a polo shirt, jeans and sandals, nothing else. He nodded and tucked the key into an inside pocket. He asked no questions and we continued our day as though we hadn't spoken of the coming evening. We sat through a brainstorming session with the team assigned to Alex's new furniture line, had lunch with a potential client, met with another client who was less than pleased with the cost of production for a series of thirty-second spots. The day ended just before five after the two of us met with Claire to update our schedules and give Claire instructions regarding letters and contracts that needed to be generated. Through all of this, he never touched me or gave me a look that was out of the ordinary. I followed his lead, but I must admit that I was a bit nervous and suffered from inattentiveness from time to time, but no one seemed to notice.

When I heard the door click and then open, I was finishing up in the bathroom. "Glory," he called in an almost whisper.

"Here," I replied. "Take a seat on the bed. I'm almost done." I heard the door close, the click of the security lock, followed by the soft swish of the mattress as he sat down. I'd slipped on the thigh-high stockings, the black thong and the thigh-length black silk robe with the pink dragon embroidered on the back. I'd already done my eyes, shading and lining them with dark colors, and brushed out my hair so that it was full and wild. I finished the makeup bit with a smudge of blush, lipstick and a smear of rouge on my nipples as an afterthought. Okay. I was ready. All I needed now was courage. He could wait. The wait would be good for him. I slipped my hand deep into my thong and stroked my clitoris and the lips of my vagina until I was moist. The blood rushed into the little nub causing it to jut out between the lips. I held on to the rim of the washbasin to steady my legs. A flush stained my face and my eyes were dark and bright. I moistened my lips with my tongue and smiled at the hot girl in the mirror. Tugging my thong back into place, I stood up, dabbed a quick towel under my breasts to remove any dampness and decided that I was ready to play.

I opened the door and stood in the tiny space between the closet and the beds. His eyes had apparently been trained on that spot. My rouged breasts and the flat of stomach that ended where the slim black triangle began burned and tingled as his eyes, like fingers, trailed over them. At first, it was difficult not to cover the expanse of exposed skin, to tug the black silk kimono closed, to hide from the hunger in his eyes, but it was exciting, too. It was exciting to let his eyes scorch my skin, to know that he wanted me like that, to see the rawness of it in his face, the way he held his lips.

I walked to him and stood in front of him, a hairbreadth from his lips, letting him smell me and feel my heat. When he closed his eyes in order to master his control, I moved forward a notch and rubbed my nipples across his lips. His lips and tongue sought my nipples like a new, still-blind puppy sucking and lapping, but his hands did not touch me. I let him suckle for a while and then I pulled away.

"I want you to make me come with your mouth and your hands," I said as I moved over to the other bed and sat down across from him. Arms straight, I leaned back and opened my legs. In seconds, he was kneeling between them, his mouth on my breasts again making the nipples long and hard and wet, his hands gripping and massaging my ass. He slipped the thong down my thighs and bent to run his tongue down the slight arrow of hair there. I opened wider to him and he began to rasp his tongue against the lips of my pussy as his fingers continued to tug and coax my nipples. I squirmed beneath his assault and his tongue slipped deeper into the moist lips and bumped into the jutting nub. A jolt passed through my body and my legs closed around his head. He rasped his tongue over the nub, nudging it back and forth, as he inserted two wide fingers into my already dripping passage. His fingers created a rhythm counterpoint to his tongue, and my body began trembling, jerking as I came, but he held me down with his mouth, and he continued to kiss and suck at the continuously tingling lips of my pussy. I had to push his head away before I screamed and startled the families on the other side of the walls. I pushed at his head, but he resisted.

"I want..." he began as he clutched at my thighs. "May I...?" he was asking, his cheek to my inner thigh as though he was afraid to look up at me.

"No," I said, and pushed hard, then harder. "No," I said louder, and kneed him in the chest. He fell back and landed sprawled on the carpet.

"No," I said as I pulled my thong back on and stood. "Don't touch me unless I give you permission," I reprimanded as I ground a spiked heel into his jean-clad thigh. Something in me wanted to laugh and say "bad dog" and smack him with a newspaper, but I didn't have a newspaper and I was glad because I was afraid that it would be too much and that I'd end up breaking character.

"Get up," I instructed. "Sit on the bed."

He did as he was told. I stood in front of him, my pussy level with his face. He leaned forward. "Don't touch me."

He sat back and waited.

"Have you ever been fucked in the ass?" I asked.

He looked away. I grabbed him by the chin and tilted his face upward, rough. His eyes evaded mine. "I asked you a question."

He didn't say anything. I released his chin and slapped him, hard across the face. My fingers left a burning red mark. He flinched and for a moment, his eyes flashed anger. My stomach jumped. *Had I overstepped? Hey, you learn by doing.*

I tilted his chin up again and claimed his eyes with mine, making sure that mine were hard, unrelenting. He nodded. I smiled. "Are you a fag?" I asked. He shook his head no. "What do you call it when you let men fuck you?"

"It was only the one time." His words were barely audible. "I was curious."

"Did you like it?"

"It hurt at first," he confessed.

I stepped back and looked him over.

"Take off your pants," I ordered. "I want to fuck you."

He stood and slowly, almost reluctantly, unzipped and removed his pants while I went to unpack the strap-on dildo I had bought for the occasion. When I turned to him, his cock was full-on and straining upward. He was well-endowed, thick and long, and for a moment I regretted the limitations I had placed on tonight's festivities.

"Come here," I ordered. "Secure this for me."

He came to me and dropped down to his knees in order

to reach between my legs to secure the straps, a set of buckles and Velcro with an underside of something soft and cushiony that allowed it to lie and hang comfortably around my hips. His fingers and hands lingered on my inner thighs, leaving trails of tingles wherever they touched. I let it go. When he was done, he sat back on his haunches and looked up at me, his thick member straining against the cotton of his polo. My own penis jutted out just where my clitoris sprouted. It was a snub-nosed hard rubber piece, about five inches or so. I didn't want to hurt him.

"I want you on the floor between the beds, your face in the carpet, your ass in the air." I pointed.

He hesitated.

"Now," I ordered.

He did as he was told.

I knelt behind him and held the weight of his balls in my hands. Then I bent down and sucked as much of them as I could into my mouth. They were tart and salty. I slid my tongue over and under them, stroking with wide, wet licks. What I couldn't touch with my mouth, I fondled with my fingers. He groaned and pushed his bottom farther up into the air. I took that as my clue that he was ready for the next step.

I stuck three of my fingers into a jar of cream that I purchased along with the dildo. The boy behind the counter said it was great for novices, "makes anything go in with ease and it tastes good," he'd said, grinning at me as he took my money. I slid my fingers down the length of his ass, over his balls and up and through the crevice. His ass trembled. He whimpered. I slid one, then two fingers into the puckered hole and he groaned. I slid another and he whimpered and shivered like a big dog. I pressed my lips to the fleshy part of his ass and took a little bite, then nipped the other side. He pressed himself closer to my face. I reached under him to tug and stroke him, my hands running the length of his rod. It was hot and tight and dripping. He was breathing hard, and I could feel his anticipation. I gripped my own penis with a well-oiled palm, tugging it with a fist a few times to ease the cream over its surface, adding an extra dab for the tip.

I rose up behind him, pressed my cock to the puckered hole, and pushed, slow at first, but he pushed back against me and I slid in farther. There was a slight protrusion built into the dildo harness that pressed against my clitoris every time I pressed my cock into Bruce. It was addictive. Before long I was banging my cock into Bruce's tight little ass and every hit sent a series of surges and shivers back to my tight little nub. It seemed to tighten and grow with each thrust. I tensed the muscles of my ass to get a harder, firmer thrust. I held on to his hips and let the rush and lightning surge through my body; it was a clean rush of power and pleasure, but I didn't surrender to it completely. Bruce groaned, a loud surrender, and nearly rose up. I reached under him, gripped, and tugged the length of sex with my slippery fingers. His body jerked and released a spray of semen, saturating the carpet. I pulled out and he fell forward, covering his mess.

I left him there, a puddle of sated man, and slipped into the bathroom, packed all of my toys in my overnight kit and slipped back into my jeans and T-shirt. When I came out of the bathroom, he was sitting on the bed, still pantless, his cock docile and quiet between a set of well-toned thighs. I picked up my purse from the dresser and headed to the door.

"Clean up this mess before you leave," I decreed as I stood near the door. He nodded without looking at me. I stepped out into the night. There were still a couple of kids and their parents around the pool. I could hear the splash as someone jumped in, the lull of conversation, a woman's laugh and the clink of glasses. I pulled the door closed and made my way back to my car.

Work was hazy with cubist edges and a fluorescent glare; I wandered around on autopilot. I was no Bruce Davies; I couldn't pretend that there wasn't something really strange going on between me and my boss. I couldn't look at him without remembering the size and length of him, the hardness of his thighs and the firmness of his backside. I would sit across from him as he sat behind his desk scanning a storyboard while I took notes, and the muscles of my sex would clinch. A dampness would creep between my legs and I'd think of little scenarios that we could act out right there on his desk with my legs wrapped around his head. I was afraid that he could sense my arousal, smell me as I sat across from him. But he was as stoic as ever. Well, not really stoic—his spirits were good, and he was quite personable to everyone he encountered. But he seemed unfazed by our episodes and impervious to my discomfort. Okay then, it was me. I had to learn to cope or to desist. I chose the latter. Oh, it had been fun, the intrigue, the fulfillment of fantasies, but I wasn't cut out for the aftermath, the lingering arousal, and yes, the guilt.

A series of cold showers and a call from Alex a week later helped me to stick to my guns. We had dinner and an evening of normal but very hot sex in his hotel room followed by a stiff morning ride before he had the town car drop me home to get dressed for work. Alex, unlike Bruce, was not one to ignore a night of hot sex.

Claire informed me that Bruce had been looking for me so I headed into his office as soon as I dropped my purse and briefcase on my desk. Alex was sitting at the circular table near the rear of Bruce's office. Bruce stood over a bottle of Dom Pérignon in a bucket of ice.

"We're celebrating," Bruce said to me. "Alex wanted to wait for you."

"You're pleased with the campaign?" I asked Alex.

He actually stood up, took my hand and drew me to the table to stand between the two of them.

"He's so pleased that he's giving us a crack at the shoes and clothing lines." Bruce popped the cork and poured the champagne into the waiting glasses.

"It means I'll have to visit more often," he said, and leaned in to plant a kiss that ended up getting lost somewhere in my hair because I tried to dodge it under the guise of reaching for the champagne glass that Bruce held out to me.

Alex laughed. "We have nothing to hide from Bruce. He's seen us at our most vulnerable."

Bruce sipped from his glass, but said nothing.

There was logic to that, but Alex was not aware of all that had transpired between me and Bruce since that night in my office. But Bruce remained silent. Maybe it didn't matter to him. Maybe he expected a woman who orchestrated clandestine perversions to have multiple lovers. Maybe he was fine with it as long as he got his share.

"To a long and fruitful alliance." Bruce held his glass out to ours. The glasses clinked. I drained mine and held it out for a refill. Maybe he thought this was normal for me. I drained the second glass.

"I'd better get back to work," I said, putting my glass down on the table.

"I thought we'd have breakfast," Alex said, capturing my hand again.

"I've got to see legal about the contracts," I ad-libbed.

"Bruce won't mind if you come away with me for a few

hours," Alex coaxed. He directed his words at Bruce, but continued to look at me.

"There are a few things pending that require Glory's touch." Bruce's words were a balm. "Maybe she could issue you a rain check."

"Tonight," Alex said, using my captured hand to draw me to him.

"I'll call you when I'm done," I said as I slipped my hand out of his, offered him a placating smile and headed back to my office. Enough already. Alex stayed another week to oversee the opening of a new store, an uptown boutique that featured his company's high-end line. It kept him busy and he didn't seem to even notice that I had been dodging him. When I showed up to represent the agency at the store's inauguration, he was affable and warm. I rewarded his nonchalance by fucking him senseless in the back of the limousine as we took a long ride along the riverfront and through the park. He was so attentive that I was sorry I had put him off all week. But I wasn't too sad when I rode with him to the airport to see him off. He held me in his arms and nuzzled my neck as the chauffeur pulled his luggage from the trunk. It felt good to bask in the shelter of his body, the heat of his chest pressed against my cheek. He was an affectionate man, a good man, and I felt sated, normal. I could go back to my life, the way it was before Mr. Davies became Bruce, before that night.

"Glory!" I could hear him through the door. I pretended not to, but his bellow was followed by the long shadow of his frame as it filled the doorway. "Why haven't you followed up on this?" He waved a folder. "You said you wanted more responsibility. I give it to you, and this is what happens." He slid the folder onto my desk and stormed back to his. I was hoping that he would slam the door behind him, but he left it open, suggesting that he wasn't quite finished with his rant. I waited, expecting a follow-up, but he'd shifted his ire to Claire. I could hear him demanding that she stay after to finish the correspondence she'd failed to complete. "I wanted to sign them before I leave," he fumed. Claire apologized, explaining that he'd only given them to her an hour ago. "Be that as it may," he said, ignoring her reasoning, "I want them on my desk first thing in the morning so they can go out with the morning mail." I looked at the folder he'd given me. Just as I suspected, it was awaiting an adjusted budget. Accounting had promised to email it to me within the week. I sent Somers, the department manager, a reminder, turned off my computer, grabbed my sweater and headed out the door.

I mouthed goodbye to Claire, and she tilted her head in Davies's direction and mouthed, "What's his problem?" I shrugged and double-timed it to the elevator. I didn't want to have to ride down with him, but I wasn't fast enough. I was standing there, pushing the button for the third time when he came up behind me.

"Long day," he said.

"Yeah," I agreed, and pushed the button again.

"A drink?" he asked.

"I'm tired," I offered, still with my back to him.

"Just one," he said, and then added, "I want to talk."

"Where?"

"Dottie's."

"Okay."

He followed me in silence onto the elevator. Neither of us said a word as we left the building side by side and walked the two blocks down the street to the seedy little bar that still boasted the tall oak booths that must have been Dottie's grandfather's pride and joy when it had opened in the 1940s. The bar, which according to Dottie had been named for her grandmother, was known for its burgers, and did a brisk lunch business with the office workers in the area. At night, the crowd was a bit more colorful, more Dickies and less Brooks Brothers. When we got there, the place was almost empty. A couple of guys nursed drinks at the bar, and there was one guy eating a burger with his beer in one of the front booths. We took the booth all the way in the back. Bruce ordered burgers for both of us, beer for him, and vodka and cranberry juice for me. It was what we always had at Dottie's. "Do you want fries?" he asked. I shook my head no. The waiter disappeared with our order.

Bruce loosened his tie. "It's been over a month, Glory," he said as though we had been in the midst of a conversation.

The waiter brought our drinks. He placed the cocktail napkins in front of us then set the drinks on them. I thanked him and he was gone. I removed the tiny straw and sipped my drink.

"Is it Alex?" he asked.

"No," I said, and took another sip.

"I don't like it," he said as though I hadn't spoken, "but I can live with it. I just don't like being shut out."

"It's not Alex. It just makes me uncomfortable."

He didn't say anything for a while. He drank from his glass, and finally asked, "What makes you uncomfortable?"

"It's just not me." I looked at him, into his eyes so he could see how I felt.

"But you're so good at it." I wasn't sure whether he was trying to cover up his apprehension or whether he was trying to blow it off.

"I'm serious."

"So am I." He stroked his glass as he watched me. After a moment of silence, he reached over and touched the back of my hand. I let him. "We don't have to play the games all the time," he offered.

I must have looked as if I was considering it because he added, "We could take turns. You could tell me what you need."

The waiter came with our food. We sat back and let him slide our plates onto the table. The young man asked the cursory, "Do you need anything else?" but scurried away when Bruce shook his head and turned his attention back to me.

I doctored my burger, mustard, ketchup, relish, and passed the condiments to Bruce, who began the process. The food was good. I chewed and smiled at Bruce. He bit his and smiled back. We ate in silence, using our napkins liberally and sipping our drinks between bites. When we finished, Bruce handed the waiter our empty plates and ordered more drinks. I sat back feeling comfortably full and relaxed.

"Come home with me tonight," Bruce suggested.

I sat up. "I don't think so," I said, and more firmly added, "Not tonight."

"Why? It isn't as though there is someone at home waiting for you."

"I'm just not ready."

"Okay," he said as the waiter placed our drinks in front of us.

"Okay," I said.

His head jerked up.

"No. I mean I'm glad you're okay with it."

He leaned forward. "I *can* be the aggressor. Do you want me to be the aggressor?"

I couldn't help but smile. "I thought you said okay."

"It's just that I know that sometimes women like..." He stopped as though he was afraid to finish.

"To be attacked?" I laughed outright.

"To be seduced," he corrected.

"Women are the only ones that suffer this affliction?"

"You have the advantage here because I am terribly attracted to you, and I haven't been with anyone since we were together. It's difficult—" he laughed and shook his head "—to think, with you sitting there."

"I'd better go," I said as I gathered my things. "It's getting late."

"I'm sorry if I made you uncomfortable. Stay. Finish your drink." I held my clutch in my hand. Resting both clutch and hand on the table, I began scooting out of the booth. He reached over, pulled the little purse out of my hand and placed it on the seat next to him. *No, he didn't.* The move completely deflated me. I sat back.

"Stay. Just for a while," he said again, his voice soft, placating. "Finish your drink."

"All you had to do was ask."

"Really." His smile was wry, as if he didn't believe me. I knew what he was thinking. *If that were true, you would have come home with me.* But, he didn't ask again.

"Okay," he said, and stood up, still holding my bag. "I'll walk you to your car."

I stood up. After pulling some bills from his pocket and tossing them onto the table, he took my sweater and draped it over my shoulders before handing me my purse.

We tried to make small talk about the office and new accounts, but by the time we reached the parking structure we had both sunk into our own thoughts. His hand rested low on my back as we entered the structure. It would have been a chivalrous thing to do, but it felt as though he was doing it more for himself than for me, as if he was giving in to his need to touch me. His hand was large and hot and burned through the cotton of my dress. I sped up a little to relieve some of the tension, but he kept pace with me and for a minute, it was as though we were both hurrying to get somewhere.

It was late. The garage, lit intermittently with fluorescent lights, was dim. It was always darkest near my car, which was parked in a corner near the elevator. I was glad Bruce was here. He stood over me. His body a half-circle fortress around mine as we waited. We took the elevator up to the floor reserved for Davies and Birch. A concrete wall separated my car from the glass enclosure that housed the elevator, a gray slab that blocked out light and created a blind spot that hid my parking space from the protective eyes of the security camera. Bruce's and Birch's cars were parked to the right, behind the other concrete wall in the spaces reserved for the executives. Because we worked for Bruce, Claire and I were given optimum spaces next to the elevator. Birch's assistants were in the same bank, next to me and Claire. It had been a not so secret bone of contention to some of the higher-earning account execs and department managers, but Bruce had dismissed their bickering and innuendoes. When one of the newer execs complained that he'd never worked for a company that gave secretaries better parking spots than the high rollers, Bruce had simply said, "They're not secretaries. They keep me functioning at my best. I need them near and on time." Since then, the guys have kept their comments to themselves.

He took my hand as we left the enclosure and led the way to my car. "I could come home with you," he said as he pressed me back against the car door and his mouth against mine. It was good. He tasted wet like beer and hot burger and man. He leaned in, and my hip nudged the door handle. I kissed him back. He groaned and pressed his luck, allowing a hand to stray behind my back and down to cup my bottom. The hard notch of him pushed into my waist and belly. I shoved at him. His hand was under the skirt of my dress. I shoved him again, but not with much force. His hand moved to the elastic waist of my panties and stopped. His mouth still claimed mine, his tongue a comfortable weight hovering at the entrance and teasing the inside of my lips.

"I just want to feel you."

I shook my head and he deepened the kiss.

"Just a little," he whispered, and kissed my cheek.

He tugged at my panties again, pulling them down my thighs. I let him, lifting first one, then the other foot so that he could slip them off and into his pocket. A breeze glanced over my newly bared skin followed by a large warm hand and fingers that burrowed into the dampness, searching and finding my center. I clutched at his shoulders, my fingers crushing the fabric of his jacket as his plucked and stroked and inflamed me. I could barely think but I could hear the clink of his belt buckle and the purr of his zipper. The subtle musk of his cologne wafted up to me as my mouth found his neck in the loosened collar of his shirt. His skin was warm and salty. The texture was slightly rough where his beard was trying to grow back. I ran my tongue over the tiny spikes and then gnawed them with my bottom teeth. He groaned and snipped my chin with his teeth. I opened my legs wider in anticipation. He lifted me up by my bottom, his hands slipping and cradling my thighs as he pressed me more firmly into the car. Only the linen of my skirt and a pair of large warm hands shielded me from the cold steel and glass. I lifted my legs to embrace his now, the rasp of his nearly naked thighs against mine in their thigh-high nylons causing a tingly friction. He slid in farther, the knob of his sex already pressing against my opening. My feet, clad in a pair of burgundy strappy heels, found purchase against the cement wall a couple of feet behind him.

He leaned forward and found home, filling me completely, the width of him leaving no room as it made a slow drag deep into my center. He hit bottom, breathed a sigh, found my mouth again and pulled almost all the way out. I waited, my pussy making clutching movements, eager for his return. He came back and I scooted toward him, trying to squeeze him, to hold him, but he had found his rhythm. Leaning forward, he secured me with his shoulders, chest and hands as he continued his assault, pounding into me. The fullness and the bliss of the slide in and out caused my legs to tremble against his. I closed my eyes as he began to swell inside me, the hardness pushing against my walls, the pace crazy, out of control, the rough hair of his groin setting fire to my too sensitive labia. I bit the thick cloth at his shoulder to keep from screaming, and then he was coming. His fingers clenched my nether cheeks as he tried to pull me even closer, and then I was spiraling. The muscles of my sex clenched and pulled at him, milking him as I came and came, my juice making a broth with his.

When I came to my senses, he was still holding me, his sex softer, but still tucked into me.

"Okay?" He grinned.

I laughed. "Yeah, okay. But we can't keep this up like this. There has to be protection."

"Fine, as long as there is a next time."

"I want to get down."

He stepped back. His sex plopped out and fell slack between his legs. I slid my legs down and pulled at my skirt, trying to right it. Linen is an unforgiving fabric. He tucked himself and his shirt away and zipped himself. When he was done he was a bit rumpled, but the lightweight wool of his suit was much more resilient than my linen.

"Come home with me?"

"Not tonight." I shook my head. "I need my bath. I need a long soak and lavender salts."

"I have a bathtub…and salts."

"I need time."

He nodded and stepped back. His foot found my purse where it had fallen. He picked it up and handed it to me. I retrieved my keys and opened the car door.

"See you in the morning," I said as I got into the car.

He nodded, and as I pulled the door closed and started the engine, he walked to the edge of the cement wall and waited for me to drive away.

The next morning I was replete with guilt and misgivings. Angry at myself for being weak, for not sticking to my guns. But Bruce was back in Davies mode, very much in charge and charming the office staff and account execs alike, bolstering them with praise for small deeds, and letting them down easy when he didn't like a pitch. On his way out at lunchtime, he stopped at the door between our offices.

"Dinner at seven. That little French place on Eighth," he said, standing in the open door, pulling on his suit coat.

"Who's the mark?" I asked.

"I had Claire make the reservations," he answered as he pulled the door to him. "I'll see you there." The door clicked closed and he was gone.

I had Cup-a-Soup for lunch, microwaved in the little kitchen down the hall, and sipped over a desk full of contracts.

Claire came back from lunch, and I gave her the contracts with my corrections and asked her who Davies and I were having dinner with.

"He asked me to make the reservations for two," she said. "I didn't know you were going. Should I make it for three?" she asked.

"No, I just thought..." And I didn't know what else to say, how to clean it up.

"Oh, maybe it's a raise or a promotion," she said, brightening as though she'd caught wind of something.

"I don't think..." I tried.

"Maybe he wants to surprise you. He can be so thoughtful," she gushed.

"Do you think you can finish the corrections before four? I'd like to make sure Legal gets them before five," I asked, changing the subject.

"Sure," she said, and turned back to her computer.

Bruce didn't come back to the office and I wasn't sure what to do about dinner. I went home and changed. I went with my black spaghetti-strapped Audrey dress. I wanted to look nice, even if I had to put a stop to this.

Bruce was there, sitting at the table, waiting for me when I got there. He looked good in the black Prada. I've always favored it because it made him look dark and rich and terribly powerful. His eyes welcomed me. The waiter pulled out the chair across from him; I sat. All this was accomplished in silence.

The sommelier broke the silence in a rapid, pointed French as he cradled a bottle of wine as if he was a proud daddy. Bruce smiled up at the intense little man and responded in kind. The man poured. Bruce sipped and actually grinned. The sommelier's smile got bigger and he poured generous amounts of the rich red liquid into both of our glasses before he left us alone.

"The dress—" he tilted his head toward me "—very becoming."

"Thank you," I said, taking a sip from my glass.

"Are you hungry?"

"Yeah, I guess."

"I've already ordered for both of us. I hope you don't mind."

"No, that's fine. Whatever. Bruce, what is this about?"

"I wanted quiet time with you, time unencumbered by work."

"Dottie's was nice."

"Yes," he said. "I enjoy your company."

We were quiet as we spread our napkins on our laps and the waiter set bowls of consommé in front of us.

"Now, you say you enjoy my company," he chided me.

"I do," I said, tasting the soup. "But I don't think it's wise to see each other without the buffer of work."

"What harm could there be? This is neutral territory. Public."

"For now."

"Are you anticipating dessert?"

"There isn't going to be any dessert tonight. Is that why you ordered me here?" I pushed the plate away, my appetite dwindling. I hated being manipulated.

"I didn't invite you here to seduce you."

"Then why?"

"I thought we could talk."

"About what?"

"Us."

"There's nothing more to say."

The waiter took the soup away. The heated plates that took its place held filet mignon, asparagus and light flaky potatoes au gratin. This man knew me. He kept the fare simple, well seasoned, and the filet mignon was juicy and so tender it didn't need chewing. We ate for a while, before he spoke again, but it was as though the conversation had never halted.

"I have more to say," he said after taking a sip of wine.

"Ah," I responded. I wanted to add, "what a surprise," but I filled my mouth with asparagus instead.

"What do you want, Glory? What can I do for you? Just tell me and I'll get it for you."

"I don't want anything." I lay my fork across my plate. "I was content before."

"Only content, Glory? I want to make you happy."

"This, whatever we've been doing, doesn't make me happy. It makes me uncomfortable."

"How can we make it comfortable for you?" He sounded so reasonable, like he does when he speaks to favored clients.

"We can't."

"What aspect of it makes you uncomfortable?"

"All of it," I blurted, feeling like a six-year-old.

"I don't believe that's the complete truth, Glory. Some parts of it were pleasing to you. I could feel you."

"I don't like the discomfort of going back to the office afterward, the pretense, the fear of discovery."

"We've been completely discreet. No one need ever know."

"That can't continue forever."

"For as long as you want it to."

"How can you be so unmoved? You sit at your desk or in the boardroom and you don't even see me."

"I see you." His words trembled and their heat sent a jolt to my core.

"I'm not as adept at hiding as you are," I said after letting the bolt pass through.

"What do you want, Glory?"

"I don't want anything. I want it to be like it was before."

"That can't happen. I wouldn't want it to."

"If we stop now, maybe."

"It's too late for that, Glory. I want you too much for that."

I sat back and looked at him. He sat, back straight, cool and poised.

"What can I do for you, Glory? What can I do to make you happy?"

Okay, so he was playing hardball here, and negotiations were in full swing. I didn't know what I expected but it wasn't this.

"Bruce, it just isn't for me. I'm just not the type."

He didn't say anything, just sat there silently. He knew that there would be more and he was waiting for me to get it all out.

"It was exciting at first, but it's not right. Not the way things are supposed to be."

He nodded and refilled my glass. I didn't even know I'd emptied it. I wondered if his crazy sex habits were the reason he and his wife divorced. If it had escalated to a point where she couldn't take it anymore. I could see how that could happen. Bruce encouraged a kind of limitless freedom.

"I don't...think...I could..." I found myself sputtering.

"It's just the two of us," he reminded me as if he knew I was considering it, considering what I could do to him. "No one else needs to know. Unless you want to include someone else. We'd have to be discreet, but if it's something you want..." He seemed shy again, like he did in the motel. My pussy twitched and moistened.

"I like my job. I like the way we were at work before," I told him.

"This has nothing to do with us when we're there. You're good at what you do. I rely on you. What we do in our free time doesn't have to affect our work."

I knew that to be the lie it was. I remembered how his mood shifted when he got what he wanted as opposed to when he was denied. I remembered Claire's face when she realized I was having dinner with Bruce alone. He must have been reading my face because he added, "As closely as we work together, there's bound to be some speculation. It's a normal by-product of having a female assistant. But again, what others choose to speculate doesn't have to affect us."

He watched and waited. I didn't say anything. I didn't know what to say short of walking away from all of it—this man, the hot sex, my job. But, I really like my job and he was something different.

"Do you need more money? A bigger apartment?"

"Monetary inducement?" I shook my head and gave him an admonishing smile.

"I just want to make you happy."

"I'm not a whore."

"You could move in with me." He completely ignored my remark, apparently dismissing it as irrelevant, and threw a fastball that hit me square in the chest, knocking the wind out of me. "I have a big house and there's only me. It feels quite hollow sometimes. You could have a wing to yourself."

When I didn't respond he said, "Come home with me."

I shot him a look. "To see the house," he added hastily.

"I've seen it."

"Only a couple of times and then only the first floor. You couldn't have seen much. You were only there long enough to hand off a few papers."

"I saw enough."

"Come on." He was smiling now. "I'd like to show you my home."

I sat there frozen, overwhelmed. *Unfair,* he was far more skilled at this than I.

"No strings," he said, trying to capture my eyes.

He lied, and he knew I knew he was lying.

I excused myself, needing a minute of near privacy to recover. When I returned, he had settled the bill and stood to help me with my shrug before fitting his hot hand onto my lower back to guide me out of the restaurant and to his waiting car.

As I sat next to him in the backseat of the town car, I was both frightened and exhilarated because I had realized that I couldn't turn this man down. I could be myself with him— pushy, demanding, cruel or loving. He encouraged it, fed off it. The prospect was intoxicating and I knew, as the car pulled out into traffic, this was just the beginning.

★ ★ ★ ★ ★

CHANCE OF A LIFETIME
PORTIA DA COSTA

Rain. Perpetual rain. I'm certainly not going to miss the British weather. I'll miss a lot of other things, but not this, not this.

I stare out of the window, down the gravel drive and out across the park of Blaystock Manor. I'm here filling in with some temp work, while I wait to take up my dream job, my chance of a lifetime working in the Caribbean at a luxury resort as a junior manager. This gig is just cleaning and helping with renovations, donkey work really, but it's all extra money to pay for my new tropical wardrobe.

Actually, it's a free day today. The marquis is pretty good about that. We get plenty of time off, plenty of breaks and other perks, and despite the fact he's strapped for cash and putting everything into this project, we're pretty well paid for our labors. Everyone else has gone off in a minibus to visit a local monastery where they brew apple brandy and make luxury biscuits and stuff, but me, I've got my own diversions here.

I'm alone in the house. Even the marquis drove off a short while ago in his decrepit gray Jag. And I'm free to indulge my wicked secret vice.

I discovered this little sitting room a couple days ago, when

I was a bit lost and searching for the Blue Salon, where I was supposed to be polishing the floor. I stumbled in here and found a room that was homely and pretty lived in, and sort of cozy. And, being irredeemably nosy, when I saw an old VCR and a bunch of tapes, I had to investigate.

Boy oh boy oh boy! What a shock I got.

And now, while the house is empty, I slip another tape into the machine and settle down in a battered old leather armchair to watch it.

It's a home movie. Filmed, I think, in this very room. And it stars my latest crush, the marquis himself, and a woman who must have been his girlfriend at the time. Obviously it was taped many years ago, because His Lordship had short hair then, and now it's long, down to his shoulders.

Here he is, possibly sitting in this very chair. His knees are set wide apart and his girlfriend is facedown across them.

He's spanking her.

He's really laying it on with his long, powerful hand, and she's squirming and patently loving it!

And I'm loving it, too, and I don't really know why. Okay, I knew people played spanking games for sexual kicks, and I'd sort of hinted to various boyfriends that I'd like to try it. But it's never happened and I've never really worried about that.

But now. Now I've seen it. I bloody well want it!

I'm so turned on now I can barely see straight. And I certainly can't stay still in my chair. I'm sweating and my skin feels like it's already been spanked, all over. And between my legs, I'm drenched, my panties sopping with intense, almost inexplicable arousal. My sex is aching, tight and hungry, as if I want to be fucked right now, but at the same time have my bottom thrashed, just like the woman in the video.

The marquis really seems to be enjoying her pleasure, even though his cool, handsome face is exquisitely impassive. It's an old, well-worn tape, but I can still see the mask of stern, beautiful composure that he affects…and the wicked dark twinkle in his eyes.

It's no good, I've got to play with myself. I can't help it and I can't bear it if I don't. My sex is so heavy and so tense, I've just got to do it.

As the woman on the screen writhes and wriggles and shrieks as His Lordship's hand comes down, I unzip my jeans and shuffle them down to my knees, dragging my soggy panties with them. There's something wickedly lewd about sitting here with my clothes at half-mast like this, and the forbidden exposure only excites me more and makes my need to touch my body ever more urgent.

"Oh, God…" I murmur vaguely as I slip my fingers between my legs and find my clit. It's swollen and ready for my touch like a throbbing button. I flick it lightly and my vagina flutters dangerously. On the screen, the spanked girl tries to touch her own sex, wriggling her hand beneath her belly as she squirms and cries, but the marquis pauses midspank and gently remonstrates with her.

"Come, come, Sylvia, you know you mustn't do that. No pleasure until you've been a good girl and taken your punishment."

His voice is soft, even, but shot through with sweet steel and authority. It pushes me closer to coming just as powerfully as the spanking show does: I suddenly wish I could get to know him better, and make this all real.

"Oh, my lord…" I whisper this time, closing my eyes and turning on an inner video. This time it's me across those strong thighs. Me who's writhing and moaning, with my bottom flaming.

Oh, the picture is so clear. And it's the marquis of today who's doing the business, not the one in the video.

He's wearing his usual outfit of black jeans and black shirt, and his beautiful hair is loose on his shoulders like sheets of silk. There's a sly, slight smile on his pale, chiseled face, and his long, cultured hand comes down with metronomic regularity.

I'm rubbing myself hard now, beating at my clit, but not stroking the very apex of it. I daren't; I'm so excited and I don't want to come yet. In my fantasy, he allows me to touch myself while he's smacking me.

I writhe and wriggle, both fighting the pleasure and savoring its gathering at the same time. I throw my thighs wide, rubbing my bottom against the seat of the creaky old armchair. The sensation of the smooth surface against my skin is even more pervy. I press down harder, squashing my anus against the leather. I imagine him spanking me there, and even though I've no idea what it would really feel like, I groan, wanting it more and more and more.

"Oh, my lord…do it…do it…" I burble, eyes tightly closed and half out of my mind with desire and longing.

"Actually, my dear, I think you're 'doing it' quite well enough on your own. Do continue."

What?

It's like I'm falling, dropping through reality into a parallel universe. I know what's happened but somehow I can't stop rubbing myself.

My eyes fly open, though, and here he is.

The marquis.

Somehow he's walked into the room without me realizing it, moving softly on the rubber soles of his black running shoes.

In a few split seconds, I take in his glorious appearance.

So tall, so male, so mysterious. Long dark hair, pale smiling face, long fit body. Dressed in his customary black shirt and jeans, his elegant hands flexing as if preparing to copy the actions of his image on the screen.

I snatch my hand from my crotch and make as if to struggle back into my jeans. My face is scarlet, puce, flaming…. I'm almost peeing myself.

"No, please…continue."

His voice is low and quiet, almost humming with amusement and intense interest. It's impossible to disobey him. Despite the fact that I think the aristocracy is an outdated nonsense, he's nobility to his fingertips and I'm just a pleb, bound to obey.

Unable to tear my eyes away from him, I watch as he settles his long frame down into the other chair, across from mine. He gives me a little nod, making his black hair sway, and then turns his attention to the images on the screen.

So do I, but with reluctance.

But I do as he wishes and begin to stroke my clit again.

Oh, God, the woman on the screen is really protesting now. Oh, God, in my mind, that woman is me, and I'm laid across the marquis's magnificent thighs with my bottom all pink and sizzling and my crotch wetting his jeans with seeping arousal.

I imagine the blows I've never experienced, and just the dream of them makes my clit flutter wildly and my vagina clench and pulse. I seem to see the carpet as I writhe and wiggle and moan, and at the same time his beautiful face, rather grave, but secretly smiling.

As his eyes twinkle, in my imagination, I come.

It's a hard, wrenching orgasm. Shocking and intense. I've never come like that before in my life. It goes on and on, so extreme it's almost pain, and afterward I feel tears fill my eyes.

Talk about *le petit mort* and post-coital *tristesse*. I've got *tristesse* by the bucketful, but without any coitus.

My face as crimson as the buttocks of the spanked woman in the video, I drag my panties and jeans back into place and lie gasping in the chair. I scrabble for a tissue. I'm going to cry properly now, not just a few teardrops, and I know I should just run from the room, but somehow I just can't seem to move.

Something soft and folded is put gently into my hand, and as I steal a glance at it, I discover it's the marquis's immaculately laundered handkerchief. Still gulping and sniffing, I rub my face with it, breathing in the faint, mouthwatering fragrance of his cologne.

Shit, I fancy this man something rotten, and I've been fantasizing about him fancying me back, and falling for me, and now this has happened. I'm so embarrassed, I wish I could burrow into the leather upholstery and disappear out of sight.

A strong arm settles around my shoulders, and the great chair creaks as he sits down on the arm beside me.

"Hey, there's no harm done," the marquis says softly. "Now we both know each other's dirty little secrets." He squeezes my shoulders. "I get off spanking girls' bottoms and having them wriggling on my lap. And you get off watching videos of it and playing with yourself." He pauses, and I sense him smiling that slow, wicked smile again. "And quite beautifully, I must admit. Quite exquisitely...."

I beg your pardon?

Hell, I must have looked awful. Crude. Ungainly. Like a complete slapper.

I try to wriggle free, but he holds me. He even puts up a hand to gently stroke my hair. I still can't look at him, even though part of me really wants to.

"I'm so embarrassed. I'm so sorry. I had no business coming in here and prying into your private things."

One long finger strokes down the side of my face, slips under my chin and gently lifts it. Nervously, I open my eyes and look into his. They're large and dark and brown and merry, and I feel as if I'm drowning, but suddenly that's a good thing.

All the embarrassment and mortification disappears, just as if it were the rain puddles outside evaporating in the sun. Indeed, beyond the window, the sky outside is brightening.

Suddenly I see mischief and sex and a sense of adventure in those fabulous eyes, and I feel turned on again, and somehow scared, but not in a way that has anything to do with an awkward situation with my employer. It's a new feeling, and it's erotic, but so much more.

"Indeed you didn't. That was rather naughty of you." His face is perfectly impassive, almost stern, but those eyes, oh, those eyes—they're mad with dangerous fun. "Do you think we should do something about that?"

I feel as if I'm about to cross a line. Jump off a cliff. Ford some peculiar kind of Rubicon. This is the chance of a lifetime, and I'm a perfect novice in the world portrayed in his video, but I understand him completely without any further hint or education.

"Um...yes, my lord."

Should I stand? Then kneel? Or curtsy or something? He's still sitting on the arm of the chair, a huge masculine presence because he's tall and broad-shouldered. Everything a man and a master should be.

I'm just about to stand, and I feel him just about to reach for me, when suddenly and shockingly his mobile rings, and he lets out a lurid curse.

"Ack, I must take this. Money stuff," he growls, and nods to me to mute the television as he flips open his phone.

I make as if to leave, but he catches me by the arm and makes me stand in front of him. With almost serpentine grace, he slides into the armchair and pulls me across his lap. Then, as he has a terse conversation that I don't think he's enjoying much, he explores the shape of my bottom through my jeans.

He doesn't slap or smack or hit. He just cruises his fingertips over the denim-clad surface, assessing my contours and the resilience of my flesh.

Slowly, slowly, as he gets slightly cross with someone on the other end of the line, he examines my cheeks, my thighs and then, without warning, squeezes my crotch. I let out a little yelp, and that's when he *does* hit!

It's just the softest warning tap…but it's electrifying. I almost come on the spot and I have to bite down on my lip to stifle my groans.

I start to wriggle and he cups my sex harder, from behind, pressing with his fingers. Pleasure flares again as my jeans seam rubs my aching clit.

I'm biting the upholstery, squirming and kicking my legs and grabbing at his legs and his muscular thighs through his jeans. He rides my unruliness, his hand firm between my legs as he owns my sex like the lord and master he truly is.

Eventually his call is over, and I'm a wrung-out rag. He flings aside his phone and turns me over, then kisses me.

I expect domineering hunger and passion, but it's soft, light and sweet, almost a zephyr.

He wants me. He's hard, I can feel it beneath my bottom. But as if his own erection means nothing to him, he sets me on my feet then stands up beside me.

"Much as it pains me to leave so much undone and unsaid at this moment, Rose, I have to go." His eyes are dark. Is it lust? Regret? Something more complex? "I need to go to London, and I'm going to have to get a bloody taxi because I've just left my car at the garage." He pauses, then leans down to kiss me on the lips again, a little harder this time. "But when I get back, we'll reconvene. If that's agreeable?" He tilts his head to one side as he looks down on me, and his exquisite hair slides sideways like silk.

I nod and mutter something incomprehensible that doesn't make sense even to me, and then he pats me on the bottom again and strides away across the room.

At the door, he gives me a wink, his dark eyes twinkling with mischief.

"Enjoy the rest of the video," he says, then suddenly he's gone.

★ ★ ★

But I don't watch it. After he's gone, I just shoot off to my room, tucked up in the eyrie of the old servants' quarters, feeling strange and weird and disoriented, as if I've been in a really vivid dream, and I've just woken up. Then I sort of snivel a bit, not sure of my emotions.

The marquis is our boss, and up until now, he's been a sort of admire/adore from afar type man. I'm not into all this hero worship or celebs and aristos for the sake of it, but he's got genuine charisma and blue-blood charm. He's also got some weird history. Apparently in the army at some time, then a dropout, and now getting his act together and sorting out the manor on behalf of his father, the duke. The whole family is strapped for cash, but Blaystock Manor is just the right size for a deluxe, high-end hotel or conference center, and the marquis has thrown just about every penny he possesses, and some he doesn't, into restoring it and bringing it up to standard.

And somewhere along the line in this convoluted story of his, he was married, but she died and now he's alone. No doubt his dad is pressuring him for progeny, to continue the family line, but so far it seems he's resisted, and there's no marchioness.

Some very silly thoughts drift into my mind as I get ready for bed and I push them smartly back out again. I've got my dream job waiting for me in the Caribbean. I won't be here all that long.

Although I would love to see what the manor looks like when it's finished.

I suppose all this pondering is to avoid thinking about the fact that the marquis has seen me masturbate, and almost, but not quite, spanked me.

Do I really want to be spanked, though?

In the video, he was doing it for real, and that woman— whoever she was, surely not his wife—was squealing and crying out. So obviously it hurt like hell. Lying in bed later, I tug down my pajama bottom and give myself a slap on the thigh. It's a pretty halfhearted effort but it makes me squawk and rub the place to take the sting away.

Immediately, though, I'm drifting into fantasy.

In my mind I'm back in the little sitting room, and this time the phone stays silent. And the marquis bares my bottom and starts to caress, caress, caress it, then lands a blow.

I slap myself again, trying to recreate the feeling. It bloody hurts, but I do it again, moaning, "My lord…"

I slap and slap and moan and moan, and suddenly I just have to play with my clitoris. I'm so turned on imagining him spanking me that my wet sex aches.

Within a few seconds I come, softly crying his name, seeing his face.

The next day, I worry. What's going to happen? Is anything going to happen? Or has the marquis quite sensibly decided to dismiss our stolen interlude as an aberration. Something of no consequence. It must be bred in his blue English blood to dally with underlings for his pleasure without a second thought.

I certainly don't see him for the next couple of days, and the cleaning, dusting and polishing goes on without incident. I work cheerfully with the rest of the team, as if nothing has happened.

But then, after a long day, when the others are all off to the pub, I slip back to my room to change, and find a little note upon my mat.

I'm sorry we were so rudely interrupted, it says in a fine, almost copperplate handwriting. *Would you care to join me in the small sitting room, at seven o'clock this evening? I feel that there's much we could explore there in the furtherance of your education and the pursuit of mutual pleasure.*

It's finished off with a single word.

Christian.

Christian? Who's "Christian"?

Then it dawns on me. Duh! The marquis is just like a normal person in that at least.

He has a first name.

I wonder if he'll want me to call him "Christian"? Somehow it doesn't seem right, or respectful. Especially in view of what we're almost certain to be doing. It'll definitely be "My lord" or "Your lordship," or just sobs and moans of pain and pleasure in equal amounts.

At seven o'clock, I'm staring at the door to the little sitting room. It was half in my mind not to turn up, to try and pretend that what happened beyond that slab of oak never happened. But doing that would be to miss...well...miss the chance of a lifetime. I might never meet a man again who's into the things that the marquis is, and I might go through life having perfectly ordinary, perfectly satisfactory sex, but still wondering what it would have been like to try the extraordinary kind with spanking and strange mind games.

I knock as firmly as I can on the door, and immediately that deep, clear voice calls out, "Enter!" from within. Crikey, he already sounds like a stern schoolmaster summoning his tardy pupil.

I tremble.

But there's nothing fearsome or intimidating when I step into the room and close the door behind me. It's cozy and welcoming, with a nice little fire burning in the grate to ward off the unseasonal damp chill. The thick curtains are drawn, and soft lamps emit a friendly golden glow that flatters the fine old furniture and makes it gleam.

It flatters the marquis, too, not that he needs it. He looks stunning.

He's all in black again, as ever. Tight black jeans embrace his long legs, and the splendid lean musculature of his thighs and his backside. As he rises to his feet from the depths of one of the armchairs, I imagine, for a fleeting second, spanking him!

Blood fills my cheeks in a raging blush, and I falter and hang back. A huge waft of guilt rushes through me at even thinking that. I open my mouth, but I can't speak, and he smiles at me.

"Come on in, Rose. Would you like a drink?" I notice that he has a glass with something clear and icy set on a little table beside his chair. Vodka? Water? Gin? Who knows....

"Um...er...yes." I flick my glance to the sideboard and a few bottles, but I can't seem to compute what's there so I just say, "Whatever you're having...please."

"Good choice...and do sit down." He gestures like a Renaissance courtier toward a free chair by the fire, and watches me as I make my way there; I'm terrified I'll trip or something, despite the fact my heels aren't high or spindly.

I take my seat, and watch him mix my drink, swiftly combining clear spirit, ice, mixer and a sliver of lemon. He prepares the concoction perfectly, despite the fact that he's studying me intently almost all the time.

I've dressed carefully.

Jeans are awkward to wriggle out of, especially if you've got a curvy bottom like mine, so I've chosen a soft, full summer skirt that almost sweeps the floor. A miniskirt would be too obvious, not ladylike, and as I'm here with an aristocrat, I'm compelled to make an effort to be worthy of him.

On my top half I've got a little buttoned camisole, pink to match the skirt, and a light cotton cardigan over that, to keep out the chills. My shoes are low-heeled and quite pretty, and underneath I'm wearing my best and sexiest underwear.

I aim to please....

The marquis comes across and hands me my drink, then retreats to his own chair. There's a moment of silence, tense for me, but apparently totally relaxed for him, and I snatch the opportunity to feast my eyes on his gorgeousness.

He sits so elegantly, even though he's totally at ease. Long legs out in front of him, booted feet crossed.

Boots? Hell, yes! They do something visceral inside me. They make me shudder and my sex clench and seem to twist and flutter with their connotations of masterfulness. They're old and soft and well polished and not all that tall, but all the same, I almost feel faint just looking at them.

And I get mostly the same feeling from the rest of him.

He's got the most exquisite black silk shirt on, full of sleeve and so fluid it seems to float on his body. The collar's fastened up for the moment, but I have the most intense urge to crawl on my hands and knees across the room and rip it open so I can kiss his throat and his chest and suck his nipples.

And not just his nipples.

His thick black hair is shiny with a fresh-washed satin sheen and his fine-boned face has the delicious gleam of a recent shave.

Bless him, he's made as much of an effort for me as I have for him. Another reason to worship and adore him.

I take a mouthful of my drink. It is gin, as I mostly suspected, and it's a strong one with very little tonic. The balsamic kick of the uncompromising spirit almost makes me cough, but I'm glad of its heat as the first hit settles in my stomach.

"So...here we are," the marquis says pleasantly, eyeing me over the rim of his own glass. As he takes a long swallow, his throat undulates, pale and sensuous.

"Yes...er...here we are," is all I can manage in reply. The gathering tension in my gut renders me all but speechless.

"Have you been thinking about what happened here the other day?"

I nod, dumbstruck now with intense lust. I don't know

whether I want him to spank me or fuck me…probably both. But I want whatever's on offer as soon as I can get it.

"So how do you feel about being spanked a little? Does that interest you?" His lips are sculpted but somehow also soft and sensual, and when they curve into a little smile, the way they are doing now, they make me want to wriggle and touch my sex to soothe its aching. So much for wearing my best knickers. They must already be saturated with juice, I'm so turned on.

"I think we could enjoy ourselves together, you and I," he continues. "I'm not offering eternal love and devotion, but we can share a little pleasure and perhaps expand your horizons in a way that doesn't involve flying thousands of miles."

Those crazy notions caper around my mind again, taunting me with the prospect of what he *isn't* offering rather than what he is.

"Rose?" he queries, swirling his glass in the face of my continued, dumbstruck silence.

I want it. Oh, how I want it. And even just the mutual pleasure if I can't have the other thing. But I'm scared. I feel as if I'm stuck between reality and some kind of weird dream. I still can't speak, but I take another swig of my gin.

The marquis frowns. It's not a cross frown, just a sad little frown, sort of regretful. "I'm sorry. I've come on too strong, haven't I?" He tips his head to one side, his dark hair sliding across his shoulders as he lets out a sigh. "Look, don't worry about it. Don't think any more about it. Just finish your gin and we'll say no more about it. It was wrong of me to ask."

I don't know whether I'm relieved or disappointed. I felt so close to him for a moment, and God, I wanted it all so much. My heart thudding, I swig down my gin and get to my feet on wobbly legs.

The marquis rises immediately, perfect manners second nature to him. He comes forward as if to escort me to the door, and does so as I make my way toward it, my heart sinking at my own craven lack of daring.

With one hand on the door handle, he touches my face. The contact is so gentle yet so meaningful, I feel quite faint.

"Don't worry, Rose, there'll be no hard feelings. It's just a might have been." He sounds so kind, so ineffably kind that it's almost like a knife in my heart. "I may have lost all my money and be a poor excuse for an aristocrat, but I do try to behave like a gentleman. We'll speak no more of this and just go back to a friendly working relationship."

"No!"

He stares at me. The frown is a puzzled one now.

"No...I mean...yes, I am interested. Definitely. It's just something that's completely out of my experience.... Yes," I repeat, aware that I'm babbling. "I'm definitely interested."

His stern, elegant face lights up as if the sun's just come out. He looks happy, genuinely happy, in a way that seems quite astonishing in a man so obviously worldly and experienced.

"Splendid!" He sets down his glass, and leans forward. "I'm so glad."

Without any warning, he leans down and dusts my lips with a tiny, fleeting kiss.

"For luck. To seal our agreement." A wry, strange smile flits across his face. It's almost as if he's surprised somehow, but not by me. "Come then."

He takes my hand and leads me back toward the fireside.

When he reaches his armchair, he sits down in it, all elegant, languid grace, and draws me between his outstretched thighs. I suddenly feel very small. Like a naughty little girl, and as that registers, I realize it's exactly what he wants me to feel. Suddenly I'm staring at my toes, too embarrassed to look at him, even though he's the most beautiful thing I've ever seen.

"Ah, now then, my Rose..." He reaches out, lifts my chin with the tip of his finger and makes me look at him. His

brown eyes are electric, gleaming and wickedly dark. Just
for a second his tongue tip flashes out and licks the center of
his lower lip, and it's as if in that instant someone's thrown a
switch and changed everything in the room.

We're playing.

"So, do you normally go around prying into people's private
belongings? Or is it just me that you spy on?"

I don't know how to answer. I don't even know if I should
answer. But he prompts me.

"Well, Rose?"

"Um…no, not normally, but I was interested. I wanted
something to watch."

"And you didn't think to ask first?"

"No, my lord…sorry, my lord…."

His title slips perfectly off my tongue, so sweet and so
dangerous in this context.

"I think I should be punished," I add rashly, suddenly
wanting to move on and get to the heart of the game.

"Really?" His voice is arch, slightly mocking, but I can still
hear the joy in it. "In that case, my dear, bold Rose, I think
we should oblige you, shouldn't we?" He's still holding my
hand, and unexpectedly he brings it momentarily to his lips
before releasing it.

For several long moments, he just watches me, peruses me,
looks me up and down as if he's planning something demonic,
and then he says simply, "Undress."

Oh, God, I wasn't expecting this. I thought it might come
afterward—after, I suppose, my first spanking. I'd been
picturing myself across his knee, maybe with my skirt up and
my knickers down…but not totally naked and exposed.

When he says, "Did you hear me, Rose?" in a soft tone of
remonstration, I realize I'm just standing here dithering.

I peel off my cardigan, and to my surprise he takes it from
me and places it over the arm of the chair. Nothing too

frightening there. But next, it's my little buttoned top, and I fumble with the fastenings as if I have five thumbs.

The marquis sighs softly, gently puts my hands down at my sides and then undoes the top himself, divesting me of it with precise efficiency as if he undresses clumsy women all the time. Maybe he does. Well, not necessarily clumsy ones…but who knows whom he sees when he's not here at the manor overseeing the renovation.

Now, on top, I'm left just in my bra, and the marquis studies it, doing that little head tilt thing of his again, as if he's grading me on the quality of my underwear. I swallow hard, wondering how my choice stands up. It's a delicate white lace number, my best…I hope it passes muster. I hope my breasts do, as well, beneath. They're not big, but they're perky, and right now my nipples are as pink and hard as cherry stones. Something the marquis takes note of by reaching out to squeeze one. I moan like a whore as he twists it delicately through the lace.

Lust and blood and hormones career wildly through my body. It's as if I've got too much energy to fit inside my skin. I close my eyes tightly, ashamed of my own wantonness as my hips begin to weave in time with the delicate tweaking. But the marquis says, "No," and with his free hand he cups my chin. "Look at me, Rose. Give me your feelings. Don't deny me them."

I open my eyes, aware that they're swimming, but it's not from the pain. It's that overflow again, that wild abundance of emotion and sensation; it's welling over in the form of sudden tears.

The marquis's eyes are amazing—deep as the ocean, unfathomable and yet on fire. He reaches for my other nipple and as he plays with that, I wriggle anew as if my pelvis had a wicked life of its own.

"You're willful, sweet Rose," he purrs, tugging, tugging,

first one nipple than the other. This simple punishment is far more testing than any amount of smacking or spanking, I sense, and suddenly I'm proud to be put to such a test.

The marquis's eyes glitter as if he's read my sudden thought, and he permits me the beneficence of a slight smile. Then he draws a deep breath and leans back in the chair, abandoning my breasts.

I feel bereft until he tells me, "Continue."

Slipping off my bra, he gives my breasts and my rosy, swollen nipples a swift once-over, as if without covering they don't interest him quite as much. I hesitate and he nods to indicate I should take off my skirt.

First I slip my feet out of my shoes and kick them away, then I unfasten the button and zipper of my skirt. For a moment, I clutch at it, suddenly nervous despite everything. Then I let it drop, and kick it away, standing as proudly as I can in just a very tiny G-string.

I keep my own smile inside, but elation geysers up inside me as the marquis can't disguise his grin.

"Oh, how splendid…how splendid…." he murmurs, and that naughty pink tongue of his slips out again, touching the center of his lush lower lip. Reaching out, he runs the backs of his fingers over the little triangle of lace, and over the fluffy pubic hair that peeks out on either side. Fleetingly, I wish I'd had a chance to visit a salon and get a Brazilian, then I change my mind as his fingertips coil in my floss and gently tug it. He seems to like me *au naturel,* and whatever the marquis likes, I like, too.

He tweaks a little harder and the tension transfers directly to my clitoris. I'm so excited I almost come; I'm so close to the edge. As it is, I let out a groan, I just can't help myself.

The marquis pulls again, making a tiny pain, a little hurt, prick and niggle at the roots of the little curl he's playing with.

But at the same time, he reaches up with his free hand and places his fingers across my lips.

"Now, now, Rose, you must learn to control yourself," he reprimands quietly but without rancor. "A good submissive is quiet and still, bearing discomfort—" he twists a little more tightly "—with perfect grace and fortitude. You have a long way to go yet, my dear, but I hope that you'll learn."

The tears trickle down my face. This isn't quite what I expected, and somehow I feel reduced to some kind of wayward little girl for a moment. But this excites me, and inside, deeper than my confusion, is a brighter glow. It's a game, and my body loves it even though my mind is still learning.

It isn't only my tears that are trickling.

As if he, too, has detected my welling arousal, the marquis's nostrils flare eloquently. His deep chest lifts as if he's breathing in my foxy, fruity smell. A slow smile curves his lips and I half expect him to lick them again, savoring my aroma.

A moment later, I'm gasping, fighting for breath, desperate to obey his wishes, and at the same time on the point of shouting out and jerking my hips.

In a sly, deft, sleight-of-hand motion, the marquis has abandoned my pubic curls and slid his fingertips into my cleft beneath the lacy triangle of my underwear. One finger zeroes in like a guided missile and pushes right inside me. He presses in deep and lifts his hand, and I rise on my toes, speared and fluttering.

When he rocks the digit inside me, I grab his shoulders, almost fainting as I come. My resolution crumbles when he squashes his thumb down flat onto my clit and I groan like an animal, lost in pleasure.

Pulsing, sweating, burbling nonsense, I lose all strength as my knees turn to jelly. The marquis's free arm snakes around my waist to hold me up, while between my legs, he both supports and manipulates me, his finger lodged inside me while his thumb presses and releases, presses and releases, presses and releases...tormenting me by lifting me to orgasm again and again.

I hold on. My body clamps down on him again and again. Time passes.

Eventually, the tumult ebbs and I flush with shame and a strange, tangled happiness as I regain the ability to stand up straight.

The marquis's strong, straight digit is still inside me.

And it stays there, his hand cupping my mound, as he speaks to me.

"You have so much to learn, sweet Rose, so much to learn." He looks into my face, his beautiful brown eyes gleaming with sex, yet somehow almost regretful. "And we have so little time, you and I, don't we? Just a week or two."

What the hell is he talking about? I could stand here forever, possessed by him, my sex his plaything.

And then I remember that all this is temporary. There's my dream job of a lifetime waiting for me in the Caribbean in a few weeks and I'll be thousands of miles away from the marquis and his hand, his eyes, his body.

The shock must show on my face because he smiles kindly. "Don't worry, my dear. All the more reason to make the most of things while we can." His finger crooks inside me and finds a sweet spot, forcing me to grunt aloud, flex my knees and bear down. "Usually, I start with a little pain before the pleasure. But in your case, I couldn't resist handling your delightful pussy and making you come."

He flexes his finger a little more.

I cry out, "Oh, God!" and come again.

It's quick. It's hard. It satisfies, yet primes me for more. But instead of either working me to more orgasms, or just pushing me down on the rug, unzipping and thrusting into me, the marquis withdraws his finger, suddenly and shockingly, and offers it to me.

My head whirling, I wonder what he means, but then it dawns on me that he wants me to clean it off.

My face flaming, I suck my own musk from his warm skin as more flows between my legs to quickly replace it.

I feel bereft when he withdraws the digit and then dries it methodically with his perfectly laundered handkerchief.

"And now to business," he says briskly, as if implying that I've deliberately kept him from it with my orgasms. "I think I'd like to bind you. Are you okay with that?"

Speechless, I nod like an idiot as he reaches down the side of his chair and pulls out a length of soft, silky cord. I feel it slide over my hip and flank as he turns me to face away from him, and then, bringing my hands behind me, he fastens them at the wrist.

I think that this is it, but suddenly he produces another length of cord and, pulling my arms back tighter, he winds it around my elbows, drawing them together.

Twice bound like this, I start to sweat even harder. While not really painful, the position is uncomfortable, and what's more, it forces my breasts to rise and become more prominent, vulnerable and presented.

When he spins me around again, I feel almost faint as he leans forward and slowly licks and sucks each of my nipples. His silky hair swings and slides against the skin of my midriff and the scent of an expensive man's shampoo fills my nostrils.

As he torments me with his tongue, I feel his fingers at my thong. He plucks at the lace and elastic and tugs the thing up tight into the division of my sex lips. When the sodden cloth is pressing hard on my clit, he reaches around behind me, working beneath my shackled wrists, and makes a little knot somehow at the small of my back, to keep it taut.

He licks at me a moment or two more, then leans back,

almost indolent in his great chair as he cocks his head to one side and regards his handiwork.

I feel like a firecracker in a bottle, an explosion of sexual energy and need contained by my bonds. I'm desperate to come again, but I'm reaching and yearning for more than just simple gratification. The marquis smiles as if he understands me completely.

"And now we really begin," he says softly, taking me by the waist and pushing me from between his knees. Then, settling himself more comfortably in the chair, and setting his booted feet more squarely on the floor, he nods to me, his eyes dancing with lights and a subtle smile on his handsome face.

I know what he's indicating. That I should assume the position.

It's difficult to settle elegantly across his lap with my hands tied, but I do the best I can, not wanting to disgrace myself. Even so, he has to more or less grapple me into place, setting me at precisely the right angle and elevation and disposing my limbs and torso in the optimum position to present my bottom to his hand.

I wait for the first spank. The first real one…the tap the other day was nothing, I suspect.

But it doesn't come yet.

"Mmmm…"

It's a low, contemplative sound, and as he utters it, the marquis gently cups my bottom cheek, testing its resilience. The feeling is entirely different this time; his fingers on my bare skin feel like traveling points of electricity, sparking me and goading me as they rove. He grips me harder and I have this sense of some kind of computer in his brain calculating, calculating. How hard to hit. How high to lift his hand for the downstroke. How many slaps is optimum.

"Ready?" he asks, to my surprise. I'd expected him to just take what he wanted. He's in charge, after all.

And yet, is he? I bet if I said "no," even now, he'd immediately desist and help me restore my clothing to decency and propriety. But no way would I do that. I want what I want and it's what he wants, too.

"Yes," I whisper, barely able to hear my own breathy voice over the bashing and thudding of my heart.

"Good girl."

And then he spanks me.

Oh, dear God! It hurts! It hurts so much!

What a shock! I'd expected a tingle, a little burn... something that's as much pleasure as pain.

Bloody hell, how wrong can you be?

It's like he's slapped me with a solid hunk of wood rather than his strong, but only human, hand. For a moment, both mind and bottom are numbed by it, but then sensation whirls in like a hurricane, I shout out loud—something indistinguishable—and my left buttock feels like it's on fire.

And that's just one blow.

As more and more land, I realize in astonishment that in that first shot, he was actually holding back....

Slap! Slap! Slap!

Spank! Spank! Spank!

The whole of my rear is very quickly an inferno, and the heat sinks like lava into the channel of my sex, reigniting the desire, the grinding longing I felt before my orgasms, and rendering it slight and inconsequential.

I know I should be quiet and still and obedient. I know I should just accept my punishment like a good little girl. Instinct tells me that a master appreciates that in a supplicant. Perfect poise. The perfect ability to absorb the punishment with grace and decorum.

But me, I'm rocking and wriggling about, struggling against my bonds, plaguing my own clit with my wild pony bucking and jerking that makes my pulled-tight thong press and rub against it.

I feel as if I'm going out of my mind, and yet I know, in some still-sane part of it, that I've never been happier in my life. Despite the pain and the strangeness and the sheer, unadulterated kink of what's happening to me, I know that this is where I should be and who I should be with.

The marquis lands a particularly sharp blow, and I let out a gulping, anguished cry. But it's not from the impact, or the raging fire in my bottom cheeks.

No, what pains me the most is that in two weeks I'll be thousands of miles away from the hand that's spanking me.

Still squirming about, my backside still in torment, still almost about to orgasm, I begin to cry piteously, completely out of control and racked by raw, illogical heartache.

As if he were plugged right into my psyche on the deepest level, the marquis stops spanking me immediately.

Strong and sure, he turns me over as if I were as light as a feather across his lap. I gasp as my sore bottom rubs against his denim jeans, but he takes the exhalation into his own mouth as he swoops down to kiss my very breath.

With his tongue still in my mouth, he unfastens my hands and elbows, then, with a swift, sharp jerk that snaps the lace like a cobweb, he wrenches the thong from between my legs and replaces it with his fingertips. His gentle fingertips that love me to a swift, sweet, pain-stealing orgasm.

I moan into his kiss, pleasure sluicing through my loins, rising through my body and my soul and soothing my aching heart. He touches me so tenderly, coaxing me to the peak again and again. As I twist beneath his touch, I realize, distantly, that I'm clinging on to him for the dearest life, yanking at his dark shirt and digging my nails into his back, perhaps inflicting a tiny percentage of the pain I've just experienced.

Finally, we both lapse into silence and stillness. He holds me. I hold him. We're two breathless survivors of a whirlwind.

How long we sit like this, I have no real idea. My entire world is his strength, his scent, his sure, steady breathing and the beat of his heart in his chest where I huddle against it. After a while, though, another physical factor begins to impress itself on me.

I'm on the marquis's lap, and in the cradle of that lap there's the hard knot of an erection.

I start to feel hot again. My cheeks flush with shame at my own selfishness. This spanking was something he wanted to do, but it was really as much my idea as his...and I've had the pleasure of it—several times—and he's had nothing in the way of sexual release.

He's been stiff all through this strange interlude and I've made not the slightest offer to do anything about that. Even though he's seen to *my* satisfaction...repeatedly!

I wonder how to broach the subject. He seems to be quite content for the moment just to hold me, despite the fact that he must be in a fair degree of discomfort. Something that's dramatically illustrated when I shift my position slightly and he draws a swift, sharp breath.

"Um...your lordship...er...shouldn't we do something about that?"

Not exactly eloquent, but I drive my point home by moving again, cautiously rubbing my sore bottom against the solid bulge that's stretching his jeans.

If I've been expecting a positive response and an enthusiastic segue into the next delicious stage of the proceedings, I'm completely wrong. He remains silent, perfectly silent, for several long moments, and when he does utter a sound it's a soft, regretful sigh.

"That's a sweet offer, my lovely Rose, and I'm very

tempted." I gaze into his face and suddenly discover that he looks quite sad. "But perhaps it's not the best idea...not really."

"Why not?" I demand, my submissive role suddenly a thing of the past. His eyes widen, and for a moment I wonder whether I should apologize and grovel a bit, but then he smiles and shrugs, the movement of his shoulders transmitting itself to me more through his erection than anything else.

"I..." He looks away, distant for a few seconds, and then returns his gaze to me. He looks rather sad, almost wistful, and then he smiles again. "I prefer to just touch and play and give pleasure, rather than receive it."

What?

"But...um...don't you need to come?"

He laughs. "Of course I do. But I'll deal with myself later, Rose." He tips his head back, as if looking heavenward for inspiration, his night-black hair sliding away from his face with the movement. "It's hard to explain, but basically, if I get too intimate, I want too much...and I'm not really a good prospect for relationships." A heavy sigh lifts his chest. "I'm a widower, but I wasn't much good as a husband. Or even a boyfriend. Too wild...too selfish.... I've settled down a lot now, of course—" he makes a vague gesture as if to encompass his responsibilities at the Manor "—but now I'm saddled with debts and commitments, and anyone who takes me on takes all that on, as well."

I can see what he means, but suddenly, in the midst of that thought, a bright revelation shatters the gloom.

Oh, God, even though he's expressing his shortcomings and his wariness of relationships, the fact that he's actually mentioned a relationship—marriage even—must mean that he feels more for me, and sees me as more than a temporary employee and a casual spanking playmate.

Mustn't it?

"Look, please, let me...let me touch you...or maybe we can

even fuck? I won't expect more than just that. All it'll be is a bit of pleasure with no commitments. Um...just friendship with a little bit of extra, really, nothing more."

It's out before I've really thought about it. But thinking about it, I know I do want more, despite what I say.

Even though it's possibly the stupidest thing I've done in my life, even crazier than agreeing to be spanked by my temporary boss, I've only gone and fallen head over heels in love with the marquis, haven't I?

And he's right, there's no future in it, is there? None at all.... Soon I'll be leaving for the Caribbean, to take up my chance-of-a-lifetime job!

He looks at me and his dark eyes are still sad, but strangely yearning. It's as if he's just read my thoughts, and feels the same bittersweet emotions that I do.

"You're a wonderful girl, Rose." He touches my face, the same fingers that punished me now a tender, caressing curve. "You're far too wonderful for me. If I take more from you, I'll just want more than that. And more...and more...and that's not fair of me."

I could weep and scream. He *does* bloody well care!

Acting on impulse, I turn my face into his gentle hand and kiss his palm. He groans and mutters, "No!"

But I know I've got him. His whole body shakes finely, and beneath me, his cock jerks and seems to harden even more, if that were possible.

"I shouldn't...I shouldn't..."

"It's all right. It'll be 'no strings,'" I whisper against his palm, then inscribe a little pattern, a promise, with my tongue.

"Oh, hell," he almost snarls, and then he's kissing me, tilting me back on his lap and going deep with tongue and lips... and heart?

I embrace him, writhing on his knee again, the discomfort of my spanked bottom forgotten. Wrapping my arms around

him, I try to silently say all the things that are too difficult
and irrational to say.

Like...

To be with him just a little while, I'll pay any price, do
things his way and never ask for more.

Like...

I'm prepared to take my chances on his lack of prospects
and commitments.

Like...

Who needs a fucking job in the Caribbean, after all?

This last one shocks me, but just as I think it, the marquis
deepens the kiss even further. His arms slide around me,
holding me tight, and yet with delicacy, as if I'm precious to
him.

And then, somehow, we're on the rug, and he's lying over
me, great and dark, like a shadow that's so paradoxical it's also
light. The light of revelation....

His hands rove over my body, exploring with reverence this
time, and great emotion. And the touch is a thousand times
more sexy than when we played. With a gasp, he straightens
up momentarily and rips open his shirt, sending buttons flying
in his impatience. Then he embraces me again, skin to skin.

His body is hot, feverish and moist, with a fine sheen of
sweat that seems to conduct electricity between us. I moan,
loving the communion, almost feeling that this might even
be as good as sex in some mysterious way. But then my cunt
flutters, reminding me I want more.

Still kissing me, the marquis deftly unbuckles his belt
and then unfastens his jeans. But just as he's about to reveal
himself, and allow me to feast my eyes on that which I've
been fantasizing about since the moment he cordially and
quite impersonally welcomed me to the manor and the work
team, he lets out a lurid, agonized curse.

Then says, "I don't have a condom. I wasn't expecting to need one."

A part of me thinks, whoa, he really did mean all that stuff about not fucking! But another part of me gives thanks for the fact that hope always springs eternal.

"Er...I've got one. It's in the pocket of my skirt."

He gives me a look that says he thinks I'm a saucy, forward minx, but he's more than glad of the fact, and then he scoots gracefully across to where my skirt landed, and locates the contraceptive in my pocket.

Back close again, he hesitates, and gives me a beautiful, complex look, full of hunger, compassion, yearning again... and a strange fear. I nod. I feel just the same.

And then he reaches into his jeans and reveals himself.

Involuntarily, I make a little "ooh" sound.

He's big. Stunning. Delicious. His cock is as handsome and patrician as his face, magnificently hard and finely sculpted. He's circumcised and his glans is moist and stretched and shiny. I've never seen a prettier one, and it's almost a shame when he swiftly robes it in latex.

I reach for him, expecting him to move between my splayed thighs. But with all the authority of his centuries-old title, he takes hold of me and moves me into his preferred position. With his arm around my waist, he scoops me up and places me on my hands and knees and moves in behind me.

It's not what I would have chosen but I'll take what I can get. And I understand his reasons. This way is more impersonal, not too intimate and less dangerous to his emotions and to mine.

At least I think so, until he moves in closer, pressing his condom-clad penis against my still-tingling buttocks while he leans over me and molds his bare chest against my back so he can reach to give the side of my neck a soft kiss.

I sway against him, loving the kiss, loving his skin, loving his scent…and loving him. His weight is on one hand, and with the other he strokes me gently and soothingly, hot fingertips traveling over my breasts and my rib cage, then skimming my waist before finally settling over my sex. He cups me there, not in a sexual sense, but in a vaguely possessive way that's almost more intimate than a blatant attempt to stimulate me.

Then his long finger divides my labia and settles on my clit.

I moan, long and low, already fluttering as he rubs in a delicate, measured rhythm. He's trying to make me come first, I realize, and perversely I resist for a few seconds, holding out for our union. But he's far too clever and too skilled, and I crumble, coming heavily and with an uncouth, broken cry.

As I'm still pulsating, he pushes in, the head of his cock finding my entrance with perfect ease.

Oh, God! He's big! He feels even bigger than he looks, so hot and imposing. I pitch forward onto my folded arms as he ploughs into me, making a firm foundation from which to push back at him.

The impact of his penetration shocks my senses for a moment, and pleasure ebbs while I assimilate what's happened to me.

I've got the marquis's cock inside me. I'm possessed by this strange, elegant, deeply personal and mysterious man that I work for. We are one, for the moment; joined by flesh.

But when he starts to move, I'm back in my body and the pleasure reasserts itself.

We rock against each other and he thrusts in long, easy, assured strokes. At first he grips my still-tingly bottom cheeks, but as things get more intense, he inclines right over me, taking his weight on one hand again while with the other, he returns his loving attention to my clit.

Somehow he manages to stroke me in exactly the way that suits me, a firm rhythm, devilishly circling, but not too rough.

God alone knows how he manages it. Maybe it's pure instinct or something? Because, judging by the way he's gasping and growling, he's just as out of it as I am.

Sublime and miraculous as all this is, I can't hold out for long. And I don't. Within moments, I'm growling, too, like some kind of she-wolf, and climaxing furiously. Dimly, I sense the marquis trying to contain himself, conserve himself as long as he can, to increase my pleasure. But I'm not having any of that—I want *his* pleasure, too!

I milk him hard with my inner muscles, and he lets out such a string of profanities—in his immaculate upper-crust accent—that I find myself laughing just as wildly as I'm coming.

Then he laughs, too, pumps hard and fast and shoots inside me. I feel the little bursts of his spurting semen even through the condom, and despite it being very stupid, I suddenly wish the rubber protection wasn't there. As we both tumble forward in a gasping, sweating, laughing, climaxing heap, I have fleeting but dangerous thoughts about one or two or three little marquises or honorables or whatever, all running around the place looking as dark and aristocratic and beautiful as their daddy.

Lying on the rug, wrapped in his arms as he cradles me spoon-style—his still partly clothed body warm and protective against mine—I fight with a huge case of genuine post-coital *tristesse* this time.

This is all there is, Rose, I tell myself. A couple of weeks of this. A bit of naughty spanking and sex play by mutual consent. Maybe a friendly, but not too personal, fuck or two.

And then you're off to your lovely new job and a new life of opportunity.

While he stays here, in the heart of England, tending to his great house.

Outside, I hear it start to rain again.

★ ★ ★

Two weeks later, it's still raining. In fact, there's a raging thunderstorm outside and it's really scaring me.

But in a way, this is a good thing. It's taking my mind off the fact that tomorrow, I'm supposed to be leaving. And though I won't miss this cold, English rain one bit, there are a lot of things I am finding very hard to leave.

This funny old house has really grown on me, and I wish I was going to be here to see it finished.

I'm going to really miss being spanked and tied up and given mock orders in a mock-stern, beautifully cut-glass English voice. Oh, I'm sure there'll be a man somewhere in the Caribbean who'll oblige me, but it won't be the same, it won't be the same.

And pleasure, oh, how I'll miss the pleasure. Not just any pleasure, but the bliss gifted to me by a man who seems to know my every thought, my every response, inside out.

I'll miss the sex, too, even if I never do get to see his glorious face as he comes inside me. But even if he won't face me, I still don't think I'll ever find anyone with his finesse, his strength, his sweetness, his consideration...and his mastery.

Yes, it's the marquis. I fear he's irreplaceable.

And it's our last night.

Lights flicker along the passage as I make my way to the little sitting room, and just as I knock on the door, as I always do now, the lights dim and then go out. There's still some rewiring to do and this happens now and again, but this is the first time the power's gone out in a storm.

There's a loud crack of thunder, and lightning flashes almost simultaneously.

I shriek with fear and the door to the study flies open.

If I wasn't so terrified of the storm outside, I would laugh out loud. It's just like a Dracula movie, with a venerable old house, a wild storm and a beautiful, dramatic aristocrat dressed from head to foot in black.

I squeak again as he gathers me to him and hustles me into the softly lit room.

"I didn't think you'd come tonight, Rose. I thought you'd be down with the others in the kitchen, all seeing out the storm together."

I would be annoyed that he'd think that of me, except that the joy in his eyes at the fact that I did come is patent. He looks as if I've just given him a supremely magnificent gift, and that expression binds me to him far tighter than any length of rope ever could.

Mad, mad thoughts gather in my mind. They're thoughts that have been circling for the past two weeks, nipping at my resolutions and my every idea of what I've always wanted for my future.

But they're so crazy that I find it hard to acknowledge them, and when thunder cracks again they disappear, along with almost all my normal ones.

The marquis wraps me in his arms, softly cooing to me in low, comforting tones, and it's only as I settle that it dawns on me that I just shouted out incoherently again.

The embrace isn't sexual, it's protective. And yet I can still feel him hard against my belly. I hope he'll make love to me tonight, seeing as it's our last time. He doesn't always. Sometimes he's still hard when he escorts me to my little room, high in the old servants' quarters, and I can only assume he deals with his own needs after, alone.

His hold on me is too nice, too sweet and tempting. I struggle out of his grip and try to sink to the floor and kneel… to begin the game.

But he holds on to me, his big, strong hands gripping my shoulders.

"Not tonight, dear. You're too frightened, aren't you?"

He gazes at me, his dark eyes full of complicated emotion. He *does* want to play. I can tell by his erection and the tension in his body that these games of ours seem to release just as much as actual sex does. But there's more, so much more on his mind.

Turbulent joy rushes through my veins. He's going to miss me! My marquis is going to miss me!

And it's for more reasons than just the obvious one—because he likes to spank my bottom....

Amazingly, for one so confident and masterful—both by birth and by inclination—he snags his lip like a nervous, unsure boy. And in this sudden, weighted moment, I sense another, far more real, chance of a lifetime.

"Where's your bedroom, Christian?"

His given name, on my lips for the first time, comes out so naturally. He looks perplexed for a moment. Not angry or confused, just amazed really. I can almost see him rapidly processing an array of new factors in our brief relationship. Then his sculpted, intelligent face lights with joy.

"Not far," he says, suddenly gruff as he grabs my hand and leads me swiftly out of the room. His long stride eats up the yards and I have to trot to keep up with him.

As we round a corner onto another corridor, a particularly violent crack of thunder seems to shake the entire manor, and I yelp again and falter, despite my eagerness to follow wherever he leads. He spins around, his long, night-black hair whipping up as he turns, and in one smooth, effortless move, he sweeps me up in his arms, and then we continue on our way, me being carried and with my arms wound tight around his neck.

The storm, his knight-errant act and his intoxicating and spicy male fragrance all make me dizzy. Everything feels unreal, yet more real than anything that has ever happened or will happen.

As he kicks open a door, there is no job, no Caribbean,

no life plan...just the marquis...no...just Christian and his bedroom and his bed.

His room is big and dark and lit by just one rather anemic bedside lamp—rather gloomy. It's nothing like what one would expect in a stately home, but then it's not a public area, just actual living space. The bed isn't even made, so I guess he does his own housework up here. My gaze skitters around and I notice there's a black shirt flung across a rather saggy armchair in the corner, a bottle of gin and a glass on the sideboard and a heap of books beside the bed, all with old, well-worn bindings.

It's like the cell of some rather libertine type of monk.

But he won't be particularly monkish for much longer, if I get my way.

Christian carries me to the bed, sets me down on it and sits down beside me.

His face is still a picture of enigmatic emotions, as if there's a war going on inside him. But at least one part of the battle is quickly resolved, because drawing in a deep breath, he sweeps his hair back to one side and then leans down to kiss me.

It starts gently, but quickly takes fire, his tongue possessing me face-to-face in a way his cock never has. Adjusting his position without breaking lip contact, he stretches out alongside me, then half over me, reaching for my hand and a lacing his fingers tightly with mine.

For a long time he just kisses me as if he were fucking me, his tongue diving in, exploring and imprinting its heat on the soft interior of my mouth. I can't believe how exciting it is, as stirring in its own way as any of the naughty sex games we've played. And yet, for all its power, it's a simple kiss.

When my jaw is aching and my lips feel full and red and thoroughly marauded, he sits up again, and mutters, "Oh, God, I shouldn't do this...."

"Yes, you should!" I insist, not sure what it is he shouldn't be doing, but every instinct screaming that if I don't get it now, I'll just go mad.

For a moment, he tips back his head and looks to the somewhat discolored ceiling moldings for inspiration. His sublime hair slides back, accentuating his profile, and giving him the look of a fallen archangel contemplating his sins. And then he swoops back down again and starts undressing me, his hands working deftly at first, and then more frantically. I swear if I didn't help him, he'd probably have torn my flimsy knickers to get them off.

Thunder peals again, and though I don't cry out, I still can't help but flinch. Instantly, he's holding me to him, stroking and cherishing and protecting, his still fully clothed body creating a piquant sensation against my bareness.

But when the noise from the heavens ebbs, I spring into action. I don't want to be just held. I want to be fucked! I want him inside me, face-to-face, possessing every bit of me.

And now it's my turn to tear at clothes, wrenching open his shirt as he first heels off his boots and kicks them away, then fumbling with his belt and his jeans button and struggling to free him from his jeans. Between us we achieve our objective and he sinuously wriggles clear of the restriction of the denim.

He's glorious naked. Utter perfection. Long and lean, yet powerful, his enticingly defined chest dusted with a scattering of dark hair. And there's more of that dark hair clustered below, adorning the base of his belly and the root of his eager, jutting cock.

He's everything I've ever wanted in a man, and I want to be worthy of him, a graceful, dexterous, intelligent lover.

But instead, I squeal like a scared kid and hurl myself at him for protection when thunder roars again, right overhead. The crack is so loud I'm convinced the manor has been struck, but it seems not to have been when all Christian does is gather me into his arms and hold me tight against his warm, hard body, stroking my back and murmuring sweet, reassuring bits of nothing.

The heavens rage and bellow, lightning illuminating the room, even though the obviously ancient and rather shabby curtains are quite thick. One powerful arm still wrapped around me, Christian tugs at the bedclothes—old-fashioned linen sheets, woolen blankets and a quilt on top—and pulls them right up and over our heads, sealing out the light show and some, if not all, of the noise.

"Better?" he whispers, his voice echoing strangely in our frowsty little nest. He tightens his arms around me again, and snuggles me close. The heat under all this bedding is really quite oppressive, but the sensation of safety, and of being cared for, more than makes up for that.

And the fact that he's still erect, and his delicious penis is pushing against my belly and weeping warm, silky fluid, makes matters infinitely more interesting and sensual.

"Yes...." I whisper, adjusting myself to rub against him and let him know that my fear of the storm hasn't killed my desire for him. In fact, the more I feel that long, hard, fabulous tower of flesh against my skin, the less I seem to be noticing the muffled booming of the thunder.

"Well, we'll have to pop out sooner or later, or we'll suffocate." He pauses, then chuckles. "And I'm going to need some air if I'm going to make love to you properly. A guy needs plenty of wind in his lungs for a good performance."

As if by magic, the next roll of thunder sounds much more muted, more distant. And the one after that even more so, far less fierce.

"I think I'll be all right now." I place my hand flat against his belly, then slide on down. When I fold my fingers around his prick, he gasps and tugs at the quilt, so we emerge.

"Are you sure? It could still come back again. We could wait a little while, if you'd like."

He's still concerned, thoughtful, caring. Even though his penis is like a bar of fire in my hand, and the satin flow of pre-come is yet more copious.

"I don't think I can wait."

It's true. My own body is flowing for him, too. I'm wetter than a river down below. The thunder chunters again in the background, and though I flinch, my need for Christian is far greater than my remaining fears.

I part my legs and he gets the message and starts to touch me, his fingertip settling lightly, yet with authority, on my clit.

The pleasure comes quickly, as wild and elemental as the storm, and just as electric. Within seconds, I'm climaxing hard, rocked by the intense, hungry spasms in my sex, and fighting a battle with myself not to grip Christian's cock too roughly.

But he just laughs kindly, and pushes toward me while I pulse and pulse.

When I get my breath back, I stare at him as he looms over me in the low light from the bedside lamp. I'm still holding his erect penis, but there's more than sex in his eyes. They're dark yet brilliant, a chiaroscuro of turbulent emotions. They seem to say so much, yet the message is still scrambled, unclear. I sense some of it, and it takes my breath away again.

"I want to make love to you." His voice is husky, low, intent. "No spanking, no mind games, no ropes or bondage. Not tonight."

I don't know what to say, but he seems to read my thoughts. He gives me a little smile, then rolls away from me for a moment and pulls open a drawer in the bedside cabinet, and fishes around in it without looking. It takes next to no searching to produce a foil-wrapped condom. He puts it into my free hand.

My fingers shake as I dress him in it, rolling the superthin latex over his silky skin and encasing the iron-hard strength of his erection. When he's covered, I hesitate.

What will he want? His usual position? Taking me from behind?

I start to roll into position, but he stops me, a firm but gentle hand on my flank.

He smiles, pushes me flat against the mattress and then parts my legs and moves swiftly and elegantly between them.

For a moment, he just rests there, the head of his cock nestling tantalizingly at my opening, almost quiescent.

"I've so been wanting to do this," he says, his eyes grave. "Wanting it, but knowing I shouldn't."

I want to say *why not?* But I think I know why.

Games of spanking and bondage are just that. Games. Beautiful and life-enhancing. Sexual fun.

But this, this is serious. This is more.

I sense a different kind of bond breaking as he enters me. It's a restriction. An artificial barrier we've set between ourselves, and it's shattered now.

All is open. All is honest, dangerous but wonderful.

"I love you," he says quietly, then starts to thrust.

I can't speak, but I show him with my body that I feel the same. By holding him in my arms as tightly as I can while still allowing him to move. By hooking my legs around his body, and undulating my hips to press against him.

If only I could mold our two forms so closely together that we could become one, be inside each other's skin.

We rock and surge against each other, our heated perspiration almost fusing us in the way I crave. Christian's thrusts are short, shallow, urgent, almost desperate. He braces himself on one arm for leverage, and clasps me tightly to him with the other, his fingers digging into my flesh, not in cruelty but in possession and fierce need.

The joining is manic, almost animal, and yet at the same time soaring and transcendent. Holding him, being held and owned and fucked by him, I'm aware of my life changing as my flesh throbs with pleasure and clutches at his.

I gasp those three words, too, as my future changes shape.

In the morning, the park outside is fresh and clean and bright with sunshine. It's like a brand-new world after the storms of last night, a tangled paradise as I stare out from the window.

On the mantelpiece, Christian's clock reads a little after 6:00 a.m., but I'm wide-awake, anticipating a busy day ahead. I've so much to do and I don't know how to start.

So instead, I return to bed…and my man.

We said very little last night. Our bodies spoke for us. But this morning, I have to confirm not just my hopes and fears but my beloved's.

I know he probably wants what I want, but will his ancestral notions of duty and honor stop him from taking it? He might feel he has to set aside his needs for what he thinks is best for me.

Time to persuade him that he can't live without me.

Lifting the sheet that covers him, I feast my eyes on his magnificent body for a few moments, loving his tousled hair and the faintly sweaty early-morning aroma of his skin. His patrician face looks younger in repose, and his long, lush eyelashes are two dark fans against his cheekbones.

I wonder whether to bend down and take his cock in my mouth. It's already thickening, as if it's awake even if Christian himself isn't quite yet.

But instead, I try something different. Lying down against him I press my bottom against his thighs, and then draw his sleeping hand against its rounded shape, hoping he'll respond.

Yours, I think as his fingers automatically curve and cup me. *Yours until the end of time, to spank and play with at your leisure.*

"You do know what you're asking for, doing that, don't you?"

His voice is sleepy, yet still full of masculine power. He squeezes my cheeks briskly, already waking and ready for his treat.

"Um...yes, I think so."

"You know, there isn't really time, my love." There's regret there, but it's tempered with typical British stoicism. As if he's bracing himself already for what he dreads. "Isn't your taxi coming at eight? Shouldn't you be packing?"

I can't speak. Now that I have to tell him about my decision, I'm scared. I know I've read him right, and I know he cares, but still...

"I'm not going."

There's a long silence. His hands are still upon me, but they're quiescent.

And then he laughs. And squeezes again.

"You're a very silly girl. You know that, don't you?"

"Yeah, I do know it...but it doesn't change things." I press myself back into his hold. "I've decided that I like rain, and I want to hang around here, stay on the team and see what this old heap looks like when the renovation is finished."

"Is that all?" I hear the smile in his voice as he rolls me onto my front, still palpating my bottom in a way that's utterly sensual and full of delicate, delicious menace. "I do hate it when someone I care about keeps things from me." He lifts his hand, and that's more menacing than ever. "Now, tell me the whole truth...or I shall be forced to punish you."

"You might think I'm a bit forward."

"I'll be the judge of that, Rose. Now tell me."

I hesitate again. Deliberately.

He makes a soft tutting sound, and though I can't see him, I imagine him shaking his head, and his gorgeous black hair rippling.

A little tap lands on my right buttock. It's light, barely a smack at all, but my sex ripples in luscious excitement. He barely has to touch me and I'm soaring toward pleasure already.

Another tap lands and I swirl my hips, rubbing my mound against the mattress, trying to stimulate my clit.

"Keep still. Don't be naughty."

He's fighting not to laugh, and his voice is so warm, so affectionate that I begin to melt in an entirely different way. My spirits sing as I work my crotch, happily defying him.

He smacks again and again, a little harder, warming up my hind parts to match the glow in my sex and in my heart.

"Tell me...tell me everything." He smoothes his free hand down my back and my flank, the other still softly slapping at my bottom.

It's hard to answer now because I'm so turned on I can't think straight to form words, and it's also getting difficult to keep my hips still against the sheets.

I grab at the pillows, clutching the linen of the pillowcase hard in an effort to concentrate.

"I...I've decided that I'd quite like to find out what it's like to be a marchioness!"

There's a pause, during which I hold my breath, then I feel a kiss settle on the small of my back like a butterfly.

"Well, I can tell you what that will be like." His breath is hot against my skin, wafting over my bottom, which is already even hotter. "You'll never have any money. You'll spend your life enslaved to a great monster of a house that'll never ever stop needing attention." He kisses me just one more time, and then straightens up again. "And you'll probably get your bottom smacked at least once a day, if not considerably more often!"

Spanks begin to rain down. Hard, loving, rhythmical and stirring. I surge against the mattress, my clit pulsating and my heart thudding and leaping with the purest love.

* * *

A while later, I've been spanked and I've been fondled and I've been comprehensively fucked…and I've been brought to climax again and again and again. And with each smack, each stroke, each thrust and each orgasm, I've been told that I'm cherished and adored.

Christian's gone back to sleep now, and I'm lying here savoring the peace and the closeness of his beloved body. Pretty soon I'll have to start making phone calls and explaining a lot of things to a lot of very astonished people. But for now, I'm just listening to my darling's breathing and the sound of a new, teeming downpour outside.

British weather? It's not so bad…in fact, I love it! Almost as much as I love the man who's at my side.

* * * * *

FOR YOUR PLEASURE
ELISA ADAMS

CHAPTER ONE

The heat was almost too much to take. Humidity robbed me of a decent breath and sweat coated my brow no matter how many times I swiped it away with the back of my hand. The misery would last for three more days, according to the radio news broadcast I caught this morning on my way to work. Three more days before we got a little relief.

Birds chirped in the trees overhead. Even their songs sounded weak. Uncomfortable. Summers in New England tended to be like this. Hot and sticky for days on end. Some people loved the heat. I hated it. Hated the way my hair and clothing seemed plastered to my body. Hated the restlessness that settled into my gut and wrapped its fingers around my throat.

Even now, I shifted in my lounge chair, wishing I'd put in a pool last summer like my sister had tried to talk me into doing. The air conditioner was on the fritz. The repairman couldn't get here for two more days. I groaned. The only place to escape the heat would be the office.

A flash of movement drew my attention and a smile tickled the corners of my lips. The slight breeze wasn't the only bonus to being outside. A light in my neighbor's window reminded me of the real reason I'd come out here after dinner. He always got home from work at eight-thirty on weeknights. And changed with the lights on.

My neighbor had yet to put curtains in his bedroom windows.

I'd seen him for the first time two weeks ago, when he'd moved into the house across the yard from mine. The second-story windows were tall and narrow, spaced three in a row with only inches between them, affording me a very nice view. For days I'd been telling myself watching the guy was only wrong if I got caught, but it didn't matter. Wrong or right, I couldn't stop.

From the first moment, I'd been obsessed. I didn't know his name, didn't know anything about him, and yet all my fantasies in the past few weeks had revolved around him. Tonight was no exception. Already I could feel my pussy getting damp. Primed. I knew what would happen next. Most nights, he did more than change with the lights on.

My skin tingled with anticipation. I ran my hands up my sides, teasing my breasts until my nipples peaked, all while wishing it was his touch instead of mine. I just wanted him to fuck me. Was that too much to ask?

Apparently. A sigh born of frustration burst from my lips. Two solid weeks of watching, and he never even looked my way.

Sad, Callie. So very sad. At thirty-two, I'd been reduced to a voyeur, wanting what I could never have, logging way too many hours with my battery-operated boyfriend. I tucked a sweat-slicked lock of hair behind my ear. My sister, the psychiatrist, would have a field day with this one.

My neighbor was gorgeous, but not in a conventional way. Toned muscles. Tanned, tattooed skin. Long, dark hair and an ever-present five-o'clock shadow. Ripped T-shirts and worn jeans, the kind of man every girl's mother warned her to stay away from.

The kind of man I needed over me, inside me, making me scream his name.

I wrapped my hand around the glass of iced tea sitting on the table next to me, stroking up and down as if it was his cock. The condensation cooled my hand and I wiped the liquid down my neck. It did little to slow the fire raging inside me, both from the weather and the man across the yard.

He stripped off his shirt and it dropped out of sight. Next, his jeans followed and he dropped to the bed in just his boxers. He ran his hand absently over the bulge there, the muscles in his abdomen flexing and bunching as he stroked his cock through the fabric. I mimicked the motion, sliding my hand over the wet bikini bottom between my legs. Two seconds in and I was already squirming, striving for release. It came quickly when I thought about him, about that big cock and what it would feel like inside me.

I waited, breath held, muscles tense, for him to take off the boxers, but tonight it didn't happen. My neighbor got up and walked away. Somehow, his absence escalated my excitement. Was he somewhere in a darkened room, watching me out a window?

I moved aside my bikini bottom, exposing my pussy to the hot night air. I brushed my finger down my slit, wishing it was his finger instead. My skin was already slick with moisture, and the dampness increased as I stroked myself with my wet fingers. My breasts tingled, my nipples ached for his lips.

How many nights had I touched myself, thinking of him? Too many, but never like this. Never outside, in full view of anyone who happened to be looking.

In full view of my neighbor, if he chose to look.

But he hadn't seen me yet, had he? Maybe he wouldn't. To someone like him, I was invisible. I'd seen his women. Watched him fuck them in his bed while they clawed at his back and thrashed their heads from side to side. An endless parade of blondes, with the occasional redhead thrown in. My neighbor liked them tall and model thin. Two things I would never achieve. Not in this lifetime.

I wasn't bitter about that, though. Five foot four was tall enough. I liked my curves. The men I dated liked my curves. If my neighbor didn't, that was his loss.

A car door slamming somewhere in the neighborhood made me freeze, but only for a second. The trees throughout the yard would keep most neighbors from nosing around, and his was the closest house to mine. If he saw me, I didn't care. Maybe I even wanted him to.

My lids sank closed, my mind already forming images of what he might be doing since he'd left the room. I continued to play my fingers across my flesh, slowly now, knowing I was getting too close to climax and not yet ready for it to be over.

The hair on my arms prickled. I opened my eyes and my breath caught in my throat. He'd moved back to the windows and was standing there with one palm pressed to the glass. The heat in his eyes made my pulse skitter. I swallowed hard. Oh, God. *Not my imagination.* He was watching me. My movements stilled. What was I supposed to do now? I started to pull my fingers away from my body, but he shook his head. One word mouthed from those full lips had me shaking in my chair.

More.

I swallowed hard. This couldn't be happening, and yet, I couldn't deny it. He didn't want me to stop.

When I didn't move, a sexy smile spread over his face and a spark of challenge lit his eyes. My whole body quivered, my pussy growing even damper. *Come on,* he mouthed now, and even though a pane of glass separated us, I could almost feel his deep voice slide over me like cool silk. Helpless to stop myself, I obeyed the command in his eyes, slipping my hand back between my legs to finger my pussy again.

I slipped two fingers inside my channel, stroking in and out. My thumb on my clit, I pressed down and cried out at the jolt of pleasure. It was too much. I wasn't this bold. I wasn't sure I could masturbate with him watching me, but I didn't want to stop. I squeezed my eyes shut, blocking out everything but the feeling of my own fingers. He still watched. I could feel his gaze all over my skin. The idea of putting on a show should have turned me off, but it didn't. All this time I'd wanted him to notice me, and now he had.

A minute or so later, strong hands moved my legs apart and my eyes flew open. He knelt between my legs, his mouth inches from my pussy. His gaze met mine and locked. The heat I found there made a wisp of arousal curl in my belly.

My face flaming, I pulled my fingers out of my pussy and started to readjust my bikini bottom, but he didn't let me finish. He grabbed my hand and brought it to his lips, sucking my fingers into his mouth. He laved them with his tongue before he let me go. I whimpered.

"What's your name?" he asked in a deep whisper.

"Callie." I didn't ask his, because I didn't want to know. It was more exciting this way, lying here so completely open to a stranger. I could barely breathe, barely move.

"Callie." He wrapped his voice around the word, dragging out each syllable. "I've been dying to taste you."

And then he did. His mouth closed over my clit and he drew the tight bud inside. His tongue flicked over me again and again, the small movement enough to drive me right to the brink of orgasm. My back arched. Seconds after his lips touched my body, I was ready to beg him to fuck me.

"Please." The word slipped from my lips, not much more than a whisper of breath on the summer breeze.

In answer, he chuckled against my skin. The thrust of his fingers inside my pussy took me by surprise, making me cant my hips toward him for more. The masterful swirls of his tongue and thrust of those thick fingers had me squirming on the chair. I threaded my hands through his hair, holding his head close while he continued to eat me out. His fingers dug into my thighs, holding me open to him.

The man was a master. Like an explosion, the orgasm took me by surprise, rocking the very foundation of my world. It tightened my grip in his hair, my head dropping back as a silent scream tore from my lips. He didn't let up right away, and tremor after tremor raced through me until all my muscles felt weak. Liquid and useless. And then he backed up and stood, leaving me cold.

Spent and trembling, I could do nothing but lie there and watch him work the buckle on his belt, his gaze never leaving mine. The heat in his eyes made me tremble all over again. My juices glistened on his chin. Once his pants were unbuttoned, he freed his cock and I licked my lips. It had been way too long since I'd had a man inside me. I wouldn't have to wait much longer. I shifted, reaching my hands toward him, but he shook his head.

"Not tonight. It's getting late, and I'm sure you have an early morning."

A little sound of protest whispered past my lips, but he said nothing. Instead, he took the length of his erection in his hand and stroked it from base to tip. His head dropped back, his eyes closing and his lips parting. It didn't take him long to get off, and he came in heavy spurts over my stomach. His lips drifted open and, gracing me with that sexy smile, leaned down and rubbed his come into my skin.

"Another time, Callie." He pressed a quick kiss to my forehead before he turned and walked away.

A long time later, I was finally able to make myself get up and go into the house. This was one night of fantasy I would never forget.

CHAPTER TWO

Three days had passed since my backyard encounter with my neighbor. I hadn't seen him since, but then again, I hadn't really been looking. Part of my reasoning could be attributed to mortification, but another, larger part relished the idea of what I'd done. What I'd let him do to me. Seeing him again might taint my memories of what had happened. Even now, as I walked up the front steps toward my door, a frisson of heat shot down my spine, settling between my legs.

I tried to brush the feeling off as I walked up the path toward my front porch. It had been a long day in an even longer week. Thank God it was the weekend. I needed time to rest. To sleep in and recharge before I had to do it all again on Monday. Funny thing was, as much as I wanted some time alone, away from people, I had to wonder what it would be like to be with my neighbor again. This time, completely with him. I didn't want his mouth, amazing as he'd made me feel with it. I wanted his dick.

An involuntary sound escaped from my lips, followed by a giggle. Being a bad girl had never really appealed to me, but I liked the way it felt. It was a heady rush of power that made me smile.

I reached the top step, keys in hand, and headed for the door, when a movement from the shadows in the corner of the porch caught my attention. I froze, the hair on my arms standing on end. "Who's there?"

"Do you always stay so late at work?"

The voice—*his* voice—made me drop my keys. They clattered to the porch, glinting in the light from the dim bulb overhead. I swallowed, bending down to pick up the ring. "You scared me. I have a project. A deadline."

"It isn't good for you. You need some downtime. Relaxation."

Easy for him to say. "Why are you here? Surely it's not to chastise me for my work habits, since you don't know me well enough to know what they are. Actually, you don't even know me at all, do you?"

He laughed. "I know what your pussy tastes like. I know what sounds you make when you come."

Already my pussy was wet, and growing wetter by the second. I'd been needing to feel his cock inside me for days now. No, longer. Much longer. Since the second I'd seen him in that upstairs window not long after he'd moved in, stroking his cock with such abandon.

"You know why I'm here," he continued, stepping closer but still clinging to the shadows. "You want me here. Want what's bound to happen between us."

"No." The denial was automatic, but untrue. He had to know it. There was no strength behind the single word. I tried to turn toward him, needing to see his expression, but his palm between my shoulder blades stopped me.

"Don't. Stay right where you are."

The command should have annoyed me, maybe even

offended me, but instead, it made me even wetter. My pussy muscles contracted, softening. Readying for him.

He dropped his hand lower until it rested on the small of my back, just above my ass. He rubbed his fingertips into the hollow there and I whimpered.

"Bend forward and put your hands on the door, Miss Jenkins."

A chill washed down my spine. I ignored his command, still trying to process what he'd said. "How do you know my last name?"

He pressed on my back, arching me forward. Fingers on my wrists, he brought my hands up to rest on the cool metal surface of the door. "I was curious, so I found out. Surprised?"

I could only nod. He moved his hands to my hips, bunching my skirt until he had the material gathered at my waist. He fit his knee between mine and nudged my legs apart. The excitement inside me threatened to bubble over, but this was wrong. Even more wrong than what had happened in my backyard. I couldn't let it continue. "Don't. We're out front, right under a light. Someone might see."

His soft laugh washed over me. "I thought you liked that. Liked to be watched. You like to watch me, too."

I went cold. No way. It wasn't possible. "You knew?"

"Oh, yeah. And I loved every second."

I licked my lips. All that time, he'd been performing. Putting on a show, the way he'd urged me to outside. I should have been upset, but then again, he should have been offended that I'd watched in the first place. The fact that he wasn't turned me on even more.

"Those other women…"

"They had no idea. But I knew. You liked watching me fuck them, didn't you?"

I shook my head, my denial emphatic. "No."

"Why not? Tell me the truth."

"Because I wanted it to be me." Every single, goddamn time, I wanted it to be me.

His fingers crept up my hip, tickling, teasing. "Do you still want that?"

"Yes."

"Good. I want it, too. Have for way too long." He slid aside my panties and ran his fingers along the length of my slit. I was so slick, so wet, that I felt hypersensitive.

He stroked my clit. Tingles spread from my pussy out to my limbs. My legs shook. I cried out, wriggled back, but every time I managed to get his fingers right where I needed them, he shifted, keeping me on edge but not letting me topple over. The tips of his fingers were callused, as if he spent his days working outside. Such a contrast from the executives I usually brought into my bed. They were all polish and class, where my neighbor was not. I hadn't realized until now that I liked it rough. Raw and sexy.

He pressed a kiss between my shoulder blades. The rich, clean scent of his cologne surrounded me. "I've been thinking about you. I shouldn't have walked away that night."

"Why did you?"

"I knew it would be better this time if I did. So much hotter."

I was on the verge of begging him to fuck me...when his other hand came down on my ass. The resounding smack echoed through the silence. Shock stole my breath. Even the crickets stopped chirping. My ass cheek burned and blood pounded in my ears. That had to have been a mistake.

A mistake that had felt so damn good. "What do you think you're doing?"

He caressed the spot he'd just spanked. "Following my instinct. You've been a bad girl, haven't you, Callie? Spying on the neighbors. Peeking into their bedrooms." Another smack, another sharp sting. Another wave of pleasure flooding my pussy. "Watching me with other women. Watching me by myself. Do you know what I was thinking about every time I jerked off?"

His raw choice of words made me shudder. My nipples rubbed against the lace cups of my bra, sending little jolts straight to my pussy. "No."

"You. I was thinking about you. About sinking my dick into your hot pussy. Making you scream my name as you begged for more."

"I don't even know your name."

Another smack, this one harder than the first two. My body pitched forward, toward the door, and I had to brace myself. I let out a gasp. *Oh, my God.* I'd never been so turned on in my life.

He pressed a kiss to my ass, right where I ached. "Actually, you do. You know more about me than you realize."

I wanted to question him, but he chose that moment to thrust two fingers into my pussy. All rational thought fled from my mind. I moaned, no longer caring if the neighbors heard. Not caring if they saw what we were doing. I was beyond embarrassment, beyond asking him to stop. I wanted him inside me, but so far, all he'd done was tease.

"Tell me what you want, Callie," he whispered, my name almost like a physical caress. His touch feathered across my hip where the skin lay exposed.

I arched my back, pushing my ass toward him. "Just... please."

"Cat got your tongue?"

I would have laughed, had I not been so needy, so ready for him. At this point, I was willing to let him do whatever he wanted to me as long as I found a little bit of relief. I reached my hand between my legs, but he stopped me with a pinch on my hip.

"Don't. I promise this will be worth the wait."

After last time, I didn't doubt it. A sexy man doing scandalous things to me outside, in public, was one of the fantasies I'd never dared confess to anyone. It felt almost shameful, but even that added to the pleasure. My senses were heightened, my skin hypersensitive as he thrust those thick, rough fingers deep into my sheath. He pushed a third finger inside, stroking them as high as they could go.

"Fuck," I muttered, my head coming close to hitting the door again. There was nothing polished about this guy, and that was exactly the way I needed it.

"Is that what you want?" His words were clipped, his voice a little breathless. I loved knowing I could affect him as much as he affected me.

"You know it is."

He pulled his fingers out of me and backed away. My body felt cold, bereft, as if all the heat had been sucked out of the air.

I gritted my teeth. "What are you doing?"

"Looking at you. I've wanted you in this position for so long."

I squirmed just knowing his gaze was focused on me. My pussy was so wet by now I was sure my cream was running down my thighs. He had to know, and still, he did nothing.

After what seemed like an eternity of waiting, I glanced over my shoulder and found him leaning on the porch railing, arms crossed over his chest. I swallowed hard. "Please."

In answer, he pushed off the railing and walked over to the door, grabbing the keys from the porch floor and inserting my house key into the lock. I stood just before he turned the knob and led me inside. My legs were shaking so hard I could barely walk. My ass still stung, but it was a good kind of pain.

The kind that made me want to tear off his clothes and have my way with him, right then and there. I didn't touch him, though. Instead, I waited, high on anticipation, to see what he would do next.

He didn't make me wait long. Once he'd closed the door behind us, he pushed me against it and pressed his body to mine. He kissed me then, a commanding attack of a kiss, his tongue forcing its way into my mouth as he took what he wanted. Amazingly, I let him. Whatever he wanted to do to me, I was his for the night. For once, I was just along for the ride rather than trying to control the situation. I wrapped my arms around his neck and hung on.

He trailed his mouth down my throat, alternating between openmouthed kisses and soft bites. Every move served to ratchet the tension inside me higher until I couldn't take any more. I ground my hips against his, desperate, needy and willing to do anything it took for him to let me come.

Seeming to sense my need, he broke the kiss and moved out of reach.

I groaned. Reached for him, even though I knew it was a lost cause. "Why are you teasing me?"

The intensity in his gaze sent a shudder through my pussy. He glanced down to where my lower half lay exposed, my skirt still bunched at the waist. A half smile lifted one corner of his mouth. "All those times you were watching me, *you* were teasing me."

"So this is payback?"

He laughed as he started unbuttoning my shirt. "No, sweetheart. Not revenge of any kind. This is all for your pleasure."

"I never really was into torture."

He laughed again, pushing my shirt down my arms until

the material gathered at my elbows, keeping me from raising my arms. "You didn't seem to mind when I spanked you."

The reminder got me hot all over again. I closed my eyes and let my head drop back against the door, licking my lips. Minded? I'd fucking loved it, though I'd never imagined having a man spank me would turn me on.

I'd never known, until he moved into the neighborhood, that voyeurism did it for me, either. Surprising what a woman could learn about herself when she opened her mind to the possibilities.

His fingers traced my bra straps, sliding to the lacy edges of the cups. Instead of undoing the front clasp, he pulled the cups down until my breasts popped free.

"You have the most amazing tits," he whispered. "I knew they would be gorgeous."

With that, he leaned in and sucked one of my nipples into his mouth. My back bowed, a moan caught in my throat.

"Damn. I love how sensitive you are."

His teeth clamped down on my nipple, not hard, but enough for me to feel the pressure of his bite. He rolled the sensitive peak around, making me squirm. By the time he moved on to the other nipple, I couldn't hold still. It was all too much, too many sensations at once, and he was barely touching me.

I wasn't a prude. I loved sex, but I'd never experienced it like this. So raw, so urgent. Maybe it was wrong to want him so much, but I couldn't help it. He tugged on my nipple and I moaned. With one last swirl of his tongue over my flesh, he stood, but didn't back away this time. Instead, he wrapped one of my legs around his hip, grinding against me. Even through the fabric of his jeans, I could feel how hard his cock was. How hot.

It felt decadent to have him touching me, teasing me while I still wore my work clothes. My heels put me closer to his height, so that every grind sent a shock through me. I undulated, sucking in every drop of pleasure.

His chest pressed against mine, his breath sawing in and out of his lungs. It wasn't long before he stopped moving, leaning in to brush his lips across my throat. "I can't wait much longer."

I laughed. He hadn't really been waiting for permission, had he? All this time, he'd taken without asking, and I hadn't been complaining. "Who's asking you to?"

His laugh rumbled against my neck before he let me go and stepped away.

I'd wanted to undress him slowly, to touch and taste him like he'd done with me, but there wasn't time. Not now. Neither of us could wait. With frenzied movements, he stripped me out of my clothes, leaving me standing there in nothing but heels and thigh-high stockings. He didn't even bother with his own clothes, just unzipped his pants to free his cock. Once he sheathed himself in a condom he'd pulled from his pocket, he was back on me, wrapping both my legs around his hips. A fast kiss and then he pushed inside me.

The width of his erection stretched me full, and the position made each of his hard thrusts feel as if they might tear me apart. I grabbed his shoulders, bracing myself as he pounded into me. His gaze never left mine, and the intensity I found there made me squirm. Tension hung thick between us, like an electric entity, snapping and popping, driving both of us higher.

My pussy muscles trembled around him as my body sped toward release. My fingernails dug into his shoulders, and the groan told me he felt the pain even through the soft fabric of his shirt. His teeth clamped down on the spot where my neck met my shoulder, biting hard enough for me to feel the pinch. I was so close, so ready. A few more thrusts and I'd find my release.

Frantic, I ground my hips against his, meeting each thrust. His breathing had long since gone jagged, his eyes closed and his forehead sweaty with the strain. He bent his knees a little, changing the angle of his thrusts, and I was done for. Stars exploded behind my eyes, every muscle in my body shaking as pleasure like I'd never experienced shot through me, from my pussy straight out to my limbs. The orgasm seemed to go on forever, wringing every last drop of sensation from me until I felt liquid. Floating. I went lax, unable to do anything but cling to him.

Not long after, he followed me into release, a shout on his lips. He pulled out and set my feet on the ground. Whispering an unintelligible sound, he pressed his palms to the door on either side of my head. "I think it's going to be a little while before I can walk."

I had to laugh. "Me, too."

"Think we could just camp out here for the night, or at least until we recover?"

As appealing to my tired body as the thought was, I shook my head. "I think I need to lie down. Why don't we take this upstairs to my bedroom instead."

A little after dawn, I finally stirred, opening my eyes to find my neighbor staring at me. His lids drooped a little, but he smiled when he saw me looking.

I cupped his cheek in my hand. "You do look familiar to me. Where do I know you from?"

"High school."

As soon as the words left his mouth, I knew. I'd seen him before. So many times, though he'd changed. He wasn't the scrawny outcast I remembered, but his features were the same.

His eyes, identical to the ones I remembered trying to avoid so long ago. I should have noticed. "Shawn Richardson."

A blush crept up his cheeks and he shrugged a little. "Yeah. Upset?"

He'd known who I was the whole time, and he hadn't bothered to tell me. I tried to muster up the proper irritation, but after the pleasure he'd just given me, I couldn't. I'd wanted sex with a stranger, and in reality, I'd come pretty damn close. I'd never really gotten to know him back in school. Hadn't even given him or his slacker buddies a second glance.

There had been a good reason for that, or at least I'd convinced myself there'd been. Looking into that intense gaze had set my nerves on edge. Not anymore. I wanted to know him now. Everything about him. I'd start by learning how his skin tasted and what sounds he made when I wrapped my lips around his cock.

"You look different than you did back then. Bulkier."

He laughed. "Yeah, outside work will do that to a guy. I'm a landscaper. I…ah, have to work in a few hours. I really should go home and shower."

He stood, gathering the clothes he'd stripped off before we'd climbed into bed and pulling on his jeans. "Will you be around later?"

I rolled onto my back and stretched my arms over my head. "That depends. What do you have in mind?"

"I dunno. I'll think of something. I can be very creative, you know."

I chuckled at the exaggerated way he waggled his brows while he zipped his jeans. "I do know."

"Sweetheart, you don't even know the half of it. I'll meet you back here around seven?"

I couldn't help myself. I got hot all over again. I licked my lips. Did he really expect me to turn him down? No way was I that stupid. "Sounds like a plan."

★ ★ ★ ★ ★

SEVEN DAY LOAN
TIFFANY REISZ

"At twenty-three years of age, I would have hoped pouting would be far behind you, Eleanor."

Eleanor turned her face to the car window and rolled her eyes. She didn't pay any attention to the soft winter woods gliding past her; she simply didn't want him to see her childish response to his rebuke. She was in enough trouble with him already. Him—she wouldn't even think or speak his name.

"I'm not pouting...sir." She delayed adding the term of respect for as long as safely possible. "Pouting is what I do when you send me to bed without supper. You're leaving me for a week and just pawning me off on some stranger. Pouting is not what this is."

She heard him sigh and felt a tug of sympathy that she quickly forced aside. She knew she was being difficult, but he was being impossible.

"Then what is it?" he asked.

Eleanor kept her jaw tight. "Righteous indignation."

"Righteous indeed," he said. "You realize that Daniel is only a stranger to you," he reminded her, but Eleanor only stared out the window again. Daniel...something. She didn't even know his last name or anything about him. He was

rich apparently. He'd sent a limo to bring her to him. She'd
thought the limo was a little ridiculous, but at least it gave her
the privacy to vent her frustration during the whole drive.
"He is an old and dear friend," he continued. "One of the
best men I have ever known. As I've told you before, his wife
died nearly three years ago. He's been something of a recluse
ever since."

"So giving me to him to fuck for a week is supposed to
mend his poor broken heart?" she challenged. "You must
think I'm pretty damn good in bed."

"Although considerable, it's hardly your prowess in the
bedroom that I imagine will help Daniel return to the outside
world again. I merely wish you to keep him company while
I'm away. Whether or not he chooses to sample your talents
is his decision."

"So I don't get a say?"

Eleanor started at the sound of the tinted window separating
them from the driver being raised. But she wasn't surprised
when he grabbed her by the knees and wrenched her toward
him. She ended up on her back stretched across the dark leather
of the seat, his hands lifting her skirt and prying her thighs
apart. With two fingers he penetrated her quick and hard.

"Who do you belong to?" he demanded, his voice quietly
threatening.

She forced herself to breathe, forced herself to meet his
eyes—eyes gray and ominous as a rising storm.

"You, sir," she answered through teeth gritting against the
sudden violation.

"And this," he said, spreading his fingers open inside her.
She felt herself growing wet at his touch and had to curse her
betraying body for being so endlessly responsive to him. "Who
does this belong to?"

"You, sir."

"Mine to keep?"

"Yes, sir."

"Mine to give away?"

She swallowed before answering. "Yes, sir."

"And mine to come claim again?"

Tears tried to form in her eyes but she forced them down. She nodded and whispered, "Yes, sir."

Slowly he pulled his fingers out of her. She sat up and straightened her skirt while he wiped her wetness off his hand with a black handkerchief.

"Now," he said without bothering to look at her, "you've had your say."

Eleanor said nothing else as the limo pulled into the long, winding driveway of a snow-covered colonial manor. *At least he's got a nice house,* Eleanor told herself. She'd almost expected it to look like a prison. But still, a pretty home was cold comfort for spending a week alone with a man she'd never met.

The limo stopped at the front door and a man, presumably Daniel, came out to greet them. She stood to the side shivering as she let the old friends exchange greetings and handshakes. Out of the corner of her eyes she studied Daniel. She guessed he was thirty-six or thirty-seven; he certainly looked no older. And, she grudgingly conceded, he was very handsome. Far from the thin pale hermit she'd imagined, he was well-muscled with a face as chiseled as an old Hollywood movie idol. His blond hair made him seem slightly less threatening but when he turned his attention to her, she stiffened in fear. His eyes were neither cold nor cruel, but flush with sorrow. The sadness rendered him immediately human to her and that was the last thing she wanted or needed. To get through this week, she needed to keep her guard up. She'd let him have her body if he demanded it of her. She'd give him nothing else.

"So this is Eleanor," Daniel said as he offered her his hand. She shook it briskly and quickly before dropping it and pulling her arms tight in around her.

"My Eleanor, yes," he said with a smile of affection and

pride. His obvious love for her didn't stop her from still thinking of him as just *him*. Faced with the reality of the week
ahead, she was more furious at him than ever.

"It's very nice to meet you," Daniel said. "It'll be nice to
have a houseguest again. I've been a bit of a Miss Havisham
lately."

Eleanor bit her lip not wanting to laugh at his astute, if
ridiculous, literary reference. She hadn't expected him to be
a Dickens fan.

"I'll be sure not to eat the wedding cake," Eleanor said
before she could stop herself. She was naturally chatty and
even a bad mood couldn't quite keep her from bantering.

"Ah, she reads," Daniel said. "Good. I'm trying to re-
organize my library this week. An extra pair of hands will
be a great help."

"Eleanor loves books," he said. "She even works in a
bookstore so at the very least you'll have a perfectly alphabetized collection."

"Oh, it's already alphabetized," Daniel said as he ushered
them inside the house. "I'm just not sure which alphabet.
Certainly not the English one."

Eleanor glanced around Daniel's home as they made their
way to what she guessed was the drawing room. The house
seemed vast but warm and would have been cozy but for
its enigmatic master. In the presence of such pain, Eleanor
doubted she could ever feel at home.

Daniel gestured toward a chair and he sat down. One glance
from him brought her to her knees at his feet. In private
she always sat at his feet. That she was to take the standard
submissive posture in front of Daniel meant only one thing—
Daniel was one of them. Or had been, at least, before his wife
died.

"Could I offer either of you a drink?" Daniel asked, taking
a seat on the sofa across from them.

"No, thank you." Eleanor let him speak for her. "I really must be going. My flight leaves in three hours."

"Back to Rome again?" Daniel asked.

"Again," he said, sounding tired of it all.

"I'll walk you out."

Usually he would never leave her without a long and intimate goodbye. But this time he merely stood, brushed a finger gently across her cheek and chin, and left her alone in the room. She waited on the floor although she desperately wanted to run after him and beg him to take her with him. But she was far too well-trained to break a submissive posture for the sole purpose of engaging in what she knew would be a futile emotional outburst.

After a few moments, Daniel returned to the drawing room. He said nothing at first and Eleanor could only keep her silence and her eyes lowered.

"Please, sit," he said, his voice kind and quietly amused. "In a chair."

"Oh, a chair. How extraordinarily generous," she said, unable to maintain her submissive comportment now that she was truly alone with Daniel.

"I understand that you're upset with this arrangement."

Eleanor smirked. Upset?

"I get it," she said as she sat in the armchair behind her. "This is good cop, bad cop, right? Bad cop works me over and leaves and then good cop comes in and offers me the milk and the cookies and the nice comfy chair. How cute."

"He warned me you were smart. He neglected to mention you were a smart-ass, as well."

She had to give Daniel some credit. He was impressively unimpressed by her sarcasm. Tougher even than he looked.

"He may live to be a hundred and the word *smart-ass* will never pass those perfect lips of his and you know it," she said.

Daniel half laughed. "He is a bit too proper for that, isn't he? I suppose he would say you were—"

"Impudent," she suggested.

"A fair assessment, I think. He could have warned me you were impudent."

"I guess he thinks it goes without saying. Since you're playing good cop, should I expect a big dinner now? A massage maybe? Or how about the sob story about your poor dead wife and how you're so sad I should blow you nine ways to Sunday?" she asked, deliberately trying to get a rise out of him. But he still seemed unmoved. That scared her even more than an emotional reaction would have. His pain was too deep to be touched. It made him seem far beyond her.

"I think we've left the kingdom of impudent and entered the realm of bitchiness."

She almost laughed. *Bitchiness*—another word she would never hear him say.

"A fair assessment," she said, repeating Daniel's words.

Daniel inhaled and exhaled heavily. She could tell he was considering his next words.

"I won't burden you with a sob story," he said. "But you deserve some explanation for your presence here. I was married, blissfully, for seven years. My wife and I were as you and—"

"If you want to get on my good side, please don't say his name. I'll make it through this week a hell of a lot easier if I don't have to hear about him or talk about him."

Daniel nodded. "As you and he are," he continued. "She was more than my wife. She was my property, my possession... and my best friend. She died three years ago. I have been with no one since. When I confessed this to S—to him, he insisted that some time with you would be therapeutic. As you belong to him, there is no threat of romantic entanglement. And as you are already familiar with the specific requirement of the lifestyle—"

"I'm kinky. You don't have to resort to euphemisms."

"Then the transition from celibacy back to sexuality would be far smoother."

"So you do plan to fuck me, then?" she asked although she knew the answer already.

"When you're ready and if you have no objection."

"I'm here, aren't I? Nobody's got a gun to my head."

"Force is for amateurs. I will sleep alone for eternity before I would ever take an unwilling partner to bed. He has shared you with others before, hasn't he?"

"Yeah, of course. But—" she said and took a breath "—he was always there."

"I understand. As I said, when you're ready. And not until then."

"So what now?" she asked after a moment's pause. Daniel stood up and went to the door. She quickly joined him.

"I'm sure you need to unpack and rest. So I suppose for the night I'll simply send you to your room."

"Send me to my room? After what a bitch I've been?" Eleanor scoffed. "From good cop to cop-out. Fine, I'll go to my room." She moved to take a step but Daniel caught her by the chin. She gasped at the unexpected movement, shocked by the sudden change in his demeanor.

He forced her to meet his eyes.

"I haven't played this game in years," he said, his voice low and forbidding. "That does not mean I've forgotten how."

Eleanor didn't dare to blink or breathe. Daniel loosened his grip on her chin but did not let her go.

"I may not touch you again for the rest of this week," he said. "Or I may fuck you blind, deaf and dumb. But you will be respectful of me while you are here no matter what the sleeping arrangements prove to be. Understood?"

Eleanor blinked and nodded. "Yes, sir," she said through trembling lips.

"Good. Your room adjoins mine. It is at the top of the

stairs, the second to the last room on the right. Your bags are already there."

"Thank you," she said, her voice little more than a squeak.

Daniel smiled but it was not a kind smile. It sent a chill into her stomach even as his fingers against her skin made her uncomfortably warm. "You flinched," he said. "This must not be how he usually gets your attention."

"It isn't. He grabs my neck. Or my wrist."

"Which do you prefer?"

She shrugged. "I hate them all the same."

Daniel's eyes momentarily brightened with suppressed laughter and Eleanor was struck again by how handsome he was. This was going to be a long week.

"Go," he said. "I'll see you tomorrow."

Relieved to be dismissed from his unnerving presence, Eleanor practically bolted toward the staircase. Taking two steps at a time she made it to the top and down the hall to her room in no time. She threw open the door and slammed it behind her, grateful to be safe and alone for once that day. Well, perhaps not safe, she told herself. But at least alone.

He had told her why she was here, what would be expected of her. But only now did the realization that she would be Daniel's sexual possession this week truly register. She went to the window and peered out, trying to see where Daniel's property ended and the outside world began. But a new snow had begun to fall and Eleanor had lived in New England all her life. She knew those heavy dense flakes dropping from a deep gray sky meant a snowstorm. She was trapped here, trapped with him. She was here and for now she was his.

Unpacking had only taken a few minutes and although her bedroom was elegant and spacious with an equally elegant bathroom attached, there was little to be explored. Eleanor tried to read—she'd packed one whole suitcase full of nothing but books—but her mind wandered too much down too many dangerous paths. She was consumed by thoughts of Daniel. Lying on her bed she stared at the ceiling, recalling the rough grip of Daniel's hand on her face. She'd felt the force in him, felt he was a man to be reckoned with. She lay there until she fell asleep and dreamed she was drowning in a sea of black snow.

An hour or a day later, she awoke shivering in the dark. She glanced around trying to get her bearings. She reached for the bedside lamp and tried to switch it on. Nothing happened. She stumbled to the wall and flipped that switch, but again the darkness remained untouched. Wearing only a white cotton nightgown, she dove under her bedclothes, desperate for what warmth they could offer her. In bed she noticed a light streaming from underneath the door that separated her room from Daniel's. How did he still have electricity when she didn't? Curiosity overcame fear and she eased out from underneath the covers and trod quietly across the floor. She considered knocking but the silence in the house seemed too pervasive to break. With a shaking hand, she turned the door handle and found the door unlocked. She took a deep breath and slipped inside.

"Can't sleep?" Daniel's voice came from a chair in front of an imposing fireplace. The orange and roaring fire was the source of the light she'd seen.

"I'm cold," she said and moved nervously toward the sound of his voice. "What happened to the lights?"

"Just a line down from all the snow." He sounded world-weary, tired. "They'll be back on by morning, I'm sure." Eleanor found him still dressed but with an extra button undone on his dress shirt and a glass of white wine in his hand. "You're welcome to share my fire. I won't even charge you rent."

She gave him a tight smile, knowing exactly what he meant by rent, and sat down on the plush rug in front of the fireplace.

She wrapped her arms tight about her and breathed the smoky heat into her lungs.

They sat in silence for what felt like an hour, the only sounds in the room the popping and spitting of the wood being consumed.

"I'm sorry." Eleanor finally broke the silence.

"For what?" Daniel asked, taking a leisurely sip of his wine.

"For what I said about your wife. That was uncalled for."

"Uncalled for? Yes, I suppose it was. Still, this can't be the most comfortable situation for you."

She shrugged. "No one held a gun to my head. I do what he tells me to do, what he wants me to do. Because I love him. That simple."

"Simple...is it? We've never met before today, Eleanor. He expects you, wants you to give yourself up to me. Not very simple from where I sit."

"He's infuriating but I've known him and loved him since I was a kid."

"You're twenty-three, yes? You're still a kid."

"But he's never taken me anywhere I was too young to go. Never asked me to do anything..." Her voice trailed off as she realized the implications of what she was saying. She took a quick breath. "Anything I wasn't ready to do."

Eleanor met Daniel's eyes for the briefest moment and glanced back at the fire.

"Are you ready?" Daniel asked and sat his glass on the table next to his chair.

She counted to ten before answering. She knew the answer at "one" but the little feminine pride she had made her wait nine more seconds.

"Yes."

If Daniel was pleased by her response, his face didn't show it. His expression was inscrutable.

He sat forward in his chair. Eleanor studied him as he moved. It seemed he was looking only at his own right hand.

He fanned his fingers out, gazed at his own palm. His hand curled tight into a fist. But it was the sound of his fingers snapping, loud and unexpectedly sharp, that really demanded her attention. He snapped and pointed at the floor. She responded with well-trained obedience, rising off the rug and kneeling again at his feet.

She inhaled as he laid a hand on the side of her face. His thumb caressed her cheek.

"I won't kiss you if that makes you uncomfortable."

"To be honest, I think not kissing would make it worse."

"Honest," he repeated. "Yes, be honest. It's been over three years for me, you realize. I need you to tell me if it's something you don't like."

"What if..." She stopped and took another breath. His hand was on her neck now, his muscular fingers kneading her skin in a way that made her stomach knot up and the flesh between her thighs damp. "What if I do like it?"

Daniel smiled at her question and for the first time she thought she caught a glimpse of the man he must have been before the pain burrowed in and made a home out of his heart.

"Then tell me that, too. Understand?"

She smiled back at him. "Yes, sir."

"Sir... I haven't been called that in so long. I've forgotten how much I like it. Stand up, Eleanor," he ordered and she came immediately to her feet. He reached out and untied the ribbon at the neck of her nightgown. The fabric loosened and gave way to his hands. He slid the gown down her shoulders and let it fall to the floor. She wore nothing under her gown so she now stood naked before him, shivering, even, despite the fire.

Daniel placed his hands against her stomach before letting them roam slowly over the contours and curves of her body. The act felt strangely unsexual. She felt as much wonder and curiosity in his touch as she did desire.

He gathered her breasts in his hands, cupping them gently.

He brushed his thumbs across her nipples and she flinched with pleasure. He took her by the hips and moved her even closer to him, close enough for him to take a nipple into his mouth. She grasped his shoulders to steady herself as he sucked at her breasts, alternating between his mouth and his fingers as he pinched them and kissed them until her nipples were painfully swollen.

Eleanor took slow breaths as he continued his assault on her senses. He slipped a hand behind her knee and lifted her leg, placing her foot on the chair next to his thigh.

Still holding on to his shoulders for balance, she looked down and watched as Daniel slid a single finger into her. She heard a sigh of pleasure but wasn't sure if it had escaped from his lips or hers.

A second finger joined the first and Eleanor began to pant as Daniel moved them in and out of her until they shone with her wetness against the light of the fireplace.

With his other hand he explored her clitoris, probing gently and slowly until he found her rhythm, the prefect pace and pressure that brought her to the edge of orgasm.

"I can't…" she gasped. "I can't stand."

Daniel immediately took his hands away from her. He gathered her in his arms and carried her to his bed. It was dark away from the fire, and cold. She wriggled under the covers as Daniel lit a smattering of candles.

She saw now that his room was both masculine and elegant; dark wood furniture contrasted with the off-white linens and rugs. But as he stood next to the bed and started to undress, her appreciative eyes fell only on him.

Daniel's naked chest was even more broad and strong than his clothes had hinted at. His stomach was a flat hard plane of muscle. Candlelight flickered over his skin, throwing every line and angle into sharp relief. Eleanor pulled the heavy covers to her chin, suddenly uncertain at the prospect of seeing all of him.

She rolled onto her back and stared into the darkness that hovered at the high ceiling as he discarded the rest of his clothing. She knew from the shifting of the bed that he had joined her. Then it was his face, his naked body that claimed her field of vision. He pulled the covers down her body, revealing every inch of her to his sight again.

"Spread your legs," he ordered and it was, without question, an order. She heard the imperative in his voice, the tenor of command. She obeyed. She was trained to obey, trained to want to obey.

As she spread her legs, Daniel reached for one of the candles that burned on the bedside table. He brought it to him, careful to spill no wax. He settled between her open thighs and looked down at her.

"Use your hands," he said. "Open yourself."

Eleanor reached down and with trembling fingers spread the lips of her vagina as wide as she comfortably could. "Your clit," he said. "Show me." Eleanor blushed in the semi-dark, but embarrassment did not stop her from using her thumb and pulling back the hood of her clitoris. Now nothing of her secret parts remained hidden from his view.

She looked at Daniel as he looked at her. His eyes seemed to devour her. She'd rarely felt so exposed in her life.

"I'd forgotten," he said quietly, "how beautiful this is."

He moved the candle to his left hand and with his right he touched her. One by one he dipped every finger into her—his thumb, his index finger...sliding one in, pulling slowly out, and then pushing in the next as if he had to experience her from every angle. With a single wet fingertip he widened her tight entrance with spiraling circles. She was so wet she could hear herself.

Again he pressed two fingers into her. She arched her hips into his hand. He probed along the front wall of her eager body. She gasped when he suddenly pushed hard into her g-spot, her inner muscles clamping down on him.

She heard his soft laughter and she blushed again, this time at her own blatant need for him.

"Responsive little thing, aren't you?" Daniel teased as he pulled out of her once more and leaned forward to set the candle back on the table. "I wonder how you'll respond to this...."

Now it was his mouth on her, his tongue inside her. She balked in shock from the sheer ferocity of it. He took her clitoris between his lips and sucked. She dug her hands into the bed, desperate to hold on to something, anything to steady herself as a current of pleasure—so strong it felt as if it would drag her under—washed over her again and again. Daniel brought her once more to the sharp edge of orgasm and stopped. He crawled up her body and pressed his lips, wet with her desire, to her mouth. She tasted herself first, then him. As he kissed her with desperate hungry lips, she felt him reach for her knees. He brought her legs up, positioning them over his shoulders. He leaned in to kiss her again, a move that pushed her knees nearly to her chest.

Now it was Daniel who reached between her legs and spread her wide. She felt the wet tip of his cock against her. She barely had time to brace herself before he thrust into her so hard, so incredibly deep that she nearly cried.

Eleanor tried to breathe as Daniel rode her with long driving thrusts. He was big but she was well-accustomed to a large size. She was shocked instead by his insistence; every thrust going deeper and deeper until it seemed he pounded into the pit of her stomach. It quickly left the realm of sex and devolved into pure fucking. And he fucked her like a starving man ate. Three years of celibacy and sorrow had turned his body into a vessel of pure hunger. He gripped her wrists as he took her, holding her down hard. If she wanted to escape him she couldn't. No part of her wanted to escape. Still some lingering defiant spark in her fought off the climax that was threatening to erupt from within her. He was so suddenly possessive of her and she so aware that no matter how he took her, she was not his, that she refused to give him the satisfaction of giving her satisfaction. But no amount of slow steady breathing could stop her. She came and when she came it felt as if her orgasm was wrenched from her. He took it from her body rather than giving it to her. His pace grew faster, harsher, and she held on to the bars of the headboard as he spent his pleasure in her, filling her stomach with his liquid heat.

Eleanor's heart still raced even as her ragged breathing settled. She looked at Daniel who still lay embedded in her. His eyes were closed and his brow was furrowed in concentration as if he were trying to imprint in his memory this one moment inside her. Eleanor stared at his face. Long blond eyelashes lay on pale cheeks like sunlight on snow, and she felt an unexpected stab of tenderness toward him.

Daniel opened his eyes slowly. Eleanor tried to smile at him but the look he gave her was one of shock. He seemed to be seeing a stranger, and Eleanor realized with a sick churning in her stomach that he was.

"It was her you were fucking, wasn't it?" she asked, her voice soft and without accusation. "Your wife, right? Lucky lady."

Daniel's only answer was to slip out of her. He left the bed and threw on his clothes.

"Keep the bed," he said without looking at her. "Tonight this is the warmest room in the house."

"But where will you—" Eleanor started to ask, but he was already gone.

She groaned in frustration and collapsed back on the bed. She blew out the candles and yanked the covers to her chin. After a few minutes in the dark, she felt the presence of ghosts in the room—the ghost of Daniel's late wife and the more fearsome ghost of the man Daniel had been before her death. Eleanor knew she lay with them in the ghost of their marriage bed. She tossed the covers aside, found her nightgown and returned to her own bedroom. She crawled back into her freezing bed where at least she knew that the only cold body between the sheets would be her own.

Eleanor awoke the next morning and heard the faint but reassuring hum that indicated the power had been restored to the house. She showered and dressed and scrounged for breakfast in the grand but near-empty kitchen. Still…although the kitchen felt abandoned, something told her she wasn't alone in the house. Last night's snow had been far too thick and heavy for the roads to be safely passable yet. Once her stomach was comfortably full, she began a cursory exploration. Ears attuned to the slightest sound, she paused outside a closed door near the backside of the house and heard the unmistakable sound of books sliding across a shelf.

She let loose a wolf whistle as she entered. The library was far larger inside than the unobtrusive door had presaged and was stocked with row after row, case after case of books. Enough books to start her own bookstore.

"I knew I heard books," she said to no one in particular.

"You hear books?" Daniel's lightly sarcastic voice came from the far left corner of the library. "Interesting. Most people actually have to read them."

"It's a gift," she said, shrugging. "What are you doing?"

Daniel stood behind a desk stacked shoulder high with books.

"I am draining all the alphabet soup out of my library." She raised an eyebrow at him as she walked to the desk. "I thought you were a bibliophile," Daniel taunted in response to her puzzled look.

"I am a bibliophile. A bibliophiend even. But I still have no idea what you are talking about."

"Well, as your book knowledge comes from the retail side of the industry then I'll pardon your ignorance." He winked at her and she fairly flushed as a sensory memory from last night hit her lower stomach with soft but insistent force. And the light, that certain white light created only by the morning sun reflecting off new-fallen snow rendered Daniel's handsome features almost luminous. She almost forgot what they'd been talking about. "Let's see, at your bookstore your books are divided by subject and then alphabetized by author's last name, yes?"

"Right. With a few exceptions."

"Well, libraries aren't allowed any exceptions. The books have to be in perfect order at all times. You can't do that with just sorting by genre and then alphabetizing."

"Yeah, that's what the Dewey Decimal system is for, right?"

"But there isn't just Dewey. There's the Library of Congress classification system. Dewey is a clean, efficient system, ten main classes divided by ten and so on. The Library of Congress is alphanumeric and based on 26 classes, one for each letter of the alphabet. Compared to Dewey it is crude and confusing, and I only had the library that way because of Maggie. It's what she was used to."

"Alphanumeric—so that's your alphabet soup."

"Yes, and this library has been disorganized soup for far too long." Daniel shook his head as he wrote out a series of numbers on an index card and slipped it inside the front cover of a book.

"Oh my God," Eleanor said, sounding utterly shocked.

"What?"

"You're a nerd."

Daniel only looked at her a moment before laughing.

"I am not a nerd. I'm a librarian."

"No way," she said, recalling again the ferocious passion and the skill he'd demonstrated last night. "Guess they were right."

"Who?"

"You know, whoever said 'it's always the quiet ones.'"

Daniel's mouth twitched to a wicked half grin. "I'm the

quiet ones," he said, flashing a look at Eleanor that nearly dropped her to her knees.

She coughed and shook herself out of the erotic reverie she'd fallen into.

"Okay," she said, walking toward him with more gusto than guts. "I can accept that you're a librarian and a sex god—"

"Well, considering your lover is a pr—"

"Nope. Nyet. Halt. I told you last night—"

"Oh, yes. I had forgotten. Our mutual acquaintance is off-limits to discussion."

"If you want me to survive this week with what passes for my mental health intact, then yes."

"Which I do. So I apologize. But as we barely know each other, finding a topic of conversation apart from our mutual friend might be difficult."

"Oh, I doubt that," she said, sitting on the table next to a stack of books. "We've got books in common, sex…" She ticked them off on her fingers.

"All of two," Daniel said skeptically.

"Well…" She stuck out her foot and tapped his leg lightly. "We've got you."

"Me?"

"Yeah. I'm curious. You're a curiosity. As long as you don't mind answering personal questions—"

"How personal?" Daniel interrupted.

"Unapologetically intrusive, knowing me. Unconscionably so."

"You have a large vocabulary, Eleanor."

"And you have a large…" She paused as he gave her a warning look. "House."

"I do."

"How does a librarian afford a house like this? That was the first unapologetically personal question, for those of you keeping count."

Daniel smiled but Eleanor saw the pale ghost of pain pass across his eyes.

"Librarians can't afford houses like this. But a partner in a Manhattan law firm can."

"Your wife? She was a lawyer?"

"She was. A very powerful attorney."

"You married a shark?" Eleanor asked, laughing.

"A corporate shark, in fact."

"Wow," Eleanor said, duly impressed. "How did you meet her?"

"At the library, of course."

"She read?"

"She gave," Daniel said with great emphasis on the last word. "She gave balls, galas, parties, charity events, fund-raisers of every stripe. She actually had a heart and a conscience. She was the human face of an otherwise very imposing old firm. She held a gala one year to raise money for a literary charity at the NYPL—"

"Holy shit, you worked at the NYPL?"

"Fifth Avenue, Main Branch," he said with barely concealed pride.

"With Lenox and Astor?" she asked, naming the two famous lions that guarded the legendary library.

"On warm days I ate my lunch outside with Astor."

"Why not Lenox?"

"He asked too many personal questions."

"I like him already. So you were both guests at the party?"

"Oh, no. She was the hostess. I happened to be working late that night in the Map Room. Lowly archivist. Not important enough for an invitation."

"So you were tucked away in a dusty corner alphabetizing eighteenth-century maps of Tierra del Fuego…"

"Something to that effect—"

"And she slips away from the suffocating crowd of the geriatrically wealthy—"

"Has anyone ever told you that you should be a writer?"

"No one who's ever tried it themselves. But back to you and her. So you're up to your elbows in Fuego and she rushes in, all disheveled elegance, out of breath, desperate for just one moment of solitude…"

"Actually I was examining a map of Eurasia for signs of wear. She strolled in quite calmly, apologized very politely when she saw me and said she simply wanted to see the library by night."

"I like my version better. But still that is romantic. You gave her a tour? It was love at first sight?"

"Intrigue at first sight. I assumed she was just a guest at the gala. She was lovely, intelligent, a very young-looking thirty-nine."

"Ohh…an older woman. I love it."

"Her age or mine was never a factor. Or perhaps it was. She was older than me, powerful, wealthy…but at night when we were alone…"

"She was your slave," Eleanor said, finishing his sentence.

"My slave. My property. My possession."

"Your possession…I know how she must have felt. Pressure to be in charge of the world. So much responsibility. The whole world on her…to let go and just give herself to you, to give up to you…"

"I'm glad you understand," Daniel said as he started sifting through another stack of books. "Few women do."

"Oh, they do. They're just afraid to admit it. Yeah, equal pay for equal work and our bodies our selves and Gloria Steinem and all that jazz…but in that dusty dark little corner of every woman's heart where we keep our maps of Tierra del Fuego lives the hunger to fetch a powerful man his slippers on her hands and knees."

Eleanor was pleased to see her words had a similar effect on Daniel as his did on her. His breath quickened just slightly as his hands deliberately stroked the leather binding of the book in his hand.

"So you," she said, meeting his eyes, "are a librarian. What does that make me, then? A seven-day loan?"

Daniel laughed as he set his book aside. He moved toward her and lightly gripped her knees.

"Seven-day loan...I'm not sure I like the thought of giving you back." He slid his hands up her thighs and took her by the hips.

"But what about the overdue fines?" she asked, playfully flashing her eyes at him.

"I think I can afford them," he said. Eleanor tried to voice another protest but his mouth was already on hers.

He kissed her with an urgency she hadn't felt last night. Last night he'd discovered, taken for his own. This morning he felt the need to have her. It wasn't about her body as a stand-in for his wife. Eleanor had made him laugh, given him a break, if only momentary, from three years of pain. This time he wasn't conquering. This time he was just grateful.

Daniel pulled her from her seat on the desk. She wondered if he would take her on the floor or take her back to his bedroom. Instead he turned her so she stood with her back to his chest. He laid one slow, possessive kiss along the length of her neck before pushing her forward onto the desk.

Eleanor forced a deep calming breath as Daniel stripped her naked from the waist down. She braced for his entrance, expecting it to be as sudden and fierce as last night's. But he waited, running his hands over her thighs, across her lower back, slipping a hand between her legs to caress her outer lips until she was so eager for him she stood on her tiptoes in readiness. When he finally penetrated her it was slow and methodical. He gripped the back of her neck as he began thrusting. He didn't go as deep today as last night either but moved in spirals in and out of her, reaching every corner inside her.

456   Tiffany Reisz

She moaned quietly, her hot breath steaming a patch of the cool mahogany of the desk under her cheek.

"You like it from behind," he said. It wasn't a question.

"God, yes," she confessed without shame.

"There's more than one way to enter from behind."

"If you think that's a threat, then you don't know me very well," she said, smug even while squirming underneath him.

"I don't," he admitted, slightly breathless, but still in control. "But that will change."

As if to prove his point, he pushed down and deep into her, eliciting both a muscle spasm and a sharp gasp.

She closed her eyes. He increased his pace. When she came she came as quietly as she could but still loud enough for Daniel to hear and laugh just before he let himself come with three final thrusts and a muffled grunt at the back of his throat.

Eleanor's breathing slowly settled. She blinked and raised her head. All she saw were thousands of books stacked and shelved and neatly scattered. Daniel was still inside her.

"God, I love a man who reads," she breathed and laid her head on the desk, spent.

The sex out of their system—for the moment, at least—Eleanor and Daniel made diligent progress on his library. Daniel sorted, reclassified while Eleanor dusted the bookcases in question and reshelved the newly Deweyed books in proper order.

Sometimes they talked as they worked: Eleanor learned about Daniel's childhood in Canada, the source of his imperviousness to New England winters, and Eleanor confessed her frustration with her lack of ambition. She wanted, in theory, to do more than work in a bookstore but was so happy, most of the time, with him that she couldn't bring herself to make any sort of profound change.

"Contentment can be the enemy," Daniel agreed and he sounded like he knew what he was talking about. "But don't worry. Life, death or an act of God will eventually intervene. Enjoy the contentment while it lasts. It won't last forever."

Eleanor shivered at the bitter truth of his words.

"You've been content to be alone for three years. So am I the life, death or act of God sent to shake things up?"

"You," he said, "are a force of nature." He slapped her bottom and ordered her back to work.

They worked mostly in silence, companionable silence after that, speaking only about the books and how they should best be arranged. During a back-stretching break, Eleanor wandered into the corner of a windowless alcove. Two dozen or more cardboard boxes were neatly stacked.

"What are these?" she called out to Daniel.

"Discards," he said, coming to her corner. "Maggie's old law books. There's a business college with a paralegal program in town. I was going to donate the books to their little law library."

"Going to?"

"Well, I still am. I just haven't quite..."

Eleanor gave him a flat, steady stare.

"How long have these been sitting here in those boxes?"

"A year, I suppose."

Eleanor continued to gaze blankly at him.

"You do recall I am the Dominant in this particular relationship, yes?"

Eleanor wasn't intimidated. "Then act like it."

"I will." At that, Daniel scooped her up and threw her over his shoulder, carrying her squirming self back to the case they'd been working on. "Back. To. Work," he ordered as he put her down, gently but firmly, on her feet.

"Yes, sir." She turned and climbed nimbly up the library ladder.

"Eleanor," Daniel said after a few minutes of actual work had passed.

"Yes, sir?"

"I'll call the college tomorrow."

Eleanor smiled a smile only the shelves could see.

"Yes, sir."

Eleanor groaned in unconcealed ecstasy.

"My God...this is so good...."

"I know," Daniel replied, taking another bite for good measure. "I have a neighbor, an older lady on the property adjacent mine. She made this."

Eleanor licked her fork and dove into the lasagna yet again. "God bless her. Did you go get this while I was in the shower?"

Daniel's eyes flashed at her innocent question. After an entire day of dusty library work, Eleanor had spent a solid hour showering and changing into her nightclothes, and when she emerged Daniel had dinner waiting for them.

"No." His voice was even. Whatever she'd seen had come and gone. "Her husband brought it by. He does some of my property maintenance. And he brought more firewood." He took another log and threw it on the warm orange fire. The wood crackled and sizzled; Eleanor breathed in the raw smoke with pleasure. She was silent for a long moment. When she was sure Daniel was watching her she said, "I was thinking."

"Always a dangerous pursuit."

"Tell me about it."

"What were you thinking about?" Daniel asked, a wary note in his voice.

"Why am I here? Really? I mean, you seem okay. Sad still. Very sad. But hardly a desperate case. What am I doing here?"

"You don't know?"

"No. I mean, he—" she still wouldn't say the name of her love who'd abandoned her here, even if she was enjoying herself far more than she wanted to admit "—he said I'd be good company for you, that I'd help you get back out into the world. But like I said, you don't seem like you need that much help."

"Back out into the world? Quite a way with words that one has. Only he could tell the absolute truth and still keep everything a secret."

"So what's the truth? And what's the secret?"

"Back out in the world..." Daniel said again. "It's a cliché. Somebody gets divorced or dumped, widowed. And after a while it's time to get back out there. Date again, make new friends, find someone new. It's figurative, not literal. But me..."

She knew the secret before he could tell her.

"Daniel? How long has it been since you left the house?"

"Oh, I leave the house all the time. But I have eight acres and—"

"When?"

"My wife died three years, five months and eleven days ago. So it's been..."

"Three years, five months and eleven—"

"Nine days. I made it to the funeral. I was on the human equivalent of a horse tranquilizer but I made it."

Eleanor shook her head. "I'm so sorry. I didn't know. But how? Over three years?"

"Maggie left me a wealthy man. Money, good neighbors and the internet is all you really need. They've been my wardens, my guards on the tower. A pleasant prison," he said, glancing around at the exquisitely furnished living room they lounged in. "No bars necessary. I suppose our mutual friend was hoping a week with you would give me a taste of what I was missing."

Eleanor snorted in derision. "He's not that altruistic. Not when it comes to me. He thinks you'll fuck me until you fall for me. Hook, line and sinker and then when I go, you'll follow."

"I've grieved in this jailhouse every day for three years and he thinks I'll be in love with you in a week?"

Eleanor shrugged and looked away from his face and into

the fire. She started when she felt Daniel's fingers slide under her hair and touch the nape of her neck.

"I don't know," Daniel said. "Maybe he's right."

He bent in and kissed the sensitive spot below her ear, misdirecting her attention as he took her plate of lasagna from her and set it aside.

"But I wasn't done," she pouted, no longer hungry for anything but him.

"Yes, you were."

"Yes, sir."

"Lay down on your back."

"Very yes, sir."

Daniel smiled down at her once she'd positioned herself on the plush rug by the fireplace.

"You could at least pretend to be intimidated."

"No offense but I've had scarier gym teachers than you. And remember who I belong to," she said, not really wanting to remember at just that moment. "He makes you look like a floppy-eared fluffy baby bunny."

"Ouch. Not even an adult rabbit but a baby bunny."

"Yup." She reached up and grazed his cheek. He really was unnecessarily handsome.

"That bad, is he?"

Eleanor shook her head. "That good."

Daniel laughed. "I keep forgetting who I'm dealing with. The Queen of Kink."

"I'm a trained submissive. More like King's Consort. I'm not worthy to hold actual rank," she said with a wink.

"Well, I'm honored to consort with you."

Eleanor gave him her best wicked grin. "Then consort with me already."

Daniel grinned back. "Yes, ma'am." He looked her up and down and something changed in his eyes like he suddenly had a very good idea.

"Where are you going?" Eleanor asked when Daniel stood and moved to leave.

"To get supplies. Stay."

Eleanor stayed flat on her back in front of the fireplace. She closed her eyes and wondered what sordid things Daniel did to his wife on this rug. She opened her eyes and saw Daniel standing over her. He sat a tube of lubricant and a towel on the floor by her hip. Deliberately he began to roll up the right sleeve of his shirt.

Eleanor didn't have to wonder anymore.

"You've got to be kidding," she said, her heart racing.

"Does it look like I'm kidding?" Daniel dropped to his knees. He eased her pajama pants down her legs and tossed them aside. With a flourish he unfurled the towel and slid it under her hips.

"Surely he's done this to you before," Daniel said.

"He has...on special occasions."

Daniel pried her knees apart. "Consider this a special occasion. Now are you intimidated?"

Eleanor took a deep breath. "Yeah. Happy?"

"Very."

She took another breath and stared blankly at the ceiling. She flinched at Daniel's first touch. "Sorry. That stuff is cold."

"I know. But it's necessary. Just relax."

"The guy always says relax. Would you be relaxed if someone were about to stick their whole hand in you?"

"I can't say I would be relaxed, but I'm quite certain I wouldn't be argumentative."

"Point taken."

Daniel stopped touching her. "Close your eyes," he ordered softly. "Just breathe in and out. Tell me if anything hurts."

She nodded but didn't answer. She began to breathe slowly—in...then out, in...then out. She could do this, had done this. If she was being honest she'd even admit that she loved this.

Daniel's fingers returned to her. He pressed her outer lips apart with his left hand while he pushed two fingers from his right hand deep inside her. Eleanor kept breathing. She'd learned the secret. She knew she couldn't allow herself to become too aroused. The vaginal muscles tightened when aroused. She had to stay calm, empty herself, let him completely in, push nothing but fear out. The perfect passive act for a true submissive.

Inside her Daniel made slow spirals with his fingers... spiraling outward pressing against her inner walls, opening her until three then four fingers were inside her.

"Are you okay?" Daniel asked, gentle concern in his voice.

"Very okay."

"Are you ready?" She didn't have to ask him ready for what....

"Yes."

If the four fingers filled her, it was nothing compared to the sensation of his whole hand, his whole fist inside her. Her calm broke for a moment and she gasped at how he now filled her. She spread her thighs wider, pressed hard into his hand. She felt her own fluid cool and slick on her thighs.

Daniel barely moved. He didn't need to. Eleanor writhed around his hand, her body torn between the twin needs to push him out or pull him in deeper and deeper.

She leaned up and gripped her own knees. For the first time she looked down and saw Daniel's wrist deep inside her. She collapsed on her back, lifted her hips and orgasmed so fiercely even Daniel gasped.

As she panted, he pulled gingerly out of her. He used the corner of the towel underneath her to dry his hand. He rolled her onto her stomach, Eleanor limp as a rag doll. She felt the cold liquid on her again, this time inside her ass. Then it was Daniel inside her thrusting hungrily. She was too tired to enjoy it. She merely waited patiently underneath him as he used her for his own pleasure and spent himself inside her once and then again when once proved inadequate to sate his appetite for her.

Finally they lay naked, near each other, sore and tired and smiling.

"I was thinking," Eleanor said, turning to drape herself over Daniel's chest.

"Always a dangerous pursuit... What were you thinking?"

"Your wife. I know she died of cancer but still—"

"Still what?"

"I kind of envy her."

Eleanor spent the next three days in a haze of sex and books and happiness. There was no room of the house they did not christen; there was nothing they were afraid or unwilling to do to each other. The fog grew so thick that Eleanor had to keep reminding herself what day it was and how long she'd been there. Arrived on Saturday, today was Wednesday, leave on Friday...leave on Friday.

Wednesday night Daniel came for her and brought her back to his bedroom. He stripped her naked and left her standing by the bedpost. She relaxed and breathed knowing exactly what was coming.

"Tell me your safe word, Eleanor," Daniel commanded as he yanked her arms behind her back, bent her over the bed, and put bondage cuffs on each wrist.

"Doesn't matter," she said. "Do your worst. You won't hear it."

"Arrogant, aren't we?"

"Not arrogant at all," she countered. "Just very well-trained, sir."

He pulled her up to her feet and chained her arms high over her head to the bedpost. The first blows of the flogger landed on her back softly. Daniel was well-trained, too. A long hard beating was always prefaced by a gentle one to desensitize the skin. Breathing in and out slowly, she let the pain wash over her as she'd been trained to do. The pressure intensified, the pain grew. Daniel paused only long enough to penetrate her from behind with short hard thrusts. He came on her thighs, pulled roughly out of her, picked up the flogger and beat her again.

An hour later he finally released her and let her fall to the floor. He was everywhere with vicious hands and probing fingers. He bit at her neck and breasts and thrust until she nearly cried from the mix of pleasure and pain. She felt Daniel coming more and more back to life every time he took her. Pushing her onto her stomach, he forced himself into her again. Her thighs were wet as his fluid mingled with hers. Her back burned with welts. Underneath him, pinned to the floor, a part of her wanted to stay there forever.

An hour…three hours later…she lost track of time. She forgot her name, forgot where she was…and most dangerously forgot momentarily who she belonged to. Bucking her hips hard into Daniel's, Eleanor came so hard he gasped from the intensity of the muscle contractions that gripped him like a hand. When Daniel came, it was with a force that tore into her stomach and sent her calling out his name. For a long time after they lay tangled together, Daniel still inside her.

She lay in his arms and tried not to say what she knew needed to be said.

"I leave Friday morning." It wasn't a reminder or a taunt. She just had to say it to remember it was true.

"Friday," Daniel said, leaning over her to blow out the two candles that burned on the bedside table. A clear signal that it was time for sleep. "Still time."

Daniel eased into the covers and pulled Eleanor close to him.

"Time for what?" she asked, already half asleep.

"Time to change your mind."

Daniel and Eleanor spent the next morning finishing his library. All the books had been recoded and properly shelved. The work progressed quickly as, for once, Eleanor toiled in silence. She couldn't get Daniel's words out of her mind. He wanted her to stay with him…here in his exquisite prison. It was unthinkable. She belonged to someone else, belonged to *him* like her heart belonged to her chest. She would no more leave him than she would amputate her own arm. Unthinkable…and yet, she *was* thinking about it.

"Want to break for lunch?" Daniel asked shortly after one.

Eleanor didn't answer.

"Elle? Eleanor?"

She exhaled slowly. "Seven-day loan, remember?"

"What was that?"

Eleanor turned to face him. "Seven-day loan. That was the deal."

Daniel nodded, but it was clear he wasn't quite nodding in agreement.

"That was the deal. The deal can change."

"No. It can't," Eleanor said, suddenly angry. "It's not a joke. I'm not a library book. I'm not a part of the permanent collection."

Daniel said nothing for a long time. "You could be."

Eleanor just shook her head. "I can't believe this. You're his friend and I'm his everything and you're doing this." She left the library and kept going down the hallway, stopping only to grab her coat. She was out the door and in the snow. She headed down the long winding driveway. Soon she heard footsteps behind her.

"Eleanor, get back in the house."

"You get back in the house. It's your goddamn prison. Not mine." She kept walking. It was cold out but she was too upset to notice or care.

"You're in a jacket and jeans and it's twenty-five degrees out."

"Well, you should have thought of that before you asked me to stay."

"That makes no sense whatsoever." They were nearly to the edge of the long driveway. "I'm not the one running away."

Eleanor turned around and stopped. She was at the end of the drive. Two steps back and she would be off his property and in the road.

"No. You're not running away. You're not running or walking or strolling or going anywhere. You're staying and rotting and hiding. And there's not much you and I haven't done together this week, but I will not do that with you."

Daniel took a step toward her. Just one but she took another step back.

"Eleanor." Daniel's voice was calm, controlled. He sounded like a jockey trying to gentle a spooked horse. "We can talk about this. Nothing has to be decided today. Just come in out of the cold. *I'm* cold, too, and I'm never cold. I know you have to be freezing. Come inside."

Eleanor only looked at him. Even so angry at him, and cold and scared, she couldn't deny he was breathtakingly handsome. Grief had left its mark on him. His eyes were haunted and his body lean and cold…like granite. She knew about granite, how you could build on it or be broken on it.

Still without a word she took the last steps back off his property.

"If you want me back in the house, come and get me." She wasn't mocking him. All she wanted was to help him.

"Don't do this to me." Daniel looked at her so gently that she was instantly ashamed of herself. But still she didn't budge.

"You're doing this to me," she countered. "I love him with all that I am and you're asking me to let that go, to leave him. I won't do it. I can't do it. I love him as much as you loved her. More maybe because if he died I would live like he would have wanted me to and not like some hermit in a cave."

"Then just say 'no' to me. Let me ask you to stay and just tell me 'no.' No frostbite or theatrics required."

"I can't let you ask me," she said.

Daniel took a half step toward her.

"Why not?"

"Because," she said looking down at the snow that caked her shoes like white icing. "I'm not sure I'll be able to say 'no.'"

"Why not?" Daniel asked again as he inched another minuscule step forward.

"Who he is and what he is…" She paused and tears flooded her eyes. "Every single second I spend with him I have to steal. I sleep in his bed and know there's no place in the world I'd rather be but it's the last place in the world I should be. I get Saturday nights with him, sometimes a Thursday night if I'm lucky. But never the mornings. What I wouldn't give for a Wednesday or a Sunday morning…"

"You're in love with a priest, Eleanor. What did you expect?"

"Not to be in love with a priest for starters," Eleanor said, half laughing, half crying. "Every morning this week you've made love to me. You're all mornings and afternoons and evenings and I didn't have to steal a single second of it. You just have them all to give. So if you ask me to stay… Please, Daniel, don't ask me to stay."

When Daniel nodded, it was in agreement this time.

"The only thing I'll ask is that you come back inside with me." He was still on his property but when he reached out his hand it crossed over to her side. She took it and hated how good her small cold fingers felt wrapped up in his warm large hand. She hated it but didn't let go until they were back inside.

Daniel let go of her hand but only so he could take her by the shoulders and pull her to him. He kissed her and undressed her at the same time. She was pinned to the front door before she knew it.

"I'll let you leave," he said into her ear as he lifted her by her thighs and pushed his cock into her. "But I'll make sure you miss me."

He was relentless. Eleanor gripped his shoulders. He was

still dressed. Only she was naked and spread out against the unforgiving front door. Only she was taking and taking as he was giving more and more of himself each time he pushed into her: she took his need, his sorrow, his determination to keep her, his anger that he couldn't, his fingers on her clitoris and finally his cum that poured into her as she shuddered from the orgasm that he'd also given her.

Eleanor wrapped her arms around Daniel's neck as he lowered her feet to the cold floor. She leaned into him and inhaled his scent—warm and clean with the slightest hint of fireplace smoke—and committed it to memory.

"Don't worry," she said, finally letting him go. "I miss you already."

Eleanor and Daniel lay in bed Thursday night, their last night, with their arms and legs wrapped around each other so that it was nearly impossible to tell where one ended and the other began. Tomorrow morning the car would come for Eleanor and take her back to the outside world and to him who she missed with every other breath and cursed with every breath in between.

"What will you do after I'm gone?" Eleanor asked, not knowing how else to keep avoiding the topic.

"What do you think I should do?" Daniel asked as he pulled Eleanor even closer than she already was.

"I don't know. You've got money, no job and it's fucking freezing outside. Go to Tierra del Fuego or something. I hear it's nice this time of year."

Daniel laughed and the movement of his chest from the laugh against her back nearly sent her reeling again. Could he stop being sexy for one moment? "Tierra del Fuego is nearly the southernmost tip of South America, a stone's throw from Antarctica. It snows there in summer."

"Wow. Anyway, you should be used to all that cold. I bet it's pretty there."

"Yes, I imagine it is. The natives burned fires constantly to ward off the cold—hence the name Land of Fire."

"How do you know all this stuff?"

"Librarian, remember?"

"I keep forgetting." She reached between his legs and stroked him. "I'm really going to have to renew my library card when I get back."

"You should," Daniel said pressing her onto her back and sliding into her. "Watch out for those overdue fines."

Eleanor laughed softly as she wrapped a leg over Daniel's back to coax him in even farther. "Oh, I think I can afford them."

Morning came too early for both of them. Eleanor awoke with her stomach pressed to the mattress and Daniel inside her, gently thrusting. He was too desperate for her to even wait for her to wake up on her own. They made love in silence, mute from the pain of having to part too soon.

Daniel pulled out of her at last with a reluctance they both felt. He ran a hot bath for her and with soap and his bare hands washed all traces of himself off and out of her. Eleanor shivered in the water despite its near scalding temperature. She would have preferred to have gone home dirty from him, stained and marked by him. She was grateful for the few black bruises he'd left on her back and inner thighs and the bite marks on her neck and breasts. She knew in a day or two this strange week with him would fade like a morning dream. She needed the marks to remind her it had happened—Daniel was real and she was more than just a seven-day loan. She had belonged to him. She had.

Daniel packed her things while she dried her hair and dressed. She felt odd letting Daniel pack up her stuff but she let him without any protest. She knew that he needed to feel in control of the situation, that her departure this morning was as much his doing as hers.

Eleanor had just finished taming her hair when Daniel came for her. His voice was low and steady, his eyes quiet. "The car's here."

She nodded, not trusting her voice, and gathered her coat and gloves. Side by side they walked in silence down the hallway, down the steps and to the front door. Eleanor reached for the door handle but Daniel stopped her with a hand on tops of hers.

"Daniel, I have—"

"Call me 'sir.' One more time at least."

Eleanor met his eyes and saw them stricken. She felt something hard in the back of her throat. She tried to swallow it but couldn't.

"Yes, sir," she whispered.

Daniel closed his eyes and opened them again slowly.

"I won't ask you to stay," he said. Eleanor could barely look at him although there was nothing more she wanted to do than memorize every line and angle of his face. "But I want to."

She inhaled sharply and forced a smile.

"I won't say 'yes' if you do ask…but I want to."

Daniel smiled back and that smile broke her heart more than any tears ever could.

"Go. Go back to him before I change my mind and keep you here forever."

"He'd come for me, you know."

"I do know. That's the only reason I won't try."

Daniel took his hand away from hers and let her open the door. The driver got out and put her bags in the trunk. He held the door open for her and she slipped inside. The driver got behind the wheel as Eleanor rolled the tinted window down.

"I won't ever see you again, will I?" she asked.

"Not unless you leave him."

"I won't," she said with merciless certainty. "But maybe," she glanced up at the great house looming behind him, "maybe someday you'll leave her."

Daniel nodded. "Maybe… Goodbye, Eleanor. Be good."

She gave him her most wicked grin.

"Yes, sir."

The car pulled away and headed slowly down the drive. Eleanor closed her eyes and leaned her head against the cold glass of the window. She would not look back at him. She knew he would still be there on the steps of the house watching her leave him, watching despite the cold, watching until every sign of her had shrunk into the distance and disappeared. That's where he was. She didn't have to look back. She just knew it.

Eyes still closed, she felt the car turn left out of the driveway and slam to a sudden stop.

"What the—" Eleanor threw open her eyes and leaned forward. Standing in front of the car in the middle of the road and completely off his property was Daniel. She wrenched the car door open and ran to him.

"Daniel…oh my God…you're—"

"I lied," he said reaching for her. "I will ask you to stay. I will and I am. I'm begging you to stay. I need you."

He kissed and she kissed back, too startled to move, too moved to speak.

She finally pulled away from him.

"Daniel, you did it. You left your house, the property. I can't believe it."

Daniel looked at the house in the near distance and laughed as if just now realizing what he'd done.

"This just shows how much I need you. I haven't stepped foot off the property in over three years but for you…here I am."

Eleanor held him just a moment longer, pressed her face to his neck and inhaled that scent that was him and only him. And in that one moment longer she saw their life together— the days among books, the nights wrapped around each other, the mornings for anything they wanted…and they would never have to be apart and there would never be another second of waiting for a door to open just enough for her to slip inside without anyone knowing...she could be Daniel's and Daniel could be hers and all she had to do was say "yes."

"No," she said and let him go.

"What? No what?" Daniel looked utterly stricken.

"If you were still in there, in your fortress, then I would know how much you needed me. That you're here, you're free...it's proof that you don't need me at all."

"Eleanor. Please."

"I'm so sorry," she said backing away to return to the car. "I know it won't help anything but you should know...only leaving him would ever hurt more than this."

She looked at him one last time before slipping back into the car and saying one terrible word—"Drive."

The car started forward again and this time nothing and no one tried to stop it.

Three months later...

She was seeing him tonight, all night. The knowledge of twelve uninterrupted hours with him left her dancing through her day. She danced home from work at eight and dropped her bag full of library books on her kitchen table. She would shower and change and in one hour, nine on the dot, she would be his, completely his all night long.

"Ellie?" her mother's voice called out from behind a closed bedroom door. "You've got mail. On your bed."

"Thanks!" she called back and danced to her room, not curious in the least what bit of junk mail was waiting for her. She glanced at the bed and saw a postcard on the corner of her quilt. She picked it up. On the front was a photo of mountains, snow-tipped and verdant. Now curious enough to care she flipped the card over and read...

Tierra del Fuego is actually quite lovely this time of year. Say hello to Astor and Lenox for me. Love.

It wasn't signed. Only *Love* and nothing else. But it didn't need a signature. Daniel...she couldn't believe he'd actually gone and left his home—gone even to the ends of the earth. The lingering guilt at leaving him so abruptly disappeared at last. He was fine and even more he was free.

Eleanor slid the postcard into a book she'd just finished reading and danced to her shower.

She knew what love was. And it was expecting her at nine.

★ ★ ★ ★ ★